A Vein Of Richness

A Vein Of Richness

Janet Wright Matthews

PIATKUS

To my husband Norman, without whom this book would not have been written.

Copyright © 1996 by Janet Wright Matthews

First published in Great Britain in 1996 by
Judy Piatkus (Publishers) Ltd of
5 Windmill Street, London W1

**The moral right of the author
has been asserted**

*A catalogue record for this book is available
from the British Library*

ISBN 0–7499–0352–X

Set in 11/12 pt Monophoto Times
Typeset by Datix International Ltd, Bungay, Suffolk
Printed and bound in Great Britain by
Mackays of Chatham plc Ltd

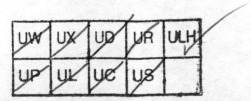

Chapter 1

Something was wrong!

Clara Pentreath pulled her trotting horse to a slithering halt, her slender seventeen-year-old body adjusting automatically to grip the pommels of the side-saddle as though it had been three days, not three years, since she had last ridden.

She cocked her head, her fingers absently stroking the dark green wool of her riding habit as she tried to identify what had caused the shiver of unease that prickled at her spine.

The high Cornish hedges, thick with May blossom and the yellow of gorse, already drowsy with the thrum of foraging bees, cut out sight of everything but the brilliant blue of the spring sky arching overhead. Only the noises, carried on the clear air, told a traveller that he was approaching one of the most successful tin mines in the St Just area.

Her green eyes half-closed in concentration, she sat motionless on her mare, the feeling of unease deepening by the moment. The mine didn't sound right. The instinct fostered by a childhood spent around the mine warned her of trouble.

She forced herself to stillness, recognising the well-known noises as easily as if the last three years at school in Bath had never been: the background thud of the tin stamps, the rattle of the iron kibbles pulling the ore 'to grass' as the miners put it.

Her hand tightened suddenly on the rein, causing the horse to throw up her head and sidle nervously.

One sound was missing.

The bal-maidens were not singing!

In fine weather like this, they always sang as they worked, breaking up the large lumps of ore into smaller pieces that the tin stamps could hammer into dust. You could always hear them, a gentle descant above the clatter of machinery, old Cornish songs and more

1

modern hymns floating out over the countryside. Now they were silent and only the blackbirds sang a melody to the rhythm of the mine.

Something WAS wrong!

Clara's heart beat faster with the knowledge of a disaster. Only a tragedy would stop their singing. Abruptly, she drove her heel into the horse's side, forcing her forward. The track was narrow and rutted, twisting crazily between the high hedges which obscured her view. It was no place for a rider to gallop but she threw caution aside. Her plan to celebrate her first morning home with a quiet hack was already forgotten, the ladylike qualities the school had tried so hard to instil wiped away immediately by the instincts inherited from her mine-captain father. Something was wrong at the mine and she had to help.

Urgently, she kicked the mare on, bending low over the horse's neck, her ash-blonde hair whipping free from her hairpins.

Rounding one sharp corner she came unexpectedly upon an old woman, a sack over her shoulders, limping slowly towards the mine. The horse shied violently, and Clara was thrown against the pommels of the side-saddle with a jerk that bruised her legs and rattled her teeth. The horse spun round, ready to bolt back the way she had come, but Clara's hand was already strong on the rein. Remorselessly, she urged the horse on again as the woman flattened herself hastily against the hedge. Clara threw a brief apology over her shoulder as she rode, her mind still fixed on the strange lack of singing from the mine, and the old woman was forgotten even before she was out of sight.

The mine was as she had remembered it, the high engine house with its great beam rising and falling rhythmically, the sheds where the still silent bal-maidens worked, clustering beneath it, the tall chimney with its plume of white smoke, the white Count House where the purser controlled the accounts. Careless of the men around her, Clara rode at full speed between the buildings, her eyes searching for whatever was wrong.

She saw them standing by the horse whim, where the patient old horse walked ever in a circle, lifting the egg-shaped iron kibbles with their precious load of ore banging and clattering to the surface. They were gathered around a battered kibble, a collection of half-naked men, their tattered canvas jackets and trousers stained with the rust-red dirt from the mines. And in their midst, lying on the ore, was another man. But the clothes of this one were stained with a different and more ominous scarlet.

Clara forced her horse through the small crowd until she could see

2

the injured man more clearly. The men drew back respectfully and one of them, older than the rest, mumbled a brief, ''Mornin', Miss Clara,' which she acknowledged absently, her attention concentrated on the still, bloodstained body below her.

It was a miner. Still in his early twenties to judge by his face, now grey-white under the smears of dirt and blood, and looking even paler for the black curls that clustered loosely on his damp forehead.

His shirt was missing and Clara could see the well-muscled chest, scored with the white lines of old injuries, and puddled now with blood which was still seeping from his side, through the filthy cloth that someone had pressed against the wound to staunch the flow. At least he was still alive, she realized thankfully, noticing the rise and fall of his chest, the rapid flickering of a pulse in his neck.

'How did this happen?' she demanded, and was proud that her voice did not show the fear and disgust she felt.

'He were ramming in the gunpowder and it exploded.' It was the old man again. His face and name came back suddenly, a memory from her childhood. Ben Pasco. But he had aged twenty years in the short time she had been away. Mining was a cruel occupation and few lived to a healthy old age.

'Reckon he won't last till the surgeon gets here,' one of the miners muttered. 'And he were a good man, and a fine tributer.'

There was a sob from a small figure crouched in the shade of the kibble. The boy only looked about nine, though it was obvious from his stained and ragged trousers that he too had been working down the mine. His helmet of stiffened felt looked incongruous above the white pinched face, its candle stuck on at a mad angle in its lump of sticky clay. The boy was clinging to the injured man's hand as if it were his only salvation.

Tears had washed white streaks down his rust-stained cheeks. 'Adam's all I got.' The words were desperate. 'What'll I do if he dies? It'll be the poorhouse for me.' He choked abruptly, leaning over the man, his tears dripping onto the motionless body beneath him.

The desolation in his voice made Clara ache for him. 'There must be something we can do,' she said, casting a doubtful eye at the injured man. The wound was still bleeding. How long would it take for the surgeon to arrive from Penzance? Three hours, possibly. The injured man would bleed to death in that time. And that was assuming the surgeon came. Although they were paid a retainer to look after the mine-workers, the medical men preferred to spend their time with the richer gentry in Penzance rather than face a wild ride out here.

3

'I've bound up the ram.' Another of the men held out a long rod, the end carefully bound with a cloth.

Clara turned her green eyes on the man and stared at the rod, momentarily puzzled. Then memory stirred. Of course! She remembered her father amusing guests one day with a talk about miners' superstitions. One had been that they would treat the item that caused an injury rather than the injured man, in the belief that he would get well by a kind of sympathetic magic. At the time it had been an amusing thought; now the reality roused her temper.

'That's ridiculous,' she snapped. With a gesture she picked out two of the strongest men standing around. 'You, and you, lift him off that stuff and lay him down.' One of the men pulled off his coat and laid it out for the injured man to lie on. The coat was filthy but at least it was better than the ground, contaminated as it was with arsenic from the mine.

Careless of her green riding habit, Clara slid from the horse and knelt to examine the injured miner. The large brim of her elegant hat hindered her and she swept it off impatiently.

Close to, he was taller and more thickset than he had seemed, crumpled up in the kibble. Even though he was unconscious, there was an aura of strength about him. The scent of male sweat and fresh blood rose to her nostrils as she hung over him uncertainly.

She had never seen a half-naked man before, never touched a male body except for chaste childhood kisses that she had planted on her father's cheek. And she knew nothing of nursing. Her school might have been progressive, but a well-brought-up Victorian lady would never dream of touching a strange man so intimately. But if she did nothing, he would certainly die.

Resolutely, she made her decision. This man was her father's employee, injured while earning money for the Pentreath family. It would be unChristian to leave him to die because of squeamishness, or the frippery customs of society.

She had to force herself to touch the blood-soaked cloth that covered his wound, but she knew it had to be done. With a quick jerk she pulled it away. The gash ran from front to back, the full width of the man's right side, over an inch wide and deep enough to lay bare the muscles. The sight made the bile rise in Clara's throat and she felt a cold sweat break out on her forehead. Desperately, she clamped her teeth together. I will not faint, she told herself fiercely. I will *not* faint!

With an effort she made herself concentrate on the wound, the fresh blood still seeping sluggishly from it. What should she do?

'I need clean cloths,' she muttered. The men stared back at her mulishly. She realized in despair that they were refusing to take any active part in what was happening. She was gentry. Now that she had arrived, it was up to her to tell them what to do. For a second, the responsibility seemed to weigh her down, then she straightened her shoulders and gritted her teeth once more. In this group, she would be the only one with clean clothes. It was up to her to act.

Swiftly, she jumped to her feet and flicked up the hem of her riding habit, exposing her white cotton petticoats. There was a shocked mutter from the men but she did not care. She pulled at the cloth, trying to rip off enough to make a clean pad to lay against the wound, but the strong material held firm.

'Here, you men, what do you think you're staring at? You turn around like good Christians.' The voice was old but still strong, and Clara, glancing up, recognized the woman she had passed on her gallop here.

'Here, miss, I'll help you.' The elderly woman turned to the men. 'A knife, you great lummoxes. You lot don't have the sense to bless yourselves. This lady needs a knife, I tell you.'

Ben Pasco passed the old woman a knife and she slashed viciously at the layers of white cotton. 'They're brem strong great petticoats you've got there, miss.'

'He needs help.' Clara gestured at the man on the ground. Even in the last few moments he seemed to have grown whiter and weaker. 'I must stop the bleeding.' She wadded the cloths into a pad and, swallowing hard against the sickness churning in her stomach, she pressed it against the gaping wound. 'I need more cloths.' Her brain was beginning to work again. 'Where's my father?'

'He took a gentleman of the press down the mine, miss,' one of the men volunteered. 'Reckon he doesn't know nothing on all this here.'

'Find me his assistant,' Clara ordered, her eyes on the man beneath her. 'Tell him I want clean rags, long strips to tie up his side. And brandy. Bring me some brandy.'

'The only brandy's in the Captain's office,' one of the men said.

'I don't care if it's on the moon.' Clara was in no mood for quibbling; fear and nausea were making her desperate. 'Bring it at once.'

'I'll get it.'

It was the young boy. He hadn't moved from the injured miner's side, his dark eyes following every move she made. Now it seemed that he had accepted her, and was willing to do anything that would help. He ran swiftly off and as Clara turned again to the injured man she heard one of the remaining men mutter, 'Just like her da, en't she?' and the reply, 'Brem bit of her mother in her too, the way she orders us around.'

'Here, my handsome.' The old woman had wadded up another pad

5

to replace the one already soaked with blood. Clara laid it carefully on the jagged wound. Was it her imagination, or had the flow of blood slowed down? And was that a good thing – or did it mean that the man was dying, even as she struggled to save his life? *Oh, don't die,* she told him in her mind. *Please don't die. Live, live, live . . .*

As if she could read her mind, the old woman said suddenly, 'We'll save him, m'dear, never you fret,' and Clara had time to flash her a brief, thankful smile before she bent again to her task.

'Miss Clara, this is most improper. You shouldn't be here.' The speaker was a young man, dressed in a dark coat and stovepipe hat, his arms full of clean cloths. Could he be the purser? He came forward, hovering nervously over Clara. 'A common miner, half-naked . . .' he spluttered. 'It is most unsuitable, immodest even.'

Clara rose to her feet. At least the fool had had the sense to bring bandages. 'This man works in my father's mine,' she said crisply. 'Should I let him die because of scruples of modesty?' Impatiently, she brushed back the blonde wisps of hair falling around her face, careless of the fact that her hand was stained with blood. 'Now, give me those cloths.'

With a quick movement she snatched them from his grip, and sorted them swiftly, kneeling to her task again, pausing only to snap over her shoulder, 'If you want to do something useful, you can send someone to fetch my father. At least he has a care for his men.'

It seemed an age before she felt the welcome warmth of a hand on her shoulder and her father's voice said softly, 'You've done enough now, Clara. Come away, girl. He'll do.'

She rose to her feet. 'The bleeding's stopped at last.' She blinked away the sweat that was running into her eyes and smiled up at the burly figure of her father, dimly aware of a thin young man, obviously a visitor, hovering in the background.

Suddenly she realized how tired she felt, drained by the effort of taking responsibility for the miner. It was as if she had used every ounce of strength willing the man to live and the bleeding to stop. Now, suddenly, she was as weak as water.

'He'll do,' her father said again. 'I've told them to bring a litter and carry him home. He needs rest now.'

'His wife can look after him,' she agreed. 'Is she a sensible woman?'

'He's not married, but I'll get one of the neighbours . . .'

Startled, Clara interrupted. 'Not married? But what about the boy?' She swung around. As she expected, the boy was still there, pressed tight against the man's body, holding his hand, his eyes glued to the white face as if his life too depended on the miner's recovery.

'His nephew,' said her father briefly. 'They live together and work as a "payre". Adam does the work while the boy works the wind-machine to give him clean air.'

So the man had been working in a distant part of the mine, well away from the ventilation systems. He must have the constitution of an ox to have survived long enough to reach the surface. She had heard how injured men were brought up, bundled on a barrow until they reached the shaft then hoisted aloft in the dangerously swinging kibble, thrown on top of the ore already loaded and hauled 'to grass', clanging and banging the shaft sides as it came. Every year young miners were killed, risking their lives on that dangerous ride rather than climb the ladders that would lead to the surface 800 feet above.

She looked at the man with fresh amazement, admiring his endurance. Seeing him now, white and strangely shrunken inside his well-knit body, it was hard to believe he could have survived such a journey.

'But he needs good nursing. Surely the other miners' wives won't have time for that.' Clara knew the demands on their time. They could not give a neighbour the constant attention that this man needed. Her eyes fell on the old woman who was gathering her few belongings about her. 'What about her? Can she spare the time? We could pay her.'

'But you don't know anything about her!' It was the young purser again. 'She's an old tramp.'

'She helped me to treat this man,' Clara returned hotly. 'She knows more about nursing than any of your miners do.'

The old woman bobbed a quick curtsy. 'Mother Downing's me name, dear, and if you was wanting someone to nurse the young man, well, I'd be more than willing. God knows, there's nothing but a piece of dry bread between me and starvation, or this sack between me and the rain.' She cackled a laugh. 'And it's been a brem time since I got my hands on a lusty young man like that. I'd do it for naught but me food, though a few pence wouldn't come amiss,' and the eye she cocked at Clara was as bright and cheeky as a sparrow's.

Captain Pentreath laughed. 'You shall have your pence, Mother, and with my blessing.' He waved at the boy. 'Phil, Mother Downing is coming to look after you and Adam until he's on his feet again. Mind you do what she tells you, and you run any errands for her. Adam'll get his money from the club, so you needn't worry about starving.'

'And I shall call in to see if there is anything you need,' Clara added. It would do no harm to make sure the old woman knew that there was someone else who would take an interest.

7

As the small procession moved slowly away, Clara felt her knees tremble with reaction. It was all too much. The first day back after three years of school and already she was deeply embroiled in the mine's affairs again – the reason her mother had insisted she be sent away in the first place.

'Miss.' She opened her eyes. It was the older miner, holding a battered basin of water. 'You want to get the blood off your hands before you go home, miss. Lady Susan would have a fit.'

She smiled her thanks. The water was warm, heated by the boilers that powered the great steam engine, and there was even a bar of coarse yellow soap.

'You, man.' It was the purser again. He strode over to the older man. 'What do you think you're doing, annoying Miss Pentreath. Get back to your work or I'll dock you.'

'He brought me this water to wash my hands,' Clara protested. She could not stand by and see the man berated for his thoughtfulness, but equally, she had no right to interfere with the running of the mine. With a smile that lit up her pale face she handed the basin back. 'You're Ben Pasco, aren't you?'

The proud grin emphasized the wrinkles and dirt ground into his skin. 'Good of you to remember me after all this time, miss. But you're like your da, a fine man. The very best. I've worked here at Wheal Susan for him ever since your father broke first ground. I mind you as a small child. I never thought then that you'd grow to such a fine great maid.'

'Well, thank you for the water, Ben. It was a kind thought, but perhaps you had better go back to work now.' As he turned away, a thought struck her. 'That man who was injured, do you know where he lives?'

'Adam Trevelyan? He's got a cottage up top of No-Go-By Hill.'

Adam Trevelyan. She savoured the name silently. It suited the man, had a ruggedness about it that matched the strong, well-knit body that she had tended so desperately.

The purser broke in again. 'I don't think you want to bother about him, Miss Pentreath. These men are tough as old boots. He'll be back at work within a week and causing as much trouble as ever. He's beneath the notice of a young lady like you.'

She turned to him, raising the dark brows that framed sea-green eyes, now cold with dislike. 'You have the advantage of me, Mr . . .?'

He removed his hat and bowed. 'Sam Grenfell, miss, at your service. I'm the purser here – I do all the accounts.' He held out his hand but she ignored it.

'Well, Mr Grenfell, I'm sure that such an arbiter of manners as

8

yourself will realize that it is my duty to take an interest in the health of my father's employees.' She ran her eyes over his thin body. 'I am only surprised that as an official here, you apparently don't feel any such need yourself.' She saw a flash of resentment and anger light his face momentarily, then he dropped his eyes, backing obsequiously away from her. Sickened by the man's behaviour she turned and searched for her father.

He was giving instructions to the men, but he moved to her side instantly. 'Are you able to ride, Clara love? If so, I think we should be going. Your mother will be worried.' But she knew he was thinking that Lady Susan would be furious with her daughter for doing anything so low as visiting the mine, and Clara was grateful to him for riding back with her. At least he would deflect some of her mother's wrath. He was always her first target.

As they rode side by side down the quiet lanes, the clamour of the mine already softened by the sounds of the countryside, Clara said hesitantly, 'I don't like that Mr Grenfell. He seems totally wrong for the post.'

Her father sighed but offered no explanation. Puzzled, she asked again, more openly: 'Why are you employing someone like that? He's so different from the old pursers that I remember.'

She had no doubt now. There was constraint in her father's face, guilt in every line of his body. It was obvious that he would have avoided the answer if he could. He leaned forward, fiddling with his horse's throatlash, his face hidden by the animal's neck. Finally, he muttered, 'We got in a bit of financial trouble last year. Nothing to worry about, but the Blacklocks suggested that Grenfell would be a good man to have, to keep an eye on the finances.'

The Blacklocks. They were the most powerful family in the district, owning as they did both the largest local bank and the smelting works that took all the tin the mine produced. Why had they taken an interest in the Wheal Susan to such an extent that they had put their own man in? Clara knew that the mine was neither the biggest nor the most prosperous in the area. It was strange that they should do such a thing.

Her father leaned across and gripped her shoulder. 'I think, Clara, that it would be a good idea if you don't tell your mother about that. I haven't mentioned the matter to her. It really isn't important. And you know how much she would dislike seeing you take an interest in anything so unladylike as the running of a mine. There'll be enough trouble just because you went there this morning. Don't make it worse.'

She agreed, but her father's attitude made her uneasy. He was

9

hiding something from her, she knew it. For a time they rode on in silence, then a turn of the road brought the high shoulder of No-Go-By Hill into view, silhouetted against the brilliant blue. Even now, she thought, that small group of men must be toiling up it, carrying the unconscious, battered body of Adam Trevelyan.

Impulsively, she asked, 'Will he live?'

'Adam?' Her father's face was impassive. 'It's in God's hands, Clara. But at least you've given him a fighting chance.'

Behind them, in the distance, she heard first one, then another of the bal-maidens, begin to sing.

Chapter 2

The house called Penalverne crouched, as it had for three centuries, with its back to the sea, as if cowering from the vicious winds that raked the coast. With its low, rambling roofline and small, dark rooms it was the exact opposite of the bright, square houses being built all over the country and already being described proudly as 'Victorian'. But Clara's heart always lifted at the sight of it, unfashionable as she knew it to be.

This time, as she pushed open the weathered oak of the front door she felt suddenly nervous. Lady Susan was waiting for them in the low-beamed hall.

Her face set with fury, she stood at the foot of the stairs, her wide, dark skirts filling the passageway, the lace of her cap elegantly setting off her silver-gilt hair.

'I should have known,' she hissed at her husband, taking in the self-conscious faces of the two standing before her. 'I should have known that you two would be out together.'

Her eyes played over them as they stood silhouetted against the light of the bright Cornish morning that streamed in through the carved oak door, and their instinctive drawing together under her gaze roused her to greater fury.

'Conspiring against me, acting behind my back.' Her voice was sour, and Clara noticed for the first time how bitterness had drawn its mark indelibly on her mother's face. 'Never mind what *I* want. Never mind that *I* had plans for Clara today. All you care about are your own pleasures, your own interests. It never occurs to you that I might have interests of my own!' Her thin lips tightened convulsively as she hooded her faded eyes with crêpey lids.

Hugh Pentreath intervened pacifically. 'My dear, we only went to the mine. After all, it is Clara's first day back . . .'

'First day back!' Lady Susan snapped, taut with anger. 'Exactly.

Three years your daughter's been away, learning to live like a lady. Learning about culture and society. Learning that there are other things in life that a woman should be interested in rather than a dirty hole in the ground and the animals who work down it. And what happens? She is back one day and already you are trying to drag her down to your level the first opportunity you have. Taking her to that filthy mine, letting her mix with all those common men. What will people think of her? What sort of a reputation will that give her, do you think? How am I going to find a suitable husband for her if you go on like this?'

She broke off to bury her face in a lace-edged handkerchief.

Clara suppressed a sigh. It was a scenario she remembered all too well from her childhood, her mother resenting any attention or affection that she had shown her father, always blaming him – but for what? Clara suddenly asked herself. Hugh Pentreath was a mine adventurer who owned a large part of the shares in Wheal Susan. Admittedly he also acted as his own mine captain, but that wasn't a sin. He had educated himself, dragged himself up from his humble beginnings, made money.

The mine would not even exist if he hadn't realized that there was almost certainly tin under the rough, cliffside moor. It had been he who had negotiated to lease the land from her grandfather, the Earl of Bodmin, and who had arranged the financing by selling shares to the other adventurers as the shareholders in a mine were called. They had invested freely because they had trusted him, both as a man and a mine captain, and Clara was proud of the fact that they had received many times the value of their original investment as a result of the success of the mine.

She turned to her father, expecting him to respond as he had so often in the past, when he would defuse the situation, flattering her mother outrageously, making her laugh so that she looked suddenly younger and gayer, occasionally even sweeping her up in his arms, despite her shocked and blushing protestations. But now he said nothing, standing mute and downcast under the lash of his wife's tongue, turning his top hat round and round in his hands.

The contrast between the masterful mine captain she had seen taking control at Wheal Susan and the submissive man in front of her now, shook Clara. He stood in the full light from the open door and she suddenly saw that he was no longer the laughing lion of a man she remembered from her childhood. There were silver threads among his tawny curls and the magnificent beard was greying. While she had been away, the laughter lines had deepened into wrinkles and there were unhealthy-looking pouches under each eye. He's old, she

12

suddenly thought for the first time, and felt her heart contract in a spasm of pity and fear.

'It was my fault, Mama.' She spoke almost before she was aware, instinctively stepping into the breach to protect her father as he had protected her so often when she was younger. 'It was such a beautiful morning, I couldn't resist going for a ride. It was pure chance that Papa and I met up.'

And that wasn't a complete lie, she comforted herself. She hadn't expected to meet her father when she had set out.

Lady Susan raised her face from her handkerchief, with no trace of tears that Clara could see, and transferred her furious gaze from her husband to her daughter.

'So, miss, you "couldn't resist" a ride, could you? Your every wish is paramount, is it, just like your father's? Is that the sort of conduct you were taught at school? Is that the sort of behaviour that I shall be expected to put up with?'

She pointed a quivering finger at Clara. 'Just look at you! No one would think you were brought up to be a lady. You look like a hoyden, filthy dirty, your hair untidy, wearing those old clothes that my maid would be ashamed to be seen in.'

Clara glanced down at the elderly habit she had pulled on with such fond memories only a few hours earlier. 'It's the only riding habit I have,' she defended herself. Her eyes took in for the first time the muddied skirt, the too-short sleeves that didn't quite cover her slender wrists, and the black military frogging straining to hold the material closed across her bosom. 'It's just that I seem to have developed a figure since the last time I wore it.'

'There is no reason to be vulgar,' Lady Susan said coldly. 'I should have thought that they would have taught you *that* at least at the seminary. Lord knows it was expensive enough. And within one day of coming home you're careering around the countryside with your hair coming down, looking dishevelled and blowzy.'

She turned again to the first subject of her anger. 'I blame your father. It's all his influence. You don't get it from my side of the family. No one would take you for the grand-daughter of an earl.'

'An earl who has never acknowledged my existence,' Clara shot back, her green eyes flashing dangerously. She was a woman now. She would not stand aside and hear her beloved father's lowly birth forever cast in his face as if it were a crime. Lady Susan's family weren't perfect.

'If he wanted a grandchild he could be proud of, perhaps he should have taken the trouble to get to know me,' she said crossly. 'If he isn't that interested, then I don't see why I should let any concern for his opinions rule my life.'

13

'You are talking about my father, miss,' Lady Susan snapped.

'A father who cast you off when you married MY father,' Clara retaliated. 'Why should I care what he thinks?' She stared angrily at Lady Susan. 'Why should you care what he thinks? If you loved my father enough to marry him, then surely you should lead your life by his principles, not by those of some selfish old man who won't even speak to you.'

'You dare to criticise me?' Lady Susan looked as if she could not believe her ears.

Clara's knees were trembling but she forced herself to stare her mother straight in the eyes. 'I learned one thing at school. And that was that when we marry, we should love, honour and obey our husbands. That we should foresake all others. And in my book, that includes parents. You can't have divided loyalties.' Her chin up, she defied Lady Susan with every inch of her body. 'When I marry, I shall give my first allegiance to my husband.'

There was a stunned silence for several seconds as the two women faced each other. Clara shook inside. She had never before dared to criticise her mother, never even dreamed of openly defying her. But what can she do to me? Clara suddenly asked herself. I'm a woman now, it's time that I knew what my principles are, knew by what rules I want to run my life. I can't spend for ever being guided by my mother.

The silence was suddenly interrupted. There was a sound of light clapping behind her, and a pleasant, tenor voice said approvingly, 'Well done, Miss Pentreath.'

Clara whirled round, her loosened hair whipping about her face. Standing in the doorway was a tall young man, his grey eyes fixed intently on her, his clothes a perfection of tailoring that she had seldom seen in this part of the world.

He smiled down at her, his height suddenly making her aware that she was only five foot two. 'If I ever marry, Miss Pentreath, I only hope that my wife will have the same loyalty to me that you intend to have to your husband.'

Clara blushed in confusion, overwhelmed at the sudden intrusion of a stranger in a family quarrel, and such an elegant one! She could only stare silently up at him, her green eyes luminous with shock.

'Mr Blacklock.' Lady Susan's breeding showed. She had recovered her poise in an instant. She swept forward, her hand held out to the visitor who bowed over it gracefully. 'I'm sorry, I wasn't aware that you had arrived.'

'Lady Susan. You are as beautiful as ever.' His eyes paid silent homage to her faded looks.

Beautiful was a word that could easily be applied to him, Clara thought, taking in his handsome face, neat moustache and the golden hair thrown into relief by the black perfection of his frockcoat. Even the gloss on his top hat and the softness of the lavender gloves he carried negligently in his hand were of a perfection seldom seen in this part of Cornwall. Yet despite his good looks there was something very masculine about him, evident in his broad shoulders and upright stance.

'You haven't been introduced to my daughter.' With a gracious smile at her visitor, Lady Susan motioned towards Clara.

Clara came out of her trance and stepped forward, aware of the blush that suffused her face. After her mother's strictures, she was all too aware of the deficiencies of her costume, especially as they must appear to such an elegant and well-dressed young man. Shyly, she held out her hand to him.

Edward Blacklock held it for a few brief seconds, smiling down at her. 'I have heard so much about you from your parents, I feel that we are friends already.'

Clara was suddenly aware of his eyes on her, lingering on her flushed face, her parted lips, travelling down over her untidy costume. She noticed his glance linger on the gaping front of her jacket as it strained across her bosom and felt her face grow hotter with embarrassment. There was something so intense in the way he looked down at her, as if she were something to eat, an object he desired, not a living person.

With a sudden effort she pulled her hand from his. 'I must go and change. I'm not really fit for society.' She felt strangely breathless, her voice thick in her throat.

'I wish you could stay, but I'm afraid that I've really come to see your father. This isn't a social call. Business, I'm afraid. Very boring but necessary if we men are to keep lovely ladies like you in the gowns that adorn their beauty.' And his eyes returned again to the swell of her bosom.

Clara was relieved when her father stepped forward to take the stranger's attention. 'Of course, Blacklock. Come on through to the study.' The words were polite but, despite the sudden excitement that had shot through her at the presence of the young man, Clara could not help but notice the heaviness in his voice. It was obvious that her Papa did not want this interview. She watched them move slowly towards the library. Was this to do with the 'bit of financial trouble' that he had mentioned on the way home? If so, she thought as she slowly climbed the dark oak stairs to her bedroom, the trouble must be worse than he had told her.

*

15

Captain Pentreath settled himself at his desk with a heavy heart. He was seeing all too much of Edward Blacklock these days. The man seemed to haunt him, but he couldn't risk offending him.

'Well, Blacklock, what is it this time? I sent you the latest figures from the mine.' Not that he wouldn't have seen them anyway, Hugh reminded himself savagely, not with Sam Grenfell as purser. Blacklock had probably known what the figures were before he did. He tried to force down the anger he could feel welling up inside him.

'Yes, I read them. Rather disappointing, weren't they? Still no sign of this new lode of tin that you keep telling me about.' Edward Blacklock settled himself in his chair without waiting for an invitation.

'Dammit, man, it's only a matter of time. It's there, I know it. I can feel it.'

Captain Pentreath leaned forward, pounding the desk top lightly with his fist, trying to make his visitor see what was so obvious to himself. 'I've been in this business now for forty years and I know it's there. When I go down the mine I can smell it in the air, I can taste it in the water. There's tin there, I tell you – and a lot of it!'

'So you've been saying for the last two years,' Blacklock reminded him, 'but I haven't seen any sign of it yet.'

'It's there all right, and you must believe it's there, otherwise you wouldn't be lending me the money to keep it open.' He glanced shrewdly at the younger man.

'Keep it open,' Blacklock repeated. 'That's exactly why I do lend you the money. To keep it working while you look for this new lode.' He tapped his riding whip lightly against the leg of his chair. 'I do not lend it to you to turn the mine into a home for decrepits.'

Captain Pentreath stared at him. 'I don't know what you mean.'

'No? What about these new ladders Grenfell tells me you're so set on spending my money on? The old ones have been there for years. They can last a few months longer, until you find this tin you're so sure about.'

A few months? Captain Pentreath felt a shiver of fear run through him. Would he be able to find that lode within a few months? Mining was a chancy business, certainly, but he knew that the tin was there. All mines went through a lean patch occasionally when the lode of tin they were following petered out, but often it was still there. Somewhere. It was just a matter of locating it.

He cleared his throat, suddenly hoarse. 'Is that all the time you're giving me?'

Blacklock leaned back. 'It's not just me, it's what a consensus of the adventurers think. And they're not going to be very happy if you have another call on the mine. They've already paid out twice to keep the place going.'

'And it's only been a fraction of the amount they've earned from the mine over the last twenty years. And a tithe of what they'll earn again.' Hugh leaned forward, his gaze boring into the younger man. 'They'll follow you, you know that. If you say that the mine is a safe bet, they'll pay up like lambs.'

'But why should I say it's a safe bet?' Edward asked, his voice silky smooth. 'I have shares as well, you know. If there's another call on the mine, I have to pay up like everyone else.'

'But you get all our ore!' Despite himself, Hugh Pentreath's voice rose. 'You make a fortune out of that! Whatever you pay us for the ore, you know you can make money on the smelted tin.'

'Times are bad,' Edward reminded him. 'Black tin is only £46 a ton.'

'And I tell you, if it were £40, Wheal Susan would still be profitable,' Hugh Pentreath broke in furiously. The mine was precious to him. He had created it, nurtured it. He could no more contemplate closing it down than he would think of harming Clara. He stared furiously at the handsome young man opposite him. How could Blacklock understand what it meant to put your whole life into something? He had inherited his money from his father and uncle. Now he ran his businesses on purely monetary principles.

Hugh set his chin, fighting to control his temper. 'Our costs aren't high,' he pointed out reasonably. 'It's just that we're not producing enough at the moment. But once we are . . .'

His voice trailed off. He could see that Blacklock was not impressed by his words.

Hugh bit down the thought that output was higher than it appeared from the figures. He was certain that Blacklock was rooking him on the ore that he sent to the smelting house, but there was nothing he could do about it. Blacklock owned too many shares in Wheal Susan to risk annoying. And these smelters all stuck together. Even if there was a way to cut himself free from the stranglehold Blacklock had on the mine, Hugh knew he was unlikely to get any better deal elsewhere.

Edward Blacklock shrugged. 'We'll see how it goes, but I can't keep paying out money. And I certainly won't pay for new ladders.'

'But they're almost rusted through.' Captain Pentreath knew that the argument would do no good but he could not stop himself. 'Those ladders have been there from the beginning. Some have had

17

water running down them continuously all that time and others are so badly sited that the men have to climb up the underside of the ladders to get to the next level. It makes sense to renew them and resite them.'

'The men climb them after their shift is finished,' Blacklock reminded him. 'It's in their own time, so why should you worry about it?'

'But if one of them breaks?' Captain Pentreath knew it was pointless but he couldn't stop himself.

'It's unlikely that they are going to break in the next couple of months, isn't it? And if you find this tin, well, then you'll be able to pay for them to be renewed yourself. But I tell you here and now that I am *not* going to pay for them.'

Captain Pentreath swung round and gazed out of the window at the heights of Carn Kenidjack rising above the garden wall, swallowing the bitterness that rose in his throat. He had been a miner all his life. He knew that the equipment in a mine should never be neglected. It cost far more that way, and not only in money. Lives could be ruined or lost by such penny-pinching. But he dared not argue with Blacklock. The man had the whip hand and he would not hesitate to close the mine if he was angered.

A couple of months. That was all the time he had to find this ore. And if he didn't find it, what then? What would happen to him, to Clara, to Susan?

He had to repress a groan. He had kept his money worries from his wife, certain that they were just temporary. But what would happen if the mine were closed? How would Susan react? Although she had defied her father to marry him, Hugh was all too well aware that she had never adjusted to his way of life, had never become reconciled to her loss of status.

Hugh ran fingers through his greying hair. She had never believed that her father would cut her off permanently for her one act of rebellion, any more than she had truly realised the difference in life style between even a poor member of the aristocracy and a relatively well-off mine owner. How would she cope if they were to lose even their present standard of living?

As if he could read the other man's thoughts, Blacklock asked suddenly, 'Will Lady Susan go back to her father if you lose the mine?'

'She will stand by me as a good wife should,' Pentreath retorted, knowing that it was not true, knowing too, that there was no way that the Earl of Bodmin would ever take back his erring daughter. But he could not say that. Blacklock's snobbery was one of the few levers he had against the man, and under the circumstances he would play it for all that it was worth.

He expected the man to leave now that the discussion was over, but Blacklock leaned at ease in his chair, seemingly happy to prolong the meeting.

'Your daughter has turned into a very lovely woman.'

Pentreath swung round in his chair and the two men stared at each other in silence for a long moment. The Captain was in a quandary. Blacklock was the most eligible young man in the district, and from a financial point of view he would make Clara a very good husband – not to mention the possibility that a courtship between the two might lead to an extension in the life of his mine. But his heart sank at the thought of his spirited daughter married to a man with the cold heart and narrow outlook of Blacklock.

'I expect you will find yourself besieged with suitors now that she is back from school.' Blacklock sounded as if had not noticed the other man's reaction. 'A young lady with her looks, her connections, the only daughter of a rich father . . .'

Captain Pentreath recognised the threat behind the pleasant words. As the only daughter of a rich father, Clara would indeed be able to choose from a host of young men, but if Blacklock were to make him bankrupt or even just put about the rumour that he was in financial difficulties, he knew that he would have a harder time trying to find her a good husband.

With an effort he rose to his feet, his face set. 'I am sorry I cannot offer you dinner, Blacklock, but we will be going out shortly.' A lie, but he was willing to say anything to get rid of this young man with his pleasant face and smoothly-spoken threats.

Blacklock followed his host across the room. 'I quite understand. So much to do, what with the mine and with your daughter home.'

Lady Susan ambushed them as they reached the hall. 'Oh, Mr Blacklock, surely you're not going? I quite hoped that you would stay for dinner.'

With a gleam of amusement in his grey eyes, Edward Blacklock noted the suddenly frozen expression on his host's face.

'I would have loved to have stayed but unfortunately, I have another appointment.' He bowed over her extended hand. 'We businessmen, you know, cannot command such leisured lives as you lovely ladies.'

She smiled down at him. He was a charming young man, handsome and so rich. She had long ago decided that he was just the man for Clara, providing her looks lived up to their earlier promise, and in this, at least, the girl had not disappointed her.

Her quick eyes had noticed Clara's sudden interest in their visitor. And his in her. Well, it was no bad thing if they were not to meet again just yet. Lady Susan knew the value of a little judicial separation.

And it would do Clara no harm if, later, Lady Susan were to imply that the young man hadn't been invited to dinner, as punishment for her behaviour this morning. It would teach the girl that she couldn't treat her mother in that way. A child owed a duty to her mama, especially if she had given up all the trappings of position that Lady Susan had had to sacrifice on her marriage. It wasn't right that a child should always put her father first, always turn to him. She would have to learn differently.

But Lady Susan was happy with their first reaction to each other, and she waved goodbye to Edward with a pleasant sense of anticipation. With the right management behind the scenes, she was sure she could marry off her daughter to the richest young man in the neighbourhood. It would help to recompense her for the unfortunate marriage she had made, letting herself be panicked into marrying a commoner by the knowledge that she might never get another chance at matrimony, as her parents had marked her out to be their carer in their old age.

Blacklock, too, rode away feeling satisfied with his morning's work. It had been good to show that jumped-up miner who held the purse-strings now. And the girl was a little beauty. She was just the type he liked – beautiful, voluptuous, with a touch of spirit.

He licked his lips. Those were the best. It was good to bring them to heel, see them bow to his will, learn who was the master. When that happened he always lost interest in them, but it was fun getting there.

He smiled as he remembered the scene in the hallway. God, she was a fiery one, taking on her mother like that. And all that hair falling down around her shoulders, fine as silk and pale as winter sunshine. It had been all he could do to stop himself stroking it.

His memory conjured a picture of Clara, standing before him as she had done then, emerald eyes flashing, chest heaving and the jacket of her riding habit straining tautly over her full breasts.

Suddenly, his mouth was dry with anticipation and his body throbbing. His mind still on Clara he turned, almost automatically, onto the path that would take him down to Newlyn and the young widow who was always willing, for a few pence, to satisfy him on these occasions and who never complained afterwards about the bruises.

Chapter 3

'Going to make your own bargains now, are you, Phil Trevelyan?'

The buddle boys stopped their constant churning of the slimy ore and water mixture to call insultingly to the nine year old as he made his way nervously across the muddy ore-dressing works towards the Count House.

'Nah! He be going for the job of mine Cap'n!' another shrieked. 'Wot else? He's bin a tributer for a year. Aimin' for the top, that's our Phil! Too proud to work out here with the rest of us.'

Phil gritted his teeth and angled away from the buddling frames as unobtrusively as possible. He should have expected this reaction, he realised. The other boys had always been jealous of the fact that he was down the mine as part of a payre while they were still employed on the surface doing boys' jobs. Helping the heavy tin ore to separate out from the lighter dust of pulverised rock was a vital job, but it lacked the manliness of actually working in the mine itself.

'Well, our Phil, and how's Adam doing?' His new track had brought him alongside the sheds where the bal-maidens worked, breaking up the ore-bearing rocks with fifteen-pound hammers until they were small enough to go to the tin stamps. He looked up miserably.

It would be Molly Willcock, he thought bitterly. Normally he tried to avoid her. It was well known at the mine that she had her bold eye on Adam. They would walk together on the rough cliffs on a summer evening and he'd escort her to the local fair, buying her fairings and taking her to see the Negro who ate live rats and the man with no arms – spectacles that he wouldn't allow Phil to see.

'He's getting on,' Phil said shortly, hitching up the too-large trousers that Adam had cut down for him. He had never liked Molly. Although she had always been nice to him, he sensed that underneath she resented him, seeing in him the reason why Adam hadn't proposed to her already.

21

She dropped her hammer and wiped the sweat off her forehead with a large, red hand. 'I would have gone to him when they brung him up, but you know that we bal-maidens would get the sack if we left our bench without permission,' she said.

'You'll get the sack if you don't keep working, too,' Phil said, looking pointedly at the hammer lying by her side.

'You shut yer mouth, you young heathen,' she snapped, but Phil noticed that she picked up the hammer again immediately. She saw the grin that spread across his face and began to laugh. 'I'll come and see him tonight,' she promised, flashing her blue eyes at him. 'Adam'll be glad of a bit of cheering up, I reckon. And I can fix you your supper while I'm there.'

Yes, and have another try at getting your feet under the table, Phil thought rudely. And if you ever marry Adam, you'll have me out on my ear, quick as greased lightning.

'You can't,' he said, and couldn't help the pleasure showing in his face. 'Cap'n's got Ma Downing looking after Adam and she says she'll not let anyone in until the fever's down.'

A worried look crossed Molly's pretty face. 'He's really bad, then?' There was no doubting her concern. 'I thought that you wouldn't be out here if he were really ill.'

'Sick as a shag,' Phil replied, happy to be getting his own back. 'He'd be a goner if it weren't for Miss Clara. It were she that saved him, I reckon. Wrapped him up in her own petticoats, she did, and poured Cap'n's brandy down his throat like there were no tomorrow.' He caught the look in Molly's eyes and pressed home his advantage. 'I reckon she were taken with him. He's a fine figure of a man, is our Adam.'

'Oh, gusson! She's gentry. She won't look at the likes of he!'

'Any more than you'd look at Sam Grenfell?' asked Phil cheekily and skipped hastily out of the way. A bal-maiden could pack a pretty punch if annoyed. But he had noticed the way the purser took every opportunity to chat to Molly. After all, she was easily the best-looking of the bal-maidens, and while he resented it on Adam's behalf, he was delighted with the opportunity it gave him to tease and annoy her.

Not that there was any comparison between the two, Phil knew that. Adam was a real man. Catch Sam Grenfell winning the boxing at the Corpus Christi Fair the way Adam had these last two years! The thought made Phil slow down.

Although Adam was less ill than the boy had implied to Molly, he was still in a bad way. And the fair was only a month away. Would Adam be well enough to defend his title again this year? There were plenty of local men who would be glad to take it away from him, including Molly's brother, Norman, who worked the other 'core', as a shift was called, on Adam's payre.

Phil slowed down even further. He was away from the main part of the dressing floors now, with only the whitewashed Count House in front of him. The happiness he had felt from his small triumph over Molly Willcock evaporated quickly. He wasn't looking forward to what he had to do now. But I am the man of the family now that Adam's injured, Phil Trevelyan reminded himself, trying to force down the nervousness he felt. If Adam could take him in after his father and mother had died of consumption, then the least that Phil could do in return was look after Adam when he was ill.

With an effort he squared his thin shoulders and knocked loudly on the wooden door.

'Well, lad?' It was Captain Pentreath, the frown leaving his face as he stared down at the small boy in front of him. 'How's Adam?'

Phil pulled off his cap and twisted it awkwardly in his hands. 'He were some ill last night, Cap'n. Raving he were and trying to get out of bed. He didn't even know me.' Despite himself, Phil couldn't keep the quaver out of his voice as he remembered the scene. He gulped manfully, forcing down the lump in his throat. 'It was all Ma Downing and I could do to keep him there, but he's sleeping quiet now.'

Captain Pentreath nodded. 'Don't worry, lad. A fever after a wound like that is only to be expected. But your Adam's a strong lad. He'll pull through if anyone can.'

'But he won't be able to work for weeks.' Phil could not stop the desperation sounding in his voice. 'And we can't live on a pound a month from the club.' He stared up at Captain Pentreath, begging him to give the right answer. 'Please, sir, can I work as a buddle boy until Adam's well again?'

It was only a few extra shillings a week but the money would help. He would willingly put up with the unkind remarks and the teasing from the other boys if it meant that he could help out. His uncle had sacrificed enough for him; this was the only way Phil could pay him back. He wanted Adam to be proud of him when he was better. Phil wouldn't even allow himself to think that there could be any other outcome to Adam's injury though he had woken up in a cold sweat three times last night without knowing why.

Captain Pentreath hesitated. 'But what about Norman? He's on your payre, alternating with Adam.'

'But I can't help him,' Phil said. 'He's already got Jan Eddy to

23

work the wind-machine. And Adam said only a couple of weeks ago that I wasn't strong enough yet to wheel the barrows.'

'That you're not, lad.' Hugh Pentreath had to force himself to hide the smile that twitched at his lips as he surveyed the scrap of humanity before him. There was no way the boy would be able to wheel barrows laden with ore along the narrow galleries to the shaft. With the temperature in the lower levels of the mine reaching over ninety degrees, it was exhausting work even for grown men.

Captain Pentreath frowned, remembering Adam's pitch. It was in the worst ventilated part of the mine. The air was so bad that a candle would only burn when it was laid almost on its side.

If he'd had his way the tutmen would have been employed to drive a ventilation shaft to that pitch. That would have saved a boy of nine working in the dark, driving a huge fan to suck the dead air out from the narrow gallery where Adam was working. Besides, he was certain that it was there, if anywhere, that they would find the elusive lode of tin. But Edward Blacklock's pennypinching meant that such work had to be put off, and a child like Phil Trevelyan had to waste his youth in hot, stinking blackness.

His tired face broke into a smile. 'I'm sure we have room for another boy on the buddles.' He reached out and pinched Phil's cheek. 'It'll do you good to get a bit of sun, lad, and at least you'll have clean feet, paddling around in the water all day. I bet you haven't washed your feet since your mother died, eh?'

Phil grinned back, relief flooding through him. It would help with the money and it was a step to being a man, as well as a way of thanking Adam for the sacrifices he had made. Phil knew that Adam wouldn't let Captain Pentreath pay Ma Downing's money while she was in the house but her wages would eat into their small savings and until Adam was well again, they needed her.

'Excuse me, Captain.' Sam Grenfell's voice sounding just behind the Captain made Phil jump. He hadn't realised that the man was in the building.

The purser leaned forward obsequiously. 'I don't like to interrupt, Captain, but I feel I must remind you. It was agreed at the last shareholders' meeting that we weren't to take on any more men.'

'Good God, Grenfell, look at him!' Captain Pentreath pointed angrily at the thin child in front of him. 'You can't call that a man.'

'With respect, Captain, "man" includes women and children in this case.' Phil could have sworn that there was pleasure in the purser's voice as he made the statement.

Angrily, he squared his thin shoulders. Cap'n had given him a job. It wasn't for this skinny skirt-chaser to take it away again. 'I ain't

24

another man,' he stated shrilly. 'I already work here. I'm just changing me job, that's all!'

'You're changing to a job that doesn't exist,' Sam Grenfell said curtly. 'We have our full complement of buddle boys at the moment. There's no room for another.' He stared down at Phil, his face taut with dislike. 'You could always get work on a farm. Or even go to school. It would do you no harm to get a bit of reading and writing.'

The injustice of this stung Phil. 'I already can read and write,' he burst out. 'Adam teaches me every evening after work. I don't need to get any more learning. And I wants the money. Adam gets money from the Club because he's hurt but I won't get none.'

'Then you should ask whoever else is in your payre,' said Grenfell. 'Norman Willcock, isn't it? He can employ you. You can't have a job here just for the asking.'

'But Cap'n Pentreath's already offered me one,' Phil protested. 'He's the Cap'n. It isn't up to you to say. You're just a jumped-up pen-pusher.' He nodded sagely. 'Yes, you are, I heard Adam say so only last week.'

Grenfell turned white with fury. 'One more word out of you, you little whippersnapper, and neither you nor your uncle will ever work here again,' he growled.

'But me job?' wailed Phil. 'What about me job?' He turned imploringly to Captain Pentreath. 'You said I could work here as a buddle boy.'

Captain Pentreath shook his head sadly. 'I'm sorry, Phil. I'm afraid I forgot. Mr Grenfell is quite right. We can't take on any more staff.'

Phil stared up at the man. He had always thought that Captain Pentreath was next to God, yet here he was, letting himself be bossed around by the purser who wasn't half the man the Captain was and who knew less about mining than Phil did himself.

'But you said,' he pleaded, his chin quivering, unable to believe that the man he had looked up to for so long wasn't all-powerful.

Captain Pentreath felt as if the bottom had fallen out of his world. He had never had his orders questioned so openly before, never been shown up as ineffectual in front of his workers. A cold fury gripped his heart. For an instant he was tempted to defy the purser, sack him in front of the boy, let the Blacklocks do their worst. But it would only lead to the closure of the mine. With a shareholders' meeting due in a few days he dare not risk it.

Embarrassed, he tried to make it up to the lad, hurt by the disillusion in his face. Sadly, he shook his head. 'I'm sorry, Phil.' He leaned forward and wiped away Phil's tear with a gentle finger. 'But you won't lose out, I promise you. I'll pay you the money you would have

25

earned as a buddle boy anyway, and you can use the time to have a holiday and keep Adam amused. What do you say to that?'

Phil backed away, horror in his eyes. 'I couldn't do it, Cap'n. I couldn't take it.'

He could feel panic rising in him at the thought. Adam would have his guts for garters if he ever thought that Phil was accepting charity. Adam was a proud man and Phil knew better than to try to disobey him on such a matter.

He shook his head firmly. 'I can't take charity, mister. I got to work for my money.'

'But it's not charity, you little fool . . .' But Phil had already gone, his thin legs pumping as he raced down the rutted track towards the cliffs.

Hugh Pentreath turned angrily to his purser. 'Did you have to do that? You could have reminded me afterwards. I'd have paid his wages for a couple of weeks. God knows they'd have been small enough, poor little beggar.'

Sam Grenfell shook his head virtuously. 'I didn't want to see you getting into further expense, Captain. Not in your present situation.'

Hugh turned away. There was a weariness in his heart that seemed to drag him down. So Blacklock had told Sam Grenfell about his financial situation. Well, it was only to be expected. And only to be expected, too, that Grenfell should use the first opportunity to throw it in his face, besides belittling his authority in front of the men. Like master, like man, he thought bitterly. He spat viciously out through the door. They were after him, like jackals after a lion. But he wasn't beaten yet. He had started from nothing and he had pulled himself up. He had done it once and he would do it again if he had to. This mine was his life and he would sacrifice everything he had to keep it.

Out of the corner of his eye he caught a glimpse of the skinny figure running, running as if the devil was after him. Poor little mite, he thought suddenly, the child's heartbreak reaching him even through his own concerns. They'll need help. It isn't enough just to pay that woman to look after them. I'll send Clara around in a couple of days with some food. That will help them out. The boy looks as if he could do with a good meal.

Phil ran until he was away from the mine workings, out onto the cliffs. Around him, the barren, poisoned earth gave way to bracken and sea-pinks, and the ground at his feet sloped steeply away until it fell in one huge drop to meet the blue restless waters of the Atlantic far below. Miserably, he threw himself down in the shade of a granite boulder and sobbed bitterly.

The world was coming to an end. Nothing was as it had been. Nothing would ever be the same again. First Adam, great laughing Adam, his glorious uncle who knew everything and who was admired by all, whose strength and stamina were legendary, who could race through the mines without a candle, who could work two eight-hour cores on end and then go fishing . . . Adam was lying weak and injured, too feverish even to recognise him.

And now Captain Pentreath was shown up, too, as a weak man. Bullied by that stick of a purser, forced to go back on his word, offering him charity! Phil fought down the sobs that rose in his throat. It wasn't just the job, it was the way the beliefs on which his whole world rested were suddenly shaken. He burrowed deeper into the ferns, curling around his hurt as if it were a precious jewel, and slowly, softly, his sobs died and he dropped off to sleep.

Phil was vaguely aware that something was tickling his nose. He snuffled slightly in his sleep, trying to get away but the tickling continued.

Crossly he dragged his eyelids open, his tired body protesting after his broken night. The golden evening sun was shining straight into his eyes, blinding him, then he rolled further over and saw, above him, a dark figure silhouetted against the brilliant sky.

With a muffled yelp he sat up, frightened into full awakening, then relaxed as he saw that it was Norman Willcock, the other half of Adam's payre.

'What did you go and do that for?' he asked irritably. 'I was having a good sleep.'

'It's all right for some,' Norman grinned down at him. 'Lying around in the sunshine like Little Lord Muck.'

'You're a fine one to talk!' Phil had got his bearings now. 'This ain't ten o'clock nor nothing like it.' He and Adam always worked the first core of the day, starting at six in the morning, while Norman and Jan Eddy took over from two until ten. Phil eyed the sun, still above the horizon. 'Your watch stopped, has it?'

'I thought I'd call in on Adam and see how he's doing.' Norman smiled easily. He was always smiling. There wasn't much that he would take seriously. He nodded at the nest Phil had made for himself. 'Haven't you got a bed at home, or do you love work so much that you can't keep away?'

At the question, Phil's misery flooded back. He remembered it all. Cap'n Pentreath promising him a place and then going back on his word on the say-so of that old woman of a purser. And then, to offer him charity! As if he were someone in the poorhouse and not a person who had been working underground for over a year!

27

Norman saw his unhappiness and sat beside him. 'What's the matter, young 'un? Is Adam bad?'

The kindness was too much for his nine years. Tears trickled down his face and dropped off his chin. 'I wanted to work buddling while Adam's ill,' he sniffed, 'but Purser said they've got no room for me.'

'Room for you?' Norman snorted. ''Course they haven't got room for you. The mine hasn't paid a dividend for nearly a year. Anyway, what are you doing, going to Sam Grenfell for a job? You've already got one.'

'Not while Adam's off,' Phil told him. 'And he said that I'm too small to wheel the ore.'

'You can work the wind-machine though,' Norman pointed out. 'As for the ore, Jan Eddy can wheel that, the great lubbercock, while you work the machine. That'll save me doing it and I'll be able to get more ore dug.' He poked Phil in the ribs. 'How about it, my beauty? You join my payre till Adam's better. With Jan pushing the barrow I reckon I can dig double what I am now. I'll be able to give Adam the same money that he always has, and still do well for myself.'

Phil considered. It was true. Jan Eddy was fourteen now and big enough to start the heavy work down the mine. If Phil kept the machine going all the time and Jan did the wheeling, they might well speed up output.

He nodded, pleased to be asked, then he looked again at the sun. It couldn't be more than eight o'clock in the evening. That meant Norman had skived two hours off his core. And how often had he done it other times? He was a happy-go-lucky person, not the sort to bother his head too much about the future. Phil felt his heart sink. Even with the arrangement Norman suggested, Phil would bet that they wouldn't bring as much ore to grass as Adam would do. But at least he would still be earning. Phil had learned some of Adam's pride in the year they had lived together. He wouldn't be living off Adam without contributing something to the household.

Suddenly happy again, he jumped to his feet and held out his small hand. 'I'll work in your payre, Norman,' he said, as if he had been a grown man. Norman shook hands to seal the bargain, his huge, calloused fist completely enveloping Phil's.

'And I'll be proud to have you,' he replied. He jerked a thumb over his shoulder. 'Now, how about we get going? You must be hungry, and I want to see Adam before I have my dinner.'

Phil danced along beside him, his troubles forgotten in the way of children. 'We're going to have Tatties and Point,' he said happily, referring to the fact that meat was so scarce in the mining villages that you had to point it out as it lay hidden amongst the potatoes.

But even though you didn't get much of it, it was still a treat to be looked forward to. And Ma Downing seemed a good sort. She had certainly supplied the Sky Blue and Sinker this morning with a free hand.

Adam might even be awake, and Phil could tell him how he was going to carry on working even though Adam himself was ill. Suddenly, all seemed to be right in the world, and Phil skipped along beside his new partner with a heart as light as the spring breeze.

Chapter 4

Clara gently shifted the basket and bowl she was holding as she gazed at the small cottage, trying to fight back a ridiculous feeling of nervousness.

It was only right that, as the daughter of Adam's employer, she should come here to ask after his injuries. She could remember accompanying her father often enough on such errands when she was younger. Even Lady Susan had raised no objection, only saying how pleased she was that Clara had learned some of the duties of a lady at her school.

But the memory of Adam's half-naked body under her hands, the knowledge that without her he might have died, made her wish that Lady Susan had taken this particular pastoral act upon herself. Her mother had been raised to be charitable, but Clara knew that she had never enjoyed the enforced closeness with those she knew to be socially and culturally inferior, and as no word of Clara's escapades had reached her, she had been delighted to hand over her duties to her usually headstrong and disobedient daughter.

The cottage was like hundreds of other miners' cottages in the area – a low, whitewashed building, the thatched roof held down against the fierce Cornish gales by long ropes tied into holed stones that dangled dangerously low beneath the eaves.

It was surrounded by its own garden, and there was a strong suggestion that somewhere round the back Adam Trevelyan kept a pig, to be fattened over the summer and eaten at St Just Feast in November. At least she had come to the right place, Clara thought with relief as she noticed Mother Downing bent double over a patch of early potatoes.

As if she could feel Clara's glance, the old woman straightened painfully and a broad smile deepened her wrinkles.

'Come in, my dear. You're welcome as a spring day.' She held out a few potatoes. 'Bit of fresh will do that young man good, and there's naught so sweet as a new potato straight from the loam.'

Clara pushed open the small gate. 'I hope Adam Trevelyan is recovering from his injury,' she said. She was aware of the rapid beating of her heart, a strange sense of apprehension that made her wish she could simply hand over the food she had brought and leave. She had to force herself to allow Mother Downing to usher her into the small, dark room that took up the whole ground floor of Adam Trevelyan's tiny cottage.

Clara halted immediately inside the door, blinking in the sudden dimness. The only light came from a single window, its shutters thrown wide, and the light which streamed in was almost obscured by the figure of the injured miner, sitting in a chair with a book in his hand to take advantage of the sun. His long legs, clad in dark moleskin trousers, stretched out across the room and he wore a white open-necked shirt from which his throat rose, strong and brown.

'Oh, you are up. I had thought that you would be too unwell to leave your bed.' She clutched nervously at the basket and covered dish she was carrying to hide her sudden embarrassment, strangely thankful that she was wearing her new pink and white striped day dress and a bonnet with a matching ruched ribbon trim.

'Great lummox,' Mother Downing broke in. 'He won't stay where he's best off, not to mention coddling his brains with all the book-learning.' She pushed past Clara and forced the man back in the wooden chair from which he was trying to rise. 'And you bide where you are. There's no call to get up. Miss Clara knows you're wisht as a winnard, none better.'

'No, stay where you are,' Clara intervened hastily. 'I'm delighted to see you so well. The surgeon must be pleased with you.'

'Him?' snorted the old lady. 'And so he might be, if he had anything to do with it. Came up here, he did, as if he was God's gift to the poor, and stinking of booze. "Help me up the stairs, good woman," says he. "I must see my patient."' Her imitation was wickedly true to life.

'"Help?" I says. "You get your fat belly up there and the floor will come down, and what help will that be to anyone?" I told him straight. "If you want to help," I says, "just you breathe up them stairs. There's liquor enough on your breath to bring life to a graveyard."'

Clara caught her bottom lip between her teeth in an effort to hold back the laughter she felt welling up inside her. She had never liked the surgeon either, a man given to pinching her cheek and breathing

31

brandy fumes all over her. 'Still,' she added, fighting for control, 'his treatment worked.'

'I never let him near,' Mother Downing said stoutly. 'Spiders' webs and honey, that's what I used. And there was plenty of both here, I can tell you, especially the webs.'

'Give over, Ma.' The man's voice was deep and there was a quiver in it which suggested that he found the old woman's description as amusing as Clara did. 'Miss Clara didn't come here to find out how often I swept the ceiling.'

'No, but she's come here to see how often *I* do,' Mother Downing retorted. 'Her da's paying me to look after you, don't forget.'

'Actually, I just came by to give you some chicken,' Clara said hastily. 'My mama thought that after your accident you might need some feeding up.' Though the roast beef they had had for dinner yesterday would have been more suitable, she thought, all too aware of the strength of the young man sitting by the window. Except for a certain stiffness in his posture and dark circles under his eyes, he did not look like the invalid she had imagined.

She held the covered bowl out towards him but he made no move to accept it. Instead, she stepped back involuntarily as she saw his hands clench suddenly on his knees, his knuckles white. He raised his head to look at her and she saw his eyes blazing bright blue in their ring of bruised-looking flesh, the only outward sign of his injury.

'That's kind of Lady Susan.' The man's voice was tight with anger. 'But there's no need. I can look after my own family without help from the likes of you. And I can pay Ma, here, for the work she does, too. I'll not be taking money from your father that I haven't earned. I'm not a charity case!'

'This isn't charity,' Clara protested, hurt by his attitude. 'It's the least I can do. You work in my father's mine and that means –'

'That means you think you own us body and soul,' he broke in. 'Well, your father's a good man and a good Captain, but no one owns me. With my own hand I've earned every mouthful I've eaten since I was eleven, and I'm not going to let someone else feed me now.'

'And you're not going to get the chance,' Clara snapped, embarrassed by the man's reaction. It was accepted that women in her situation in life should give help to people like him. Who was he to throw her good actions back in her face?

She stared straight at him her emerald eyes blazing. 'There are plenty more deserving people who would be grateful for this help,' she said furiously. She dropped the bowl and basket on the ground at her feet, her chin raised as she prepared to tell him just what she thought of him and his stupid, bigoted pride.

There was a sudden flurry of movement and Mother Downing stood between them, facing the sick man. 'Now, you just listen to me, you great lummox.' She stuck her hands on her broad hips, her bosom heaving under her sackcloth apron. 'You may have earned every mouthful you've ate, but who gave you the chance? Her da, that's who. And who gave you the chance of paying me to look after you, you ungrateful lout? Who even gave you the chance to act like a pig with a sore nose?'

She pointed a quivering red finger as broad as a sausage in Clara's direction. 'She did, that's who! If it wasn't for her, you'd be six foot under by now, and don't you forget it, my handsome!'

'She won't let me forget it, will she?' he answered, his eyes narrowed with fury below the black curls that tumbled untidily onto his forehead. 'She comes round here playing the Lady Bountiful. First she gives me my life, then she gives me my dinner.' He poked the bowl angrily with a foot encased in a heavy boot and it tipped and fell, the chicken pieces cascading across the bare earth floor.

'That's right,' Clara exploded, 'spoil good food. You're too proud and pig-headed to eat it yourself so you make sure that no one else will be able to eat it either.'

'Proud and pig-headed, am I?' His hands gripped the arms of the hard wooden chair. 'Well, maybe I am. Too proud, anyway, to live off the slops from a rich man's table.'

He pointed furiously at the door. 'Get out,' he told her. 'You don't own me and you don't own this house. I'm not going to sit here and let myself be insulted by some chit of a girl.' In his anger he rose to his feet, careless of the book in his lap and gasped suddenly, doubling up in agony as the sudden movement caught at his wound. In an instant, Mother Downing was at his side, her strong arms supporting him as she held him until the pain subsided.

Clara's anger disappeared instantly at this sudden revelation of his pain and weakness. She did not dare to help him herself, afraid that any approach on her part might drive him to make another unwise movement. She could only watch, her heart twisted with concern, as the older woman held him.

Suddenly he gasped, 'What in God's name is that?'

He was staring down into Clara's basket from the space of a few inches.

Clara bent down and picked up the book that he had dropped at her feet, glad that the action gave her a reason for looking away from his furious blue stare. 'It's a puppy I found. I think some boys had been stoning it.'

33

Adam Trevelyan settled back painfully in his chair and gestured at the basket; she lifted it onto his knee. Carefully, his big hand suddenly gentle, he reached into the basket and lifted out a small black and white puppy. It whimpered softly at the movement, its body gashed and bloody, one leg hanging at an awkward angle.

Adam Trevelyan stared up at Clara as she stood above him, her fingers white around the book she still held unconsciously in her hands. 'Another of your charitable acts, I suppose?' His voice dripped sarcasm. 'You just thought that it would be an honour for this puppy to die bouncing about in your basket?'

'I thought nothing of the sort!' Clara cried. 'I just couldn't leave it to suffer.' The crows had been gathering around it already, waiting for the courage to attack the dying creature. She couldn't have left it there, to have its eyes pecked out while it was still alive.

Clara already despised herself for the weakness she had shown and gazed fixedly out of the window, unable to look him in the face. 'I know it should have been put out of its misery but I couldn't do it. I thought that the best thing to do was to take it home, and ask one of the gardeners to do it.' She waited for the sneer that she knew she deserved. No woman of his class would have thought twice about such a matter. Nor would they have put themselves to any trouble about such a useless scrap of life.

Adam stroked the small head with a gentle finger then laid the pathetic body carefully on the floor by his chair. 'Don't you worry.' His voice was suddenly gruff. 'You're a lady. No one expects you to do things like that.' He glanced up at her. 'I'm sorry I said what I did. You were right to bring it with you. But you needn't worry any more. Leave it with me and I'll see to it for you. After you're gone,' he added swiftly, seeing the sudden look of horror on her face. 'It'll save the poor wretch the pain of being bounced around in your basket.'

Gratitude flooded through her. She had known that she must have been hurting the puppy with every step that she took but there had seemed no alternative. And he hadn't sneered at her weakness, either in rescuing the puppy or in being unable to put it out of its misery.

She smiled at him, her elfin features suddenly lit up by relief. 'I'm sorry too,' she confessed suddenly. 'I hadn't realised you would recover so quickly. I thought you would be too ill to mind if I brought you the chicken.'

'I heal quickly.' For a moment they smiled into each other's eyes, then Clara dropped her gaze, her heart for some reason beating faster, her breathing erratic.

'You've bent some of the pages in your book.' She began to straighten them out with shaking fingers, grateful to have an excuse

34

to look away from him, then her fingers paused. She lifted her head, staring at him startled. 'It's a book on geology! My father has this in his library.'

'Well?' The defensiveness was back in Adam's voice. 'Aren't I allowed to have books that he has got?'

'Of course,' Clara stammered. 'It isn't that. It's just that . . . it's such a difficult sort of book!' she blurted out.

'And I suppose that you think that I can't read difficult books? That I'm just a miner, just a lot of muscles to hump ore, with the body and brain of an ox?' Anger roughened his voice. 'You despise us utterly, don't you?'

'Certainly not.' Her light, incisive tones cut through his fury. Chin up, she stared back at him. 'How dare you say such things to me? My father was a tributer when he was younger, just like you. He was born near here but he was no animal. He educated himself, worked his way up.'

Her neat boot tapped furiously on the bare earthen floor. 'But he was unusual. No one else round here has managed that. He owns the mine now, but he has men working for him that he grew up with, men who are still no better off than they were when they started. So, seeing you with the book, I was just surprised, that's all.'

Lifting her long skirts clear of the spilled chicken and the puppy, Clara stepped forward and handed him the volume. 'You must want more out of life than most miners.'

'Far more.' His pale face lit with sudden enthusiasm. 'Your father is my inspiration. I tell myself that I can do what he has done.'

He stroked the binding with a reverent finger. 'I'm learning. Geology. Engineering. There's so much to know if you want to be a good miner. And I'm going to know it.' His gaze ran round the small, dark room, played over the crude furniture, the dark dresser with its few earthenware plates, a table and a couple of stools, the smoke-blackened hearth and rough-hewn shutters that could be pulled closed to cut down the draughts that whistled around the ill-fitting window with its thick, distorting glass.

'I spend every penny I can on these books. They're the key to a better life. I want to do what your father did – learn all I can here, then go abroad, make money, become a mine captain. Maybe, one day, even have my own mine.' His eyes glowed with a vision that only he could see.

'But first I have to make money – a good find.' He laughed bitterly. 'It's a funny thing. Under any other captain but your father I'd have done it already. In the past I've found new lodes. But your father is too good. Each time, he saw the signs as soon as I did and dropped

35

the rate for the work so I never made the money I needed to, to get a start.'

He leaned forward cautiously, eager to make her share his feelings. 'I don't blame him. He has a duty to make the mine profitable and he does his best. He's got an instinct for tin. But so've I, and I bet I can beat him to it. That's why I'm working the western gallery on the 130 level. I reckon there's tin there and I'm going to find it.'

He grinned at Clara conspiratorially and she found herself smiling back at him. She knew what he meant. At the beginning of each account period the tributers would bid for their pitches. On a good pitch, where there was plenty of tin, they might agree to take two shillings for every pound's worth of tin they raised in the following two months.

But there was always a need to find new seams of tin, to follow an unpromising lode in the hope that it would suddenly produce something better, and a tributer on this sort of pitch could earn sixteen shillings in every pound. It was every tributer's dream to bid for an uninspiring pitch and the next day discover a rich lode. They could make nearly £1000 in that account period and would work the clock round, knowing that at the following account they would be offered that same pitch for only a few shillings in the pound.

'They are crying out for trained miners in Australia.' Clara had heard her father discussing it over dinner the previous evening, half-wishing that he were young again, and poor, ready to stake his all on hard work and luck. She nodded at the books stacked on a small shelf nailed to the rough wall of the cottage. 'For the cost of those you could buy a ticket.'

'And not know enough to make use of it.' His voice was harsh. 'I know about tin mining in Cornwall but you need to know more than that. It may not be tin that you find – it could be copper, silver, even gold. You need to know where they're found, how to get them out and dress them. Even how to run your own pumping engines. There's so much to know!'

He gestured wearily at the dark little room. 'And there's not just me to consider. There's my nephew Phil. I'm all he's got and he's too young yet to earn his own keep. I've either got to stay here until he's old enough to earn a man's wage for himself, or make enough money to pay someone to look after him while I'm gone.'

Clara could hear the pain in his voice and in a sudden flash of sympathy she realised the limitations of his life; his spirit curtailed, with time, youth and strength passing while his ambition burned in him like an all-consuming flame.

Although she had known of her father's background, somehow she had never before understood that there were other men like him – dynamic, full of ambition, anxious to better themselves and their families. For her, Captain Pentreath had always been unique, rising alone above the common men who were content to wear out their lives in the dark for a mere pittance.

And now, in Adam, she could see the man her father must once have been, a man longing for a new and better life; a life with sunshine and safety in it, a life where a man had more than the choice of dying young in a rock fall or coughing his lungs out at the age of forty. But to achieve this, Adam needed two things, things she herself had always taken for granted but for which, she now realised, Adam had had to fight: money and education.

Well, perhaps she could help him with the latter. Impulsively, she asked, 'Do you need other books?' His startled glance took her aback but she struggled on, 'Father knows you. I'm sure he wouldn't mind if I were to borrow some of his books for you; providing he got them back again, of course.'

Adam's face glowed. 'My God, do you think he would?' He gestured at the tiny shelf. 'I want so many. I only buy the ones I can't do without, but there are so many others, books I'd love to read but can't afford.'

'Tell me what they are and I'll try to get them for you.' Clara was sure that Captain Pentreath wouldn't mind. 'You'll need something to occupy your time. It'll be a while before you're fit enough to work down the mine again.'

'Anything to keep him occupied,' Mother Downing broke in from the hearth where she was preparing the next meal. 'Though why he wants to wear out his head and his eyes with all those dirty old books I don't know. What good did they ever do anybody? That's what I ask him, but he can never tell me.'

Clara and Adam exchanged a swift, secret smile, then Clara bent to pick up the basket. 'I must be going.' She looked uncertainly at Adam. 'If my father agrees, will you mind if I bring you the books?' A mischievous smile quirked her mobile lips. 'I wouldn't want you to think that it was charity.'

'I'll recognise that you're just doing your Christian duty,' he said, and quoted, '"I was sick and Ye visited me." But I'd rather you came with books than chicken.'

Suddenly daring, she held out her hand and he clasped it in his strong, brown fingers. She could feel the calluses rough against her soft skin, and his hand was warm and firm despite his injury. 'I'll come as soon as I can,' she said, and wondered if the promise was to him or to herself.

Adam watched her pick her way carefully down the garden path to the road. Her full, swaying skirts and ash-blonde ringlets swinging below her small bonnet gave her an air of fragility so that she looked almost like a child dressed up in her mother's clothes. But she was a woman, he had recognised that at once, and a strong one. Ma Downing had told him how Clara had saved his life, staunching the bloody wound because there was no one else to do it.

He smiled suddenly. She was tough enough to act like that, bullying miners twice her age and handling his wounded body, but she was too soft-hearted to kill an injured puppy, and too sentimental to leave it to die.

At the memory he reached down to the floor. He could move around a little as long as he took it slowly and, though he hated the thought of killing the puppy as much as she did, he could not let it linger in pain.

To his surprise, the puppy was not there; it had crawled forward and was wolfing down the chicken pieces spilled on the earth floor.

It couldn't be that badly hurt, he decided, letting his gaze wander back out of the window and follow Clara as she made her way back down the road, her basket swinging easily now that she no longer had to worry about the puppy.

A gentle lick woke him from his reverie. The puppy had crawled back to his side and its small pink tongue was rasping at his thumb.

He picked it up and examined it. The puppy would always limp, but its wounds were less severe than they had seemed at first glance and the food seemed to have done it good. It no longer looked as if it were about to die.

He reached a sudden decision. 'How are we off for cobwebs, Ma?'

'You know very well there isn't a cobweb in the place,' she said tartly, 'and there won't be as long as I'm here.'

'Then you'll just have to go next door and get some,' said Adam, suddenly cheerful. 'There's another injured creature in need of them. And the honey.' And he stroked the puppy's head with a gentle finger while his eyes followed Clara until she was out of sight.

Chapter 5

Clara breathed a sigh of pure pleasure as she gazed around the crowded room. The Manor was as old as Penalverne but carried its years more gracefully. With its diamond-leaded windowpanes and tall, Elizabethan chimneys it had always struck her as romantic rather than simply old when she had visited the house as a child.

But now she was seeing it as an adult for the first time – the rooms decked out in their party best, the low beams shining softly in the gentle candlelight, the white shoulders of the women in their low-cut gowns gleaming amidst the severe black of the men's evening clothes . . . The low hum of conversation and the crackling of the fire was under-laid by the rustle of silk and taffeta as the women moved slowly through the company, their wide skirts sweeping the thick carpets.

Clara felt her chest tighten as the golden hair of Edward Blacklock caught her eye. She had hardly dared to hope that he would be here. It was a long ride in the dark from his home near Newlyn, even though the weather was mild for early May and the full moon, shining in a perfectly clear sky, had lit the rutted Cornish roads as clearly as if it had been day.

She heard his laugh ring out above the buzz of conversation, then he moved slightly, and Clara saw that he was talking to Isabelle Kings-ley, the daughter of the house. Stupid of her to feel that pang of disappointment, she chided herself, forcing her attention back to the young Naval Lieutenant who was detailed to lead her into dinner. He was less tall and attractive than Edward but less intimidating, too, his dark eyes gleaming with appreciation as he bowed over her extended hand.

But it was a thrill to discover that she was seated at the table between the two of them. Clara had found her thoughts constantly turning to Edward since their brief meeting at Penalverne three days earlier. She could still remember the shiver that had run through her as she felt his eyes on her, a sensation that was half excitement, half fear.

At least she had the confidence of knowing that now she was attractively and appropriately gowned. Her hair was done in the latest style, hanging in ringlets around her face, with just a couple of white rosebuds to emphasise her innocence. Her low-cut evening dress showed off her deep bosom to perfection and echoed the emerald of her eyes. She had already caught the Lieutenant giving it an appreciative glance.

She was suddenly aware that the man opposite was smiling at her as if he knew her. As he caught her eye he rose slightly in his seat and bowed to her. 'You won't remember me, Miss Pentreath, but I was at Wheal Susan three days ago. James Henson at your service. I'm a reporter for the *Mining Quarterly*.'

Clara stared at him blankly. He smiled back. 'I'm not surprised that you can't remember me, but please believe that I shall never forget you. You were magnificent – a heroine!'

'You must tell us more, Mr Henson,' Isabelle Kingsley broke in from where she was seated on the far side of Edward Blacklock. 'A *heroine*? I have heard nothing of this. I didn't even know that Clara is in the habit of visiting the mine. My papa never lets me near any of the men who work in his business,' and she preened herself slightly, her eyes sliding to Edward as if to see how he approved of this evidence of good breeding.

'If Miss Pentreath had not been at the mine that day, I am convinced that a man would have died.' Mr Henson's voice was warm in praise. 'I have never seen such quick thinking, nor so much resolution. A miner was brought up from the mine, badly injured. It is no exaggeration to say that he was bleeding to death. There was a gash right along his side where the ram had been blown into his body by the gunpowder prematurely exploding.'

'Mr Henson!' Isabelle fanned herself furiously. 'Please. We are eating!'

'Aye, so you say, and so would all of today's young ladies. But Miss Pentreath is made of sterner stuff. No fainting or hysterics for her! She realised what had to be done, and, by George, she did it.'

As he spoke, Clara was aware of a pool of silence spreading out from him along the table. Everyone was listening to the reporter's story, the enthusiasm in his voice catching their attention. She risked one look and met Lady Susan's furious gaze, then lowered her face again, wishing she could die. This was the end of her social career, finished before it had begun. Who would ever invite such a brazen female as she had proved herself, to respectable dinner parties?

40

'But what did she do?' Lieutenant Laity asked, leaning eagerly across the table.

'She stopped the bleeding. The men were useless – you know how they can be without leadership. But Miss Pentreath took charge. She stopped the bleeding single-handedly; she even ripped up her own petticoats to staunch the wound.'

Even through the drumming of blood in her ears Clara could hear Isabelle's outraged gasp. Her face burning, she stared fixedly at her plate, unwilling to see the condemnation in the eyes around her.

'The man died though, I suppose?' Christopher Kingsley, the owner of the Manor, raised a questioning eyebrow at Captain Pentreath.

'Not at all. Clara went to see him yesterday, took the fellow some chicken, and he's up again and recovering.' Hugh picked up his glass. 'I'm glad of it too. He's Adam Trevelyan, one of my best tributers and a good man to boot. When the mine picks up I'm planning to make him a captain under me.' He drained the glass in one swallow. 'You'd better hope he gets well quickly, Kingsley, or you may find you'll be paying more for your brandy than you're accustomed to.'

There was a moment's frozen silence. Clara risked a glance up, trying to see the cause. Her dinner partner saw her bewilderment and took pity on her. He turned towards Hugh Pentreath. 'I don't think we've been introduced, sir. I am Lieutenant Laity of Her Majesty's Royal Navy. I am presently stationed at Pendeen in charge of the Preventative Station there.'

Clara saw her father colour. Her whole family would be ostracised after tonight, she thought miserably, imagining what her mother would say to the two of them when they were alone in the carriage. To her relief, the reporter took up the conversation as though there had been no dreadful faux pas. He eagerly addressed the Lieutenant. 'I hadn't realised that there was a Preventative Station here. I thought that smuggling had stopped now that the excise duty has been reduced?'

'There is certainly a great deal less of it since Sir Robert Peel removed the duty on many of the goods that used to be smuggled,' the Lieutenant replied, 'but down here it has become almost a tradition, and I expect it will continue as long as those who should know better encourage it.' His eyes rested casually on his host as he spoke and Clara was amused to see a tinge of red brighten Christopher Kingsley's cheeks.

'The miners do it to supplement their income, and to provide the local inns with spirits to which they are not entitled,' he continued.

The reporter nodded. 'I've already found out about the kiddleywinks down here and the fact that they are only supposed to sell beer.'

Lieutenant Laity went on, 'In fact, our role is changing. Now we are as concerned with the safety of shipping as we are with smuggling. The Longships Lighthouse is wonderful, but there are still too many wrecks. We assist whenever we can, and at the very least we help stop the wrecking.'

The reporter was shocked. 'You mean that still goes on?' he asked.

'No, ships aren't lured deliberately onto the rocks, if that's what you mean, but down here you will often hear men talk about wrecking – that is, collecting stuff that is washed off the wrecks onto the shore. Sometimes they go further and board a stricken vessel to carry off any of the valuable cargo that they can get. That is what we try to prevent, but it is a hard business. Cornishmen have lived this way for years and can't see why it is suddenly illegal to do something that their families have done since time immemorial.'

'And what will you do about that man Miss Pentreath saved?' asked the reporter. 'It will be hard for him if she saved his life, only for him to be thrown into jail because of a careless remark at a dinner party.'

Clara also turned to the Lieutenant. She had been concerned about this.

He shrugged. 'I can do nothing. I know the names of many men who are supposed to be smugglers, but unless I can catch them in possession of smuggled goods, or I have trustworthy witnesses, I am helpless. The laws of the land apply to smugglers as much as to anyone else.' He turned to Clara with a smile. 'So you can rest assured, Miss Pentreath, I shall not be arresting the man you saved just because of a careless remark by your father, which I am sure, in any case,' and he looked severely at Mr Kingsley, 'that he meant as a joke.'

She breathed a sigh of relief, forcing herself to nibble at the food on her plate. She had refused the roast veal and saddle of lamb, but even the capons in white sauce, the lightest of the dishes, seemed to stick in her throat after the stresses of the last half hour. At least, she thought, the conversation had moved away from Adam Trevelyan and smuggling. Then, to her horror, James Henson finished his plateful of raised pie and brought up the subject once again.

'I would have thought that you would be out patrolling tonight, Lieutenant,' the reporter said thoughtfully. 'The weather must be ideal for catching smugglers.'

'Too good,' said the Lieutenant dryly. 'They're not fools. You won't

42

find them out on a clear night like this doing anything worse than a bit of fishing. No, the times for smuggling are when there's a new moon and the sky is cloudy. Weather like this, I can relax. There won't even be a shipwreck with these light winds and full moon. But in a fortnight's time, when the nights are dark and you can't see your hand in front of your face – that's when I shall be busy!'

'You say that this Adam Trevelyan is recovering?' the reporter asked Clara. 'He must have a strong constitution! And from what your father says, he is obviously an unusual man.'

'I think he is,' Clara agreed enthusiastically. 'When I visited him yesterday, I expected that he would still be abed but he was sitting up and could move around with care.' She could hardly believe what was happening. Lady Susan had always told her that to attract a husband, a lady should be frail and meek, but she hadn't acted at all like that at the mine, yet both the reporter and the Lieutenant seemed to admire her for it.

Edward Blacklock broke in from her other side: 'These uneducated men are little better than animals in many ways, and their powers of recovery show that. A gentleman would have been laid up for weeks with a wound of comparable severity.'

Clara was delighted for a chance to speak to him again. 'Mr Trevelyan isn't a gentleman,' she admitted, 'but he certainly isn't uneducated either. When I called round yesterday he was reading a book about geology. In fact,' she took a deep breath, 'I promised to ask Papa if he could borrow some of the mining books in our library to read while he is convalescing.'

She had been unsure how to raise the subject with her father, but the support of the men around her gave her courage.

'And what would you think about that, sir?' asked the reporter, peering down the table at Clara's father. 'Would you be willing to lend any of your valuable books to a common miner?'

'If it's Adam Trevelyan, I don't mind at all,' Hugh Pentreath replied easily. 'I'd trust him with my life. If Clara is willing to take them to him, I will lend them willingly.'

'Of course, Papa,' Clara answered demurely, her elfin features lighting up at the thought of the pleasure such a loan would give Adam.

To her surprise, Edward asked stiffly, 'You don't feel any repugnance at seeing the man again, then?'

'No, of course not. Why should I?' She stared at him, startled.

'I only wondered.' There was a strange glitter in his eyes. 'You were so closely closeted with him, touching him so intimately . . .'

'There were other people around all the time,' Clara pointed out quickly. 'We were never alone. And the injury was so bad, I didn't have time to think of myself.'

'There was a lot of blood, then?' he asked. His voice was husky and he seemed almost breathless.

'Quite a lot,' Clara answered, trying to fight down the feeling of unease that was sweeping over her.

'You must have got it on you,' he continued. 'You must have got your hands covered with blood. Did you have to bind him up? Did you have to pull his torn skin together?' He was staring down at her hands as if he could see the blood still on them, as if he could see her touching the unconscious body of the injured man.

'Mr Blacklock.' Clara was beginning to feel frightened. 'I don't think this is a suitable subject for the dinner-table.' She glanced at Isabelle for support.

'No, indeed.' Isabelle was bored with a conversation in which she could play no part. Clara had acted like the underbred little hussy she was. Why should the men all get so excited about it? She might be the grand-daughter of an earl, but it was easy to see that the common blood of Captain Pentreath ran strongest in her veins. 'Besides, Mama is about to lead the ladies out so that you gentlemen can drink your brandy in peace.'

Clara smiled. 'I shouldn't think Lieutenant Laity will enjoy his very much – not if he thinks it might have been smuggled.'

He smiled back at her. 'There's no evidence, my dear Miss Pentreath. And without evidence I shall give our host the benefit of the doubt and enjoy it with a clear conscience.'

Clara burst out laughing then stopped abruptly as she caught her mother's eye. Laughing out loud was another of the interminable things that a lady shouldn't do. But the Lieutenant was laughing with her and even Edward Blacklock was smiling with a warmer look in his grey eyes, stroking his golden moustache with one finger as he took in her amused face.

Why were there all these stupid rules? she wondered, rising obediently to her feet as Mrs Kingsley collected the ladies with her eye. Sometimes it seemed as if everything she wanted to do was banned, and everything she *didn't* want to do was compulsory!

She met Edward Blacklock's gaze as he held the door open for the ladies to pass through. Well, he was a gentleman, and he didn't seem to mind that she kept breaking the rules. Perhaps she should just ignore her mother and keep on doing as she liked. She flashed him a smile as she passed by.

Edward mopped his brow as he closed the door behind her. His hands were shaking. That girl! He could see her in his imagination even now, crouched over the miner, her hands covered with blood. The picture stirred him as he had seldom been moved before.

What was it about Clara Pentreath that so excited him? She wasn't as pretty as Isabelle, nor as charming. He compared them mentally, contrasting Isabelle's slender figure and elegant, smooth, dark hair with Clara's shorter, riper figure and that strange ash-blonde hair, baby-fine, that refused to stay confined in the neat chignon that fashion dictated but insisted on curling in loose, soft wisps around her elfin face.

Logic said that Isabelle was the woman for him. She was everything that society expected a man in his position to desire. But it was Clara who excited him as no other woman he had ever met.

He would talk to her afterwards, when the men moved to the drawing room for tea and coffee, he decided. He would fathom out the strange attraction she held for him, then, maybe, he would be able to dismiss it and let his life return to its usual calm course. He drained his brandy in a single gulp, then turned his attention to the conversation that had been flowing, unheeded, around him.

Christopher Kingsley leaned back in his chair, his waistcoat comfortably unbuttoned.

'Well, Pentreath, I hope you are going to have better news for us at the shareholders' meeting tomorrow.' He pulled at his cigar. 'It's a year now since we've had a dividend in your mine. You'll have us all bankrupt at this rate.'

'Are you a shareholder too?' asked James Henson inquisitively.

'Of course.' Christopher Kingsley winked at him. 'I am, and Blacklock here is too. So's the surgeon at the mine but he, er, can't be here tonight.' Because there was no way he would have his wife insulted by that alcoholic loudmouth, he added to himself.

'But as a chandler that means that you are doubly at risk, surely?' the reporter probed. 'If the mine closes, you'll lose your money *and* your trade.'

'No danger of that,' said Kingsley comfortably, without noticing that Pentreath had not replied to his earlier question. 'We've got a good Captain and a good mine there. Just a temporary worry. As to losing trade – there's no way! I'm too good a businessman for that, and so's Blacklock here.'

He leaned forward confidentially. 'The thing is, you shee, er see, we've got trade by being shareholders. There's plenty of chandlers around, and quite a few smelting works, so why should Wheal Susan come to us rather than the rest?'

He waved his cigar in a large motion, spilling ash onto the table. 'I'll tell you why. Because we're shareholders, that's why. So we get the trade. Isn't that right, Blacklock?' He hiccupped gently.

'That's right,' Edward agreed sourly. Why couldn't the drunken fool finish his glass so that they could join the women?

Kingsley went on, 'We get the business and we get paid at once. I don't allow tick, and as for Blacklock,' he grinned lopsidedly at his companion, 'he doesn't pay until the stuff's been assayed and stamped, so he's all right.' He banged his glass on the table. 'I tell you, I've done well out of the mine over the last ten years, damn well.' He hiccupped again. 'And that's without the dividend. The good ol' dividend.' He peered owlishly at the glass in his hand. 'Le'sh drink to the dividend.'

Captain Pentreath stared at his host. Kingsley had done well out of the mine. They all had. But the way they had complained last time just because he had asked them for a payment of fifteen pounds a share! What would they say tomorrow when there would actually be a call? When instead of taking their profits out of the mine, they would have to pay out even more money to keep it going? Would Kingsley and the others remember then how rich the mine had made them?

But it didn't matter what they thought, or how they felt; he knew there was tin there! He would keep the mine open if it killed him. His hand clenched round his glass and the delicate stem snapped between his fingers.

'No harm done.' The Lieutenant was there, a handkerchief ready to wrap round the gash in his hand. 'You'll live to fight another day, Captain, and to have another talk with your charming wife. Talking of which, shall we join the ladies?' He gazed enquiringly at them all.

'You're right,' Captain Pentreath agreed heavily. 'We've sat round the table long enough.' He glanced at Blacklock, who seemed mesmerized by the drops of blood that spattered the table in a small half-circle. 'Still after my blood, Blacklock? I'm surprised I'm not sucked dry by now.'

Edward jumped. He had been lost in his thoughts, remembering again his vision of Clara with the injured miner. Eagerly, he leaped to his feet and moved towards the door. He wanted to talk to that girl and he wasn't going to let that blasted Navy man get there first.

Conversation was languishing in the drawing room when the men made their appearance. The women mostly clustered as close together on the sofas as their voluminous skirts would allow them, exchanging desultory gossip. Clara sat by herself by a small table, turning the pages of a book of prints of Classical sites and fighting down the fury that threatened to overwhelm her.

How dare the women treat her like dirt, just because she had sullied her hands by helping a common miner? She swung her small foot angrily under her full green skirts, not taking in any of the pictures as she turned the pages.

Her ears were still ringing with her mother's condemnation. 'Lowering yourself . . . touching a strange man . . . half-naked . . . unladylike.' Clara gritted her teeth. Why did none of them see that she had saved the man's life? And he *wasn't* a common miner. She had realised that almost as soon as she had met him again yesterday. She was glad that her father had given her permission to lend the man his books, though she had better not let Mama know what she was doing, or she would be forbidden ever to see Adam again. And Clara wasn't going to risk that.

Adam was an interesting man, a man like her father must have been when he was young. He piqued her curiosity. He was a lot more interesting than the boring, so-called ladies who sat around her making small talk.

Clara scowled at them, her emerald eyes fierce under her surprisingly dark brows. They should be proud that she had acted so promptly, not condemn her for breaking some silly rules that were meaningless anyhow.

At least the men didn't despise her for what she had done, she comforted herself. Her father had been proud of her, and the reporter had been impressed. As for the Lieutenant, she had definitely noticed a glow in his eyes as he had looked at her after he had heard the story. She glanced up as the door opened, grateful that the after-dinner tedium was to be broken at last.

Edward and the young Lieutenant were the first men into the room, defying the usual custom of following their elders. Clara watched them approach. She had already realised that Isabelle Kingsley considered Edward to be her own particular protégé, and wasn't surprised when she moved forward to intercept him. But Edward sidestepped easily, leaving her to face the Lieutenant while he made his way over to the little table where Clara was seated.

'Is this seat taken?' His voice was soft and cultured, his moustache golden in the soft candlelight. Startled, she indicated the empty chair beside her.

'I am just looking at some pictures of Greece. Have you ever been there, Mr Blacklock?'

'No, unfortunately.' He smiled at her. His light grey eyes looked almost transparent in this light. 'I have always had a strange idea about Greece. I have always thought that it would be a wonderful place to visit with a woman you love, perhaps on a wedding journey.'

Strange men did not usually mention such things to a lady on short acquaintance. Clara felt a small shock at his words but she would not let him see it. 'That is a very romantic notion, Mr Blacklock. I didn't realise that gentlemen thought things like that.'

'Not think about marriage? And why should we be different from yourselves? You are still a young lady, but I know that you have thought very seriously about the matter.'

'You know nothing of the sort,' Clara protested.

'No? Then I didn't hear you tell your mother that you would love and honour your husband above all men?'

Clara felt herself blush. 'You are unfair, sir. I didn't realise that you were listening or I would never have said such a thing.' She fanned herself, aware that her low-cut dress was revealing that more than her cheeks were red. Her blush deepened as she saw Edward, too, had noticed the fact.

'But why should you be embarrassed? Surely that is just what every man would want his wife to think?'

'Then when I am a wife, I won't be embarrassed to let my husband know what I think,' she said tartly. 'Until then, I would have hoped that my thoughts and beliefs were known only to my family.' Her green eyes challenged his, half-daring him to take offence at her assertive attitude.

But Edward was delighted with her. She was a spirited little thing. And she did not seem to know how to flirt. She was probably so innocent that it would be easy to take advantage of her, he thought, his eyes again following the fading pink of her blush until it was hidden by her dress. He would definitely not let any Naval man take this little peach away from him. He stroked his golden moustache thoughtfully. 'Would you be in if I were to call tomorrow after the shareholders' meeting?'

Clara shook her head. She had already promised herself that she would visit Adam tomorrow. He must be bored sitting still all day, and this would be an ideal time for him to catch up on all the knowledge he yearned for.

'Then the day after?' Edward suggested. 'Perhaps, if the weather is fine, I could take you and your mother for a picnic on the moors.'

Clara could feel herself grow hot again. He seemed so eager. 'If Mama will approve,' she murmured correctly, then glanced up at a movement beside her.

Isabelle Kingsley was staring down at her, and her eyes were full of hate.

Chapter 6

Captain Pentreath rose reluctantly to his feet and let his eyes wander over the crowded Count House. In the old days he had always looked forward to these regular bi-monthly meetings of the adventurers, when he would tell of the profits that the mine had made, talk excitedly of his plans for expansion, and announce the dividend to loud cheers.

Now, the faces that stared back at him were closed and suspicious. Even the walls of the building seemed to be reproaching him, their once pristine whiteness now marred with patches of damp and the marks of wear. Above, cobwebs moved in the slight draught, mute testimony of the mine's decline.

He cleared his throat uncomfortably and began to speak.

'You're only here for one thing, so I won't keep you in suspense by going over my usual rigmarole of how much ore we've brought up and how the search for new lodes is going. You want to know how this mine will affect you individually, so I'll tell you.'

He took a deep breath. 'I am proposing a call on this mine of twenty pounds a share.'

There was a moment's stunned silence then Christopher Kingsley leapt to his feet.

'You're mad! Twenty pounds? It's too much! We've already paid out twice before to keep the mine going because you told us we were going to find that new lode any day. Now you come back and ask us for twenty pounds a share!'

His red face was mottled with anger. 'I'm not paying out good money in this way. If Wheal Susan can't earn its keep, then let it fold. Knack the bal, I say.'

Others were on their feet, shouting: 'Knack the bal! Knack the bal!' The cobwebs fluttered crazily from the beams as the time-honoured phrase echoed round the room.

49

Hugh Pentreath hammered on the table in front of him with a sample of tin-bearing rock. *'Quiet!'* he thundered.

He waited until they were back in their seats, then forced himself to speak quietly and reasonably. 'In the last twenty years you've had over a thousand pounds dividend on each share. And that's on top of all the money most of you have made selling us supplies or buying the ore. Surely you can pay out another twenty pounds? Once we find that lode, the dividends will start again and you'll all be sitting back raking in the money.'

'That makes over fifty pound you've asked from us,' Kingsley shouted back. 'How do we know that you won't be coming back in two months' time and asking us for another twenty pounds? And another? How long do we have to pour money into that hole outside before you finally come to your senses, Pentreath? This mine is finished! There IS no tin there. I say knack the bal. We can sell off the pumping engine and get a bit of our money back that way.'

There was a murmur of agreement from the other men. One after the other took up the cry once more: 'Knack the bal! Knack the bal!'

Hugh hammered on the table again. 'Sell the pumping engine? Don't you realise we're in the worst recession that tin mining has ever known? Three mines have closed in this district in the last six months. No one will buy our engine. It will rust where it lies.'

'If three mines have closed, then that shows that there's no point in trying to keep this mine open,' another man shouted. 'Knack it!'

Hugh struggled for control of the meeting. 'Gentlemen, you can trust me. I told you there was tin here when other miners thought this place was barren. I found that tin, and I've made you a profit. A very good profit.'

He paused, surveying the angry faces in front of him, trying to make them see what was so obvious to him. 'The reason that our profits were so good was not just because we found good tin, it's because our costs are low.' He enumerated on his fingers. 'Wheal Susan isn't a deep mine and it's a relatively dry mine; that keeps down the pumping costs. It's in good, hard granite so we don't have to waste time and money propping up long stretches.'

He waved a hand out of the window. 'Those other mines have been closed because their costs were so high that they can't make a profit unless the price of tin is high as well.'

He leaned towards them, urging them to believe him. 'But Wheal Susan is different. Our costs are low. Even if the price of tin dropped another ten pounds a ton, we could still make a profit.'

'Then why aren't we?' a voice shouted out. 'Why aren't we making this profit? Why are we paying out all this money?'

'Because we've lost the lode,' he explained patiently. 'I told you this last time.' He held his hands up palm to palm, then slid one of them forward to try to illustrate the problem. 'The tin lode has fractured. We have been following one half and reached the end of it, but the rest of it is out there somewhere, tantalisingly close. It could be a foot beyond where we've reached, it could be a yard to the left of the gallery we've dug. Once we find it, this mine will make a profit again – and a good one, at that. I just need money to keep going for another couple of months.'

'That's what you said last time,' Christopher Kingsley shouted out. 'I don't believe you. Yes, she's been a good mine, but now she's sucked dry. Knack her, I say!'

The others took up the shout. Hugh Pentreath turned to Edward Blacklock, knowing that the men would follow where he led. But Edward was leaning back against the wall, his arms crossed, his light-grey eyes empty of all emotion as he stared at the shouting men.

A sudden fury gripped Hugh. The mine meant nothing to them. They were jackals, content to take the money that he and his workers had sweated for. But it was life to the miners who worked in the mine and life to him. He gritted his teeth. He would not let the mine go.

He hammered on the table again. 'This is a meeting of gentlemen,' he reminded them, 'and I expect you to behave as such.' He half-heard a whispered remark mentioning his antecedents but he closed his ears to it. There was more at stake here than mere personal pride.

'This mine was established as a cost-book company,' he stated formally, 'and under those rules, before the mine can be closed, any outstanding dividends must be paid, and any outstanding calls must also be collected.' He bared his teeth wolfishly at them.

'So, gentlemen, whatever your feelings in the matter, you owe this mine twenty pounds for each share you own, and the mine cannot be closed until that money has been paid.'

'That's a formality, Hugh, and you know it,' Christopher Kingsley bellowed angrily.

'It's the law,' Hugh retorted implacably. 'That money is due from you, and I expect to get it.'

'It's due from you, too! You own as many shares as any of us.' Kingsley was bitter.

Hugh pulled a wad of notes out of his pocketbook and laid it on the table. 'There is my money already. I don't avoid my responsibilities,' and his eyes challenged them all.

There was a low muttering of discontent, then men reached for their pocketbooks. They had all come prepared, Hugh realised wryly. They had guessed what the situation would be, or else Blacklock had

51

made sure that they knew. Most of the men here banked with his bank and he knew them all socially as well. There was plenty of opportunity to make sure they all knew which way the wind was blowing. No wonder he didn't need to speak himself at these meetings.

The pile of banknotes and notes of hand and guineas grew rapidly on the table and Sam Grenfell moved from his quiet corner and began to count them with quick efficiency.

'There now.' Christopher Kingsley threw his money on the growing pile. 'That's the last money this damned mine is going to take from me. Now let's close her down and good riddance.' There were nods of agreement throughout the room. None of the men there enjoyed parting with good money.

Hugh stood at the table again. 'It is of course your right to close the mine down if you wish it,' he stated. 'I have to do what the majority of the shareholders in this company decide. But I would like to point out that there might be another way out of your troubles.'

'If it costs more money, I'm not interested,' one man cried, and there was a general murmur of agreement.

'But if you were to make money by it?' Hugh let the words drop into the sudden pause.

'Make money? What do you mean?' He could feel their attention sharpening at the thought.

He said, 'If you knack the mine, your shares are worthless. No one will ever buy them. But if you don't vote immediately to close the mine, I am willing to buy them from you for ten pounds a share.'

There was a moment's stunned silence then someone objected, 'We paid fifty pounds for those shares.'

'And if you close the mine you'll get nothing for them,' Hugh retorted. 'I'll give you ten but not a penny more.'

There was no reaction for a long time, then a muttering began. Hugh smiled grimly to himself. They were a suspicious lot, who would never take anything on face value.

'Why are you doing this?' The surgeon was on his feet, urged forward as spokesman by the others.

'I'll tell you why.' Hugh stood proudly in front of them. 'I'm doing this because *I* believe in this mine. I believe that she has a future, and a rich one. I won't let all that tin that God put there go to waste just because there are a few men here who haven't the guts to stand a few squalls.'

His faded blue eyes surveyed them, trying to gauge their reaction. 'I will use my own money to keep her going if necessary, and by God, when I find that tin, those of you who chickened out now are going to feel pretty sick about it.

'And I'll tell you another thing.' He stared at Christopher Kingsley directly, challenging him. 'Anyone who sells their shares can forget about supplying the mine or working for her.' He transferred his gaze to the surgeon. 'I will not deal with cowards who don't believe in what I am trying to do.'

He took a deep breath, pushing his hands into his coat pockets so that no one could see that they were trembling with tension. 'Well, gentlemen? What are you going to do?'

Most of the men turned to their neighbours, discussing, commenting, anything to put off being the first to make a decision. Christopher Kingsley leaped to his feet.

'Say as you please, Pentreath, I'm not tying myself to a useless hole in the ground. You can have my shares and welcome to them.'

'Give your name and the number of shares you are selling to the purser,' Hugh said calmly. 'I will settle up with you later.' He turned back to the others. 'Well? Is anyone else going to follow Mr Kingsley and sell me his shares?'

More men rose to their feet but, to his relief, about half of the adventurers stayed where they were. Hugh pretended to busy himself with his papers, his ears straining to follow the low conversations that were going on around him.

'Pentreath is a wily fellow,' he heard the surgeon say. 'It's my guess he's made a rich find. This is just a ruse to increase his profits.' The other man nodded agreement, making no move to come to the table where Sam Grenfell was rapidly writing down names.

They wouldn't believe that I was just doing this for a dream, Hugh thought. They can only understand pounds, shillings and pence. He glanced out of the corner of his eye at Edward Blacklock. The young man was still standing as he had before, his arms crossed, but this time his light-grey eyes were fixed appraisingly on Hugh himself.

At least he hadn't made any move as yet to sell his shares. Hugh knew that if he had, every man there would have followed Blacklock's lead. Nor had he tried to stop Hugh's rash offer to buy any shares for sale. What's he after? Hugh wondered. Does he, like the surgeon, think that I have found a new lode? Or is he playing a deeper game? He shivered slightly.

When all those who had wanted to sell their shares had returned to their seats, he spoke again.

'It is the custom, after these meetings, for the shareholders to enjoy a good dinner together, and so we always have done. Up until now.'

His lips twisted as he caught the flash of faces turning towards him at the mention of the meal.

'However,' Hugh went on, 'some of you are no longer shareholders and so are not entitled to the dinner.' He grinned at Christopher Kingsley, noting the disappointment in his face, 'And those of you who are still shareholders will, I expect, be glad to hear that one of the economies I have made is to scrap the "free" dinners until the mine is in profit again. Gentlemen, I wish you all good afternoon.' And he turned and walked from the Count House without a backward glance.

Around him, the mine was still working smoothly as it always had done. Above the sound of the tin stamps he could hear the balmaidens singing. With luck he had saved their jobs, but for how long?

He made his way to the engine house where the great beam rose and fell with monotonous regularity against the sky, pumping water from the lower levels so that the men could continue to work in peace. Hugh Pentreath always found comfort here. Despite its huge size, the engine was virtually silent, the loudest noise being the soft gurgle of water in the pipes.

Ben Pasco slammed the door to the firehouse shut as Hugh came in. 'She's going well, Cap'n.' There was honest pride in his voice. He nurtured the machine as if it were a sick wife.

Hugh dropped a hand on his shoulder. 'Then go outside for a pipe, Ben. I can look after her for half an hour.'

He knew that there was no way to avoid the confrontation he was expecting, but if it had to be faced, then he wanted it to take place here, here in the heart of the mine, where the huge steam engine sighed softly as it worked like a giant asleep.

He breathed deeply, drawing in the smell of hot oil, taking pleasure in the sight of the shining wood and softly gleaming brasses. This epitomised all he loved about the mine, all he had struggled for. The final step on the road he had chosen would be taken here.

Hugh heard the step behind him but he did not turn around even when Edward Blacklock spoke. 'That was a dangerous game to play, Pentreath.'

He fought to keep his voice neutral as he answered his opponent. 'Risky, perhaps, but I reckon it paid off.'

'Do you know how many shares you've just agreed to buy?'

'Near enough,' said Hugh heavily, 'though no doubt you know exactly.'

'And the cost of those shares?'

'I'm no fool. I can work it out.'

'And what,' asked Edward Blacklock, his light tenor voice pleasant and casual, 'do you intend to use for money?'

Hugh turned to him then. 'Are you saying you'll not support me?'

'You have nothing in the bank.' Edward Blacklock spoke as calmly as if he were discussing a sample of ore. 'You have just bought over fifty shares in a mine which is to all intents worthless. Unless a miracle happens, you will have to make another call on the shareholders in two months' time, and you will be liable then for the ten or twenty pounds due for each of the fifty shares you have just bought, as well as the shares you already own. Would I be wise to continue to support you?'

'You know I have other assets,' Hugh spoke angrily. 'I own shares in other mines besides this one.'

'Mines which are also doing badly,' Edward retorted. 'Only one is paying a dividend. The shares in the others aren't worth a tithe of what you bought them for.'

'I have other assets.' Hugh reached out and placed a hand on the control handle, fondling the smooth iron. 'I'll pledge those if you need extra security.'

'And what are those assets?'

'You know damn well what they are!' Hugh lost his temper for a moment. 'I own Penalverne and the farm around it. You can have the deeds for security to cover the loan to buy the shares.'

'And if the mine doesn't make money in the next few months?' Edward asked.

'Then I'll be bankrupt.' Hugh's voice was rough with pain. 'Bankrupt, God help me, because I know that you won't.'

'Just as long as you realise the position.' There was a note in Edward's voice that Hugh could not place. Amusement? Triumph? Silently, he stood and watched as his tormentor left the engine house and picked his way carefully across the muddy floor of the dressing yard to his waiting horse.

Alone again, Hugh leaned his head against the whitewashed wall of the huge building and closed his eyes in pain. What had he done? He had bought time for the mine – but at what cost to his family? If they didn't find tin within a couple of months, the Pentreaths would lose their home.

He thought of the way they had looked at the Kingsleys' party, Lady Susan in her element, making the most of her superior social position, Clara fêted and admired by all the young men. What would their lives be like if his gamble failed? He knew that he could earn enough as a mine captain to keep them from starving, but they would lose everything they had been brought up to expect from life if he didn't find that lode within the next four months. And his best tributer was injured.

He buried his face in his hands. 'Oh God, forgive me,' he muttered, but as he looked up again at the huge beam nodding against the sky, he knew that he had had no alternative.

Chapter 7

There was no way that Clara could have backed out of the meeting even if she had changed her mind at the last moment.

Adam Trevelyan was sitting in the sun outside his front door as she approached the lonely cottage, mending a broken fishing net. He glanced up as he heard her footsteps and she saw his face become still and unreadable as he recognised her.

'I am glad to see that you are feeling better,' she greeted him, wondering briefly what to call him. 'Mr Trevelyan' seemed too respectful, 'Adam' too intimate, and she suspected that to simply call him by his surname would be resented by him as a sign of her superior social position.

'Not more charity?' He was looking at the basket swinging from her arm.

'Books,' she informed him succinctly. 'You didn't tell me what you wanted so I have brought a selection.' She would have died rather than let him know that she had spent nearly an hour in her father's library that morning, trying to pick the right books for him.

She had dismissed any that seemed to be elementary, guessing that he would consider this to be another form of condescension and the ones she had chosen were, she discovered, almost meaningless to her, with their talk of killas, heamatite and cassiterite.

She held out the basket and he reached for its contents eagerly, his hands reverent as he fondled the leather bindings and turned the stiff pages.

'Aren't you going to ask me to sit down?' Clara was half-amused, half-irritated by the way he seemed to forget her so completely, becoming lost in an instant in the treasures she had brought for him.

He looked up, startled and guilty, but Mother Downing was already bustling out of the cottage with a rough wooden chair.

'You sit here, my handsome, and put up your pretty parasol to keep the sun off your face. Make yourself comfortable and I'll bring you out some Sky Blue and Sinkers for your tea.'

'Some what?' Clara had never heard the expression before.

Amused, Adam explained. 'Skimmed milk and bread. It's what all the miners eat before they go down the mine. Ma, here, has taken to giving it to me for tea as well. She seems to think I need feeding up or something.'

'You did lose a lot of blood,' Clara agreed unthinkingly, then blushed as the words brought back the memory of this man's body under her hands, his strong muscles and soft skin.

She tried to hide her sudden embarrassment by settling herself busily on the chair, spreading out the sweeping skirts of her new apple-green walking dress around her. When she looked up, Clara was surprised to see that Adam was looking as uncomfortable as she felt. Did he, too, feel embarrassment at the thought that she had touched him so intimately? That he had been helpless under her hands?

It was a relief when Mother Downing broke the awkward silence, bustling out with two earthenware bowls.

Clara stared doubtfully at the strangely coloured liquid. It did seem to be a light-blue colour.

Adam cleared his throat. 'It's barley bread in warm skimmed milk and water. It's filling.'

'But not very nourishing, I imagine.' Clara dipped the pewter spoon cautiously in the mess, grateful that there were no other cottages nearby. If her mother ever heard that Clara had been sitting in the sun in a cottage garden, eating with a common miner, she would probably never let her leave the house unaccompanied again.

A light pressure on her slipper made her look down. A small black and white puppy gazed up at her with pleading eyes.

'You didn't kill him!' She turned to Adam, her face alight with pleasure, then stooped to lift the little animal into her lap.

'Be careful with his leg. It's broken and it still pains him,' Adam said quickly.

'But you saved him. Oh, thank you! I never thought he would live.'

'It was that chicken you brought that did it.' Adam laid the books carefully down by his side. 'He dragged himself over to the meat and wolfed it all down. I reckon he was starving as much as anything, because after that he perked up. I got Ma to put cobwebs and honey on his cuts and he'll be as good as new in a week or so.'

'Well, I'm glad that the chicken didn't go entirely to waste.' Clara hid her face in the puppy's soft coat but he wiggled free and began to lap busily from the leftovers in the bowl in her lap.

'He still seems to be hungry,' she said worriedly, watching the triangular stub of a tail waggle madly as the animal ate.

'Him? He's a proper little bustguts,' Adam remarked caustically, watching the puppy eat as though it hadn't been fed for a week. Then, realising what he had said, he added hastily, 'I beg pardon. I shouldn't have used that word in front of a lady.'

'No,' Clara agreed, and they burst out laughing in unison. 'But I know what you mean,' she added, feeling the puppy's stomach, round with food.

She put the bowl and the puppy on the ground and sat back with a comfortable sigh. She felt at ease with this man, released from the tiresome conventions of a Victorian young lady. She gestured at the net. 'Do you do much fishing?'

'I share a boat with Norman Willcock who works on my payre. She's drawn up at Priest's Cove but we go out in her on summer evenings to catch a few pollock and mackerel. And in the autumn we can get enough pilchards to see us through the winter.' He glanced worriedly at the sun. 'Are you sure you're comfortable there? You can go inside if you'd prefer.'

'I am quite comfortable,' Clara said cheerfully. 'Besides, I'm not that fragile. Mama and I are going on a picnic tomorrow with Mr Blacklock so I shall be out in the sun all afternoon, then.'

There was a moment's stillness from the man at her side, then he said, his voice carefully neutral, 'Mr Blacklock is a fine-looking gentleman.'

'Almost like someone out of a novel.' Clara was careful to keep her voice as unemotional as his own. She found herself simultaneously attracted to Edward and scared by him. Sometimes he looked at her so intently, as if he couldn't keep his eyes off her.

She felt a chill as she remembered again his strange questions about how she had treated Adam. Was that how men were when they liked you? She longed to discuss her feelings with someone, but her mother would merely repeat that Edward Blacklock was the richest man in Penwith and her father seemed too preoccupied these days to answer any of her questions.

Perhaps she could find out something from the man at her side. Clara said carefully, 'My father seems to see a great deal of Mr Blacklock. I find it strange that one man can be both a banker and own a smelting works at the same time.'

Adam laughed harshly. 'All smelters are bankers! It's the only way they can use up all the money they make. The mines work for a pittance and they are going bust all the time but you never see a poor smelter.'

He wondered at her interest in the man. Was she seriously attracted? His heart bled for her if that were the case. He had heard rumours about some of Edward Blacklock's more unpleasant quirks from the Newlyn fishermen.

It would be a pity if a lovely, innocent girl like Clara Pentreath were to find herself married to a wretch like Blacklock. But what could Adam do about it? He could not have offered her advice on such a delicate subject, even if he were of her own social class. And Clara had made it all too obvious at her last visit that she considered him to be scarcely higher than the pig he kept in the back garden.

Clara twisted her fingers together, wondering how to continue with the subject. 'I understand that Mr Blacklock is one of the largest shareholders at the mine,' she ventured.

Adam bent again to his netting. 'That's so.' His expression was unreadable once more.

Clara tried again. 'I don't suppose the mine will be declaring a dividend today.' She knew that it was not done to discuss such matters with the men employed at Wheal Susan, but Adam would know how the mine was doing. The constant attendance of Edward Blacklock and her father's preoccupation had left her with a feeling that the mine was in more trouble than her father had revealed.

'I doubt it,' said Adam shortly. Didn't she know that there had been a call on the shareholders for the last two accounts? And there would be another today; of that he was certain. But if Captain Pentreath wanted to keep his financial difficulties hidden from his womenfolk it wasn't up to Adam to tell them the bad news.

Clara sighed. She was getting nowhere, learning nothing. The silence between them stretched out interminably. It seemed that neither of them could think of anything to say. And time was moving on. She should be leaving, but she felt a strange reluctance to go.

'Is there anything I can do for the puppy?' she asked. 'I feel that I have imposed him on you. If you would prefer me to take him . . .?'

'That won't be necessary,' Adam replied. 'Phil has taken a fancy to him now, and it does the boy good to have something to play with.' He looked at the lonely moorland that surrounded the cottage, where huge granite boulders thrust their hard shoulders through a veiling of bracken and yellow gorse. 'There's no one here for him to mix with, and he's alone down the mine except for me most of the day. A dog will be company for him.'

'I see. I am sure you're right.' There was nothing else to say, no reason to prolong her stay. Reluctantly, she rose to her feet. 'Well, I had better be going.'

'You'll be late back, otherwise,' Adam agreed.

Clara walked slowly to the gate. Adam watched her go, willing her to stay, willing her to turn around, but she seemed determined to leave. It was as she was shutting the gate that the thought struck him. 'About these books . . .'

'Yes?' She turned eagerly, her face alight.

Half-despising himself for his weakness, he said awkwardly, 'I'm a fast reader.'

She was there before him. 'And you'll need more books soon. That is no problem. I can bring more, and I can take back any you have finished with. Shall I come in a couple of days' time? Will that suit you?'

'That'll be fine.' Their eyes met and he felt as if he were drowning in her emerald gaze. She smiled broadly at him and walked down the road, more quickly now, with a spring in her step that hadn't been there before. Just past the turn in the road she passed another woman climbing the hill, a black-haired girl with the bright pink cheeks of one who worked in the open air.

Molly Willcock turned and stared after Clara as she passed. She felt a shiver of unease. Surely Phil hadn't been telling the truth when he spoke of Clara's attraction to Adam?

Then commonsense asserted itself. If she had been to see him for any reason, it would have been to bring him charity, and she knew how Adam would react to that! She remembered the long summer evenings that she and Adam had spent in each other's arms, lying on the cliffs above the restless sea, and tossed her head. No, she had nothing to fear from a namby-pamby lady like that.

Adam was a red-blooded man, as she knew to her delight, and he wouldn't be satisfied with the passionless couplings of the gentry. Not that Lady Susan would ever allow anything like THAT to happen. Clara would be destined for someone completely different, someone like Edward Blacklock. Molly's mouth stretched in a cruel smile. Miss Pentreath was welcome to that one and good luck to her! So it was with a light step and lighter heart that Molly approached the cottage.

'Well, look at you!' She leaned over the gate and grinned at Adam. 'There was me thinking you was at death's door, and here you are, as right as ninepence, with your head in some dirty old book!'

She swung the gate open and walked over to him, planting a hearty kiss on his lips. 'How are 'ee, me handsome?'

'Much better.' He hadn't even heard her approach. He had been lost in thoughts of Clara, trying to damp down the happiness that rose in him when he thought that within a few days he would see her again. After her cool innocence, Molly's loud brashness was like a slap in the face. With an effort he forced himself to smile at her. 'It was good of you to come and see me after working all day.'

She sank into the chair Clara had vacated and leaned back, spreading her legs out in front of her. 'It's a hot day for it, as well. I'm wet leaking.' She mopped her brow with a dirty piece of cloth. 'But I wanted to see how you were getting on, my dear, and anyway, Norman asked me to give you a message.'

'Yes?' Adam sat up, alert. A message from Norman could mean only one thing.

Molly spoke quietly now. 'He's heard from that Frenchie.' Even here she would not put it more plainly. 'The stuff will be laid on the night of the new moon, weather permitting.'

Adam nodded. He and Norman had a regular arrangement with a Frenchman in Brest; smuggled goods were dropped at a regular spot every month throughout the summer when the weather was good enough, then he and Norman would collect it the next night and bring it to shore.

'Norman says it's too late to try to stop it. He wants to know if he should get Ben Pasco or one of the other men to help him this time.'

'Of course not!' Adam was indignant. 'The fewer people who know about this the better. That's what we've always agreed.'

'But now you've been injured, he's got to have someone to help him,' Molly insisted. 'He can't get the kegs on board by himself.'

'I'll do it the same as always,' Adam said confidently.

'But you're injured!' Molly almost wailed it. 'You can't do things like that. My soul and body, you'll break the wound open and then where shall we be?'

'It's a fortnight to the new moon,' Adam pointed out. 'I shall be much better by then. Norman might have to do the heavy lifting but I shall be all right to steer the boat and I'll help out where I can.'

He patted her shoulder reassuringly. 'Don't you worry, Molly. I'm not going to risk myself. It's Corpus Christi Fair in a month's time and I'm not going to let that brother of yours beat me at the boxing. And it'll be safer this way. You use Ben Pasco this once and the next thing you know, he'll be down the kiddleywink, out of his mind on scrumpy and telling the world how he got the stuff ashore and where we stowed it. We'll have the revenue men down on us before you can turn around. It's better this way, trust me.'

'But if anything goes wrong?'

'It won't. We've done this a dozen times before and it all goes like clockwork. Don't you worry.'

'But they've got a new man in charge of the Preventatives at

62

Pendeen.' Molly still sounded worried. 'They say he's got eyes like a hawk.'

'Well, even hawks can't see in the dark,' Adam said comfortingly, 'and that's when Norman and I will be out.' He shifted uneasily in his chair. 'But Norman will have to make all the arrangements. There's things to be sorted out as soon as possible, and I can't do it this time. I'll have to leave all that to Norman.'

Why did this injury have to happen now? he asked himself fretfully. He knew Norman of old – a good enough man but not one to worry about details. And in a business like this, it was the details that could get you caught.

'I'll tell him,' Molly promised. 'He won't let you down.' She leaned forward and put her hand on his knee. 'So you're planning on going to the Fair next month. Will you be buying me some fairings?'

'I did last year,' Adam reminded her. He felt a strange reluctance to commit himself to any future plans which involved Molly. What's the matter with me? he wondered. I've been happy enough with her for a couple of years. Why, suddenly, does she seem loud and common?

He knew the answer in his heart. It was ever since he had met Clara. But Clara was not for him, could never be for him. She was gentry, out of his sphere. He would be a fool to throw away a woman like Molly because of an impossible dream.

He forced himself to smile at the woman. 'We'll share a bag of clidgy-nicies, I promise you.' She loved the sticky sweets that stuck your jaws together so that it was impossible to talk. Now that he thought of it, that was the only time she did stop talking, except when they were making love.

The memory suddenly sickened him and he rose abruptly to his feet.

'I've been out too long. I'm not as strong as I like to pretend.' He made his way slowly to the door, emphasising his weakness for her benefit. 'You will give Norman that message, won't you?'

She watched him worriedly, as if sensing that he was hiding something but unable to guess what. 'Do you want some help?'

'Ma Downing will look after me,' he said. 'I don't need anyone else. Goodbye, Molly.'

He went inside and closed the door, leaning back against the rough, whitewashed wall with closed eyes. Clara Pentreath! he thought miserably, Clara Pentreath! She had saved his life but she had poisoned his mind. Now, suddenly, all the simple things that he had wanted out of life were no longer enough. He had a new, bigger ambition. And one which it would be impossible to fulfil.

Mother Downing came over and stared at him. 'You're brem

63

wisht,' she said. 'I reckon you've been overdoing it. Two young ladies in one afternoon is too many.'

He opened his eyes and managed a faint grin. 'You're right, Ma. Definitely one too many!'

But which one?

Chapter 8

Molly walked morosely down the hill, kicking a loose stone in front of her with her thick working boots.

There was no doubt about it, Adam hadn't been his usual, welcoming self. She wanted to put it down to his injury but the remark that Phil had dropped at the mine kept coming back to her. Could it be true that Clara Pentreath fancied Adam? She clenched her fists in fury and kicked the stone so viciously that it rolled and bounced between the high Cornish hedges. With a final leap, it disappeared around the next corner and she heard a sudden cry of pain.

When she rounded the corner herself her mouth broke into a pleased smile. Sam Grenfell was rubbing his ankle fretfully. Molly was well aware of his weakness for her. A bit of a flirt with another man was just what she needed to salve her self-esteem, and besides, he was a power at the mine. It would do her no harm to keep in with him.

She hurried forward, her face a mask of concern.

'I'm brem sorry, Mr Grenfell. I wouldn't have hurt you for the world.'

She leaned down and rubbed his ankle gently, letting her fingers run slowly up and down his lower calf. 'Is that any better, Mr Grenfell?'

'A little.' He leaned against the hedge, enjoying the touch of her fingers. 'I think it needs more rubbing, though.'

She smiled up at him, her blue eyes bright above ruddy cheeks. 'I reckon it can't hurt that bad, Mr Grenfell. I can't have hurt you that much.'

'But your touch is so soothing.' He closed his eyes as her fingers slid an inch further up his leg.

'From where I am,' Molly said tartly as she crouched at his feet, 'it looks as if you found it more exciting than soothing.' She stood up, well pleased with the reaction she had seen in him. 'I don't think that I've broken anything, Mr Grenfell.'

'Only my heart!' He rolled languishing eyes at her. She was an attractive wench, bold and brassy. Her skin was tanned from the sun and her shoulders broad as a result of the heavy work she did all day, but she had a ready tongue and her bright glance showed that she was not unwilling to indulge in a flirtation.

She laughed deeply. 'Gusson with you! I know you from old. If you're so smitten why don't you come over for a chat? I'm there at the mine all day and I never see sight nor sign of you.'

'I'm afraid of that great hulk who's been courting you, that Adam Trevelyan.' And that wasn't entirely a lie. The man had a temper if roused and was as stubborn as the devil.

Molly tossed her head, setting her black curls dancing under her bonnet. 'Courting, is it? And if I was courting proper, don't you think that I'd have been wed by now, with a house and all of my own?'

She smiled encouragingly at the purser. It had rankled her that Adam was so slow to get round to the question of marriage. She blamed that Phil, battening onto him. Adam would soon forget him and his stupid promise to look after the boy once he had babies of his own. Phil should be in the workhouse – that was where orphans went who couldn't look after themselves. But Adam's babies, that she so much wanted, hadn't come and Adam was still dragging his feet about marriage. And now that blamed Clara Pentreath was on the scene!

Sam Grenfell read something of her discontent in her face, and felt encouraged. He had no intention of getting really involved with a woman of this class but there was no doubt that she was an attractive wench, and obviously, one with plenty of experience.

'You've just been to see the young man,' he pointed out.

She laughed. 'Well, my brother works in his payre. I was told to find out when he would be fit for work again.'

'And when will that be?'

'Not for a brem while. He's still not fitty.' She looked disconsolate for a moment, missing the evenings that they had had together.

'It's not surprising.' Grenfell shook his head. 'When I saw him brought up, I thought he was a goner. That was some injury he had. It was only Miss Pentreath that saved him.'

His face darkened as he remembered the scene at the mine. Arrogant little bitch! How dared she put him down like that in front of the men. And her father hadn't stopped her either. Well, they would both be brought down soon enough. As from today's meeting, the Pentreaths were responsible for almost the whole financial burden of the mine and he didn't think they had the money to stand that sort of expenditure for long. They'd soon learn their lesson, and he would cheer when they did.

As if she had read his mind, Molly said crossly, 'She went to see Adam today.' She kicked at the hedge, her bitterness too strong to be contained. Grenfell was intrigued. The Pentreaths were looked on almost as angels by everyone at the mine. Had he found a kindred spirit at last?

He said cautiously, 'You can't be happy with another woman seeing your young man,' and watched with pleasure the anger that showed momentarily on her face.

'He's not my young man,' she snapped, 'and I don't care what that whey-faced little bitch does. What good are the likes of she to a red-blooded man?'

'A red-blooded man would be much better off with a fine healthy woman like yourself,' he agreed. He took off his hat and bowed to her. 'I can't claim to have the strength of an ox like young Adam Trevelyan but even I can appreciate your claims over Clara Pentreath's!' And he let his eyes travel openly over her deep chest and down to where her full skirts hid her strong thighs.

To her surprise, Molly found herself blushing at his frank appraisal. He noted and took advantage of her confusion.

'If I met you at the Fair next month, would you let me buy you some fairings?' It was the custom of every young man to buy these sweet biscuits for his lady-love, and if Adam Trevelyan was going to be laid up for several months it would do Sam no harm to stake his claim to this armful of delight.

She shook her head coquettishly. 'I might at that,' she answered. It would serve Adam right to see that she had other admirers, and one who wasn't just a common miner either, but a purser with education and a good position in the mine. Almost a gentleman, in fact. That might make him realise what he was missing and make him come running back.

Reaching a decision, she smiled warmly at Grenfell. 'But I reckon that if a gentleman's going to buy a girl fairings, he ought at least to walk her home if he meets her in the road.'

Sam Grenfell took off his stovepipe hat and bowed again. 'Miss Willcock, it will be a pleasure.'

Molly smiled happily as she took his arm. It would do her no end of good if the neighbours saw her arm-in-arm with the purser at the mine. And with any luck, word of it would get back to Adam and make him jealous. If anything could turn his thoughts away from that stuck-up Clara Pentreath, that would.

*

67

Clara smiled shyly at Edward Blacklock from below the fringe of her parasol. 'Do you think we ought to waken Mama?' she asked quietly. She gestured with her eyes at the slim figure of Lady Susan slumped against the granite outcrop in the shadow of which they had been picnicking.

Edward shook his head definitely. 'I think we should let her rest. We've rambled a long way this afternoon and she must be tired.'

Inwardly, he was pleased that his plans had gone so well. The coach and servants had been dismissed until later in the afternoon and he had poured Lady Susan's wine with a generous hand, hoping for just this result. Now he was as good as alone with Clara. He jumped to his feet and pointed at the headland before them. 'They say that you can see the Scillies more clearly from there than from anywhere else around,' he lied. 'Shall we see if it is true?'

He noticed her hesitation and hastened to reassure her. 'We won't be alone, really, you know. Your mother will be within calling distance and can easily see us when she wakes up.' He held out his hand, smiling pleasantly. 'Come, Miss Pentreath. Surely you are not afraid of me?'

Clara let him help her to her feet but inwardly she knew that the suggestion he had made sound so ludicrous was really true. She was afraid of him. There was something about him that made her heart beat faster. Was it just that he was so good-looking? That he was so rich and respected? Or was there something else?

When they reached the headland, she stood silently for several minutes, gazing around at the expanse of sea and cliffs. Below her, white froth edged the feet of the rocks even though the sea was calm. The constant roar and hiss of the breakers filled her ears, interrupted only by the raucous scream of gulls wheeling and circling in the blue sky overhead.

She breathed a deep sigh of contentment. 'I didn't realise how much I missed this part of the world until I came back again,' she confessed. Her eyes followed a soaring gull, high above her. 'Before I went away, I never thought that wild seas and cliffs could be beautiful, but now I find a romantic pleasure in the very savagery of the scenery.'

'And I find a romantic pleasure in watching you.'

There was sincerity in Edward's voice and it made her feel confused and uneasy. She glanced back anxiously at the sleeping figure of Lady Susan.

'Have you ever been away from Cornwall, Mr Blacklock?' Anything to keep the conversation on normal everyday lines, to stop immediately any emotional scene with the tall, handsome man beside her.

'Like you, Miss Pentreath, I went away to school. To Rugby, in fact, under the great Doctor Arnold, and then on to Oxford, though I had to come back when my father died, to look after the business.' He reached out and took her hand in his. 'But I would like to think that we will be friends. Won't you call me Edward? Mr Blacklock sounds so formal and I don't want to think that there should be any distance between us.'

Clara felt herself blush. She was unprepared for this. She had admired Edward Blacklock when she first saw him, but he had seemed like an unattainable dream and she had quickly realised at the Kingsleys' party that Isabelle Kingsley believed she had a right to his attention. But he seemed determined to be friendly, even *over*-friendly with her. She glanced away in confusion.

The headland was exposed, and a gust of wind, stronger than the others, caught at her full skirts which flattened against her despite her five petticoats, indicating briefly her flat stomach and slender legs and making her stagger slightly.

Edward's grasp on her hand tightened. 'I am afraid for you there. It is too exposed. Come and sit in the shelter of this rock.' He sat quickly, pulling her towards him.

Half-scared, she resisted. 'Mr Blacklock . . .'

'Edward,' he insisted. He pulled again at her hand, so that she had no choice but to drop beside him in the lee of the rock. He leaned over her, his eyes shadowy and unreadable. 'You must call me Edward.'

He was so close that she could see the golden stubble on his cheeks where he had shaved that morning. His red lips were inches from hers and there was a faint sheen of perspiration on his upper lip.

'Edward,' he insisted again.

She could not breathe, could not move. She felt like a rabbit mesmerised by a stoat. He leaned closer. 'Say it,' he whispered, and his breath fanned her cheek. Then in a sudden, convulsive movement he reached out to her. His hand twined painfully in the soft wisps of hair at the back of her neck and he pulled her towards him. His mouth descended on hers, hard, wet, demanding. She felt his tongue forcing its way between her lips while his other hand grasped at her breast.

Revulsion swept through her. In a sudden rage she reached up and dug her nails hard into his cheek and raked them down, feeling the flesh catch and tear. When Edward jerked his head back, reaching

69

with incredulity for his gashed face, Clara took the opportunity to tear herself from his embrace and jump to her feet.

Immediately, she saw Lady Susan, looking towards the couple with no sign of sleepiness in her eyes. Clara hesitated, casting a quick glance at Edward where he sat at her feet, dabbing at his bleeding cheek with a handkerchief. She could rush back to her mother, but that would cause an open scandal. Besides, now that she thought about it, it was unusual for Lady Susan ever to sleep in the afternoon. Could it all have been a ploy? Clara had no doubts that her mother's greatest wish was for her to marry the man beside her. She made her decision.

Taking a deep breath, she said coldly, 'I think that you had better get up, Mr Blacklock. My mother is awake and looking for us.'

She began to hurry back but he caught her arm. 'Not so fast, Miss Pentreath. If you rush back now, your mother will realise that something has gone wrong and we wouldn't want that, would we?'

'Yes, we would,' she snapped. 'I am going to tell her what you did anyway.'

'But you haven't thought of the consequences, have you?' he asked gently.

She stared at him uncertainly, her green eyes clouded under dark brows. 'I don't understand what you mean.'

'I mean,' he said, 'that if you tell your mother what has happened I shall be barred from visiting Penalverne.'

'Well, that is perfectly all right by me,' she said furiously. 'I never want to see you again as long as I live.'

'But how will that affect you? How will that affect your father?'

She hesitated. 'What are you talking about?'

He dabbed at his face. 'I'm talking about society, Miss Pentreath, and I'm talking about a woman's reputation. Everyone will guess what has happened, and if I know the people around here they will guess more than actually did happen. And do you know what they will say, Miss Pentreath?'

She shook her head silently, her eyes dark.

'They will laugh and say that I am a typical man. But they will label you used goods, a slut, no better than she should be.'

'But . . .' Clara was bewildered. 'How can I be in the wrong? I didn't do anything!'

'Only crept away with a man while your mother's back was turned. Only let him take advantage of you.' He stared down at her stormy face and played his trump card. 'And then, of course, there is your father to consider.'

'He doesn't come into this,' she said hotly.

70

'On the contrary, he is the linchpin, at least as far as you are concerned.' His grey eyes studied her, enjoying her fury and confusion. 'I buy all your father's ore, Miss Pentreath, and I lend him the money necessary to keep the mine open.'

'Well?' She confronted him, her chin lifted. 'There are other smelters, other banks.'

'Not one that would take on your father if I suddenly stopped dealing with him. And there is no way that I could carry on our business partnership if I was forbidden to enter his house.' He smiled at her. 'I hope that that explains the position.'

Her eyes dropped. She understood it all too well. This was blackmail. If it had just been herself she might have called his bluff, might have challenged him to do his worst. But she could not risk her father's business. The mine meant everything to him. He loved it more than life itself.

Through gritted teeth, she said, 'You think you've won, don't you, Mr Blacklock?'

He laughed. 'I know I've won.' He gestured at the figure of Lady Susan still sitting by the rock. 'Now, don't you think that you should act like a perfect lady and attend to the cheek I so unfortunately scratched while rescuing the parasol you dropped? After all,' he added, 'if you can soil your hands with the blood of a filthy miner you can hardly claim to be too squeamish to help a gentleman.'

He moved, carefully placing himself so that his tall body completely shielded Clara from her mother.

Unwillingly, she took the handkerchief that he held out to her. 'I would never consider you a gentleman, Mr Blacklock,' she said coldly.

He caught her wrist in a painful grasp. 'Edward,' he insisted. She remained silent. He twisted her wrist slowly, deliberately, watching her teeth bare as she fought against the pain. 'Edward,' he repeated, then twisted further, harder. '*Edward.*'

'Edward.' She spat the word out, unable to endure the agony in her wrist any longer and despising herself for giving in to him. He released her, watching with pleasure as she rubbed at her tortured flesh.

'I'm glad that you've decided to be friends, Clara. I anticipate our courtship with very great pleasure.'

'Courtship?' She felt her voice shake.

'Courtship,' he repeated, smiling down into her pale face. 'I really can't remember when I met someone who has moved me the way that you do, Clara.' He reached out and ran a finger down her cheek. She stared at him stonily. He reached the corner of her mouth and inserted the tip of his finger between her ripe lips, pressing on her teeth until she was forced to open her mouth.

'I think that we will share very many interesting times together in future, Clara.'

She wished she had the courage to bite down hard on his finger, to sever it and spit the end in his face, but she did not dare. Anything that she did like that he would take out on her father, she had no doubt of that at all.

He took his finger out of her mouth and licked her saliva off it as though it had been a delicious sauce. 'A token,' he murmured, 'of all the other juices we will exchange between us in the future.'

Sickened, she turned away, her green eyes filling with tears. She knew that this had been just the first of many clashes between them.

Chapter 9

'Ready?'

Adam braced himself against the bow of the boat and prepared to push. Above him, dark clouds scudded swiftly across the sky, hiding the new moon and revealing only intermittent glimpses of the stars. In the darkness it was barely possible to see the fretted foam that laced the bottom of the Priest's Cove slipway where the waves sucked and crashed only a few feet from the stern of the small fishing boat.

'Ready,' he said shortly. The change in the weather made the expedition safer. It was unlikely that they would meet the Preventative boat tonight, but he did not welcome the extra strain that the rough seas would put upon his side. If the wound broke open again he could be off work for weeks.

'Heave,' Norman ordered. He pulled at the stern as Adam pushed and the boat began to slide backwards down the slipway, the grating of the iron keel clearly audible even above the wind. Adam felt the change in the boat as the stern met the water and carried on pushing. For once Norman had the tricky job of keeping the stern from swinging round and crashing onto the slipway Adam knew how difficult it could be, with the waves threatening to sweep you off your feet and the boat bucking under your hands like a live animal.

Then the boat was properly afloat and he struggled to hold her straight as Norman towed her into deeper water. A pause, while Adam waited for a helpful swell and then he was aboard, shipping the rudder and letting the single sail flap as Norman pushed the bows round to face the open sea.

'It would be a black easterly!' Norman pulled himself breathlessly into the small boat. He was wet to his waist in the short, choppy seas that the wind kicked up. 'Let's hope it's too lively for that new Lieutenant over at Pendeen. They say he has the Preventative boat out almost every night, these days.'

'He'll have trouble seeing us, even if he is out.' Adam guided them away from the dangerous rocks around Cape Cornwall. 'But we'll have a problem seeing the Frenchie.' A spatter of rain slapped into his face and he grimaced. That was all they needed. In this darkness the only point they had to navigate by was the Longships Lighthouse off Land's End. If the weather really came in and hid the light they could find themselves in trouble, unable to land until after dawn. It was not a happy thought, not with the hungry Brisons half a mile offshore, the deathbed of a hundred ships.

'*If* the Frenchie comes,' Norman responded morosely.

'He'll come.' Jean-Pierre was the best sailor in Roscoff. Adam would bet his life that even now, the Frenchman was out there somewhere, eyes peeled for the small Cornish boat that would take the contraband brandy into shore.

The easterly wind filled their old brown sail as they headed out to sea. 'I never thought you would be here today,' Norman remarked, wringing out his wet clothes. He pulled dry trousers out of a canvas bag that Adam had stowed under the thwart. 'I'd have thought that injury would have kept you laid up for at least another week yet.'

'I heal quickly,' Adam said shortly, hoping that he had made the right decision. 'And I couldn't let anyone else in on this. Nobody likes the Preventative men but there are too many loose tongues in a place like this, and secrets get out.'

He squinted at the few stars that had appeared in a gap in the clouds, altering tack slightly as he re-orientated himself. 'It isn't just us, there's Phil to think of. If I am caught, it'll be the workhouse for him, and if they catch him with the mules it'll be prison.'

'He'll be there tonight, then?'

'Waiting above Priest's Cove. I told him not to come until one o'clock but it'll take him until then to grease them.' He grinned at the thought. Although nothing was ever said, Christopher Kingsley always left seven or eight mules in a field by the road on dark nights. And if they turned up tired and covered with grease the next day, just when, coincidentally, his keg of brandy appeared in the byre under some hay, no one ever mentioned it. Nor did they wonder why he would ride alone up No-Go-By Hill every month or so and, afterwards, Adam would find a cache of money under a certain stone.

Phil liked the excitement of it all, as Norman did, but he hated the mules with a deadly loathing. They had to be greased before use. It helped them to escape if the Revenue men should catch them, as a greased and frightened mule was almost as difficult to keep hold of as a greased pig. But the mules hated the process as much as Phil did. Many was the day he had turned up at the mine with bruises and toothmarks that he couldn't explain to the other boys. Adam smiled to himself. Phil would never make a stockman.

Norman said jokingly, 'I'm surprised that you still come on trips like this, now that you've joined the gentry.'

'I don't know what you mean.' Adam was glad that the darkness hid his face.

'Oh, gusson! You do know very well what I'm talking about! That Miss Clara. Phil says she's brem taken with you.'

'She just comes round to see how I am doing and to lend me some books.' Adam fought to keep his voice neutral. He hated the thought that the miners were discussing her, discussing them. She was too pure to have her name sullied on their lips. Her visits were the highlight of his days. He looked forward to them as to the springtime; the smile that lit up her elfin features, the faint aroma of lavender that hung around her, the way her chin lifted when she was drawn into one of their frequent arguments, and the way her emerald eyes betrayed every shade of emotion as they talked and laughed together.

It was all too precious, too special to be talked over with other men, as if she were a common woman, like Molly or one of the other bal-maidens.

'I reckon that's the way the gentry do their courting,' Norman chuckled. 'Not like us, a bit of slap and tickle on the cliffs, just reading to each other and letting someone else's words say what they can't.' He put on a high-pitched, ferociously genteel accent. 'Mai deer, isn't this pome just too, too lovely.'

Adam ground his teeth. 'It's books on mining she brings me,' he said irritably. 'You can't make that sound romantic.'

'You still want to watch out,' Norman advised. 'You could find yourself hitched before you know where you are, and what will our Molly say then?'

Adam changed course slightly, refusing to answer, refusing to let his secret dream be tarnished by the touch of common banter.

They sailed on in silence, keeping a lookout for any sign of another boat but the sea around them seemed empty, the only sign of life the distant flashing of the Longships Lighthouse.

'We should have found him by now,' Norman fretted. 'If he's here.'

'He's here. He's not going to send up flares, is he?' Adam changed tack again, moving nearer to Land's End. He wondered what the time was. Late, he knew. Later than they had ever been to a rendezvous before. The short summer night would be over soon. At sea it grew light earlier than on land; they had to be ashore before half-past two. But Jean-Pierre would wait as long as he could.

'If we can't find him we'll have to try again tomorrow. Perhaps it'll

75

be warmer then.' Norman hunched his shoulders against the cold wind.

'There!' Adam pointed to a pinprick of light off their port bow and adjusted their course slightly. 'Signal with the lantern to show him that we know where he is.'

Norman reached for the curiously-shaped lantern. Where the glass should have been there was only a long, narrowing spout. When lit, it was impossible for the light to be seen from anywhere except directly where the lantern was pointed. As he moved it, Adam heard the slop of oil in the container. 'That's almost empty,' he said accusingly.

'There's enough oil to let the Frenchie know that we're here.' Huddled in the bottom of the boat out of the wind to light the wick, Norman sounded defensive. As well he might, Adam thought. Even though it was Norman's job to make sure that the boat was properly equipped for these trips, Adam had usually double-checked everything. Now, on the one occasion when he hadn't been able to because of his side, Norman had skimped on the work.

'We were about to go.' The French accent could be cut with a knife but Jean-Pierre's English was functional. He threw a rope to the smaller boat, pulling it alongside.

'It's as black as your hat,' Adam said, tying it firmly while Norman waited for the other. 'If you hadn't shown the light we'd still be looking for you.'

'Better me than you, eh?' They saw the flash of white teeth above them. 'The Preventatives can't touch me.'

'We're grateful, anyway,' Adam said. 'What's the time?'

'It will be dawn in less than an hour. You will have to hurry, *mes amis.*' Already the French crew were appearing at the side of their boat, kegs of brandy in their arms.

Adam reached for the first one, feeling his side pull as he moved, struggling to keep his balance in the tossing boat. Beside him, Norman was moving smoothly, reaching and stowing the kegs with easy regularity. He hadn't realised how much his injury had affected him, Adam thought, straining to lower the heavy barrel. Last time he had gone smuggling the work had seemed so easy; now he was sweating heavily despite the cold wind, and his side pained him every time he stretched and bent.

'Hsst! Capitaine!' The sibilant whisper startled them all. Jean-Pierre stopped and turned to one of his sailors but he was back within seconds.

'My men say there is a boat approaching. Bigger than this. No lights. They only saw her because she was silhouetted for a moment against the horizon.'

'The Preventative boat?' Adam felt his heart beat more quickly.

'Probably. Who else would it be?'

Adam thought fast. The Preventative boat was the fastest boat around, faster than the French boat and far faster than his small fishing boat, laden down as it was with contraband brandy. 'How many kegs left?'

'Only five.'

'Then give them to us.' Careless now of his side, Adam stretched and lowered frantically, taking the casks as soon as the fishermen had hoisted them above the gunnels.

He gasped as he worked: 'You can help us, Jean-Pierre, if you will.'

'How, my friend? What shall we do?'

'Lead the Preventatives away.' Adam gulped at a fiercer-than usual pang in his side. 'Make sure they see you, then act guilty. Try to lead them round Land's End out of sight. If we stay quiet they may pass us by without seeing us.'

'But you won't have time to get to the shore and unload the kegs. It will be light soon.'

'Don't worry about us. We'll find somewhere to hide before they come back. But it depends on you.'

'We'll do what we can.' Jean-Pierre handed down the last keg. 'God willing, we shall see you in a month's time.' The Frenchman took the purse Adam handed him, sketched a salute and disappeared into his ship.

Adam reached for his knife and slashed through the ropes that tied him to the French boat's side, and even as the last rope fell free the bigger boat moved away and he heard the rattle as the sails were raised.

Now they could only wait.

They huddled in the small boat as it wallowed uneasily on the choppy seas, weighed down by the kegs that they had taken on board.

Already it seemed less dark, the sky to the east showing the first glimmer of false dawn. Adam breathed a sigh of relief as he saw faintly, the outline of the French boat's sails against the horizon. If they could see it there was a chance that the Preventative boat could also see it. It was important that she should be lured out of sight before the light grew any stronger. If she didn't follow the French boat there was a stark choice between getting caught with the contraband or ditching it over the side.

A flash of light showed briefly on the French boat and was instantly doused. Adam grinned. Good old Jean-Pierre. Enough to catch the Preventative's eye but so little that it would seem an accident. That should lure them after her.

Silently, he stared at the horizon, eyes watering with the effort of trying to see into the darkness. Suddenly there was a hiss of shearing water and the Preventative cutter was almost upon them. She swept past, sails up but still not showing any lights. She doesn't realise that she has been seen, Adam thought. She's relying on her superior speed to catch up with the Frenchies before they know she's there. He buried his face as the boat swept by, afraid that even the glimmer of his white skin might catch the eye of someone on board.

He waited until the cutter had sailed into the darkness, then shook Norman. 'Quickly. Get the sail up, but keep it quiet.'

'We won't make it to Priest's Cove, I tell you.' Norman fought to raise the sail in the darkness. 'Even if we get there, we won't have time to unload before the Preventatives are back.'

'Who said anything about Priest's Cove?' Suddenly, Adam was enjoying the trip. 'There are other places to land.' He swung the boat round, feeling her answer sluggishly to the helm. The barrels were making her slower. The boat was lower in the water and the choppy sea slopped dangerously close.

He grinned to himself in the darkness. Jean-Pierre would lead the cutter a merry dance and they would be safe before the ship returned. Confidently, he set sail for the shore.

The light was growing stronger by the minute. Already he could see the shadowy mass of Cape Cornwall hunched against the sky. Adam swung the tiller over, turning the boat towards the east.

Norman peered into the darkness. 'Adam, for God's sake, come over a bit. You'll have us on the Brisons in a moment.'

'That's exactly where I intend to put us.' Adam laughed at the note in his voice. 'Don't sound so frightened. Ships often land on the Brisons.'

'Only by mistake.' Norman sounded panicky. 'Adam, you're mad. The wound has affected your mind.'

'I've never been saner.' Adam could have roared with laughter. It was suddenly so easy, the right answer. He had recognised it as such as soon as the thought had come into his mind.

'Ships often land on the Brisons after a wreck, either to take off survivors or to get what they can salvage from the ships. We're just going to land there to leave the kegs. Unless there's a wreck in the next twenty-four hours, they'll be quite safe and we can collect them tomorrow.' He looked at the rocks looming ahead of them in the pre-dawn greyness and turned the boat into the wind. 'Down sail. We'll be safer sculling.' He took out the single oar and fitted it into the half-circle cut out for it in the stern of the boat.

'We'd be safer heading for the Cove,' Norman muttered, obeying him. 'What is Phil going to do?'

'He's had his orders, and he knows better than to disobey them. If we're not in sight by first light he's to turn the mules free and head for home.' Adam spoke absently, his eyes searching the black rocks that jutted from the sea in front of him, rising sixty feet in a series of jagged spikes. He gazed down at the blackness below him. He would have preferred more light to make this landing, for the sea beneath him was inky, hiding its secrets, but there was no telltale swirl to speak of hidden rocks that he could see.

'Get ready to jump ashore the moment we touch,' he commanded, steering them for a narrow gully in the rocks. There was a bumping grind as the boat touched, then Norman was ashore, the mooring rope in his hand. 'This isn't safe.'

'Do you want to live for ever?' Adam grinned at him, his teeth flashing white in the gathering light. 'See if you can make her reasonably secure. I'll stay in the boat and hand you out the kegs but you'll have to hide them above the tideline.' He balanced himself, using his hands to fend off the boat in the choppy seas as Norman climbed away to reconnoitre a hiding place.

'Got it.' Norman was panting slightly. He gestured behind him. 'If you move to the other side of this gully there's a place I can stow them, and quickly.'

Adam looked at where he pointed. The only foothold for Norman was a narrow ledge well above the bows of the boat. He pulled the boat across to it, gazing up at him. 'Be careful.'

Norman flashed his usual smile. He seemed to have forgotten his bad temper earlier in the night. 'Want to live for ever?' he echoed. He balanced precariously, reaching down. 'Now, give us a keg before we have to share it with the Preventatives.'

Adam handed it up, feeling his side catch uncomfortably as he stretched. He felt so helpless here. Normally it would have been him, climbing the rocks, manhandling the fifty-pound kegs. Now he was having to act as if he were an old man. It chafed him, wounded his self-esteem. Not for much longer, he reminded himself. Next month I shall be as good as ever. He bent and handed up the next keg.

The light was growing appreciably stronger now. They worked in silence except for the gasps of effort as the heavy kegs were hefted. They had nearly finished when Norman paused, straightening his back and staring off to the east. 'The cutter's coming back.'

'Let's get out of here then.' Adam passed the next-to-last keg to him and watched as he dragged it back out of sight, the last keg already at his feet.

'Ready.' Norman leaned over and Adam lifted it towards him. As he grasped it, a larger than usual wave lifted the boat and then dropped it abruptly. Norman, his hands already on the keg did not let go and the sudden pull unbalanced him. For a moment he teetered desperately, trying for balance on the narrow ledge, then he fell, sliding down between the rock and the side of the boat.

Adam grabbed for him, trying to haul him on board to safety but he was a dead weight. Then the boat rose on another wave and, his hands still grasping Norman's arm, Adam was pulled forward with a jerk and felt the jolt of sudden pain and gush of hot blood as his side tore open.

Chapter 10

Adam set his teeth and hung on grimly, holding tightly to Norman's arm with one hand while with the other he fended the boat off from the sheer side of the gully in which they were moored.

The sea swelled and gurgled beneath them, sucking at the boat then trying to throw it viciously against the rocks. Norman dangled helplessly for several seconds, his back rubbing against the barnacle encrusted granite, his chest inches from the side of the pitching boat.

Dropping the keg, he clutched with his free hand at the gunwales of the boat. Adam grunted, and with a final, supreme effort that brought the sweat to his brow, hauled him bodily onboard. They collapsed together, panting, in the bottom of the boat as the next wave swung her broadside against the rocks, crushing the keg as though it had been made of matchwood.

The sharp smell of spilt brandy brought both their heads up. Norman heaved himself to his feet and stared at the pieces of wood floating around them. 'Shite!' He turned to Adam. 'Who do you reckon that one would have belonged to?'

Adam pushed himself painfully into a sitting position and wiped the sweat from his eyes. 'Jan Pendryer,' he said shortly. 'Last time I had a drink up Kenidjack Kiddleywink, I swear he'd watered the beer. If anyone has to go short, he can. That'll teach the bugger to mess with my drinks.' He put his hand to his side and it came away red with blood. He grimaced. No time to do anything about it now. The broken keg was evidence and if the Preventative boat saw it they would search the rocks and find the rest of the cache.

'Let's get out of here.' He picked up an oar and fended the boat off the rocks with it.

Norman swung round. 'You've split your side again.'

'And you've skinned your back.' Norman's shirt was hanging in tatters, stained with blood where the barnacles had scraped his skin off. 'We'd better get away from here before that cutter comes.' He inched the boat backwards out of the narrow gully that had sheltered her, then they hoisted the sail and set course for the cove.

'Here.' Adam reached into his pocket and produced a small flask. He handed it to Norman. 'Don't drink it, just throw some over your clothes so that you stink of the stuff.'

Norman sniffed it, carefully. 'But this is good brandy!'

'And we're two soused miners out for a quiet night's fishing away from our womenfolk.' Adam splashed seawater over himself, hoping that the light would not be strong enough for anyone to tell the difference between clothes stained with water and those stained with blood. Reaching for the bag he had placed under the thwart he up-ended it swiftly. Dead mackerel slithered out to lie washing to and fro in the bilges.

He grinned at Norman, pulling up his shirt and emptying the stinging brandy onto his newly-opened wound. 'Phil went out with Ben Pasco yesterday morning and caught them special.'

'Then I hope the Preventatives don't look too closely at 'em,' Norman growled, eyeing the fish caustically. 'A few hours more and they'll be high enough to fly home by themselves.'

Adam laughed, letting the boat turn more into the wind so that it slowed down, sails flapping. The Preventative boat must be nearly on them now, hidden only by the bulk of the nearby Brisons. In a tuneless voice he began to sing, 'Christ the Lord is risen today.'

'A-a-a-a-allelu-oo-lia!' Norman joined in with more enthusiasm than skill. He slumped against the bows, looking artistically drunk. 'They're coming.'

Adam waited until he could hear the ship's keel scything through the water then he stood up unsteadily in the boat and waved dramatically. 'Ahoy!' He lurched and recovered himself. 'Any chance of a drink?' He held out the flask to the Lieutenant who was peering suspiciously down at them.

The Preventative boat hove to. 'It's a strange night to go fishing.' A lantern played over the small fishing boat and its two occupants.

Adam sat suddenly on the thwart as the boat rocked and had to stifle a gasp as the jolt hurt his side. 'It's a strange night to go out for a sail, if you ask me.' He stared boskily at them. 'But it's a lot be'er night for fishing than it is for staying home with women gettin' at you all the time, yack! yack! yack!'

'What women?' enquired a local voice. 'I do know you, Adam Trevelyan, and you haven't got no wife.'

Cursing under his breath, Adam hiccupped loudly. 'Tha's what you

82

think.' He waved broadly at Norman who was sitting in the bows with a lopsided grin on his face.

'There's his Molly after me morning, noon and night, wantin' to be wed. And there's Ma Downing back home telling me off for a lazy lout 'cos I can't work. But I'm hurt.'

He stared hard at the flask. 'Captain Pentreath gave me this 'cos I was hurt. An' now it's all gone!' He turned it upside down and gazed miserably at the few drops that splashed into the boat. 'Got any more?' he asked hopefully.

'We're wasting our time here.' The Lieutenant rapped out an order and the bigger boat turned away, moving smoothly through the water. The two men gazed after it in silence until it was well out of earshot.

'Look at them go, like a cat out of a bonfire,' Norman said admiringly. 'But I reckon we had them diddled all right there.'

Adam took the tiller again and began to steer for home, making sure that even from a distance his erratic steering could still be appreciated. 'Thank God. Are they going near the Brisons?'

'Straight back to Pendeen, I reckon,' Norman said cheerfully. 'They don't suspect nothing.' He grinned at Adam. 'The weather's improving. Shall we get those kegs tonight?'

Adam thought. They could not wait too long, as there was always a danger that a storm could wash the kegs away, and in a few days the moon would be giving more light, making the short summer evenings even more dangerous. He felt his side carefully and winced. The kegs had to be collected but there was no way that he could do it. Already he was suffering from the after-effects of the long night and there was a danger that he might have infected the wound.

He asked, 'How difficult is it to get them back on board?'

'Easy as pie,' Norman said comfortably. 'I can manage it myself if you can't do it.'

'You'll need someone in the boat, even if the seas are calmer tomorrow. There will always be a swell in that gully.' He took a chance. 'Would Molly do it?'

'For you, 'course she would. And she were good in a boat when she were a maid.' Norman nodded. 'It'll keep it all in the family.'

'That's what I want.' Adam moved uneasily, trying to find a position where his side didn't pain him. He could still feel the slow seep of blood and was beginning to feel light-headed. The two-mile walk home suddenly seemed impossible and he wondered if he would even be able to help pull the boat up the slipway.

The light was stronger now. It was less than half an hour to sunrise. Peering ahead, he saw a small familiar figure standing waiting for them in the cove. As the boat ran aground, Phil waded out to help pull her up.

'I saw it all,' he said excitedly. 'I saw the Preventatives come for you. What happened? Didn't you meet the Frenchie?'

'We met him all right.' Adam bit back a groan as he swung his legs over the side. 'Only we'd got rid of the stuff before they caught us.' He rubbed Phil's hair. 'Just don't ask what we did with it, all right?'

'I know better'n that.' Phil stopped and stared at Adam. 'Your side – it's bleeding!'

'A bit of an accident.' Adam suddenly saw them both as they must appear to Phil – Norman wet through, his shirt torn almost off his back, while Adam was pale and weak, scarcely able to stand. He turned to the boy. 'What happened to the mules?'

'They're still here, up on the hill.' Phil gestured behind him. 'I could see you coming back so I thought that I'd better hang onto them.' He glanced nervously at Adam, half-afraid of a telling-off.

Adam forced himself to grin. 'Then for God's sake go and get the one with the least grease on it. I'm not going to be able to walk home.'

Then his legs gave way suddenly and Norman caught him in strong arms as he collapsed in a faint.

'Fishing?' said Clara. She angled her parasol so that he could see clearly the disbelief on her face.

'Fishing,' Adam stated definitely. He walked beside her up the twisting path that led to Chapel Carn Brae, restricting his long strides to match her shorter steps. Around them, the bracken unfurled fresh green leaves, hiding the harshness of the granite in a veil of softness that exactly matched Clara's walking outfit.

'And I thought that the Cornish were a kind race,' Clara mused, her emerald eyes watching him closely. 'I always thought that if someone was injured they would help him out, bring him food, bread, fish . . .' She shook her head sadly. 'Strange how one can be mistaken.'

'Strange,' he agreed, biting his lip to stop it from quivering. The little minx! She knew, all right! It was easy to see that she was just teasing him, but if she knew so much about his activities, how much did other people know? Not that it mattered, he reminded himself. They could suspect as much as they liked, but without evidence they could do nothing. And any evidence was long gone, dispersed to the surrounding kiddleywinks and farms, thanks to Norman and Molly. There was no chance that anything could be pinned on him.

'You haven't thought of teaching Phil to fish?' Clara asked, with spurious sympathy. 'It would be such a consolation to you in your old age,' and her eyes travelled meaningfully up his well-muscled body, noticing how quickly he had recovered from his setback, how easily he walked beside her up the steep path.

'Phil?' Adam gave a grunt of laughter. 'He could earn his living fishing any day. Better than any of the lads from Newlyn already, he is.'

Clara was surprised. 'Then why don't you send him fishing?' she asked. 'Surely it would be better for him than spending all his time in the mine. It can't be healthy.'

'And I suppose fishing is?' Adam queried, irritated by her implied criticism. 'I suppose you haven't seen the number of men with only one leg in our fishing villages? Or the number of widows?' He turned to stare at her. 'Mining isn't healthy, but usually it kills you slow, a lot slower than fishing does. And the hours are shorter.'

He gestured angrily. 'Phil is down the mine for eight hours, say nine allowing for getting down and up after our core. Then he's free. Free to go fishing with me or work in the garden in the fresh air, and free to learn his books. How much time for those things would he have if he was a fisherman?' His blue eyes surveyed her.

'Confounded little,' he answered himself. 'If it wasn't the fishing it would be cleaning the fish, or mending the nets, or tarring the boat.' He shook his head. 'For the moment, he's better off where he is. You don't get rockfalls in our mines and as long as you're careful it's quite safe – except for the consumption.' He turned his back to hide the emotion he could feel showing on his face.

Clara stared up at his broad back, the coarse cotton shirt that stretched uneasily across his shoulders, the black hair that curled just over his collar. 'You really care for him, don't you?' She could not keep the surprise she felt out of her voice. He was so different from the way she imagined. It would be easy for Adam to resent the nephew he had taken in, but his voice expressed real concern, even love for the dirty little imp who grinned so engagingly at her when they met.

'He's all I've got,' Adam said shortly. 'And I'm all he's got. If anything happens to me . . .' His voice trailed off and she was suddenly aware of the desperation that lay so close below the surface of all these men. One accident, one slip on the ladders or misfire of the gunpowder, and their families were exposed to a living death in the workhouse. Cut off from education, from society, from the chance of a good job, they lingered in a limbo, despised and pitied by everyone.

He should not have this worry, she thought suddenly. He should not have to go down the mine every day, afraid for the boy whose only hope for the future lay in him. Moved by an impulse she scarcely understood she clutched at his sleeve, bringing him to an abrupt halt. As he swung round to face her, she blurted out, 'If anything happens to you, well, I'll look after Phil for you. I swear it.'

Her green eyes stared up into his, blazing with sincerity. 'I won't let him go to the workhouse,' she said earnestly, willing him to believe her. 'I won't let you down. Whatever happens, you needn't worry about Phil. Please,' her voice quivered, 'I know you don't think well of me, but please, trust me in this.'

His hand, warm, brown, rough, closed over hers. 'I believe you, love.' The voice was suddenly rough, hoarse. 'I'd trust you with my life.' The words jolted through her. The world suddenly contracted to the two of them alone. She was lost in the blueness of his gaze, the touch of his hand. Her breath caught in her throat. She was aware of him as she had never been aware of a man before, of his physical presence, his nearness. She felt as if the air had suddenly become too thick to breathe.

'Miss Pentreath.' The light, drawling voice behind her made her jump. She snatched her hand free and spun round to stare up at Isabelle Kingsley where she sat on her black horse.

'I do hope we didn't startle you.' There was no mistaking the sneer on her pretty face as she glanced meaningfully from Clara to Adam and back again.

We? Clara had not noticed Lieutenant Laity sitting quietly on his horse just behind Isabelle. With an effort she gathered herself together, bowed politely to him. 'Miss Kingsley, Lieutenant. I see that you are out exploring the ancient chapel as well.' She cursed herself for not hearing their approach.

'I am showing the Lieutenant some of the historical sites in the area,' Isabelle said. 'I think it's so important that we should make such a pleasant new neighbour feel at home.'

She allowed her eyes to run slowly over Adam, taking in the black curls that tumbled over his forehead, the coarse white cotton shirt and rough trousers which ended above heavy boots. 'And your friend, Miss Pentreath?' She raised her brows mockingly and Clara could see that she knew very well who Adam was but was using the opportunity to try to embarrass her.

Clara raised her chin, defying the other girl. 'Mr Trevelyan,' she said, as formally and as proudly as if he had been the Prince of Wales. 'He is the best tributer at Wheal Susan.' She stared at Isabelle Kingsley, defying her to make any comment.

Lieutenant Laity nodded briefly at the other man. 'We have already met,' he said quietly. Then, seeing Clara's enquiring look, he added, 'He was out – fishing.'

It was patently obvious that he no more believed that Adam had been fishing than Clara had done, and she had to bite her lip to hide the smile that his words conjured up.

Adam nodded briefly back. 'That's right,' he said, and Clara noted that there was no servility in his voice. 'We'd had some luck as I remember.' His blue eyes met the Lieutenant's, full of guileless query. 'And you? Did you catch – anything – that night?'

'Nothing,' the Lieutenant said shortly. 'Even less than yourselves.' He stared down at Adam thoughtfully. 'You didn't see any other boats that night, I assume.'

'I did,' Adam said, and grinned as the Lieutenant straightened suddenly. 'One near ran us down as we were fishing about half an hour before we met you.' He shrugged. 'Going like a bat out of hell, she was, and no lights on. Came from Pendeen as well.' He grinned innocently at the Lieutenant. 'You didn't see her, I suppose?'

'We didn't.' There was a trace of a flush in the Lieutenant's face that Clara could not account for. She glanced from one man to the other, aware that there was a by-play here that she did not understand, feeling the tension that crackled between them.

Isabelle Kingsley broke in. 'You must be the miner whose life Miss Pentreath saved,' she said sweetly to Adam. 'She told us all about it. At great length,' she added, her eyes marking the sudden angry flush in Adam's face.

'I seem to remember that it was that reporter, Mr Henson, who told us about it,' said Lieutenant Laity politely. 'Miss Pentreath was the acme of modesty about her achievements,' and he bowed to her over his horse's neck.

Clara felt herself blushing. What would Adam think of her after this? she wondered. The Lieutenant was so obviously gallant, Isabelle so catty. What sort of impression would he have of her? Would he think her shallow and stuck up? She said boldly, 'Mr Trevelyan and I were walking. Now that he is recovering from his injury, a little gentle exercise will do him good and I am delighted to have someone to walk with.' She stared defiantly at Isabelle, daring her to comment on her choice of walking companion.

The Lieutenant broke in quickly. 'You are recovering, then?' he said to Adam. 'But I don't suppose that you will be at the Fair this year?'

'I shall be there,' said Adam shortly. 'And I shall win.'

The two girls stared at him blankly but the Lieutenant laughed.

'I'm relieved to hear it. I put a guinea on you before your accident and I hate to lose.'

Adam said, 'It was foolish of you to bet on a man you don't know, and so far in advance.'

'Not so foolish.' The Lieutenant patted the horse's neck as it pawed impatiently at the ground. 'I had heard good reports of you from my men, and you get much better odds so far in advance.' He fixed his eyes meaningfully on Adam. 'I go by a man's reputation, Mr Trevelyan. And I find that is a very good guide to a man. In all things.'

Adam met his glance without flinching, lifting his chin proudly as his eyes crossed with those of the Preventative Officer's. 'Then I shall do my best to live up to my reputation, sir. In all things.' They stared at each other across the heads of the two women.

'But what is all this about?' Isabelle broke in. 'I don't understand what you are talking about.'

Lieutenant Laity smiled. 'We're talking about pugilism, Miss Kingsley. This gentleman has won the prize for being the best fighter at Corpus Christi Fair in Penzance for the last two years, and I have my money on him to win again.'

Isabelle gave a small scream. 'Fighting! Lieutenant, you can't be serious. Surely the magistrates don't allow such things.'

'Down here, it's one of the highlights of the Fair,' the Lieutenant said. 'But, of course, there are many other attractions, stalls and theatres and sideshows. Have you never been?'

'It is hardly entertainment for a lady!' Isabelle looked affronted. 'I believe that the servants have a day off, and the workmen, people like that.'

'Then I won't have the pleasure of seeing you there?' asked the Lieutenant. 'Not at the fighting, of course, but at the rest of the entertainments.'

'I don't go to such things, Lieutenant,' Isabelle said coldly. 'I find the very idea unpleasant.'

'You are very different from your father,' Adam said quietly. 'He comes every year.'

'And isn't he a magistrate?' Clara broke in, flashing a swift, secret glance at Adam. Their eyes met for a brief second and she sensed in him the wicked joy that she felt in baiting the pious Isabelle. Encouraged, she added, 'Perhaps your father will take me if Papa is too busy.'

'Captain Pentreath usually goes,' Adam assured her, 'and bets on the fights.'

'Then I shall see you there, Miss Pentreath.' The Lieutenant smiled at her. 'Why don't we make up a party? Then perhaps we can persuade Miss Kingsley to come. With myself and Mr Blacklock to look after the ladies, there can be no danger to them.'

'As long as I don't have to mix with,' Isabelle said pointedly, 'the *lower classes*. But I can't imagine Mr Blacklock will want to come to such an affair.'

The Lieutenant grinned. 'He was a well-known amateur pugilist when he was at Oxford. I should think that he would definitely be there.'

'Really?' queried Isabelle faintly, 'I would never have thought it.' She turned her gaze onto Clara. 'You seemed very interested in Mr Blacklock at our party,' she said brightly, glancing at Adam to see his reaction. 'It seems that you are attracted to men who are, er, addicted to violent sports.'

Clara felt her face freeze at Blacklock's name but she would not let the slur pass unchallenged. 'No more than you, it seems, Miss Kingsley. In your case it apparently also includes gentlemen with violent occupations,' and she let her eyes rest momentarily on Lieutenant Laity's face, giving him a dazzling smile to take the sting out her words.

The Lieutenant loosened his reins, allowing his horse to sidle restlessly. 'I think we should be moving on, Miss Kingsley. The horses are getting cold.' He smiled down at Clara. 'I shall make arrangement with your parents regarding the Fair, Miss Pentreath.' His eyes moved on to Adam. 'And doubtless I shall see you there, if not before.'

'You will certainly see me – at the Fair at any rate,' Adam responded calmly. 'And don't worry about your money, Lieutenant. I shall do my best to win it for you. I am proud of my ability to live up to my reputation. Whatever it might be.'

The eyes of the two men locked, then the Lieutenant bowed. 'I am sure, Mr Trevelyan,' he said courteously, 'that your reputation, in every area of your life, is well earned.' He touched his hat to Clara and turned his horse, following Isabelle as she spurred her mount towards the ruins of the chapel that crowned the steep hill.

'Well!' Clara turned to Adam. 'What was all that about? And do you really intend to fight at the Fair?'

'Oh yes, I intend to fight,' Adam said grimly. 'And I intend to win.' A sudden smile lit his face. 'And God help anyone who tries to get in my way.'

Chapter 11

Clara sniffed the air, her eyes luminous with excitement.

The soft Cornish air vibrated with exotic smells. Ginger and cinnamon produced a heady note above the rougher scents of strange animals and unwashed humans, and the normally quiet road at Alverton, on the outskirts of Penzance, echoed with shouts and bewildering cries.

All around her, people pushed and shouted; servant girls wearing their Sunday best, old women from small farms around Land's End looking for a bargain, their traditional white starched headdresses or 'gooks' standing out amongst the small, close-fitting bonnets that were the present-day fashion.

A crowd of fishermen walked past, talking amongst themselves in the loud voices common to those who spent their lives shouting over the noise of wind and waves. They, too, were wearing their Sunday best – of black frockcoat and grey trousers, just like the gentlemen wore. But their muscular shoulders and thighs deformed the clean lines of the cheap material as no gentleman's would ever do.

And all around her, the excitement of the Fair itself! Clara turned to stare at the brilliant paintings that covered the outside of the booth that they were passing. In glorious, unlikely colours they promised wonders within. A man swallowing a poker! The living skeleton! The bearded lady! It was all so thrilling. She wanted to see it all! This minute!

'The best gingerbread-nuts are sold by Hamlyn, down this way.' Edward Blacklock caught her arm, pulling her aside as a group of drunken fishermen staggered past, their thick accents making the remarks they threw at her incomprehensible.

Now she knew why the locals had looked forward to the Fair with such anticipation. It was a world she had never entered before, one in which she wanted to immerse herself. No wonder Lady Susan had not wanted her to come, she thought, reluctantly allowing Edward to lead her to the quieter stalls at the side of the road.

The atmosphere of the Fair was intoxicating. Suddenly, the boring rules of everyday life didn't apply. For the first time she could see a world where conventions did not matter, where excitement and the joy of living were paramount. She could feel herself responding to the animation of the scene, flowering in the heady environment.

Edward led her to a stall where fairings of gingerbread-nuts and burnt almonds were for sale, ready packed, the mouths of the white cotton bags rolled down to show their contents. 'These are the best,' he said, and she could feel his eyes taking in her flushed cheeks and wide eyes. 'The best for the best!'

Clara laughed recklessly, breathing in the spicy smell that rose from the array of goodies before her. What did it matter what he said? She felt drunk on the life that barged and bustled around her, enthralled by the strange booths and tents.

'Then we'll have the best!' she said, knowing that Edward could not stop staring at her, but no longer caring.

She turned to smile brilliantly at the stallholder. 'Four bags please,' she said, and chuckled as he blew a kiss at her while folding the packets.

'This is insufferable!' Isabelle had arrived, clutching Lieutenant Laity, her face angry. 'Really, I must have been mad to come! All these people!' She broke off with a little scream as a couple barged into her, throwing her into the Lieutenant's arms.

Clara threw back her head and laughed. 'Enjoy yourself! This is life!' She handed Isabelle the bag of fairings that Edward had paid for, but Isabelle turned away in disgust.

'You can't eat those!' she gasped. 'And in public!'

'I can!' said Clara, positively. She eagerly dug into the bag she was holding, hungry for the sticky goodies within.

Isabelle said haughtily, her face flushed with anger: 'I shall certainly not –' but could get no further. There was a sudden burst of noise that made Clara clutch at her ears and a brass band appeared on the platform in front of Wombwell's Menagerie and burst into a spirited version of the 'Hallelujah Chorus'.

Edward tugged at Clara's arm and she followed him willingly as they moved further off. Even here, the noise was astounding. Every theatre had a group outside, clowns throwing insults at the passers-by, actors showing a taste of the wonders to be enjoyed inside. And each booth had its showman. 'Walk up, walk up, just about to begin!'

'You are enjoying yourself.' His eyes took in her vivacious looks, the pretty pink cheeks.

'I love it.' For some reason, she did not feel afraid of him here as she did when they met at home. In this rumbustious atmosphere he seemed somehow diminished, paler. Suddenly she felt strong, capable of anything. She returned his stare challengingly.

He said, almost wonderingly, 'You are so alive, Clara, so vibrant.' There was something in his voice that reached her even through the heady excitement she was experiencing. He sounded almost reverent, his eyes seemed to be glued to her face. As if he could not help himself, he reached out a finger and drew it gently, worshipfully, down her cheek, following the delicate hollow of her cheekbone.

Isabelle's gasp interrupted him. 'Clara!' the girl hissed. She was staring at Edward as if she had seen a ghost, her face pale under the shade of her becoming bonnet. 'You called her Clara!'

Clara swung round, glad to dismiss the puzzle of Edward Blacklock and his behaviour to her. She was tired of Isabelle and her missish ways, her constant harping on ladylike behaviour. It was nearly as bad as having Mama standing beside her all the time. Worse, because at least Mama was the daughter of an earl and had a right to criticise Clara's behaviour; Isabelle Kingsley was only the daughter of a tradesman even if he was a rich man and a magistrate, and she had no authority over Clara at all.

Back straight, chin up, she challenged the other woman. 'And why shouldn't he call me Clara?' she demanded tartly. 'I have a right to let my friends call me what they will.' No reason to let someone like Isabelle Kingsley in on the secret of the scene on the cliffs; that was part of the private battle between herself and Edward Blacklock.

'Friends?' enquired Isabelle. 'As far as I can see, you are willing to be friends with anyone.' She corrected herself, her blue eyes fastened coldly on Clara's face. 'Anyone of the male gender, at least.'

Lieutenant Laity intervened swiftly. 'Miss Kingsley, take care. You are about to drop your fairings,' but his voice was lost in Clara's angry reply.

'And only you are allowed to have such friends, I presume.' She looked quickly from Edward to the Lieutenant. 'It seems to me, Miss Kingsley, that you have as many such friends as I.'

The Lieutenant intervened again. 'Miss Kingsley, Miss Pentreath, this is not the place for such a discussion.' He reached out deftly and caught the bag that was dropping from Isabelle's uncaring fingers. 'Why don't you try the fairings, Miss Kingsley? I can assure you they are very good.' He held the bag out to her.

Isabelle swept it away impatiently. 'I do not eat in the street like a common woman, Lieutenant. Nor will I lower myself by bandying words in public.' Her stare altered, became fixed on someone behind Clara, and when she spoke again her voice was honeyed with malice.

'I don't think I have quite as many friends as you, Miss Pentreath, and certainly not from such a wide range of backgrounds. For instance, another of your very best friends is arriving just at this moment.'

The eyes of the whole group swung round to follow her gaze. Adam Trevelyan, with Norman Willcock beside him, was walking towards them.

Reckless fury flamed through Clara. She had recognised Isabelle's jealousy and until now, had felt sorry for the girl. Edward Blacklock might be the catch of the district but the more attention he paid her, the less Clara liked it. Not all his wealth and good looks could make up for the strange way he treated her. When he looked at her, it was as if he wanted to devour her; when they were alone, he seemed to take pleasure in forcing his will on her. There was something about him that frightened her. If Isabelle wanted Edward, then, as far as Clara was concerned, she was welcome.

But Isabelle had no right to vent her malice on Adam Trevelyan. Clara could look after herself, but he was prohibited from retaliation by the difference in their positions in society. Clara gritted her teeth. She would not allow Isabelle to get at her by humiliating Adam.

Ignoring the stares of her companions she stepped forward boldly. 'Mr Trevelyan.' Ignoring the conventions of her class, she held out a daintily gloved hand to him. 'How nice to see you again. I hope that you are quite recovered from your injury?'

Adam paused and for a second she was afraid that he would not respond to her friendly overture. She saw his blue eyes sweep over her companions, narrowing as he took in the array of gentry lined up before him, then, to her relief, he responded in kind. With a grace she had not expected of him he took her hand in his and bowed over it.

'Miss Pentreath.' He raised his head and she saw a gleam of humour light his face. 'I am quite recovered now, thanks to you and your admirable nursing.'

Still letting her hand lie in his, Clara turned to her companions. 'Mr Trevelyan, you have met Miss Kingsley and Lieutenant Laity, I know. Please allow me to introduce you to Mr Blacklock.' Her smile broadened as she heard Isabelle's surprised gasp at the way she was treating a workman as though he were an equal but she did not care. Adam was worth ten of her.

Adam hid his surprise at her action, bowing politely to her companions. 'Miss Kingsley, Lieutenant.' There was a pause as he faced Edward, then, his voice neutral, he added quietly, 'Blacklock.'

93

Clara glanced quickly up at him. The omission of Edward's title had to be deliberate, Adam had already proved that he knew the conventions of polite society. Perplexed, she turned to Edward. His light-grey eyes empty of all expression; he was staring at the miner, his fingers softly caressing the golden hairs of his moustache.

Lieutenant Laity broke in swiftly. 'I hope that you are going to be defending your title in the boxing ring today, Trevelyan.' He turned to Edward. 'Trevelyan holds the title for the last two years.'

Still with his eyes locked on Adam's, Edward said slowly, 'Something tells me that he will be beaten this year.'

Clara stared at the two men. They seemed to be locked in a battle that she could not understand. The air between them was thick with tension. For a moment she was strongly reminded of two dogs circling each other, hackles raised.

They contrasted strongly; Edward, his height set off by the elegance of his costume and emphasised by his top hat, shiny black above his golden hair, and Adam, a couple of inches shorter, his black curls riotous on his forehead, his broad shoulders and strong thighs pushing his Sunday clothes out of shape and making him seem shorter than he really was.

At Edward's words, Adam's hands clenched involuntarily. 'And something tells me that you will be proved wrong in that prediction, Blacklock.' The atmosphere was electric.

Following his usual role of peacemaker, Lieutenant Laity said cheerfully, 'I hope he will be, too. Don't forget, Trevelyan, I have my money on you.'

For several seconds more, the eyes of the two combatants stayed locked, then Edward moved, breaking the current that flowed between them. He turned to the Lieutenant. 'I shall have to leave the ladies to your protection for a few minutes, Laity. I have just remembered something I have to do.'

He glanced down at Clara and she shivered at the cold emptiness of his gaze. 'Will you go with the Lieutenant, my dear? I shall meet up with you as soon as I can, but there is plenty to amuse you here.' He glanced again at Adam, still standing near him, taut and defiant.

'Since predictions are in the air,' Edward said to the Lieutenant with a sneer, 'why don't you take the ladies to one of the fortune-tellers? They are only gipsies but they can't be any worse at prediction than a miner.' He bared his teeth at his companions in a brief smile, then moved swiftly away, his elegant hat showing his progress for several seconds before it was swallowed up in the laughing, noisy crowd.

'Miss Pentreath.' Lieutenant Laity held out his arm to her. 'I think that a fortune-teller sounds like a good idea, don't you?' He nodded briefly at Adam. 'Good luck in the fight this afternoon,' then he turned away, taking the women with him.

Norman let out his breath in a whooping sigh. 'What in God's name was that all about?' he asked Adam.

Adam was still watching the place where Edward had disappeared amongst the throng of Fair-goers. 'I'll call no man "sir" who doesn't deserve respect,' he answered. 'And that – louse – will get no respect from me. Ever.'

'Be careful,' Norman advised him, his usually cheerful face clouded with concern. 'Blacklock would be a bad enemy.'

Adam laughed and clapped him on the shoulder. 'Well, I can tell you, Norman, that I shall be a bloody good one!' He glanced up as Molly pushed her way through the milling mass of people, responding to the whistles and calls that her pretty face and bold eyes invited.

'Some people have posh friends,' she announced, clutching at Adam's arm. 'I were just passing the time of day with Mr Grenfell, and that Mr Blacklock came up to talk to him. Wanted him to take a note to his bank for him.' She shrugged. 'You'd have thought he'd have known to bring some money with him to a place like this. Or perhaps his ladyfriends want expensive presents?' She flashed her blue eyes challengingly at Adam.

Norman said roughly, 'He's not the only one with posh friends.' He nodded at Adam, who stood lost in thought at Molly's news. 'We've been talking to Blacklock too, *and* the Lieutenant from Pendeen, not to mention Miss Kingsley and Captain Pentreath's daughter.'

'So I've got rivals, have I? Two of them, no less?' Molly pressed herself close against Adam's side, nestling her breast against his arm. 'Well, I reckon there's safety in numbers. And if you buy me some clidgy-nicies, I'll forgive you for talking to other women.'

Adam looked down at her and forced himself to smile. 'One packet of clidgy-nicies coming up.'

Isabelle backed away from the small tent. 'I'm not going in there,' she said nervously.

'Come on, it will be an adventure.' Clara looked again at the crude paintings that decorated the sign. If what they indicated was true, the Great Alhambro had all the rulers of Europe as clients. Hardly likely for someone whose tent was tucked away in one of the quieter by-roads of a West Cornwall fair. She gave a shiver of anticipation. It would be fraud, of course, but that would not stop her enjoying it.

The Lieutenant patted Isabelle's hand. 'Don't worry, Miss

Kingsley. I shall be with you. There's nothing to fear.' He glanced at Clara. 'Are you willing to try it?'

'Of course!' Ignoring the Lieutenant's proffered arm, she shouldered her way eagerly through the black draperies that masked the doorway, her face sharp with curiosity.

Inside, the tent was also swagged with black material that cut out the daylight. The only illumination came from a small pan of grease in which floated a large cotton wick. The air was thick with the smell of burning fat overlaid with the scent of something richer and more exotic. The black hangings seemed to close in on Clara, making the tent seem even smaller than it had appeared from the outside. In the flickering light, the draperies were full of menacing shadows and half-unseen objects that hovered on the edges of her vision. Despite herself, Clara felt a nervous shiver run up her spine and she was grateful for the comforting presence of the Lieutenant.

'Well?' Clara jumped at the fretful query which seemed to come from nowhere. 'What do you want?'

She saw him then, a small, dark-faced man in a gaudy turban, squatting on a low pile of cushions at the back of the tent, almost out of the fitfully-flaring lamplight. He took the pipe out of his mouth and pointed it at them. 'Don't stand there like dummies. I said, what do you want?'

Lieutenant Laity moved forward. 'That's for you to tell us, old man. That's what we're here for.'

'To have your fortunes told, eh?' the old man cackled. 'Disbelievers one and all, coming in here to make fun of a poor old man.' He coughed wrackingly, and spat. 'And what sort of future does a man like you have?' he demanded, staring up at the Lieutenant's tall figure, towering over him. 'You, you'll do your duty, keep out of debt, act like a gentleman and live till you die. What sort of fortune is that?' He spat again.

'The best a man could have,' said Lieutenant Laity heartily, 'but not the kind that is going to find favour with the ladies.' He rattled some coins in his pocket meaningfully. 'I think that they would like something rather more interesting.'

At the sound of the coins the old man's eyes glittered in the shadow of his turban. He heaved himself more upright. 'Fortunes are for the fortunate,' he snapped. 'What makes the young ladies think that they are fortunate, eh?' There was an indefinable menace in his tone.

Clara stepped forward, her head up. 'I'm not afraid. I want to hear what's going to happen to me.'

He echoed, 'Want? Want? All the gentry think about is what they want. The rest of the world worry about what they need.' His eyes, rheumy and slitted, studied her in the flickering light of the single lamp. 'Well, little miss, you'll find out what the difference is between wanting and needing, aye, and all too soon I reckon.'

Clara felt a chill run through her. It was all very well to laugh at the expected prophecy of a handsome and rich husband; the forecast of poverty seemed suddenly all too real.

'And what about you?' The old man turned suddenly to Isabelle who sank back against the Lieutenant with a gasp. 'What does the future hold for you, eh?'

'I don't want to know,' she said hastily, clutching at the Lieutenant.

'Want again, eh?' He pulled himself to his feet with the help of a black stick. 'Want! Want!' He hammered his stick onto the ground. 'Well, you'll never know want, my pretty miss. But you'll never get what you want, either.'

There was a sudden increase in the light as the door curtain was moved aside and Edward entered, the drapes falling back into place behind him. His golden hair gleamed as he leaned towards the old man threateningly. 'I heard your fortunes for the others, Father, and I don't like them' he said coldly. 'Perhaps you would like to try again?'

The Great Alhambro seemed unaware of the threat implicit in his words. 'Here's another wanter,' he screeched, 'well, you'll get what you want, my young friend. But by that time you won't want it any more!' He cackled maniacally and as Edward moved forward to grab him, he knocked against the table and the lamp expired with a last flicker and a smell of dead fish.

The sudden blackness was smothering, overwhelming. Clara could hear her own heart beating fast even above Edward's muffled curses and the sound of Isabelle's incipient hysteria. She stood still, listening to the sound of blundering as the men moved around in the darkness.

Then, suddenly, the Lieutenant found the doorway and drew aside the curtains. Daylight flooded in, turning the mystic black draperies to tawdry, badly-dyed cheap cotton, letting out the choking stench of the lamp, showing that the tent was empty of anyone save themselves.

With an oath, Edward leaped forward, but the old man had gone, and when they searched outside, there was no sign of him.

Chapter 12

Lieutenant Laity hammered on Edward Blacklock's shoulder as he joined in the cheering. The striped canvas walls of the boxing booth vibrated to the sound of male shouts and claps; the rough voices of the miners and fishermen rising above the more moderate cries of the gentlemen who stood in the more exclusive roped-off area around the boxing ring.

'What did I tell you?' Lieutenant Laity shouted into Edward's ear over the hullabaloo. 'I knew he'd win. By God, sir, he's got some bottom. That's a real man!' He watched Adam as he stood panting in the middle of the ring, an arm over Norman Willcock's shoulders. The scar along his side blossomed red and ugly, but it hadn't hindered his fighting.

Edward shook himself free from the Lieutenant's grasp. His face was set and hard. 'He's a barbarian.' He hissed the words between gritted teeth. 'An animal. He has no finesse, no science. He fights like a badger in a pit, because that's all he knows how to do.'

'Oh, come,' the Lieutenant protested. 'That was the best fight I've seen for years. He's not a professional, you know.'

'He's not even a man!' Edward stared at his companion. Slowly, a smile twisted his handsome mouth. 'You want to see a real fight?' he asked. 'Follow me.'

Without waiting to see what the Lieutenant would do, he made his way over to the two contestants, ducking between the twin ropes slung on posts driven into the earth that marked the boundary of the ring. Laity followed him, intrigued despite himself.

As Edward entered the ring, Adam saw him. He pushed himself clear of his friend and erstwhile opponent, balancing himself warily on the balls of his feet as he watched the other man approach.

Edward halted immediately in front of him. The two men eyed each other aggressively. The tension between them was so palpable that it communicated itself to the watchers round the ring, and the cheers and conversations quickly died away as the audience crowded forward to hear what was going to happen.

Keeping his eyes on Adam, Edward Blacklock reached inside his coat and pulled out a small linen bag which Grenfell had passed to him earlier in the evening. With a flourish, he threw it down in front of Adam. It landed heavily, the clinking sound as it hit the turf clearly audible in the suddenly silent tent.

'There's a hundred guineas in there.' Edward Blacklock's voice was clear and carrying. 'I challenge you to a fight. The winner to get the money.'

There was a sudden buzz of excited talk. Laity grasped Edward's shoulder and shook it lightly. 'You can't do that, man.'

He nodded at Adam who was standing silently in front of them, his eyes fixed on the bag of golden guineas lying at his feet.

'He's already had four bouts this evening. You're fresh. You can't fight him when he's tired like this.'

'Four bouts!' There was scorn in Edward's voice. 'That's nothing. I'm not talking about boxing here, wearing gloves, pussy-footing around for a few minutes to amuse the spectators. I'm challenging him to a prize-fight. Bare knuckles. To end when one of us can't come up to scratch.' With his toe, he pointed at the line scored into the earthen floor of the ring.

The noise rose to an excited crescendo, then died away as another man shouldered his way through the gentry gathered in a roped-off circle around the boxing ring itself.

Christopher Kingsley climbed into the ring. 'Prize-fighting is illegal,' he stated to the boos of the miners and fishermen gathered round the walls of the tent. 'As a magistrate I cannot condone such a thing.' He turned to Edward. 'Take back your challenge.'

Edward shook his head. 'You condoned it two years ago when Slater and Briggs fought.'

'And nearly had to try Briggs for murder afterwards,' Kingsley replied. 'Give it up, Blacklock.'

Edward shook his head. 'I'll fight this man,' he stated. 'If necessary, I shall move to the next district to do so. But fight him I will. As long as he has the guts to accept my challenge, of course.' His grey eyes, light and cold, watched Adam like a snake watching a rabbit.

Adam raised his head slowly and moved to stand close to Edward. His voice was quiet, heard only by those standing in the ring itself. 'You know I cannot match that purse.'

Edward's finely moulded lips moved in a twisted grin. 'If you beat me, you are welcome to the money,' he said. 'But if I win . . .' His voice

99

died away and he stroked his moustache with a gentle finger. 'If I win,' he repeated more strongly, 'I will have had the pleasure of beating the hell out of you. Believe me, no mere money could buy that.'

Their eyes met and clashed, then Adam said in a loud, carrying voice, 'I accept.'

There was a concerted cheer from the common men. Lieutenant Laity pushed forward anxiously. 'But you cannot fight now,' he said to Adam. 'You are exhausted. If you must fight, why not put it off for a day? Or even a week? You've been injured. There's no reason you have to fight today.'

'He has challenged me now, I fight him now,' Adam stated flatly, then he grinned wolfishly. 'And when I win, it will feel even sweeter.'

'You'll lose,' Edward snapped. He turned to the Lieutenant. 'Laity, you'll be one of my seconds?'

'If you insist,' the Lieutenant said heavily.

Kingsley broke in hastily: 'Don't ask me, Blacklock. I'm a magistrate. I won't stop the fight, but you can't expect me to act for you.'

A rough, dark-skinned man pushed himself forward. 'There's no hurry, gentlemen.' He turned to face the crowd. 'This fight was not included in the programme,' he bawled. 'Everyone clear the tent. Admission for the fight which starts in – one hour?' – He turned to get the agreement of the two principals – 'will be one shilling for the inner ring and threepence for the rest.'

There was a howl of outrage from the miners and fishermen which died away as the professional boxers employed as stewards, moved menacingly forward, clubs in their hands. Slowly, with mutters and a few scuffles, the tent emptied.

'I never thought I'd be grateful to a Romany!' Norman muttered as he pulled Adam to the side of the ring. 'Trust them to have an eye for the main chance.'

'They only hold the local boxing competition because of the money it brings in.' Adam spoke almost without thinking, his mind on the coming fight. 'You can't blame them for wanting to cash in on a prize-fight. It's not something that happens every day.'

'No. And why is it happening now? That's what I want to know,' Norman demanded forthrightly. 'What is it between you and that Blacklock, Adam? Why does he hate you enough to want to beat the shit out of you? Because that's the only reason he's doing this. If I had won he wouldn't have challenged me.'

Adam closed his eyes as, unwished-for, a small figure appeared to his imagination. A girl with a slender, almost childlike waist which belied the womanly curves above and below. He could see again the ash-blonde wisps of hair that he longed to stroke, see the flash of her emerald eyes, the elfin grin that lit up her face. For a moment, he could almost smell the flowery perfume that rose from her skin.

With an effort he forced the vision from him. 'I don't know,' he lied. 'But if he wants to fight, I'm willing. And if he wants to fight dirty, I'll fight dirtier. I won't be beaten by a so-called gentleman with the instincts of a rat.'

He ducked between the ropes and reached for his shirt, shrugging it over his sweating body. 'I'm going for a walk. If I don't move, I shall stiffen up. But tell His Lordship over there,' he threw a contemptuous glance at Edward Blacklock, 'that I shall be back in time to meet his challenge. And I shall win.'

When Adam returned, the place was full to bursting. He had to force his way through the mass of male bodies crammed into the tent. A prize-fight was a rare occurrence anyway, and a contest between two local men, one of them a respectable businessman, added spice to the occasion.

The air was thick with the stench of stale beer and unwashed bodies. The owner had brought in more lights, crude wicks floating in bowls of fat, and these added their stink and heat to the already noxious atmosphere.

'He's working himself up.' Norman pulled off Adam's coat, nodding briefly at Edward. Glancing across the ring, Adam could see the sheen of sweat already on his chest and shoulders. Edward stripped better than he had expected. His height and the elegant tailoring of the black coats that he always wore had disguised his breadth of shoulder. He would have a longer reach, Adam thought, trying to analyse his opponent dispassionately. And he would be full of tricks.

Norman massaged Adam's shoulders, loosening the muscles. 'Ben Pasco's your other second, and I've agreed with the Lieutenant that we have the same referee and umpires as for the boxing.' He paused. 'I thought it better not to risk having someone who might be crooked.'

'Like Grenfell, you mean.' Adam could see him in the other corner, hovering obsequiously. 'But where's Ben?'

'Visiting his favourite dancing girls.' Adam glanced up, startled out of his preoccupation. Ban Pasco wasn't a womaniser. Norman winked meaningfully.

'I see.' Adam stifled a grin. Dancers would use resin on their shoes, and resin, rubbed into the palms, helped a tired fighter grip his hands into fists after the muscles had become weak through exhaustion. Obviously his seconds had no objection to bending the rules a little where they thought they could get away with it.

101

The professional boxers cleared the ring of spectators then the umpire moved forward. 'Gentlemen, please come up to the scratch.'

Adam moved forward, his heart beating furiously. He had fought before, and won, but this fight would be different. This time he was facing, not an opponent but an enemy. Carefully, he aligned his feet with the mark, taking up the appropriate stance. From a distance of a few inches, Edward Blacklock's eyes bored into his.

'I'm going to teach you a lesson, Trevelyan.' The words were quiet, but full of venom. Then a fist pummelled into Adam's stomach, a bare quarter of an inch above the belt, and the fight was on.

'First round to him.' Norman massaged Adam's solar plexus as he rested on Pasco's upraised knee.

'It isn't who wins the rounds, it's who wins the fight.' Adam squeezed cold water from the sponge over his head. Blacklock was quicker than he had expected and more knowledgeable, and Adam knew that he hadn't yet adapted to the change in fighting methods. Unlike in boxing, throws were perfectly legal in this type of fighting and Blacklock's swift movement had caught him by surprise, hurling him to the ground and so ending the round.

But it had been a tactical error, he decided, forcing himself to analyse the fight objectively. It was too early yet for a throw to do any real harm. Blacklock should have kept his skill in reserve. If he had suddenly unleashed it when Adam was tired and weak, he might have done more damage.

The referee was staring at his watch. 'The thirty seconds are up. Come to scratch, gentlemen, please.'

Blacklock was there first. He had refused the offer of his second's knee, spending his thirty seconds' grace walking about, talking to his friends and showing how little he was affected by the brief flurry that had made up the first round. Adam gritted his teeth and moved to the mark.

This time he was ready for Edward's initial blow and the round lasted for nearly five minutes. Edward was determined to inflict as much pain as possible. Time and again he tried to grind his knuckles into Adam's eye or aimed at the throat, but Adam's reflexes were still honed from his earlier battles and he avoided serious hurt. For the moment, the other man's longer reach prevented him from retaliating as he wanted, but Adam knew that this would alter as the fight took its course.

Again, it was Adam who was thrown to the floor, but he had the measure of his opponent now. Edward was motivated by hate, by the desire to inflict pain. It gave his fighting an edge that Adam could not combat. But the heightened emotion was taking its toll. Edward was

102

bathed in sweat, far more than could be justified by the activity in the ring. Adam knew that if he could only hang on, sooner or later Blacklock would suffer from a reaction.

A third time the men came up to the scratch. Again, Edward taunted Adam; 'No miner is going to lust after my woman.'

The surge of anger which ran through him at this enabled Adam to inflict the first real damage. He had aimed at Blacklock's eyes but a swift movement saved his opponent from the true force of the blow. Instead, Adam split his cheek, and smiled grimly as he saw the blood run down Edward's face and spatter onto the earth floor of the ring.

The rounds began to merge in Adam's mind. There was only the constant giving and taking of punishment, the rapidly growing feeling of exhaustion which the thirty second rests between rounds did little to alleviate. Pain was a constant companion that he had to live with; pain from the cuts and bruises inflicted by Edward's blows, but much worse was the pain from his own battered hands.

Adam stared down at them as he rested after one particularly long bout. The knuckles were swollen, the skin over the left hand split open where he had connected with Edward's nose. His fingers would scarcely unclench at the end of the rounds and he knew it was only a matter of time before the exhausted muscles refused to work any more. Then, with every blow, he would risk a broken finger.

'How many rounds?' He had no breath left for unnecessary talking.

'Fourteen so far. You've been going for just over forty minutes.' Norman handed him a flask of brandy and water and he swigged it gratefully. Blacklock had stopped his posturing between rounds, Adam was pleased to see. He, too, was slumped on his second's knee, with Lieutenant Laity sponging his face and shoulders with cold water.

As if he felt Adam's glance, Blacklock looked up and the two opponents stared at each other across the width of the ring. Suddenly, horribly, a rictus grin contorted Edward's face and he was on his feet even before time was called.

Until now, Blacklock had kept just within the rules; now he ignored them blatantly. The round ended, as so many of them had, with Adam being thrown in a cross buttock to fall heavily on his back. He felt his breath knocked out of him by the force of his landing, then saw Edward falling onto him, his knees aimed at Adam's stomach.

With a last reserve of strength he didn't know he had, Adam rolled swiftly sideways, away from the falling body.

'Foul! Foul!' Adam could hear Norman's shout even above the roar of the crowd. He could see the disappointed malice in Edward's eye as he knelt beside him, but when the referee came to object, Blacklock was all apologies.

'Sorry,' he gasped, and Adam knew that he was exaggerating his breathlessness. 'A bit tired. Overbalanced.'

He would never have got away with that earlier in the fight, Adam knew, but there was just enough possibility that he might have been telling the truth for the referee to back off. Adam climbed slowly to his feet and this time he did not refuse when Ben surreptitiously offered him some powdered resin to rub onto his hands.

'Think you can hold out?' Norman sponged the sweat and blood off his face with rough tenderness.

'Yes.' But for the first time, Adam felt a doubt. He hadn't worked for a month. In that time, he seemed to have lost half his stamina.

It was not only the heavy work, boring holes single-handed in granite with a hammer and iron borer that had kept his muscles in trim. The twenty-minute climb back to grass at the end of each core, carrying his tools, had given him extra fitness. But this last month he had done none of that, and he could feel his body, that he had always trusted implicitly to do what he wanted, weaken and flag just when he needed it most.

'He keeps aiming at your wound,' Norman said, and Adam nodded. It had been obvious. In the boxing matches, the miners and fishermen who had been his opponents had avoided the glaring scar with an innate chivalry. With Blacklock the opposite occurred. Every body blow was aimed at that one spot, and Adam was aware that his need to protect the recently-healed flesh handicapped him in the fight.

Blacklock was slower to come to the scratch this time and the taunts with which he began each round had sunk to gasped imprecations. 'Coward. Animal.'

In sudden fury, Adam reached out, clutching a handful of the golden hair, pulling his enemy's face forward onto the blow he aimed at him. He got in two good punches, then Blacklock dropped to his knees and the referee caught at Adam's raised arm as he aimed another punch. 'You mustn't hit a man when he's down.'

'But he did it on purpose,' Adam gasped. 'He's not that badly hurt. He just did it to stop the round.'

The referee shrugged. 'The rule is, you mustn't go to the ground unless a blow has been struck. You struck the blow. There's nothing I can do.'

Thirty brief seconds, then out again. Adam could feel his strength disappearing by the minute. The bouts earlier in the evening had taken more out of him than he realised, and it was obvious to him now that Blacklock had deliberately goaded him into the fight to take advantage of the fact.

Another round. Another fall. The rounds were over more quickly now. Neither man had the strength left to sustain a real attack. Adam knew despairingly that he was weakening more quickly than his opponent. If the fight went on, as they often did, until one man was too exhausted to drag himself to the scratch after the thirty seconds' rest, then he knew that it would be Blacklock, and not he, who would win the fight.

His only hope was to incapacitate Blacklock before he got to that state. But it was too late for a knock-out blow. His hands were swollen to twice their normal size, purple and raw. He would never get the force behind them now to knock Edward out. Many lighter blows might achieve the same thing in his opponent's weakened state, but he had already shown that if that appeared likely he was willing to drop immediately to his knees on the earth, just to put an end to the round.

Another fall, another round. Adam could see that Blacklock had read the situation the same way that he had. There was an air of jauntiness about him as he stumbled back for the start of the next round, a suspicion of a smile on the cut and swollen lips under the golden moustache. He could even spare more breath for his taunts. 'You'll never get her, miner. How does it feel to know that you'll never have a decent woman?'

Never get her. Never get her. The words seemed to whirl round and round in Adam's battered head. He slumped, for the first time exposing the recently-healed wound in his side to direct attack, and Blacklock went for it. His hands were in the same state as Adam's but they could still inflict severe damage. Adam turned half-away, as if trying to protect his side and Edward moved in for the kill, his teeth bared in a grin of pleasure.

With a sudden movement, Adam whirled back, his arm reaching out, not to punch but to hold. His arm locked firmly around Blacklock's neck, his hip jutting out to support the man's body.

With his right hand, Adam rained blow after blow upon his enemy's face. He felt Edward's body sag as he tried to touch the ground with his knees to stop the round, but Adam's grasp was too strong. He pulled the man further across his hip to stop him slipping to the floor, continuing the barrage of punches into his captive face. It was his one chance. He closed his mind to the agony in his hands, even when a sharper pain warned him that he had broken a finger.

The man's face was covered with blood now, but whether it was his

105

own or from Adam's torn hands, Adam no longer knew or cared. Where strength was missing, then guile must do the work instead. Half-unconscious himself, he closed his mind to everything but the need to beat his opponent. Then the referee pulled his arm free from around Blacklock's neck and he dropped to the floor beside Edward's unconscious body.

The seconds raced to their fighters, Norman almost carrying Adam back to his corner. Thirty seconds. That was all he could think. Thirty seconds in which he had to recover himself enough to walk unaided to the scratch mark across the ring. And thirty seconds in which Edward Blacklock might recover enough to get there himself. And if he did, Adam knew, the fight was over. He had used up the last of his strength. If Edward came up to scratch this time, he would win the match.

Time. Adam's legs were buckling under him. The tent seemed to sway to and fro before his eyes. Reeling like a drunk, he forced himself to walk the few feet to the mark on the turf. He blinked, trying to clear the blood out of his eyes. The mark on the earth swam and wavered giddily in front of him.

With an effort he got himself in position and stared into the opposite corner. The Lieutenant was standing back. It was the rule that a fighter had to get up to the scratch-line unaided. But Grenfell was pushing Blacklock to his feet, lending him a shoulder. For a few seconds, Blacklock stood supported, then he took his hand off Grenfell's shoulder. Slowly he walked towards the centre of the ring. One step. Two steps. Then his knees buckled and he fell headlong, to lie motionless on the grass.

The noise was a physical assault. It battered ears, it pressed against his swollen eyes, vibrated in his useless hands. Adam was vaguely aware of someone raising his arm, of the shout of delight that went up from the watching miners, but inside his head the same words kept running round and round. *I've won. I've won.*

Keeping his knees from buckling by sheer force of will, he said to the referee, 'You've got the gold?' He had to say it three times before his bruised and broken mouth would make intelligible words.

'My dear sir, it's yours. And well-deserved.' The referee reached down and took the bag that someone had been keeping safe for him.

Adam's hands would not work. 'Open it for me,' he ordered shortly. The referee gave him a startled glance, then fumbled with the knots that held the neck closed. He pulled it open, showing Adam the softly gleaming coins inside, running his fingers through them so that the miner could see that there were no base coins at the bottom.

106

Adam held out his puffy, twisted hands and the referee lowered the bag gently into them.

Norman was by his side. 'I'll look after that for you, Adam. Let me take it.'

Adam shook his head. 'I'll take it.' His mouth moved more freely this time.

Concentrating on every step, he made his weaving, reeling way across to the other corner. Edward Blacklock was conscious now. His nose was bloody and misshapen, his eyes almost closed, but he could see Adam and forced himself into a sitting position as the miner approached.

Adam stared down at him. Articulating as clearly as his smashed lips allowed, he said loudly, 'Keep your money, Blacklock. I wouldn't take anything from you if I was starving.'

He tipped the bag up. In a golden, glittering stream, the sovereigns poured from the bag, bouncing off Blacklock's body, rolling across the ring in shining arcs.

At the sight, a sudden silence fell and the clink and rattle of the coins could be heard throughout the tent.

When the bag was empty, Adam flung it contemptuously in Blacklock's face, then, with grim determination, he staggered back across the expanse of the ring to his own corner.

And he never saw the hate that peered out through the swollen, bloody eyelids of the man he left behind him.

Chapter 13

'Dear God!'

Clara came to an abrupt halt immediately inside the cottage door as she caught sight of Adam. In the two days since the fight his face had blossomed into a kaleidoscope of colours, veined by the puckered scabs of cuts and split flesh.

'I was told you'd won!' She couldn't believe that it was possible for a face to look so battered. She moved forward, unable to take her eyes off his face and Adam moved uneasily under her probing glance.

'And so he did win, the great lummox!' Ma Downing pulled a stool forward for Clara. 'That's men for you all over. No sooner do you get them fit than they go and cripple themselves again. And for what, that's what I want to know.' She stood squarely in front of Adam, her hands on her ample hips. 'For nothing, that's what! All that fighting and you're not a penny the better off for it.'

'What does the money matter!' Clara felt her stomach churn as she examined his face. She was simultaneously revolted and moved to admiration by his injuries. How much courage it must have taken to go voluntarily into a ring, knowing that you would have to suffer like that. And how futile and barbaric it all seemed.

'Of course the money matters,' Ma Downing said indignantly. 'It's only they who've never lacked it who think it's not important.' She snorted and pointed at Adam. He glared back defiantly through eyes swollen almost shut. 'He only does it for the money. And then he goes and throws it all away!'

'But if he won . . .' Clara couldn't understand what the older woman meant. 'He must have got a prize if he won the boxing.'

'Boxing!' the old woman retorted. 'You don't get marked like that by boxing! Prize-fighting, that was, for all it's supposed to be illegal. And all the gentry there to see it, magistrates and all!'

Clara felt sick. Was this what her father went to the Fair to see? It was hard to think that he enjoyed seeing a man get beaten like this. And the only magistrate around was Mr Kingsley, who had always chucked her under the chin and given her sixpence when she was a child. How could men who were kind and considerate to their families and friends stand by to see such brutality?

Ma Downing wiped her hands on her sacking apron. 'And at the end of it he went and threw away all that money. Good money that he'd already won.' She was almost breathless at the enormity of the action.

'It isn't as if we don't need it,' she pointed out furiously, turning to Adam. 'You can't expect the club to pay you this time, you great lummox. You didn't get these injuries down a mine. And heaven knows when you'll be able to work again with hands like that!'

'Oh!' Clara could not restrain the moan of horror that broke from her as she noticed Adam's hands for the first time. They looked like raw meat, purple and swollen to twice their normal size, the fingers so fat the skin shone as it stretched painfully across the battered flesh.

Unable to stop herself, she reached out a gentle finger and ran it with a gossamer touch over the poor, bruised hands. Glancing up, she caught Adam's eye. For a long moment, she felt as if time had been suspended, as if the two of them were alone in the world, then, suddenly, she returned to the present. She sat up hastily, feeling her face flush with embarrassment as if she had exposed herself to him.

Ma Downing broke in, 'If you think he looks bad now, you should have seen him when that Norman brought him home last Thursday. I tell you, he were like a dying duck in a thunderstorm.'

She shook her head, making her fat cheeks vibrate. 'It's a good thing young Phil were asleep in bed – he'd've been proper upset to see his uncle like that. And all for what? He could have got a hundred guineas for it but he throwed it all away. Daft as a brush!'

'What is all this about a hundred guineas?' The sum was enormous. Surely it wasn't usual to win such a huge amount of money? Clara looked from Ma Downing to Adam, glad to break the sudden moment of intimacy that her touch had created. 'I haven't heard anything about this.'

'Nor should you,' Adam broke in hastily. His words were distorted through swollen lips. 'Fighting isn't a fit subject for a young girl to hear about.'

'In that case,' Clara said tartly, 'men shouldn't indulge in it.' Her eyes met his challengingly. 'Well?' she demanded. 'What's all this about a hundred guineas?'

He stared fixedly at the floor, unwilling to answer her. Furiously, she stamped her foot. 'Tell me!' she demanded, then, more quietly, 'Don't you think I deserve to be told?'

He looked up then, acknowledging tacitly the hold she had over him. 'I had won the boxing,' he began unwillingly. 'I beat Norman in the final and then there was a challenge from the floor.'

He looked past her and Clara realised that he was seeing again the scene in the boxing booth. 'I was offered a hundred guineas for a prize-fight.' He shook himself slightly, and focused on her. 'I don't fight like that normally.'

She nodded, understanding him. To her, it all seemed brutal and ugly, but she could see that it mattered to him that she should be aware that there was a distinction between the two types of fighting, and that he knew it. 'So you fought?' she prompted him.

'And I won.'

He made no attempt to tell her the details and she recognised and welcomed his natural delicacy. She had seen the results of the fight; she had no wish to hear a blow-by-blow account.

'And they refused to hand over the money?'

'I got the money.' His voice was harsh. 'I gave it back.'

For a second she could not believe her ears, then she jumped to her feet. 'You gave it back!' Her voice rose in disbelief. 'For heaven's sake, why?'

She knew how much that money must have meant to him. With a hundred guineas he could have afforded to emigrate; he could have paid for someone to look after Phil until he was capable of earning his own living. The hundred odd pounds could have given him freedom, made his dreams come true . . . And yet he had thrown it all away.

He would not look at her now, would not meet her eye. Exasperated, she leaned over him, shaking him by the shoulders. 'Why did you do it?'

He was still silent. Something about him brought her up short. There was a mystery here, one which he did not want her to unravel. The thought calmed her, made her more determined than ever to find out the truth.

Clara took a deep breath, settling herself again on the chair, spending time adjusting her long skirts until they flowed around her feet in the correct, elegant folds. When she spoke again, her voice was quieter, more restrained.

'A hundred guineas is a great deal of money.' She spoke slowly, her mind working hard though she kept her emerald eyes fixed on his face. 'No working-class man would have money like that; it can only have been put up by a gentleman.'

He was deadly still now, and she knew that he was trying to

dampen down all response to her words so that she would not be able to read the answer in his reactions. Mentally, she reviewed the men in the area who might be willing to pay such money.

'Edward Blacklock!' It wasn't a guess. Suddenly, she knew it as certainly as if he had said the name, and Adam Trevelyan's small, involuntary movement at her words only confirmed her instinctive knowledge. Stunned, she said, 'But why would he want to fight you?'

As soon as she had asked it, the answer came to her. She felt the crimson flood her face, felt her heart jump and thud as embarrassment burned through her. *Edward had fought Adam because of her.*

And Adam had given back the money because of her. She did not need to ask him, did not need to have his reasoning spelled out. She knew it as clearly as she knew her own name. He had refused Edward's money because, in some way, he saw that by accepting it he would have compromised her!

She felt the enormity of his sacrifice wash over her. She would have called the action romantic or chivalrous in another man, but she could not apply those words to Adam. He was too down to earth, too normal. Only his pride would have made him act that way, his pride, and in some way she could not fully understand, his feeling for her.

She could not look at him, could not speak. She was grateful that Ma Downing was bustling around behind her, clashing pots together as she cooked the evening meal over the open fire. The noise helped to hide the silence that grew between Adam and herself, becoming every second more impossible to break.

It was Ma Downing who finally broke the tension. 'I didn't see your Da at the Fair.'

Clara jumped nervously, and swung round. 'He didn't go this year. He was working. He only rode in to escort Miss Kingsley and myself home.' Her mother had been furious when she discovered that he had given the servants leave to go to the Fair. An earl's daughter wasn't accustomed to being left without servants to attend her every wish. Her lips twitched at the memory of the row.

Adam grunted. 'Strange time to be working.' He, too, seemed glad to leave the subject of the fight.

'He seems to be working all the time these days,' Clara admitted. She would never have considered discussing her father with anyone else, but somehow, Adam's actions at the fight had moved him into a different category. After what he had done for her, she could not continue treating him as if he were a stranger.

Tentatively, she said, 'He works late in his library every night.' She glanced up at Adam for the first time since the revelation about the fight. 'Is the mine in trouble?' Her voice was quiet but controlled.

111

He paused for a long time before he answered and she felt her heart sink. 'I reckon that they'll have to knack her in a couple of months at most.'

Clara could scarcely breathe. The news was even worse than she had feared. 'Knack?' Her throat had closed up and the word was scarcely audible.

He nodded. 'The rumour is, your Da's in hock to Blacklock. If the mine doesn't start paying her way in the next couple of months . . .' He made an abrupt chopping motion with one swollen, purple hand.

Clara winced. No wonder her father had told her to be nice to Edward. Perhaps it was only his feeling for her that had reprieved the mine even this long. Because Edward did have a strong feeling for her. She knew it even while she was revolted by his expression of it. She could not call it love, it was too strange and dark for that. But he was attracted to her. And in her, now, lay her father's one hope of keeping the mine open until a new seam of ore could be found.

The thought both frightened and excited her.

Thinking of Edward, she said slowly, 'Mr Blacklock won't be pleased with the way you treated him. Do you think he will get my father to lay you off?'

Adam shook his head. 'He won't do that. That's too petty for him, and not personal enough.' He moved painfully in his hard chair, trying to ease his cramped and battered muscles. 'He'll try to get some sort of revenge, I'm sure, but he won't do it that way.'

Clara nodded. She already knew that he could be vindictive, but Adam's words reassured her. Edward wasn't petty. Quite the opposite. When he took revenge, it would be something dramatic and vicious.

Without thinking, she reached out and touched Adam's sleeve. 'Be careful, please.' She could not hide the fear in her voice.

His swollen hand covered her small white fingers. 'I can look after myself, I promise you.'

She looked up into his face and her mouth quirked into a tremulous smile that lit her face with an elfin beauty. Then it was gone. She sighed and rose restlessly to her feet, walking silently about the tiny room, her worries too great to let her sit still any more.

He watched her sympathetically for a while, then, 'Are you still worried about your father?'

She swung round to stare at him, biting her lip to stop it from trembling. 'If he loses the mine it will kill him. The Wheal Susan is his life.' She could not disguise the quiver in her voice.

Impulsively, she came back towards him, her fingers twisting nervously together. 'I suppose there's no chance of finding tin before the mine . . . in the next few weeks?'

112

Adam was silent. After a long moment she turned away and began walking restlessly to and fro again.

Doubtfully, he said to her, 'There's just one thing . . .'

Instantly, she turned back to him, her face alive with hope. 'Yes?'

'I'm not sure that I should tell you,' he said, and she could hear the reluctance in his voice.

She dropped to her knees beside him on the layer of sand that covered the earth floor, careless of any damage to her skirt. 'I won't tell anyone, I promise.'

He could not hold back. If his words could give her any hope, he had to tell her, even though he knew that it might rebound on him.

He said, 'I don't want to get your hopes up. I don't know that there's tin there. I haven't seen the signs myself. But Phil has been working the pitch with Norman and Jan Eddy. When it's just Phil and me, I have the candle so that I can see and Phil works the wind-machine in the dark.'

'But he's only a boy.' Despite herself Clara could not stop interrupting. 'Are you telling me you make a child like that work for hours alone in the pitch blackness?'

'Candles cost money,' Adam reminded her. 'More, they take as much air as a man. We can't afford to waste good air down there. He knows I'm nearby. He's not afraid.'

Clara subsided though she was still shocked. It had seemed cruel enough to make a child of nine work down the mine anyway. She knew that Phil would not have been allowed to work in a coal mine or a factory. But to leave him without a light for hours on end seemed brutal beyond belief. For the first time she wondered about the good life she had led, paid for by mites like Phil breathing foul air in the darkness.

Adam did not seem to realise how shocked she was. He went on, 'When I had my accident, we all moved round. Phil works the air-machine for Norman instead of Jan, and Jan now wheels the barrows to the shaft. He needs a candle for that.'

Clara nodded. She knew from her father that the galleries were narrow and twisting. It would be difficult to push a heavy barrow if you could not see where you were going.

'Whenever Jan is loading up, Phil can see round the area where he sits.' He cleared his throat. 'Phil reckons that he can see a sign of quartz.' Adam paused and looked at her expectantly.

Clara stared back, blankly. 'But quartz isn't tin.'

'But tin is found in quartz,' Adam told her.

'So you mean, the vein everyone's been looking for is there all the

113

time? You've only got to dig where Phil said and you've found it?' Clara's green eyes burned with excitement.

Adam shook his head. 'It's not that easy. In the first place, I was looking for signs of a lode when I cut that gallery and I never saw it.'

'But you might have missed it,' Clara objected.

'It's possible. If I was just a millimetre away from the vein, I might have missed it. But it's more likely that Phil is wrong. He's learning, but he's not trained yet. It could be something else in the rock, a piece of mica or something. Or even just wishful thinking.'

'Or it's there!' Clara would not let him dampen her happiness.

'Even if it's there, it doesn't mean the mine is saved,' Adam said shortly. 'Not every vein of quartz has tin in it. And even if it does, the ore could be poor quality, or in such small quantities that it wouldn't make any difference to the mine.'

He leaned forward, trying to temper her enthusiasm with his knowledge. 'The mine is in a bad way. You need a good find if your father is going to keep it open. And, in a way, a bad find is worse than nothing.'

She nodded. 'Because you've found the vein everyone knew was there but it's no good. I can understand that.'

'And, in any case, there's nothing we can do about it at present.' He lifted up his swollen, bruised hands. 'I can't climb ladders like this. To get to my pitch I have to climb down the underside of some of the ladders because of the way the shaft bends. I need to have good hands.'

'But Norman . . .' Clara began. Now that she knew there was a chance that the tin was there, she wanted something to happen immediately.

Adam shook his head. 'He's not the greatest miner in the world, nor the most subtle. One hint that there's tin there and he'll smash a great chunk out of the rock to check. And if there *is* tin there – well, we're nearly at the end of the account period. Even if it's a real find, a "sturt" as we call it, we won't get much up this account, especially with me off. And next account – we'll be given a couple of shillings for every pound's worth of tin we raise. And bang goes my chance of making some money.'

She stared at him, her face pale. 'You mean you're deliberately keeping it from my father?'

'I'm keeping nothing from him,' Adam pointed out, his voice rough. 'I don't know that there *is* tin down there.'

Clara rose slowly to her feet, staring at him. 'But you think there might be!' Her voice was shaking. 'My father is making himself sick with worry and all you care about is your pay!'

He stood up, too. 'I care about my family,' he snapped. He pointed at Ma Downing who had stopped her work and was staring at them in bewilderment. 'My earnings keep three people out of the workhouse,' he said, 'not to mention feeding the dog you landed on me. If I don't earn, we all starve.'

'And if the mine closes down, you'll starve as well,' Clara said passionately. 'And so will Norman and half the other people around here. And so will I. And it will all be your fault!' She could not keep the sob out of her voice.

'If the mine closes,' said Adam coldly, 'it will be the fault of Edward Blacklock and your father.'

'My father! Papa is the only reason that mine was ever opened.'

'And he's going to be the reason it's closed down,' Adam said bitterly. 'He knows mining. He should have started looking for new lodes long before this. And renewing the ladders. They're rotten! You say that mine is his life, but it's *our* lives that we're risking every day.'

'He doesn't have the money,' Clara said furiously. 'How can he renew ladders when the mine is in such a bad way?'

'He should have done it years ago,' Adam said. 'And he should have had payres looking for new lodes years ago, too. But he didn't. And do you know *why* he didn't?' The blue eyes bored down into hers. 'Because he was draining the mine of every penny he could, to keep you and your mother in luxury.'

Chapter 14

The following Monday, Clara rode to the Wheal Susan, her face serious and determined.

She had been unable to sleep after Adam's revelations. Restlessly, she had argued with herself half the night, uncertain what she should do.

All her love for her father urged her to tell him about Phil's findings. Even if the boy was wrong, the news might still lift the trouble from her father's face for a few brief hours. But the thought of Adam, refusing the hundred guineas that he had already won, that he so badly needed, always stopped her.

She knew in her heart that he had made that quixotic, irrational gesture because of her. How could she now betray his trust and possibly deprive him of the money he could earn if he made a good find?

She had not realised until now how much she had come to rely on Adam's easygoing companionship. The thought had made her sit up in bed abruptly. Nor had she realised how much support he had provided. She had gone to him, telling herself that it was her duty to a sick miner. When had the relationship changed? When had she begun drawing on him for strength?

She laid her head on her knees, her pale hair, braided for the night, falling across the lacy counterpane. It was wrong. He was someone she should never even speak to unless she was being charitable. Yet, somehow, Adam Trevelyan had become more important to her than anyone else in her life; she cared about his worries and concerns as she cared about no one else's.

Except her father's, Clara reminded herself. She owed her first duty to her father. She would tell him about Phil's discovery first thing in the morning. Relieved to have reached a decision, she finally slept, but her dreams had been broken by Adam's bruised and swollen face. The next day, she had kept silent.

Now she was determined to find out the truth. She already knew that her father hadn't stinted in spending on her mother or herself recently. In church yesterday she had allowed her attention to wander, mentally pricing the rich figured silk in her mother's new dress and the deeply fringed cashmere shawl that she wore over her shoulders.

Afterwards, she had examined with a new eye the furnishings in the drawing room, the fresh silk curtains and elegant knick-knacks. Everything was of good quality. Even her own horse was far better bred and trained than Isabelle Kingsley's, Clara realised with a faint shock, as she turned into the mine and dismounted.

Suddenly worried beyond endurance, she flung open the Count House door without knocking. Two figures leapt guiltily apart – Sam Grenfell and a pretty, black-haired girl whose face seemed vaguely familiar. Clara stood in the doorway, tapping her riding whip lightly against her riding habit, letting her eyes rest coolly on the red-faced couple before her. 'Busy, Mr Grenfell?' Her voice was honeyed with malice.

'Never too busy to see you, Miss Pentreath.' His obsequious words made her even angrier. He smoothed down his hair with a shaking hand and turned away from the other woman, pretending to busy himself by straightening some papers on the table. 'Thank you for letting me know, Molly. You had better get back to work now.'

Molly pushed her way past Clara with a defiant toss of her head, slamming the door behind her. Something in her attitude told Clara that it wasn't the first time she had visited Grenfell in this way.

Once she had left the room, Grenfell recovered some of his aplomb. He moved forward, smiling ingratiatingly. 'I'm afraid your father is busy at the moment, Miss Pentreath. He's at the sampling.'

Clara nodded her understanding. She had timed her visit deliberately. The sampling took place once in every account period, when the ore brought up by each 'payre' was sampled to check the quality and quantity of the tin contained in it. Every able-bodied person, above and below ground, would be gathered around the dressing floors to check that the samplers were not cheating the miners.

'Then, perhaps, Mr Grenfell, it might be a good idea if you were to be there, too. Aren't there records to be kept of the results?' She raised her fine dark brows at him.

He looked confused. 'Your father . . .' he began.

'. . . Is a busy man,' she interrupted swiftly. 'I am sure that he would be grateful if you were to take this work, at least, off his shoulders.'

He hesitated, glancing around the office uneasily. She said calmly, 'You have no need to be concerned, Mr Grenfell. I shan't steal

117

anything. And please tell my father not to hurry back on my account. I know he likes to keep an eye on the samplers and I shall be quite comfortable here.'

She moved into the middle of the room, laying her whip and gloves on the table. Still he hesitated; with a haughty lift of her brows, she sped him on his way. 'Goodbye, Mr Grenfell.' He had no option but to go.

Clara collapsed in a chair, breathing a sigh of relief. That man always made her feel uncomfortable, for his toadying personality brought out the worst in her. But she had got rid of him, that was the main thing – and now she had the run of the office to herself. But what should she look for?

Throwing her elegant riding hat with the curled ostrich plume onto the great wooden table, Clara glanced around the room. The walls were covered with plans of the mine as they had been when she was a child, but they couldn't conceal the marks of damp that now disfigured the whitewash. Thoughtfully, she gazed up at the cobwebs in the roof. Those, too, were new. But they could just be a sign of rational cost-cutting.

With an expression of distaste she reached for the heavy ledger books lying on the table. If the truth were anywhere, it would be here.

When Hugh Pentreath hurried through the door an hour later, Clara was sitting with her head in her hands, her fingers entwined in her pale golden hair. Loosened tendrils curled in front of her ears, framing her white face. At the sight of her, he stopped, appalled. 'Clara! Are you ill? Is something wrong?'

She wanted to scream at him, '*Yes. Something is wrong! You've bankrupted us! You've ruined the mine!*' But the sight of Sam Grenfell's weasel face peering over her father's shoulder stopped her. What she had to say couldn't be said here, with the workmen passing outside the window and Grenfell listening to every word.

With an effort she forced herself to answer calmly. 'I'm feeling unwell, Father.' She did not need a mirror to know that her face was white and strained, her eyes dark with despair. 'Could you see me home?'

'Of course, my dear. Or shall I send for the carriage? You don't look well enough to ride.' The concern in her father's face made her want to cry.

'I can ride,' she said flatly, swallowing the lump in her throat that threatened to choke her. At all events, she must not let him send for the carriage. This was the one chance for them to talk confidentially and she knew that if she didn't talk about her findings soon, she would lose courage.

It seemed an age before her father's horse was brought round, a century before she could allow him to help her into the saddle. Then he mounted his own horse and reached for her reins. 'I'll lead you, Clara.'

'No.' She could not bear the thought of not being in charge of her own movements. Abruptly, she turned her mare towards the road and home, her mind still racing in circles, shocked by what she had learned.

She knew that this was not something that could be discussed with her mother present. She needed to know the facts, the true reasons behind her father's actions and she could not do that with Lady Susan in the room, alternately blaming him and lamenting the way she had come down in life.

With sudden energy, Clara pulled her horse to a sudden halt. Her father was instantly by her side. 'What's the matter, Clara, love? Are you feeling faint?'

His kindness made her want to weep, but instead she said quietly: 'I looked at the ledgers while I was waiting for you.'

An expression of unease crossed his face but was instantly gone. He forced a laugh. 'You must have been very bored, Clara. I would have thought a novel was more suitable reading for a young lady.'

'I may be a young lady, Father, but I'm not a fool.' There was real anger in her voice now. Her eyes blazed. 'I can read and I can add up.' She turned to him, strengthened by her feelings of outrage. 'The mine hasn't paid a dividend for over a year, has it?'

'All mines go through a rough patch.' He could not meet her eyes.

'Rough patch!' Her voice was exasperated. 'It's more than a rough patch, isn't it? Especially when you've had three calls in a row!' She bit her lip, fighting for control. Losing her temper would not achieve anything. More quietly, she asked, 'Does Mama know of this?'

'No!' Her father jerked upright in his saddle. 'And I forbid you to tell her, Clara.'

'But you can't keep it hidden from her,' Clara protested. 'It isn't fair on her to let her believe that all is well when –'

'Fair! Fair!' He pounded the pommel of the saddle with his fist and his horse moved restlessly. 'Clara, I ruined that woman's life! Through my selfishness I took from her everything she holds dear. Money is all I can offer her in exchange. How can I tell her that we could be bankrupt in a few months?'

'You underestimate yourself, Father.' Clara was shocked by the bitterness in his voice. 'If Mama chose to marry you, that was her decision. You cannot hold yourself responsible.'

'I can.' The voice was little more than a groan. Captain Pentreath stared out across the rough moorland that surrounded them, the yellow gorse in full bloom now contrasting with the thrusting chimneys of the engine houses that marked the erratic courses of the tin lodes. Dimly, Clara could hear the distant clatter of the tin stamps at Wheal Susan, hammering the ore-laden rock to a pulp. How long before that sound would be stilled for ever?

'I had no right even to look at her.' He was speaking to himself rather than to her, Clara realised, straining her ears to hear the quiet words. 'She was all I had ever dreamed of in a woman. She had elegance, breeding, style. She was so different from the women I had grown up with.'

He turned to look at her. 'I always wanted more from life than anyone else I knew, Clara. I always wanted more than the poverty and despair into which I was born. I wanted riches; I wanted respectability; I wanted success.'

'And you got them, Father.'

He shook his head. 'I thought I had them. I thought I had it all. And then I went to the Earl of Bodmin because he owns the mineral rights for the land where Wheal Susan stands and I met your mother. As soon as I saw her, I knew that there was still something more to strive for, something that would crown everything else.'

He turned to her, and Clara could see the tears standing in his eyes. 'I had no right, Clara. She was too far above me. And she was a person. It was wrong to use her just to fulfil my ambitions. And yet, I loved her too . . .' His voice choked and died away.

Embarrassed and upset, Clara turned away from him. She had never seen her father cry, had never believed that he could cry. The weakness, the honesty of his confession shook her. Staring at the looming, ruin-topped mass of Chapel Carn Brae high above them, she said reassuringly, 'You shouldn't blame yourself. Mama knew what she was doing when she married you.'

'No.' There was desolation in his voice. 'We were both aware that her father would be angry, but if I had known that he would cast her off entirely I would never have married her, never have proposed. Oh, not for my sake,' he waved a hand dismissively as Clara turned to him, a question on her lips. 'For her sake.'

He paused. 'I wanted her to hold on to everything she had ever had. I wanted her to be able to see her family, stay with them whenever she wanted to, live the life of an earl's daughter. Not for myself. I would never have forced myself on her family, God knows. But I wanted her to keep the old life too . . . but she lost it all.'

He turned to her, holding a hand out pleadingly. 'Money was all I could give her, Clara. It couldn't make up for what she had lost, but at least I could ensure that she wouldn't miss the pretty clothes she had been used to.'

'And so you took in dividends money that should have been reinvested in the mine.' She spoke flatly. Adam's accusations were true. The mine was in its present state because of the way her father had run it.

He didn't ask her how she knew that. He said sadly, 'The mine is my life, Clara, but your mother is more than that to me, more than my soul.' He gestured, helpless to explain his feelings.

She gathered her courage. 'And if the mine is knacked?' It was the hardest thing Clara had ever had to say in her life. Her mouth would scarcely move to fashion the words. But it had to be said. The picture painted by the ledgers had been bleak. She had to know the truth.

'It was nearly knacked at the last meeting. I had to buy up most of the shares to keep it open.'

She stared at him, stunned. It was worse than she had thought.

He went on, more strongly now, 'If we find that lode I shall make a fortune.'

'And if there's another call?' She was angry now. 'That mine provides us with our money. How can you keep it going single-handed?'

'We'll find that tin. I *know* it's there!' He beat his hand lightly on the pommel again.

He's mad, Clara thought. Surely he can't be gambling with our lives like this – all to keep my mother from having to give up her new dresses and furniture.

'And how long do we have, to find this elusive lode?' She could not keep the bitterness from her voice.

He looked at her. 'That's up to Edward Blacklock,' he admitted. 'And up to you, Clara, love. He won't bankrupt me while there's a chance he can marry you.'

Her throat was tight; her corset seemed to be constricting her breathing. 'Has . . .' Her voice croaked and she had to start again. 'Has he said anything to you?' She pleated the skirt of her habit with nervous fingers, anxious for his reply.

'Not yet. But it is easy to see how he feels about you from the way he looks at you.' He paused. 'Shall I ask him about his intentions?'

'*No!*' It came out more forcefully than she had intended, and Clara corrected herself. 'I mean, it is too soon yet. I hardly know him.' She kicked her horse into a walk, her worries making her restless. 'Tell

121

me, Father, what would you think of Edward Blacklock as a son-in-law?'

'He has plenty of money.' Her father sounded eager, as if that was the only quality that mattered – and, Clara realised sadly, to him it probably was.

'And do you think he would make a good husband?'

'He loves you, Clara. Anyone can see that.'

She rode in silence, thinking about his words. Possibly Edward did love her, in his way. But she was uncomfortably aware that his way was not the way of most men. She remembered again his questions at the party, the way he had treated her on the cliffs. He was attractive and he was rich, but she was afraid of him as she had never feared anyone before in her life. And he had deliberately challenged Adam to a fight. Had he recognised her interest in the miner even before she was aware of it herself?

Clara waited until they had clattered through the tiny hamlet of Truthwall before she risked her next question. 'And supposing I don't want to marry Edward?'

Her father reached out for her rein, pulling her horse to a halt. 'Clara.' His voice cracked with emotion. 'For God's sake, don't let him know that. Keep him dangling for a little while longer. A few weeks, a couple of months even.'

He saw the look of anger on her face and went on, 'You must, Clara. For your mother. For me. We . . .' he took a deep breath, 'we depend upon you.'

'You mean you'd sacrifice me to save the mine?' she asked disbelievingly.

'Not sacrifice, Clara.' She could see the anguish in his face. 'I'm not asking you to do anything you don't want to. Just to keep him sweet for a few weeks more.' He cleared his throat, staring at her intently. 'It's not much to ask.'

Just for me to lose all self-respect, she thought indignantly. Just for me to act a lie, pretending to like a man I *dis*like and fear.

But she knew that she could not bring about her father's downfall – especially not when there was a slim chance that in a few weeks more the mine might be saved, if the vein that Phil had found really did contain tin. Then they would be free of Blacklock's threats for ever.

'I'll do as you ask.' The words were bitter. 'I won't refuse him definitely until you have found your lode of tin. But don't expect me to encourage him. I can't do that. Not even for you.'

Then she dragged her reins from his restraining hand and whipped her mount into a reckless gallop.

Chapter 15

Captain Pentreath stood outside the Count House, a box of small pebbles in his hand. His entire workforce were gathered around him, dressed in their best clothes. At the rear, the bal-maidens chattered quietly, unrecognisable in their white aprons, with their goffered traditional 'gooks' hiding their hair.

'Setting and Pay Day' was always a holiday, a day when the workforce received their pay for the last working period and when the tributers made their new bargains for the coming two months. Only the huge beam engine still nodded up and down against the summer sky, continuously sucking water from the depths of the mine.

Once, Hugh had looked forward to these days. He had bantered with the men as he negotiated their new bargains, enjoying the battle of wits as they tried to barter up the price and he tried to reduce it, the last bid before a tossed stone hit the ground taking the pitch. He doubted whether he would have to use the stones today; the men were subdued and quiet, aware that the mine was doing badly. They would not bid eagerly for their pitches as they had when times were good. He sighed heavily. Would this be the last Setting Day the Wheal Susan would ever see?

All the money being paid out was coming from his own slender resources. If that elusive lode wasn't found in the next two months, he would be bankrupt. Hugh glanced up at the black-coated figure of Edward Blacklock leaning negligently against the wall of the Count House, the sun gleaming on his bright hair. A crow waiting for a corpse.

Hugh Pentreath turned to Sam Grenfell, who stood beside him holding the book with details of the last period's bargains, and with an effort, he launched into a description of the first pitch on offer.

'West end, one hundred and thirty fathom level. Presently worked by Adam Trevelyan's payre.' He searched through the crowd. Adam was there, thank God. He hadn't worked down the mine since his accident. Hugh consulted the book Sam Grenfell held. 'Last account, we paid fourteen shillings in the pound.'

Adam walked forward, his hands in his pockets. 'It'll have to be more this time, Cap'n. We didn't make enough to live on, last account.'

Hugh jerked his head up and stared at the tributer. Didn't the man realise how badly the mine was doing? Adam met his eyes defiantly. 'If we don't get more,' he continued, 'I'm not taking that pitch.'

'But . . .' Hugh gritted his teeth. He was sure that the new lode of tin was in Adam's pitch if it was anywhere. He daren't risk the man refusing to work it. At the same time, he couldn't be held to ransom like this, not with the mine in its present state. 'You were off for most of the last account,' he pointed out harshly. 'That's why the earnings are down.'

'I missed six weeks.' Adam's voice was firm. 'The earnings are only a quarter of what they were the account before.' He grinned, his teeth white in his tanned face, the marks of his recent fight already faded. He'd obviously been making the most of the fresh air during his enforced convalescence. 'Eighteen shillings.'

It was a ridiculous sum. 'Fifteen,' Hugh countered. He had to have that pitch worked. It was his one chance of saving the mine.

'Eighteen shillings.' Adam's blue eyes were steady.

Hugh could feel the tension in the miners as they stared at the two combatants. There was something going on here that they didn't understand. Dammit, *he* didn't understand it. Adam had worked that pitch for months and had been quite happy with the going rate. He knew, better than anybody, that if the earnings were down it was because Norman Willcock worked no harder than he had to.

'Fifteen and six.' Hugh could feel the sweat on his brow. He tore his eyes away from the miner slouching confidently before him. By the Count House Edward Blacklock had pulled himself to his full height, his grey eyes almost colourless in the bright sunlight as he stared at Adam, his face wiped clean of all expression. Hugh Pentreath was suddenly aware that Clara had ridden in, in defiance of her mother's explicit instructions. She sat motionless on her horse, behind the silent group of miners, her eyes fixed on Adam Trevelyan, and Hugh could see the tension in her body.

'Eighteen shillings.' Adam's voice was still calm and clear. He stared challengingly at Hugh.

He had to have that pitch worked. Was it worthwhile offering it to someone else for a lower sum? But the men remained silent, witness

124

to this battle of nerves that they did not understand. Adam was their unofficial leader, Hugh knew. They would never bid against him.

'Sixteen shillings – and that's my last offer.' Hugh could feel his hands shaking. If he didn't find tin in this account period, he was bankrupt. All he had worked for, gone. And Susan . . . he dared not think how it would affect her. He *had* to have that pitch worked.

Adam's blue eyes met his, and Hugh could have sworn that he saw a lurking smile in their depths. Then the miner shrugged. 'If I don't get eighteen shillings, I'm not working it.' He turned his back and began to walk out through the crowd that parted silently before him. In desperation, Hugh glanced at Norman. 'You'll take it?' His voice sounded almost pleading and he despised himself for his weakness.

For a second Norman hesitated, and Hugh felt his heart leap, then Norman shook his head. He gestured at Adam. 'He's the boss.'

Adam was almost through the crowd now. As Hugh watched he saw the miner suddenly catch sight of Clara. The man checked slightly. Clara was staring down at him, her face white. As their eyes met, her fingers tightened involuntarily on the reins and Hugh saw the horse toss its head and sidle uncomfortably, its tail swishing angrily from side to side. For a second, the two of them stared at each other, then Adam shook his head slightly and broke their glance, angling to pass behind the horse and away, out off the dressing floor.

He had to have that pitch worked! It was their one chance! 'All right, eighteen!' Hugh heard his voice crack on the word.

Adam Trevelyan stopped. For a few seconds he stood motionless, then he turned slowly. 'It's a bargain.' His voice was calm and controlled. He sketched a brief salute at Hugh, caught Clara's eye briefly, then turned on his heel and walked away from the mine.

Hugh closed his eyes and felt himself go limp with relief, scarcely aware of the disbelieving murmur that ran through the crowd. He still had a chance! Adam might still find that lode and save the mine! He opened his eyes just in time to see the look Adam gave Clara. Hugh was shocked at the smile that lit her face. That's not right, he thought. I didn't drag myself out of the gutter so that my only child could throw herself away on a common miner. How many times had she seen Adam when he was ill? Hugh wondered suddenly. He had been too preoccupied with his own problems to keep an eye on Clara.

Anxiously, he glanced at Edward Blacklock. He, too, had seen the look that passed between the pair, and the expression on his face made Hugh shiver. Edward was not a man to anger. I must warn Clara tonight, Hugh resolved, turning back to the bidding. She mustn't alienate Edward now, whatever happens.

Clara sat limply on her horse, shaking with reaction. She had been

125

so sure that Adam had thrown away his chance to work the pitch. And it was vital that he got it and found the new lode of tin – for both their sakes. She closed her eyes, trying to control the beating of her heart.

'Clara.' The voice made her jump. Edward Blacklock was standing by her horse, his cold grey eyes freezing her blood. He gestured at Adam Trevelyan's retreating figure. 'You seem to be very friendly with that – miner.'

Clara raised her chin defiantly, sitting straighter on her horse. 'And what right have you to interest yourself in my friendships, Mr Blacklock?' she asked, raising her brows haughtily.

He placed his hand on her ankle, his body hiding his actions from any passers-by, and she felt his fingers digging in through the thin leather of her boot. 'The right of a friend to whom you owe a great deal,' he said coolly.

'Still harping on about your money?' She was in no mood to be pleasant. 'Isn't that rather underbred?'

His mouth was a thin, white line. 'And you, of course, are an expert on good breeding, Miss Pentreath – your father being what he is.' He turned to look at Hugh where he stood in front of the miners, continuing the bidding for the pitches.

'I know that you can always tell a gentleman by the way he behaves.' She tapped her whip significantly against his hand. 'Kindly release me, Mr Blacklock.'

He tightened his grip and she had to bite back a gasp of pain. 'I thought we had agreed that you were to call me Edward.' His voice was implacable.

'I have changed my mind.' Her green eyes blazed down at him.

He was silent for a moment, then his teeth showed in a wolfish grin. 'Angry because I beat up your beau?'

'I rather thought that he beat you up,' she snapped angrily. 'And he is *not* my beau.' Even as she said it, the truth dawned on her. Edward was right. That last look had laid Adam open to her. He loved her. A feeling, half fear, half exultation, flooded through her, leaving her suddenly breathless.

Edward said fiercely, 'He had better not be.' His other hand had been stroking the mare's neck. Now he moved it onto her knee, creeping slowly up to the soft flesh of her thigh. 'Because if I thought that he were, I should put my hands around his neck and kill him – like this!' His fingers dug spitefully into her leg.

'I want you, Clara.' The words were almost passionless in their intensity. 'And I am going to have you. Whatever the cost. You are mine. You belong to me body and soul.'

126

She licked her lips, suddenly afraid. His fingers still dug into her thigh.

'No one is going to stop me, Clara. No one. And if someone tries, I shall break them.'

With a swift movement he released her leg and snatched at the whip she still held, then, his eyes on hers, he doubled it slowly between his hands. It bent, quivered then snapped with a sudden crack that sent the horse plunging nervously.

He flung the two parts of the whip aside and caught at the horse's reins, jerking cruelly at her mouth to bring the mare under control. 'You understand me, Clara? No one. And that includes you!'

She lashed out at his face with her booted foot and as he ducked to avoid the blow, she whipped up the horse with the ends of the reins. In a rattle of gravel the horse leaped for the entrance to the mine, Clara urging her on with heels and voice. Behind her, clear in the summer morning, Clara could hear the rising note of Edward's mocking laugh. Furiously, she lashed the horse into a gallop, passing a running bal-maiden unheeded as she put as much distance as she could between Edward Blacklock and herself.

Adam heard the galloping hooves in the distance but he paid them no attention. His heart was bursting with exultation. He had done it! He had got his pitch at eighteen shillings in the pound. At that price, he knew, he could make up the money he had lost while he was ill just working the present lode. And if there was a new vein of tin down there . . . he felt his skin crawl at the thought. Riches. At last. Enough to set him on his way. Enough to enable him to take a step towards achieving his ambitions. And at the end of it . . .

He saw again Clara's white face as she sat on the horse, watching him walk away from the bargaining. She hadn't told her father. He had realised that as soon as Captain Pentreath had offered him the pitch at the old price. But the tension on her face hadn't been because she was worried that he was pushing her father, it was because she was afraid he would lose the pitch, and with it his chance of making his fortune.

He tried to force down the joy he felt bubbling through him, but it was impossible. His heart leaped. Clara was not out of his reach. He had as much chance of making good as her father ever had. And she loved him. He had seen it in her eyes, in the very way her body had leaned towards him as he approached her. She might not know it yet, but she loved him, as he loved her. Nothing could keep them apart.

Lost in his thoughts, he did not notice the running footsteps behind him and he started when Molly slipped a hand under his arm from behind. She was panting, her cheeks redder than ever under the traditional white gook that tied under the chin then spread over her shoulders like a nun's ornate wimple.

'My soul and body,' she gasped. 'What did you go and do that for, Adam Trevelyan? You scared the living daylights out of me.'

'Stand out for the money, you mean?' His white teeth flashed in a grin. 'Oh, just to see.'

'To see?' she yelled. 'You nearly saw the the sack, my lad.'

Adam shrugged. He had wanted to know how desperate Captain Pentreath was and he had found out. Eighteen shillings was a ridiculous price for that pitch, and they both knew it. But if Captain Pentreath was so desperate to find that vein of tin that he would pay Adam eighteen shillings in the pound to work the pitch, then the mine must really be on the verge of bankruptcy.

Such calculations were beyond Molly. She clung to Adam, her face beaming. 'Still, eighteen shillings,' she breathed. 'You'll make your fortune! You'll be rich!' Her fingers tightened on his arm. 'We'll be able to get married on that.'

Adam stiffened. He had seen little of Molly since his accident, deliberately discouraging her from coming to the cottage. He had heard rumours that she had been in the company of Sam Grenfell, and he had been relieved that she herself had made the first steps to ending their relationship. Now that he had met Clara, he was suddenly sickened by Molly's earthy lustiness.

She had not noticed his instinctive withdrawal. Happily, she chattered on. 'We can build another room on for young Phil. Or even send him to stay with Norman.' The idea caught her fancy. 'Norman wouldn't mind him. He's easygoing about things like that. Especially if you're both earning that sort of money.' She hugged his arm, pressing her swelling bosom against him. 'It'll be good to be wed at last, Adam. I've waited too long.'

'Molly . . .' His voice husked and he had to clear his throat. He could not let her carry on like this, could not, for her sake, let her expose her feelings to him when he knew that he could not reciprocate them. 'Molly.'

She laughed up at him. 'Lost your voice, have you?' She patted his shoulder. 'I do know that it's a man's job to propose to a maid, but what do it matter? We both know we'll wed sometime, and now you've the money, where's the reason for waiting?'

'Molly.' The words would not come. Tongue-tied, Adam stared down into her pink, glowing face. He had meant to marry her once, long ago, in those distant days of two months ago, before Clara Pentreath had come into his life. She was pretty and lively, and he had enjoyed the evenings they had spent entwined in the secret places on the cliffs above the restless Atlantic.

But now he had met Clara, and his life had changed. His ambitions had grown, become dreams, large and powerful enough to drive a pumping engine. He had outgrown Molly. And she hadn't realised it.

'Well, come on.' She was staring up at him, her brows drawing together. 'Spit it out. Aren't you going to kiss your bride?' She snorted. 'Anyone would think that you didn't want to marry me!'

There was no easy way to say it, no way to break it to her gently. Adam pulled himself away from her. 'Molly – I can't.'

Her face hardened. 'Can't? What do you mean, can't?'

'What I said.' He stared at her, unwilling to hurt her, unable to do what she wanted. 'I can't marry you.'

'But you can't be married already?' she asked, stupidly, then the truth hit her. 'It's that bloody Clara Pentreath, isn't it?'

For Clara's sake, he could not confirm her suspicions. 'It's just me.' He cast around for a reason. 'It's been since my accident. I – I think it changed me.'

Molly blinked back the tears that beaded her long black lashes. 'The only thing that's changed you is that stuck-up little cow. I was good enough for you until then.'

'You're good enough for anybody, Molly,' Adam said gently, unwilling to see her belittling herself.

'Oh yes,' she jeered. 'Good enough for anybody – even good enough for the great Adam Trevelyan, just as long as all we're talking about is a quick roll on the cliffs of a summer's evening.' Her voice broke. 'But not good enough to marry, oh no. Not nearly good enough for that.' The tears quivered, hung for a second then rolled, living diamonds, down her soft cheeks.

'Molly.' He couldn't bear to see her hurt like this, but he couldn't bring himself to say the one thing that would mend her hurt.

She turned on him, careless of her swollen eyes, her red nose. 'Don't you "Molly" me,' she snapped. 'You've no right, no right at all.' She sniffed angrily. 'You've used me, Adam Trevelyan. You've used me, and now you've thrown me away. But I won't stand for it, Adam. I won't! I won't!'

He reached out a hand to restrain her but she darted away. 'I won't be treated like this.' Her voice was thick with sobs. She sniffed again, dragging the back of her hand across her nose. 'I'll show you you can't do this to me, Adam Trevelyan. I'll get you, I will, if it's the last thing I do!'

'Molly . . .' he began again, but it was too late. With a broken-hearted wail she turned and ran back up the road, and long after the sound of her footsteps had died away in the distance, Adam could still hear the gulping of her convulsive sobs.

When Sam Grenfell came into the Count House after the last of the bargains had been made, Edward Blacklock was waiting for him. 'Pentreath?' Edward asked.

'Gone home.' Grenfell's teeth showed in a foxy smile as he threw his stovepipe hat onto the table. 'Can't stand the heat.' He nodded at the door. 'Today, the men were like sheep. They took the pitches they were offered at the prices the Captain said. They know the mine's on the way out, and he knows they know.'

Blacklock nodded. 'None of them followed Trevelyan's lead, then?'

Grenfell spat accurately into the corner, raising a brief spurt of dust. 'Him? He'd get the better of the Devil, given a chance.'

'As he got the better of Pentreath?' Edward smiled a twisted smile. He caught Grenfell's eye on him and reached out suddenly, catching him by the lapels, pulling him closer. 'As you think he got the better of me?' The menace in his voice was palpable.

Grenfell hung helpless in his grasp. 'No, sir. Not you, sir. No one gets the better of you, Mr Blacklock.' His voice was squeaky with fear. Sweat beaded his loose upper lip.

Blacklock stared at him for a second then flung him away in disgust, turning to walk restlessly up and down the room, his booted feet echoing on the bare boards.

'You're damn right no one gets the better of me!' His voice was harsh. 'And that includes Adam Trevelyan.'

'Yes, Mr Blacklock, of course, sir.' Grenfell was eager to please but Blacklock ignored him, lost in his thoughts.

'And no one must be seen to get the better of me, either.' He swung round to stare at the purser. 'Do you understand what I mean?'

Grenfell's brows creased with effort. 'You mean . . . You're talking about . . .'

'I'm talking about Trevelyan,' Edward said flatly. 'He won that fight. He – he threw back my money!' That was the thing that stuck in his maw. He ground his teeth as he heard again the heavy tinkle of gold sovereigns, poured over him. Money, money that illiterate oaf should have died for, being spurned as if it were rubbish.

'I'm going to break him.' The words were barely audible but Grenfell had guessed what they were going to be.

'I can sack him,' he offered eagerly. It would be good to get rid of Adam Trevelyan. Grenfell had enjoyed Molly's favours, but with Adam around he knew that at best his opportunities for meeting her would be severely curtailed if not stopped altogether. He wouldn't be surprised if the silly bitch went back to him after all. Women were too stupid to recognise a good thing when they saw it. He could offer Molly Willcock far more than that oaf, but women were all the same; they couldn't see further than a pair of blue eyes and some brawny muscles.

'Sack him?' Edward's lip curled scornfully. 'What good would that do? He'd get work in another mine the next day. He's too good a worker to be left to rot.'

He resumed his restless pacing. 'I don't just want to hurt him, I want to break him. I want to see him reviled, despised, crawling.' His voice cracked with desire as the hot rush of hate filled his head. 'I want him lower than the lowest beast.'

Grenfell said doubtfully, 'There's always prison.'

Blacklock stared at him and for a second Grenfell expected another outpouring of scorn, then Edward's lips twisted into a faint smile. 'Prison.' He tried the word on his tongue as if it were a fine wine. 'Hard labour. Solitary confinement.' He stroked his golden moustache with a gentle finger while he considered the idea.

Anxious to build on a sure foundation, Grenfell said eagerly, 'They're very law-abiding round here, you know. Lots of them are Methodists. They wouldn't respect a man who had been to prison.'

'They wouldn't, would they?' Edward asked dreamily, his eyes fixed on a pleasant vision that only he could see. 'And I know just what we can get him for. Smuggling.'

'You're going to inform on him?' Grenfell whispered.

'Not yet. First I have to get the right information.' His glance sharpened, focused on Grenfell. 'And you're the man to get it.'

'Me?' Grenfell stepped quickly backwards. 'I don't know anything.'

'No? Well, you soon will – if you know what's good for you.' Edward drummed his fingers on the table. 'Everyone seems sure that this Adam Trevelyan is a smuggler. I just want you to find out when he's doing it.' He laughed. 'I want him to get caught with the stuff actually on him. There's no way he could wriggle out of that.'

'No one will ever tell me that.' Grenfell was horrified. 'Even the Methodists don't think smuggling is wrong, not round here.'

'Whatever they think,' Blacklock said coldly, 'it's against the law, and if Trevelyan is caught he will go to prison. And that's where I want him. No respectable woman would look at him after that.' He cracked his knuckles, smirking at the thought.

'But how will I find out?' Grenfell whined.

Blacklock raised his brows. 'That, my dear fellow, is for you to work out for yourself.' He grinned. 'But rest assured, I shall make it *very* worth your while.'

131

Grenfell's pale pointed tongue flicked across his lips at the thought of money, but he said worriedly, 'A lot of people will be upset if Trevelyan goes to prison.'

'And *I* shall be upset if he doesn't!' Blacklock snapped.

Grenfell rubbed his hands together, thinking. 'Mind you,' he said, 'I don't know but what it won't be a good thing to upset some of them.' His thin lips cracked into a mean smile. 'Captain Pentreath and his uppity daughter, for two.'

The slap took him by surprise, rocking him back on his heels, then the second buffet caught him from the other side. Whimpering, his hands over his burning cheeks, he backed towards the door. Blacklock followed him, looming over the weaselly fellow, his eyes colourless chips of ice in his frozen face.

'You are speaking of the woman I love.' His voice shook with anger. 'Of the woman I am going to marry.' He reached out and caught Grenfell by the throat, lifting him almost off his feet.

Ignoring his terrified whimpers, Edward said softly, 'If I ever hear you speak of her in that way again, I shall kill you. Do you understand?'

Chapter 16

It was two hours before the normal start of the morning core, and the mine was silent apart from the constant noise of the unceasing pump and the clatter of their boots on the iron ladders as Adam and Phil made their way down to their pitch.

Adam flexed his hands and grimaced as he stepped off the last ladder into the foetid darkness. Six weeks away from work had weakened him, and his legs were shaking from the effort of climbing down nearly a thousand feet on vertical or even underhung ladders, many of them running with water.

A glimmer of light showed where Phil was still climbing down above him, the boy's short legs making hard work of the steep rungs. Even though Adam always made the journey in darkness, saving the candle and trusting to his body to remember the necessary manoeuvres to get on and off the ladders, he insisted that Phil should use a light. Impatiently, he watched the boy's progress, beaconed by the growing aurora of light from his candle and the blue flashes as the iron studs on his boots scraped against the rusty ladder.

'Right, lad,' Adam lit his own candle, attaching it to his felt helmet with a lump of slimy clay, 'let's see this new lode you've found all by yourself.'

Phil danced ahead down the narrow gallery, squeezing past the iron barrow that took up most of the space between the rough-hewn walls. 'It'll be there, Adam, you'll see.' He dropped to his knees and pointed to a patch of wall that looked no different from the rest. 'It were only a small bit, but I covered it up with dirt, just in case the Cap'n saw it.'

Adam grunted, lowering his small barrel of fresh water, bag of tools and small keg of gunpowder carefully onto the ground. Bending, he examined the place that Phil had indicated, wetting the rock with spittle and wiping it cleaner with the corner of his stained canvas jacket. There was a trace of whiteness in the depths of a small depression in the rockface. Quartz? Even if it were, there was no guarantee that he had found a seam of it, and even less that it would contain any tin ore.

'Stand back, lad.' Adam took his pick and gad and chiselled at the rockface. A small piece fell away, exposing more whiteness. He hit again and again. More quartz. A seam of the stuff. He examined the fallen pieces closely in the light of the candle.

'Is there tin, Adam? Have we found a new lode?' Phil hopped excitedly from leg to leg.

'No sign of tin, lad.' With an effort Adam rose to his feet and his candle guttered dangerously. 'And what do you think you're doing, bouncing around with your candle lit? Don't you know a candle uses as much air as a man?' He pointed at the huge fan that lay nearby. 'Blow your candle out and start working that machine or we won't live to find the tin, even if it's there.'

He bent again to the white scar in the wall, chipping out more rock until he had a clear idea of the size of the quartz seam. It ran roughly northwards, as far as he could judge, which meant that it was unlikely to contain tin. The miners called them 'cross-seams' as they often ran between one seam and another. And the seam it led to might contain tin. Might.

He straightened and walked further down to look at the face where Norman had been working alone for the last six weeks. It bore silent testimony to the fact that his partner hadn't put much effort into his mining. Had Adam been working, they would have made nearly three times the progress.

He ran his hand down the exposed quartz seam that they were working on, a narrow seam that ran diagonally across the rockface. Looking up he could see where it ran centrally along the roof of the gallery.

Thoughtfully he dug his nails into the thin, black streak at the centre of the seam. Tin. Good quality, though not enough of it to make a fortune. Or to save the mine. But at eighteen shillings in the pound, he could make a reasonable wage mining it.

He turned again to the white scar that defaced the wall behind him. It could mean heartbreaking work in the hundred-degree temperatures for no return at all. Or it could mean a fortune. The candle guttered again and he moved it so that it was almost horizontal, the only way it would burn once the air had been used up. He could feel the lazy draught from Phil's wind-machine. It moved the air around slightly but they were too far from the shaft for fresh air to reach them, even with its help, and it did nothing to cool him.

134

Almost unconsciously, he pressed himself against the rock, his ear against the wall, trying to use the instinct that had motivated generations of his ancestors. Silently, he let his thoughts roam through the living rock that bounded him on every side. He felt the weight of it pressing down upon him, the walls closing around him. Granite. And through it, thin veins of black richness. Tin.

He quested for it, trying to hear it, trying to feel its pull in his blood and bone. He emptied his mind of everything but the thought of tin – and saw only the face of Clara Pentreath.

With an oath, Adam swung away from the rock. 'I'm blasting here.' His voice was harsh, his hair already wet with sweat in the stinking, airless heat.

What did the odds matter? It was his one chance of winning her. He had to take the risk.

With an effort, Adam took up his borer and hammer, and began, with a muttered prayer, to bore the first holes in a new venture that must, one way or the other, decide his future.

'It was good of you to walk out with me this evening, Miss Willcock.' Sam Grenfell always spoke to her as if she were a lady. It was his main attraction for her.

Molly smiled up at him from eyes still red-rimmed and swollen from a night's crying. 'Charmed to be asked, and by such a gallant gentleman, too.'

She took his arm, nuzzling her breast into him as if by accident. If she couldn't marry Adam, she would do her utmost to catch Sam. A purser was a good step up the social ladder from a miner, even if he was a poor stick of a man with damp hands and a slobbery mouth. 'Where are you going to take me?'

'I know a farm the other side of Carnyorth where they are willing to provide saffron cake and cider – for respectable people, of course.'

'Of course,' she echoed, unable to suppress the thrill that ran through her. Respectable people! A bal-maiden was looked down on by all the yeomen farmers in the area. She knew that it was only because she was with Grenfell that she would ever be allowed on the farm for anything more than a cup of water at the back door. She breathed an ecstatic sigh.

Grenfell suppressed a satisfied smile. He had deliberately chosen the farm to appeal to her vanity – and because it was down a long, country lane.

After his meeting with Edward, he had struggled hopelessly to think of a way to get the information Blacklock required. Grenfell had no illusions about his standing with the men. He knew that they distrusted him, seeing in him the catspaw of Edward Blacklock. Only his higher social position kept them from openly showing their dislike.

Molly was the only one with whom he had struck up any kind of relationship since Edward had installed him at the mine almost a year ago. Sam knew that she only went out with him because Adam Trevelyan had been laid low and that her vanity was gratified by his attentions. He was quite clear about their relative importance in her life. She had amused herself with him while Adam was ill, but she was a hard woman who judged to a nicety the favours she must grant to keep his attention while not allowing him one inch further than necessary.

The sight of her red eyes this morning had given him an idea. He had noticed the look that passed between Clara and Adam, noticed, too, the way Molly had run after Adam. And now she was tear-stained and miserable. He could think of only one explanation. Immediately, the plan had leaped into his mind by which he could obtain the information Blacklock required and enjoy Molly's favours as well. The speed and genuine pleasure with which she greeted his tentative offer of an evening walk confirmed his suspicions. Molly and Adam had argued. This was his chance – in more ways than one.

He hugged her arm closer into his side, relishing the touch of her firm young body. 'You won't be too tired to walk to Carnyorth?'

'Me?' Molly's laugh rolled out, a little forced and shrill. 'My handsome, I could walk there and back three times before nightfall!'

Grenfell smiled to himself. If all went well, he would have Molly eating out of his hand by then.

The road to Carnyorth was almost deserted. The early core of miners were at home, eating their dinners, and the late core still working. Only a farmhand leading a couple of mules laden with bulging panniers of potatoes passed them as they followed the road that climbed high above the sea.

Below them, the land was scarred with mine workings, the tall chimneys and huge pumping houses each surrounded by acres of rough sheds and wooden buddling frames, the ground around them bare and stained rust-red from waste iron ore. Beyond that, the restless ocean ate away at the towering cliffs and stretched in variegated shades to the horizon, only interrupted by the pinheads of the Scillies, thrusting up infinitely small against the sapphire weight of the sky.

Grenfell paused to catch his breath, surveying the scene. 'The gentry . . .' he began, then changed swiftly at the thought that to Molly he probably was one of them. 'The ladies are always in raptures about this view.'

'Ladies!' Molly kicked at a boulder in the hedge with her heavy boot. 'What do they know about anything! Gadding around on their great horses where hardworking women have to walk on their own two feet. And they don't have to clean them, either.' Her suppressed rage overcame her pretensions to manners and she spat accurately into a clump of grass at the side of the road.

'All they have to think about is looking pretty and being pleasant,' Grenfell agreed, egging her on. 'And even so, to my eyes, they can't match the appeal of a real woman.' He openly showed his appreciation of her buxom charms, letting his eyes linger on her deep bosom and strong neck.

Molly preened under his gaze, her reddened eyes brightening perceptibly.

Grenfell took her arm again, pressing his advantage. 'The trouble with women like that is, they can't do anything else but flirt with men.' He coughed meaningfully. 'Men of their own class, they know how to take it, but a workman, a fisherman or miner maybe, they think it means something and it goes to their head.'

He could see by the way Molly blinked rapidly that he was on the right track. When she spoke, her voice was choked and uncertain. 'Blamed fools!' She swallowed loudly. 'They don't know what's good for them.'

'They certainly don't,' Grenfell agreed warmly. 'Any man, any *real* man, would be far better off with a loving, generous woman who can be a helpmate to him, a companion, the mother of his children.'

He recited the words almost without thought, his eyes watching her face greedily as the tears glistened for a second on her black lashes before sliding down her cheek. She gave a convulsive sob and tore her arm from his, hiding her face as the unhappiness she had thought to hide from him poured out in a blubbering wail.

'Miss Willcock! Molly!' Grenfell looked around with satisfaction. They were above the limit of the small Cornish fields now. Only rough moorland stretched away on either side, the scrawny grass and gorse interrupted by boulders of grey granite thrusting up through the thin soil.

He put an arm around her heaving shoulders. 'You are unwell. Let me help you off the road where you can't be stared at by passers-by.' He led her along a rough track of tussocky grass to the shelter of a boulder where they were hidden from the road, then he assisted her down into a sheltered hollow.

Molly hiccupped loudly and rolled onto her face in the long grass, hammering her fists into the ground, her voice rising in a wordless lamentation.

Grenfell watched her for a few seconds, fighting his distaste at the sight of her blotchy face and running nose. He had planned for something like this, but the reality of an hysterical woman was more than he had bargained for.

'You must calm yourself, please. You'll make yourself ill if you go on like this.' He reached into his pocket and pulled out a flask. 'It is fortunate that I have something here that will help you.'

Molly broke off in mid-wail. 'Spirits? I c-c-can't!'

'It's medicine,' Sam Grenfell told her smoothly. 'In the mine, we call it "The Doctor". Captain Pentreath never goes down the mine without taking a flask of this with him.' The difference was, as Grenfell well knew, that "The Doctor" was watered down until it was no more than a mild stimulant, while this was Captain Pentreath's best brandy, stolen a little at a time from the store in his office, and of full strength.

He sat down beside Molly and helped her into a sitting position. 'Here.' He placed the mouth of the flask between her teeth and poured a measure quickly down her throat.

Molly twisted away from him, coughing and catching her breath as the harsh spirit burned her tongue. 'My Lor', Mr Grenfell. That's brem strong!' She could scarcely speak, her voice weak with crying and the effect of the liquor.

'That's because you are a lady. "The Doctor" is well watered down, I assure you. Ask anyone at the mine.' He held the flask out to her again. 'Take some more. It is only a restorative, just like the *sal volatile* that Miss Pentreath and the other ladies take whenever they feel unwell.'

The name of her hated rival acted on Molly as he had hoped and she gave another sob before quickly applying herself to the flask. 'I'm as good as they,' she muttered crossly as she lowered the small leather bottle. 'If they can have that *sal* stuff, I can have this.' She hiccupped again.

'Of course you can,' Grenfell said soothingly. 'It's only medicine, after all.' He watched her carefully. It would take good judgement to get her drunk enough to be amenable without making her too drunk to talk. He allowed her one more swallow before taking the flask firmly away.

'Forgive me if I am impertinent, Miss Willcock.' He used his most formal voice, sitting with his hands wrapped around his bony knees, his gaze on the far distance lest she take fright at his close proximity

138

in such a lonely spot. 'But I suspect that something has upset you. Or someone,' he added, stealing a quick glance at her.

He saw the swollen eyes glisten again as tears began to well up in them. She pulled up a clump of grass and began to rip it apart with her strong red fingers, ignoring the bits of earth and leaf that fell on her best skirt. Her mouth was clamped shut as if she were trying to hide the quivering of her lips.

'Is it, could it perhaps be – Adam Trevelyan?'

She nodded abruptly, her face stony.

Grenfell placed his hand lightly on her arm. Whatever happened he mustn't alarm her. 'I hope you won't take it amiss if I say that – well, to put it crudely – you are far too good for him.'

It was too much for her self-control. With a sudden wail she flung herself onto him, burying her head in his shoulder. 'It were that stuck-up Clara Pentreath,' she gasped. Her breath was heavy with brandy fumes. 'She's bewitched him! She's all he can think about.' She burrowed her head deeper into his shoulder. 'I hate her! I hate her! I hate her!'

Grenfell put his arms around her shuddering body. He felt the same about Clara, but it was Adam he wanted her to talk about now. He said sympathetically, 'I can understand how you feel, but if he were a real man, who truly loved you, nobody could have turned him from you.'

She said, brokenly, 'I loved him.'

He stroked her shoulder, calming her. 'I am sure you did.' Inwardly, he doubted it. Adam was a good-looking man and a good miner. He was the best she was likely to catch and that was why she had set her sights on him.

Grenfell handed her the flask again. 'You're getting distraught. Try a little more of "The Doctor". It will help you recover yourself.' And become more talkative, he prayed.

She did not hold back this time, swallowing the brandy eagerly. He could see that her eyes were slightly unfocused and there was a sheen of sweat on her forehead under the cheap bonnet.

Grenfell said thoughtfully, 'I can't understand how anyone could throw over a woman like you. I know you. You are,' he racked his brains for a suitable description, 'generous and loving.'

She nodded drunkenly. 'That's right. I were good to him, I were.' She swallowed another sob. 'I gave him a good time, out there on the cliffs. Whenever he wanted it, I were ready. He won't get that from that whey-faced miss he's took up with now.'

Grenfell felt his body stir at the thought and he tightened his arm around her shoulders. But this was business. He had another purpose for this meeting.

'The love of a woman like you,' he said, pulling her towards him, 'is above rubies. I would think that any man would find it impossible not to confide in you. Any woman with your looks, your kindness, your feminine sympathy – well, it makes a man want to pour out his troubles to you, knowing that you would always understand, always want to help.'

Molly hiccupped and applied herself once more to the flask. 'Tha's right! The things he told me! An' I never told nobody. Nobody!'

'I believe you.' Grenfell said. 'And you'd never betray a friend, *I* can tell that. You would always stand by me, wouldn't you, Miss Willcock? Or may I say Molly?'

'M-Molly.' She drained the flask and held it upside down, looking sadly at the last few drops that spattered onto the ground. "S gone,' she said. 'All gone. And tha's the first brandy I ever had, even though I helped him bring it in when he were hurt. Risked myself for him, I did, and what do I get out of it?'

She turned to Grenfell and he nearly flinched at her brandy-laden breath. 'Nothin',' she said. 'Not one li'l thing. I just get dumped. Bye-bye, Molly, you're not good enough.' Tears came again to her sore eyes.

Hiding his sudden excitement, Grenfell asked, 'He couldn't have been so ungallant as to put a wonderful woman like you in any danger, surely?'

'Did,' Molly asserted, nodding violently. 'When he were hurt, it was. He opened his side out smuggling when Norman fell off the Brisons an' I had to get them barrels back for him. An' what thanks do I get? Nothing. Not even any brandy.' She stared mournfully at the empty flask.

Grenfell pulled her closer to him. 'He didn't make you go to the Brisons, did he? Surely that could be very dangerous?'

Molly leaned heavily against his shoulder. 'It were dangerous,' she said sleepily. 'No one goes there. Tha's why it were a good place to stow the stuff. Anyway, it were only for one night.' She nestled closer. 'But never again. I got a real gentleman now. Next time there's a new moon he can risk his own skin. I'm through with him. Through.' She made an extravagant gesture and toppled slowly backwards.

Grenfell leaned over her. He could feel the excitement rising in him. 'You have got a real gentleman this time,' he said hoarsely, his hand moving to her breast. 'The kind of gentleman who appreciates a real woman like you.' Ignoring the rank smell of brandy on her breath he kissed her mouth, rejoicing as it opened slackly under his.

This was his night, he thought. He'd got the information Blacklock had wanted, and now he'd get his way with her. All for a few mouthfuls of brandy that he'd stolen anyway.

And he hadn't even had to take her to the farm and put up with their shocked expressions when they saw him with a bal-maiden.

Chapter 17

Clara put her book down and began to pace the drawing room restlessly, automatically threading her way between the small tables that stood by each armchair.

Since her brief meeting with Adam at the mine she had no longer been able to ignore her true feelings for him. Somehow, foolishly and reprehensibly, she had fallen in love with him.

The angry swish of her petticoats made a rustling counterpoint to her thoughts. She despised herself for her weakness; he was impossible. She hated herself for what it would mean to her father; Edward was the only man she should be thinking of.

She still shuddered when she remembered the way she had kicked out at his face, driven by her fear of him and still shocked by the realisation of her feelings for Adam. She had half-expected him to make her father suffer for her actions but Edward had made no move to punish her. Sometimes, she thought, turning swiftly as she reached the end of the room and making her skirt fly about her with the speed of her movement, it almost seemed as if he liked her to fight him.

Lady Susan's entrance was a relief. Anything was better than going over and over the same thoughts, caught everlastingly between her duty and her desires.

'I think, Clara, that it is time we ordered some new evening gowns for you.' Lady Susan settled herself elegantly on the sofa and surveyed her daughter critically. 'Mr Blacklock must be sick to death of your green silk. Something in the latest style, I think,' she added thoughtfully. 'A deep lace collar would emphasise your slim figure. Something that Isabelle Kingsley could not wear without making her look like an elephant.'

Clara took a deep breath. She had been wondering for days how she could talk to her mother about the financial situation. This seemed an ideal opportunity.

'Mama,' she said hesitantly, standing in front of her mother, her fingers intertwined to stop her hands shaking. 'Is it wise to spend more money? Just at this time, I mean,' she added quickly, seeing the look on her mother's face.

Lady Susan sat more upright on the sofa. 'Your father has never interfered with the way I run my household, Clara. I see no reason for my daughter to do so.'

'But that was in the past,' Clara said awkwardly. 'Under the present circumstances . . .'

'What circumstances?' her parent demanded. 'As your mother, I am the best person to decide when your wardrobe needs to be increased.'

'I was thinking about the extra cost,' Clara blurted out. 'Surely it would be wise to retrench until my father's financial situation improves?'

'Your father's financial situation?' repeated Lady Susan coldly, raising her eyebrows with aristocratic hauteur. 'That is no concern of yours, miss. Your father, I am pleased to say, has always allowed me a free hand and has never queried the accounts I present to him.'

Clara fought down a feeling of panic. Before she could lose her courage, she stuttered, 'But with the mine doing so badly . . .'

'The mine!' Lady Susan's voice was icy with disdain. 'Surely you have learned by now, Clara, that a lady does not interest herself in matters of trade.'

'But you must!' Clara cried. She threw herself to her knees beside her mother, reaching out for her hands as she hadn't done since she was a small child. 'Mama, don't you understand? The mine is almost bankrupt. There is no money for new evening gowns. There is scarcely enough money to pay the miners! If a new lode is not found soon, we will be bankrupt.'

Lady Susan pulled her hands from Clara's grasp and rose to her full height. 'You are rambling, girl. What would you know of such things?' She stared down at Clara where she knelt on the floor. 'Your father promised me, when we were married, that I would not lack for material things. He has kept his word. There is no need for you to concern yourself with such matters.'

Clara leapt to her feet. 'Yes, he has kept his word,' she repeated hotly. 'And do you know how?' She raised her chin, staring defiantly at her mother. 'Because he has starved the mine of the investment it has needed over the years, in order to pay for your clothes, and carriages and furniture.'

143

She stared into her mother's set and furious face. 'I've seen the books, Mother. I'm not mistaken. We *are* on the verge of bankruptcy.' She hesitated before adding unhappily, 'I had to tell you. It is unfair that you should not know the true position.'

Lady Susan reached out with strong fingers and caught Clara's chin in her hand. 'You've seen the books?' she demanded. 'You've been to the mine?'

Clara nodded briefly, thankful that her mother was accepting her words as true. The next moment, she winced as Lady Susan Pentreath slapped her furiously across the face with her free hand.

'You disobeyed me, miss. You deliberately disobeyed me.' Her hand slapped again across Clara's cheek. 'How dare you!'

Clara tore herself away from the clutching fingers. 'I dared because I had to,' she retorted angrily. 'You can't just hide away from facts, Mama. The only way to deal with a situation like this is to find out what the truth is.'

'And how would you know anything about truth?' Lady Susan demanded. 'You promised me you would never go to the mine and now I find that you have spent half your time there. Where's the truth and honesty in that?'

Clara said spitefully, 'I thought you wanted me to see more of Edward Blacklock? I see more of him at the mine than I do anywhere else.'

Lady Susan paled. 'He's seen you at the mine?' Her voice was weak with horror. 'What sort of a female will he take you for?' she lamented. 'How will I ever persuade him that you are a suitable wife when you act like a common hoyden?'

'Personally,' Clara retorted, 'I don't think he wants a lady. It seems to me that the less I act like a lady and the more I defy him, the more interested and excited he becomes.'

'Mr Blacklock,' Lady Susan snapped, 'is a perfect gentleman. He would only find behaviour such as you describe as unseemly and revolting.'

'A perfect gentleman!' Clara gasped. 'Well, just see what your "perfect gentleman" has done to me!'

She bent and began to fight with her voluminous skirts and petticoats, anxious to show her mother the five individual bruises on her thigh that marked Edward Blacklock's painful grasp.

Lady Susan said coldly, 'Kindly lower your skirts at once. No daughter of mine should be so eager to display herself in this unseemly fashion.'

She strode towards the door. 'You will be confined to the house for the next week, miss, unless you are accompanied by me.' She paused.

144

'I obviously cannot rely on your father as a suitable chaperon. And I shall arrange for the gowns to be made up without reference to you. You do not deserve to have your wishes taken into consideration after your behaviour today.'

Her eyes swept coolly over her angry and passionate daughter. 'I only hope,' she added, 'that Mr Blacklock does not judge from your sluttish behaviour that you are too unladylike to make him a good wife.'

She whirled round the sitting-room door with a swish of silk skirts and slammed it behind her.

Clara stared miserably at the doorway. 'Oh, there's no danger of that,' she said bitterly. 'No danger at all!'

'What in the name of Almighty God do you think you're doing?' Norman Willcock demanded angrily.

Adam rubbed away the sweat that was trickling into his eyes with an equally sweaty forearm. 'Working,' he said shortly. He turned again to the rockface, the borer in one hand, the hammer in the other, and began to pound yet another hole in the hard granite.

'But that's not where we're working!' Norman grabbed him by the shoulder and pointed at the original workface. 'That's where we're working, remember?'

'I haven't been away that long,' Adam snapped. 'I know perfectly well where we were working. If you remember, I was the one who got us eighteen shillings in the pound for working it.'

'Then what the hell are you doing here?' Norman pointed at the white quartz vein, unmarked by any sign of tin. 'You won't find tin in that. It's a cross-vein. They never have ore in them.'

'But they might lead to other veins that do,' Adam said.

'Might! Might! But when?' Norman's face was red with rage. With an effort he controlled himself. 'Look,' he said, fighting to keep his voice calm, 'you got us eighteen shillings in the pound and I'm brem grateful. But let's make the most of it, eh?' He pointed at the original workface. 'Let's work that for all we can this period. We can make a good bit of money out of that.'

'A good bit,' Adam agreed. 'But not enough.'

'Enough?' The exasperation in Norman's voice was palpable. 'Not enough for what?'

Clara's face floated briefly into Adam's consciousness but he ignored it. It was too precious and distant a dream to be spoken of yet. 'Enough to get a start in life,' he said harshly. 'Enough to set Phil up in safety so that I can go to Australia and make my fortune mining

145

copper. Enough to save this mine for all the other miners who depend upon it for a living.'

He pointed at the quartz vein that shone a ghostly white in the light from their guttering candles. 'That's our only chance.' Then he pointed at the face they had been working on. 'You get going on that, Norman. What you can raise will cover our expenses and a bit over at the rate I've got us. Meanwhile, I'll get cracking here.'

He rubbed a hand over the white, silky rock. 'I'll do a double core every day for the next month, to follow this. If I haven't made a find by that time, I'll come back to working our original pitch. We won't be worse off than we usually are.'

'And what do you think Captain Pentreath is going to say when he sees what you're up to?' Norman demanded.

'He'll agree with me,' Adam said wearily. 'He needs the find as much as we do. He'll recognise that this is our best chance.'

Norman stared at him. 'Because the mine is almost ready to be knacked?' He hammered one fist into the palm of his other hand. 'But don't you see, that's why we should be working our original pitch. If the mine's going down we need every penny we can earn.'

'I've made my decision,' Adam said heavily, 'and I'm sticking to it. If you don't like it, join another payre.' He made his way stiffly to the small barrel of water he had carried down with him and took a deep draught. After eight hours down the mine the water tasted warm and stale, but it was necessary to replace the sweat he had lost doing hard physical work in the hundred-degree temperature.

He put down the barrel and saw that Norman was still staring at him, his broad features eerily lit by his flaring candle.

'It's that blonde piece, isn't it?' he said slowly. 'Our Molly came home last night screeching like a whitnick. She wouldn't say nothing but I could guess what it were. You'd thrown her over. And all because Captain Pentreath's pretty daughter used to come round to see you when you were hurt.'

Adam said nothing, staring at his companion under lowered brows, his lips compressed into a hard line.

Norman went on, 'You must be daft as a brush. She'll never look at the likes of you! Her mother's set on having her wed Blacklock.' He paused. 'You've lost your way, Adam,' he said with rough kindness. 'You always had dreams, but you used to know when to stop. Now you don't.'

He laid a hand on Adam's tense shoulder. 'Forget her, Adam. Clara Pentreath's a pretty little thing but she's not for the likes of you. Our Molly will forgive you like a shot, I know her. And she's a good girl. Maybe not ladylike but she's strong and a good worker and keeps a good house. She's what you need, Adam.'

'What I need,' Adam grated between clenched teeth, 'is for you to hold your tongue. I'm the only one who can decide what's right for me and what isn't. And I'm the head of this payre. And I'm warning you, Norman Willcock, you either agree to the plan I suggested or you join up with someone else.'

He picked up his borer and hammer again, turning back to the quartz vein as a clatter of heavy boots warned him that Jan Eddy was approaching to work the wind-machine for the second core. Then he began to hammer the borer into the hard granite as if it were Blacklock's face that he was hitting.

It was late evening when Sam Grenfell walked tiredly up the Newlyn Coombe towards Edward Blacklock's elegant Queen Anne House.

He had been hoping all day that Blacklock would pay one of his frequent visits to the mine and save him the walk. But there had been no sign of him. That was typical, Grenfell thought resentfully as he made his way up the drive. He had been tempted to wait another day, hoping that Blacklock would ride out to the mine in the meantime, but he hadn't dared. Blacklock expected prompt service, and Grenfell had a feeling that he was more than usually impatient over this matter.

'Well?' Blacklock was sitting at his ease in a large armchair, turning a glass of fine brandy between his fingers and surveying Grenfell as if he were something brought in by the Persian cat that lay motionless on his knee.

The smell reminded Grenfell of last night, of Molly's warm lax body under his, and the memory aroused him. He cleared his suddenly tight throat. 'I've found out what you wanted, sir.'

'And?' The voice was almost bored.

'He goes out on the dark of the moon. Last time, they stowed the casks on the Brisons and collected them the next day. Mol – my informant thinks that they will do the same again this month. The nights are so short this time of year there isn't enough time to meet the ship and bring the stuff to shore and get it away before dawn.'

Edward Blacklock's face did not change but his free hand caressed the beautiful animal lying on his knee and Grenfell jumped at the full-throated purr that vibrated through the room.

'Is that what you wanted, sir?' he asked nervously, unable to read Blacklock's closed face.

'It's exactly what I wanted.' There was a brief gleam in the cold grey eyes. 'I've got the bastard now!' His voice was vibrant with suppressed emotion. 'I've got him just where I want him!'

'And you'll tell the Preventative men?' Relief made Grenfell suddenly talkative.

'Preventative men?' Blacklock stared up at Grenfell. 'Of course. But I want to be involved myself. Every day that Trevelyan is in prison, every day for the rest of his life, I want him to know that it was *I* who ruined him.' A smile twisted the handsome lips.

'But, you can't . . . I mean . . .' Grenfell stammered to a halt under the hard gaze.

Blacklock said clearly, 'You and I will watch to see him go out. You and I will visit the Brisons afterwards to check that the kegs are hidden there. Then, and only then, do we tell Laity. And when the Preventative men arrest them, you and I will be there with them. And, speaking personally, I shall enjoy every second of it.'

His teeth gleamed white in the candlelight. 'And then to top it all, you and I will stand up in court and give evidence that will put him away for seven years.'

'Me, sir? But – but – but . . .' Grenfell had not expected this. Adam was a bad person to cross and he had many friends, friends who would delight in making Grenfell's life a misery if he were known to be involved in this betrayal.

Blacklock rose to his feet in one fluid movement, the cat springing to the carpet as he moved. He took a step towards Grenfell who backed hastily away.

'You will do as I say.' The voice was little more than a whisper but it was all the more frightening for that. 'Trevelyan supplies at least one magistrate that I know of. They'd love to find an excuse to let him go free. And they know I am supposed to have a grudge against him because of that fight.'

One long forefinger reached out and bored painfully into the centre of Grenfell's chest. 'But you work for Captain Pentreath,' Blacklock went on. 'The highly respected and admired Captain Pentreath. You could have no possible grudge against Trevelyan.'

'N-no, sir.' Grenfell's voice rasped in his throat. He swallowed nervously, afraid to move away from the pressure of Blacklock's finger. Thank God the man didn't know about Molly, he thought, feeling the sweat gather on his brow.

Blacklock smiled. 'So with you to back me up, and the evidence of Lieutenant Laity, they won't be able to throw the case out.' For a moment his face relaxed, and Grenfell shuddered at the cruelty he saw revealed there.

Blacklock continued: 'And Trevelyan will know it was I who ruined his life. And he will know why. And do you know what will be the worst punishment of all?'

Grenfell licked his dry lips. 'No, sir.' His voice was a strangled gasp.

'It will be knowing that the beautiful Miss Pentreath is my wife. Mine! To do with as I like. For the rest of her life.'

Chapter 18

'That's the lot.' Norman climbed easily down into the small boat which Adam held against the steep rockface of the Brisons. 'Doing it in two trips like this we can deal with more barrels as well. More profit for the same risk.'

'At the cost of two sleepless nights instead of one.' Adam suppressed a yawn and began to edge the boat backwards out of the narrow gully.

'You didn't go to work today, surely?' Norman swung round in astonishment. 'I didn't bother.'

'So I noticed,' Adam said shortly, taking the tiller and watching as Norman raised the brown sail.

'But you did a double core yesterday!' Norman sounded stunned. 'You'll kill yourself, my handsome, going on like that.'

'Kill myself, or make my fortune.' Adam grinned as the wind caught the sail, the sea creaming along the small boat's tarred side as she sped for the shelter of Priest's Cove. 'Any sign of the Preventatives?'

'Nah! Given up on us, I reckon.'

'Or lying in wait somewhere. With clear skies like this, they could see us from the land.' His eyes ran over the conical mass of Cape Cornwall, searching for any sign of movement, but the land was black against the starlit glory of the sky and he could see nothing.

'Why should they?' Norman asked comfortably. 'There are no ships around at the moment. Jean-Pierre has gone back to Falmouth. There's no one around for us to get the stuff off. How could we be smuggling?'

'Unless they've cottoned on to the fact that we've stowed the stuff offshore overnight.'

Norman snorted. 'I reckon they're too thick for that. Or too lazy.'

Adam grunted, unconvinced, his eyes still searching the shore for any sign of life. He felt uneasy. Some instinct that he could not explain warned him that all was not as it seemed. Or was it just the fact that he knew that this might be the last such trip that they would have to make? That he could achieve his ambitions now without the risks that smuggling entailed?

He surreptitiously patted his coat, feeling the drag of the heavy weight in one pocket. 'I'd have showed you something if you'd come to work today.' He had to strive to keep his voice casual.

'And what was that?' Norman's voice was bored and Adam grinned to himself. Once Norman knew what he had found . . .

'Tell you when we've got rid of this little lot.' The shore was closer now. Adam could see the waves breaking on the slipway, receding with a sigh and a tracery of bubbles. Somewhere an owl hooted, and his head jerked up, but there was no other sign of life. Not even a sign of Phil. Adam cursed silently. Surely he wasn't having trouble with the mules tonight of all nights?

'Lower the sail, we're going in.' Stifling the instinct that warned him something was wrong, Adam turned the boat to the shore.

'They're coming in.' Lieutenant Laity spoke under his breath but Blacklock could hear him. He grinned to himself in the darkness, stroking his moustache with a gentle finger in his habitual gesture. It was all working out just as he had planned. Tonight that bastard Adam Trevelyan would be behind bars, and he would know who to thank for putting him there. Blacklock shivered with suppressed excitement, keeping his head down behind the low Cornish hedge lest the gleam of his golden hair should alert the men in the boat.

Behind him he could hear the harsh, nervous breathing of Sam Grenfell. Blacklock's smile grew broader. The man was a rat, happy to betray anyone as long as it was behind their back and he wasn't involved himself. It was a pleasure to see him here, sweating with fright as he waited for the showdown.

There was a splash from the bay as one of the smugglers jumped into the water, and Edward could hear the keel grating as the boat was beached onto the slipway. 'Now?' he breathed.

Lieutenant Laity shook his head. 'Not yet.' His voice was so low that it was almost inaudible. 'Let them land the stuff first. We don't want them to escape by sea.'

Biting his lip with impatience, Edward waited. He could hear the faint thuds as the barrels were unloaded from the boat, the muffled instructions and finally, the grunting of straining men and the screech of metal upon rock as the now-empty boat was manhandled up the steep slipway, beyond the reach of the waves.

151

'Now, men.' Laity's shouted command made him jump. The dark lantern was suddenly opened, its beam lancing out across the beach as the Preventative men leapt to their feet. By its light, Edward could see Adam and Norman, shocked into stillness by the surprise attack.

Grabbing the reluctant Grenfell by one arm, Edward ran after the others. Adam must see him here, know that he was the one to whom Adam owed his downfall. And if Blacklock could personally make sure that Adam was captured tonight, that would make his victory even sweeter.

It had only taken Adam a second to recover from the surprise that had gripped him at Laity's shout, then he swung into action.

'Swim for it,' he shouted at Norman, reaching into the boat for an oar. 'I'll hold them off as long as I can.'

Norman grunted. 'I'm staying with you, boy. I'm not going no-where.' He groped round his feet, searching for something that could be used as a weapon. Side by side, the two men advanced on the approaching soldiers.

'Least Phil's not here,' Adam said thankfully.

'Unless they got him already.'

'We are Preventative officers.' Adam could recognise the Lieutenant's voice in the darkness. 'I order you to give yourselves up, in the name of the Queen.' The figures were closer now, six in a row and another two behind. The lantern wavered wildly as the running man tried to keep its beam focused on them.

Norman swung his arm and the stone he had picked up flew hard and true. There was a yell and the lantern spun off into the night, hitting the ground and expiring in a sudden blaze of spilt oil. 'One down, seven to go,' Norman said with satisfaction.

There was a ring of steel as swords were drawn and the men advanced more slowly down the steep path. Behind them, Adam heard a voice shout, 'Don't kill them. I want them alive.' His lips twisted bitterly. Edward Blacklock! So this was how he had decided to take his revenge. He hissed at Norman, 'Get away while you can, you fool. I'm the one they want.'

Norman reached for another stone. 'One and all,' he reminded Adam. 'I've got the one. Now let's get them all.'

'With stones?' Adam had to fight to keep the untimely laughter out of his voice. 'I didn't know you were called David!'

There was another shout as Norman's stone found its target. The remaining men advanced more slowly, starlight gleaming on their drawn swords. 'Laity will have a pistol,' Adam said, hefting the oar thoughtfully.

'Then he's next.' Norman took aim again but the stone flew wide in the uncertain light.

This is impossible, Adam thought. We may hurt one or two but we can't win. He darted forward, swinging the heavy oar. The first man ducked but it caught the second in the neck and he dropped instantly. The other men backed away nervously.

'Get them.' It was Blacklock's voice again. 'Cowards. Fools. They're unarmed – *get them*!'

'Silence!' Laity's roar shouted down the other man. 'We do this my way and I will not have unnecessary loss of life.' He moved forward, a dim figure in the starlight. 'Surrender at once or we fire.'

Adam swore and backed away towards the boat pulling Norman with him. 'Now will you swim for it, you damn fool? There's no point in us both getting shot.'

'You go,' Norman said shortly. 'You're the one Blacklock wants.'

'Listen.' Adam cocked his head. There was a noise of hooves in the distance, rapidly getting louder. 'Phil with the mules? Or reinforcements?'

'Reinforcements,' Norman told him. 'They're going too fast for the mules.'

In the uncertain starlight they caught sight of the animals coming down the steep track from St Just. A jostling, heaving mass of heads and backs, racing down the narrow, twisting road. A rout of animals, mules leading, horses behind, heading remorselessly for the Preventative men standing horror-struck at the bottom of the track.

The men did not need Laity's shouted instruction. They threw themselves bodily against the hedges as the herd thundered past. The animals swept them aside as though they were no more than grasses as they galloped by, slithering down the slipway and churning the sea with their frantic hooves.

'It's Phil,' Adam yelled above the braying of the terrified mules. He could see the boy, clinging inexpertly to the mane of one of the horses, trying to hang onto the reins of the other while the mules milled around, their headlong race stopped abruptly by their sudden immersion into the sea.

He barged his way through the seething herd, Norman just behind him, and hauled himself on to the back of the wildly circling horse behind the boy. Norman struggled onto the other horse. 'Now what?'

'Now we get away.' Adam whipped the nearest mule with the end of the reins, sending it plunging back up the hill. The other animals, following their instincts, raced after it, the horses in the midst of the mêlée.

Adam saw the revenue men, who had just picked themselves out of the hedge, dive for cover again as the herd galloped back up the hill towards them. Only Blacklock and Laity stood firm. Adam saw the Lieutenant knocked to the ground by a glancing blow from a terrified mule, but Blacklock was still on his feet and as the horse Adam was riding approached he leapt out for it, grabbing at the reins.

The horse jibbed, throwing its head up, and Adam slithered sideways in the saddle as the animal swung completely round, anchored by Blacklock's grip on the reins. The plunging horse crashed against the high Cornish hedge and Adam used the unexpected foothold to thrust himself back in the saddle again.

One hand locked into the horse's mane, the other arm holding Phil tightly to him, he swung his foot viciously forward and heard the crack as his toe connected with Blacklock's chin. The hold on the reins loosened suddenly and the horse swung round again, racing instinctively after the other animals, its ears flat to its head.

A volley of shots from behind them brought a frightened gasp from Phil but the bullets went wide in the uncertain light and only made the animals gallop faster.

'Where the hell are we going?' Adam gasped as the herd suddenly dived down a small farmtrack.

'Back to the field the mules are in, I expect.' Phil's words came unevenly, jolted out by the motion of the horse.

Adam could see the crouched shape ahead of him which meant that Norman had not yet fallen off. He grunted, 'Well, at least we're going in the right direction,' and concentrated on staying on top of his plunging horse as it rocketed after the other animals.

It was a mile further on before the horses slowed first to a bone-jarring trot and then a walk. Adam thankfully pulled his to a halt and slid off, hauling Phil after him.

Norman appeared beside them, walking uncomfortably. 'First time I been on a horse since you and me stole Farmer Trenbath's ponies when we was lads and raced them up Carnyorth,' he said to Adam with a rueful grin, rubbing his behind. 'God knows why the gentry do ride for pleasure. It's a lot more comfortable walking.'

'Let's get on,' Adam said tersely. 'They'll be after us as quickly as they can.'

'But they haven't got no horses,' Phil broke in. 'I chased all the others off before I came for you. They was hidden in a field. They neighed at the mules, see – that was how I knew they was there.'

'You're a good lad.' Adam ruffled his hair. 'You saved our skins all right.'

'Yes, but what do we do now?' Norman broke in. 'They know who

154

we are, right enough, and they'll be after us for more than smuggling now. We've given they Preventative men a couple of sore heads between us at best, and if they didn't get up before the horses came down – well . . .' He shrugged.

'We have to get away.' Adam's face was dark. 'It would have to happen now of all times!' He considered. He was the one Blacklock was after. If Norman was found alone, he would probably get off more lightly. Edward had no quarrel with him.

'Let's split up. I'll hide in the adit of the old Wheal Tempest, you go to the disused Wheal Anthony workings. We'll be safe there until tomorrow night. They won't think of looking for us there. And you, lad,' he turned to Phil, his face sad, 'we'll have to rely on you to sort things out for us.'

''Course, Adam.' Phil's face was alive with excitement. He was too young to understand, Adam thought. To him this was just an adventure.

Adam glanced at the sky. Already it was growing light. 'You'd better be on your way,' he said to Norman. 'You've further to go and we don't want anyone on their way to work to see us.' He thought briefly. 'We'll meet on the dunes at Wherry Town after midnight tomorrow night. I'll see if Phil can arrange a boat for us. If not, we'll have to risk going off with one of the Newlyn fishermen. We've got to get out of this district. And fast.'

Norman nodded. 'Seven years' deportation we'd get otherwise,' he stated gloomily. 'And that's supposing none of them got killed by the mules. If they did . . .' He tightened an imaginary noose around his neck and his head dropped sickeningly to one side. Phil choked slightly.

Adam dropped a comforting hand onto the boy's shoulder. 'On your way, Norman. I'll see you tomorrow night.' He stood silent, watching as the other man disappeared into the pre-dawn dimness, his fingers caressing the boy's shoulder. 'Don't worry, Phil. It won't come to that.'

The boy said stoutly. 'You're cleverer than any Preventative man, ain't you, Adam? Cleverer and braver.'

Adam's mouth twisted in a wry smile. 'Perhaps. But it's you who have to be clever and brave now. And without any breakfast. You mustn't go back to the cottage until Norman and I are well away from here, do you understand?'

Phil nodded, his eyes fixed on Adam's face.

Clearly and concisely, Adam gave Phil his instructions and made sure the boy understood. 'There's just one other thing.' His voice was quieter, less certain. He shifted uneasily under Phil's curious stare.

155

'I want you to give a message to – Miss Pentreath. And to her alone, mind. Not to anyone else.'

'But they got servants up there.' Phil made it sound as if they were dragons. 'How am I going to see her?'

'You'll have to find a way. Go there first thing this morning. Tell her what's happened tonight.' He paused. 'Tell her I must see her. That it's important. And I want you to bring her to the Wheal Tempest adit tonight. If she will come.' His voice trailed away uncertainly.

'Suppose she do tell someone?' Phil asked doubtfully.

'She won't tell. I'll stake my life on it.' It suddenly occurred to Adam that if one of the Preventative men had died under the horses' hooves, then that was precisely what he was doing, but he had no qualms. She might not come, but she would never betray him. The way she had kept the secret of the cross-seam even from her father told him that.

'Tell her,' his voice broke suddenly, 'tell her that I've got to go away. That I need to see her first. Tell her it's important. Do you understand?'

Phil nodded. Adam stroked his hair with a tender hand. 'You'll do your best, I know. You always do. Now go.'

The child ran off, his strong legs pumping fiercely as they carried him out of sight. Adam sighed, turning to the cliff path that would lead him to the disused mine working that would shelter him through the coming day.

His life was ruined, his dreams falling in tatters. Ahead he could see at best, a lifetime of poverty and unremitting labour, at worst, disgrace, imprisonment, even death at the hands of a hangman.

And it was all through Edward Blacklock. He had recognised at once what the man's presence had meant tonight, him and Sam Grenfell. Laity could not have set the trap up like that. He did not have the men to stake out every small cove, watch each small boat as it left to bring home fish or more valuable catches.

It had been Blacklock who had targeted him, had him watched and followed and then set the trap tonight. Blacklock who hated him enough to want him ruined, disgraced, even dead.

And all because of Clara. Adam closed his eyes in anguish as he saw again her face, the impish smile, the narrow waist around which he longed to clasp his hands. The baby-fine ash-blonde hair, the soft tendrils curling loose around her face and the soft, tender nape of her neck.

Losing her was the worst part of it all.

She had to come tonight. *She had to*. His fingers closed with brutal force around the rock that weighted down his pocket.

Chapter 19

'How much further?' Clara hissed. She leaned against the dark rocks, trying to catch her breath.

Beneath her feet, the cliff appeared to drop away sheer to the rolling Atlantic, and she could dimly see in the darkness the white-laced edge of the breakers as they rolled and sucked at the towering cliffs.

'Nearly there. Come on.' Phil's hand plucked frantically at her skirts, his voice scarcely audible. 'We can't stop here. We might be seen.'

Clara forced herself to stumble after the boy through the velvet night. Her light boots slithered dangerously on the steep slope and she had to clutch at the rough tussocks of grass to keep her balance.

Improbably, there seemed to be steps cut into the steep slope which descended into one of the 'zawns' or narrow crevasses that edged the coast. They occurred, she knew, where veins of tin or copper ran into the cliffs. The seething Atlantic wore away the soft ores, leaving the hard granite on either side. The result was these narrow, precipitous chasms thrusting into the land like tearing fingers, their steep sides falling almost sheer to the hungry sea.

Her nerves were so on edge that she almost screamed when she felt Phil's fingers unexpectedly catch at her boots. 'Here.' He guided her foot to a platform to one side, and suddenly she was standing in a low tunnel cutting back steeply into the side of the zawn. An old adit, perhaps, designed to drain water from the upper reaches of a now-disused mine.

In the dim light, Clara gazed round eagerly. Her hands were shaking and her breath caught in her throat. 'He's not here.' She could not keep the desolation out of her voice. She had wanted to see Adam so much, longed for the sight of his strong, trustworthy body, ached to hear again his deep Cornish voice.

But he was not here. She felt herself slump against the tunnel wall. 'Perhaps they caught him.' Her voice trembled. 'Perhaps he couldn't get out.'

'And perhaps there are more pessimistic women.' The deep voice rolled out of the darkness, quivering with laughter. 'But if there are, I never met them!'

'Adam!' Laughing, crying, not knowing how she got there, Clara found herself in his arms. 'You're safe! You've escaped!'

She felt his arms tighten around her, holding her close to him for a heart-stopping second. She could feel the strong chest under her cheek, hear the regular thud of his heart, then his hands moved to her shoulders, putting her gently away from him and she had to bite her lips to hide the disappointment that she felt as he parted her from him.

'You've done as I asked, Phil?' His voice was businesslike and calm. In the dim light that hid his rough clothes, he seemed far more self-possessed and more gentlemanly than she remembered him. She felt again the ache that ran through her body at the thought of losing him, and she closed her eyes in anguish, fighting for self-control.

'Done it all, Adam.' There was pride in the boy's tone. He was too young to appreciate the disaster that had occurred. At nine, he saw only the fun and the excitement. 'Nobby's boat'll be beached at Wherry Town before morning. He's quite happy.'

'Good lad.' Clara watched as Adam's strong hand reached out, ruffling the boy's already untidy hair. His nephew nudged his head trustingly under the man's hand, like a cat wanting to be stroked and Clara could see how much they meant to each other.

'Adam,' Phil's voice was choked suddenly. 'Can't I come with you? I'll do everything you tell me. I wouldn't be no trouble.'

'No, lad.' His voice was heavy with sadness. 'It's no life for you, I've told you that before. As soon as I'm settled, as soon as I can give you a home, I'll let you know. You can trust me. Until then,' Clara saw his shoulders move in a bitter shrug, 'stay with Ma Downing as long as the money holds out. The cottage is for my lifetime and Ben Pasco's, so even if you don't hear from me again, they can't turn you out. After the money goes, I'm afraid it'll be the workhouse. But I'll get you out of it Phil, as soon as I can. I promise you.'

'There'll be no need for that!' Clara reached out and touched his arm. 'I promised you once before . . .' Her throat tightened as she remembered that day in the sunshine on the moors, that day before she knew she loved him, when life was so happy and easy and promises were lightly given.

'I'll look after him,' she promised again. 'He won't go into the workhouse while I can help it.'

'And what about Ma Downing?' Phil interrupted swiftly. 'She'll be there, too, before long. She ain't got tuppence to rub together.'

'Her, too,' Clara said. 'I promise.'

'And Tehidy?' Phil pressed.

Clara was puzzled, and Adam said roughly, 'The dog! Now look here, young Phil . . .'

'And the dog,' Clara said quickly, 'But that's all.'

'I should think so!' Adam reached out for the boy. 'You hear, Phil? Miss Pentreath will do her best for you. And I'll send for you as soon as I can.'

He crouched by the child, their eyes only inches apart. 'There'll be hard times, Phil, and you'll be alone . . .'

The boy shook his head. 'Not with Ma, and Tchidy, and Clara.'

'Miss Pentreath,' Adam corrected automatically. 'But the thing is, Phil, life isn't that easy. Things go wrong. They may go wrong for a while before I can send for you.' Clara could see the tears sparkling in his eyes as he tried to prepare the boy for what was ahead of him.

She blinked in sympathy. Phil would not have an enviable life. Even with the help that she could give them, Ma Downing and Phil would be basically living on his meagre wages. And she knew that he would miss Adam in ways that he did not even anticipate yet. She had seldom seen a father so close, so supportive, as Adam was to his young nephew.

'I can manage, Adam,' the boy said, wriggling in his grasp. 'It'll be an adventure. I'll manage.'

Adam pulled him closer, burying the boy's head in his broad shoulder. His voice was rough with unshed tears. 'But when – if things go wrong, Phil,' Clara could hear the break in his voice, 'don't lose faith in me, Phil. I love you, boy. I'm doing my best for you. Remember that.'

''Course I do know that, Adam.' Phil pulled free. 'I got other things to do tonight.'

Adam stood up slowly. 'I know, lad. And thank you for what you've done already. Not many boys are as trustworthy as you.'

'I won't let you down, Adam. You'll see.' With a grin and a wave of his hand, Phil nipped quickly out of the mouth of the adit. For a few seconds they could see him, climbing the steep sides of the zawn as nimbly as a monkey, then he was gone.

Adam leaned against the wall, his head buried in his arm. 'I wanted to tell him . . .' His voice broke suddenly.

Clara dug her nails into her palms, struggling to keep her self-control, to prevent herself from taking him in her arms and comforting him.

'He's too young to understand.' She could hear her voice shaking slightly and she stopped. Adam had enough problems. He should not have to put up with her as well. There could be no future for their relationship. It was best if she acted as if she were still unaware of her feelings for him.

Gently, she said, 'I won't let him forget you. I'll always talk to him about you.'

Adam was still upset. 'He's so young. He thinks this is a game – that I shall come back in a few days with my pockets full of money. He doesn't realise . . .'

'It's best that way.' Clara reached out a tentative hand and laid it on his arm. 'And I shall look after him. You have my word.'

Soundlessly, he groped for her hand, his warm fingers folding around it with bruising force. She buried her teeth in her lower lip as tears came to her eyes. Still with his face averted, he said, 'You are my only hope.'

Clara waited until she had control of her voice, before asking, 'What are you going to do? Do you have any place where you can be safe?'

His back to her, staring out across the black Atlantic, he said, 'I'm going to Australia. They want men with mining skills. Norman will come with me.'

She had expected it but the bald announcement still made her heart contract. She said awkwardly, 'For that you will need money . . .'

'Phil's arranged that.' He still had his back to her. His broad shoulders were silhouetted against the scattering of stars. 'I'm leaving our boat for Nobby and taking his. When we get to Plymouth we'll sell it. There's money in the house but I daren't get it, and anyway, Phil will need every penny.'

'Even if you get a subsidised passage, you'll still need money,' Clara insisted. 'The food is poor unless you can bring some of your own, and you'll need clothes.'

She reached into the pocket tied around her waist. 'Here. These are for you.'

He looked at her then, staring down motionless at the items she held in her hand.

'They're for you,' she urged. She sorted them with fingers that shook slightly. 'This is a chit from my father giving you and Norman a reference. Oh, don't worry,' she added as he made a sudden movement. 'It isn't in your real names.'

160

He took the piece of paper, printed with the Wheal Susan heading. 'How did you get that?'

Clara smiled in the darkness. 'I didn't tell the truth,' she said, 'but my father is no fool. I remembered what you had said once about going to Australia. When I asked what sort of a reference men would need to get an assisted passage, he wrote this to show me.' Her voice wavered for a moment. 'You appear to be called Sam Cornish.'

'A good manly name.' He folded the paper and stowed it away carefully. 'And those other things?'

Clara lifted her chin, forcing herself to meet his eyes. 'My pearls. For you.'

'I can't take them.' His voice was harsh and angry, his face set like granite. It took all her courage to stand still in the face of his blistering fury.

'They are mine,' she repeated. 'I can do with them as I choose. And I choose to give them to you.'

'You think I am the sort of man who would take a woman's jewels to save his skin? What a high opinion you must have of me, Miss Pentreath.'

She knew how to deal with him now. 'I have a very high opinion of you,' she said firmly. 'And I hope that you have just as high an opinion of me.'

That brought him up short. He paused, peering at her in the dim light. 'What do you mean?'

Clara took a deep breath. 'I mean,' she said, clearly and distinctly, 'that I am the reason for Edward Blacklock treating you like this. If it hadn't been for me, you would still be a free man, able to work and live as you please.'

He made a sudden negating movement but she interrupted him. 'No. Let me go on. It's foolish to hide behind lies and pretences. We both know why Edward has treated you like this and it is all my fault. If I hadn't brought you to his attention, made him aware of you . . .'

'You treated me as you would a man of your own class, Miss Pentreath,' Adam said shortly. 'You don't know what that meant to me – to be seen as an individual rather than just one miner among many. To know that *you* saw me as an individual . . .'

Clara found it difficult to breathe. With an effort she steadied herself, and her voice showed no sign of the turmoil within her. 'I treated you as a friend,' she said, hoping that he would not look at her or he would see the tears coursing down her cheeks. 'And that is how I offer these pearls to you. As a gift to a friend. If you don't accept them, then I'll know how little you value that friendship. And I

161

cannot blame you at all, knowing as I do, that it is my friendship that has led you to this.'

He was silent, standing motionless, his eyes fixed on the clear sky ahead, the stars lancing the darkness in a pattern of diamonds. She stifled her sobs, wiping her cheeks dry with hasty hands, her eyes fixed on him.

Finally, he said quietly, 'I cannot refuse such an offer.' He seemed to find it difficult to speak. 'I will take your pearls in the spirit in which you offered them, but, believe me, Miss Pentreath, Clara . . .' His voice died away.

Clara pushed the suede bag into his hands. 'Take them,' she whispered, 'and God go with you.'

They stood for long seconds, side by side, still and silent as the waves below them rushed in and out through the rocks. It was Adam who spoke first. 'You must be going,' he said gently. 'I'll see you to the top.'

With a single stride he was on the rough-hewn steps that led up the side of the zawn, his hand reaching out to her. She took it, feeling again the thrill that ran through her at the touch of his warm fingers, and the confidence as they made their way silently up the slippery, treacherous path to the cliff-top.

Here, the sky was an arch of brilliance, the Milky Way a cloud of light. As she reached the cliff-top, Adam released her hand, turning to face her. 'Can you find your own way home from here?' His voice was a whisper in the black and silver radiance of the night.

Clara nodded silently. For long seconds they stared at each other, their eyes locked together.

'You must go,' Adam said at last.

She nodded again, making no movement except for her slender fingers, pleating and unpleating the material of her skirt, her eyes fixed on his face as silver tears glistened on her lashes.

'Please.' His voice was harsh. 'Go now.'

She could bear it no longer. With a sudden sob she flung her arms around his neck, pressing herself to him as her tears ran onto his neck.

For a second he stood rigid, his body as unyielding as steel, then, with a groan, his arms folded around her, loving, gentle. His mouth sought hers as she lifted her lips to him, trusting and willing.

As their lips met, Clara felt a thrill run through her. Her arms tightened about him, pulling him closer to her. She was aware that he was struggling against her in some deep pocket of his mind, holding himself back.

She ran her fingers through the black curls that fell forward onto

162

his brow. 'I love you.' The words came of their own volition. 'I love you so much.'

He responded then, crushing her against his strong chest. His mouth met hers, demanding, this time, and hungry. She gave herself up to him, letting the storm of her feelings sweep her away. When she felt his hand fumbling at her bosom, she responded in kind, brushing back the coarse shirt that he wore, fastening her mouth to the tiny buds of his nipples.

With an easy movement he swung her off her feet, laid her gently on the ground. Her heart hammering, resentful of every second they were apart, she watched as he stood above her, stripping off his clothes. In the starlight, his body was a silver statue. She caught her breath in an agony of expectation as he dropped to his knees beside her.

'Clara. My darling.' His lips met hers again and she moaned, reaching out for him. With trembling fingers she traced the gleaming curves of his muscles. Her body responded to him with a wisdom beyond her knowledge, opening itself to him.

'Clara. His voice was urgent. 'Are you sure?'

'Yes! Yes!' She clutched him to her, moaning as he lowered his body onto hers. The question was meaningless, she did not know what he was talking about. All she knew was that she wanted him, she needed him. She was lost in the magic of his touch. His caresses drove away all fear, all modesty, all thought.

The sudden pain when he entered her was unexpected, terrifying. She drove her nails into his back in a convulsive grip, biting back an instinctive cry. Instantly, he was still. 'My God! Clara!' She could hear the anguish in his voice. 'I never thought . . .! I didn't know . . .!'

She stared up at him, shocked out of the spell that had kept her mind in thrall. But already her body was recovering. Her hips moved against his instinctively, her fingers silenced his lips. And when he cried out in a long, shuddering climax, she cradled him gently to her, knowing that never again would she love any man as she loved him.

'Clara.' He was staring down at her, his blue eyes black in the starlight. 'If I had known . . .' He started again. 'I should have known. You are so young, so innocent.'

She stroked the curls back from his damp brow. 'I wanted it.' She said it as simply as a child. 'I wanted you.' Her eyes filled with tears. 'You are going away for ever.'

'Not for ever, my darling.' He held her close. 'If you want me, I am yours. For the rest of my life. For ever.' He ran a gentle finger down her face, tracing the delicate indentation of her cheek. 'I'm not worthy of you, Clara, God knows. And I can't give you the sort of things that you deserve. But, one day, I promise you . . .'

'Oh, what does it matter!' she said impatiently. 'What does any of that matter? You are going away and I shall never see you again!'

'I'll be back,' he promised. 'Somehow. Some time. To come for you – if you still want me.'

'I'll always want you.' Her lips met his, sealing the promise with a kiss. 'However long it takes, I'll always want you, always love you.'

He helped her up, struggling with the unfamiliar fastenings on her clothes. 'You must go. It's late.'

'I never want to go.' She leaned against him, revelling in his closeness, knowing that she would never feel whole until they were together again.

'You must go.' He held her close for a few seconds longer then put her from him. 'Please, Clara.' There was desperation in his voice. 'Don't make it harder for me. Just go. *Please.*'

She could not refuse such a request. Could not add to his torment.

At the last moment, he reached briefly into his pocket and handed her something cold, hard and heavy. 'Take this,' His voice was no more than a whisper. 'Remember me, Clara.'

Blinded by tears, she nodded and stumbled away from him across the rough headland. It was only when she woke the next morning, her eyes swollen from crying, that she remembered the object Adam had thrust into her hand as she left him.

She groped for it where she had placed it on her bedside table. It was instantly recognisable. Captain Pentreath kept a similar specimen in pride of place on the mantelpiece in his study.

It was a lump of rich black tin ore.

Chapter 20

'Mr Blacklock, miss.'

Clara came out of her dream with an effort, still feeling Adam's hands on her body, his lips on hers. She blinked uncertainly at the small maid standing in the doorway. 'Send him in, please.'

She rose swiftly and went to the glass above the mantelpiece. She felt as if her experiences last night were marked indelibly on her forehead for all to see. Surely Edward would realise at once what she had done? She felt a shiver run through her at the thought. His anger would be terrible. But she had more cause for anger, she decided. It was he who had brought about Adam's downfall, he who had betrayed the man she loved to the Preventative officers.

And, besides, she need not fear him any longer; he had no power over her any more. The lump of tin ore, lying hidden in her bureau upstairs, guaranteed that. Once her father had seen it, knew that the elusive lode for which he had searched for so long had finally been found, then the family would no longer be in Edward Blacklock's power. Even if he withdrew his financing, her father would be able to get a loan from another bank on the strength of the find.

As the door opened, she turned to meet him, the colour rising in her face.

'Mr Blacklock.' She nodded at him distantly.

'Clara.' His handsome face was wreathed in smiles, his hands outstretched towards her. 'I have asked you so often to call me Edward.'

She pointedly refused to shake hands with him. 'I must do as I think fit, Mr Blacklock. I don't feel that friendship towards you that would entitle me to call you by your first name.'

He searched her face. 'You know about Trevelyan.' It was a statement, not a question.

'I know what happened to him, and about your part in it.' Her voice was steady, her eyes met his defiantly. 'I suppose you think what you did was the act of a gentleman?' She could not keep the sarcasm out of her voice.

'What I did was the act of an honest man and a lover,' he retorted. 'Do you really think that I should have kept silent when I had evidence that someone was flagrantly breaking the law?'

Her mouth tightened. 'I think that if it had been anyone else breaking the law, you would not have felt so honour-bound to deal with it.' Her voice lingered meaningfully on the word 'honour' and she was pleased to see the colour rise in his pale face.

He retaliated instantly. 'You think that I only acted because it was Trevelyan?'

'I am certain of it.' Clara forced herself to meet his cold grey eyes. 'You disapproved of my friendship with Adam so you deliberately persecuted him.'

'Disapproved? Of course I disapproved.' He smiled thinly. 'It was hardly fitting that Miss Pentreath of Penalverne should have a friendship with a common miner.'

'Then,' Clara said sweetly, 'it was up to my parents to make their wishes felt, Mr Blacklock, not you.' She straightened, lifting her chin to stare belligerently at him. 'I have never given you the right to monitor or control my behaviour.'

'But I have that right anyway, Clara,' he said quietly. 'I have the right of an affianced husband to approve or disapprove of your friendships.'

The shock ran through her body like a blow so that she had to clutch at a chairback to steady herself. 'Affianced?' Her voice was a whisper.

He nodded. 'Affianced, my dear. I have just spoken to your mother and she has agreed – subject to your father's approval, of course. And under the circumstances I can't see him disapproving, can you?' He grinned wolfishly at her.

Clara felt herself relax slightly. The situation was awkward enough, heaven knows. There was sure to be an argument with her mother, and possibly with her father as well, but at least Adam's discovery of the lode of tin meant that she did not have to accept Blacklock's offer.

The thought of marrying him filled her with disgust. He was totally to blame for Adam's predicament, wholly responsible for separating her, perhaps for ever, from the man she loved. And now he came here, confidently expecting her to marry him without a murmur. She would soon teach him to think differently.

'There is one person you have forgotten, Mr Blacklock,' she reminded him tartly. 'Myself. As the person most intimately concerned, I should have thought that I would have had some say in the matter.'

166

He bowed mockingly. 'Of course, Clara. But I can hardly see you refusing. Not when I have the agreement of your parents. And not when you know what the consequences of such a refusal will be on your family.'

She raised her dark eyebrows questioningly. 'And not when you have made sure that your only rival has been forced to leave the field?'

She saw the red rise in his fair skin, mottling his cheeks. 'Rival?' he snarled. 'Adam Trevelyan was an animal, a crawling pest. And I got rid of him as I would any such pest.'

Clara gave a brief smile. 'It seems to me, Mr Blacklock, that you can't have been very sure of your charms if you didn't dare to propose to me until you had "got rid" of Adam Trevelyan.'

He moved then, his hand shooting out to catch her chin, twisting her face painfully to stare up into his. 'I am well aware of my charms, Clara. You seem to forget who I am, what I can offer you.'

His free hand swept in a half-circle, encompassing the low-ceilinged room, the small seventeenth-century windows. 'I can offer you a home to be proud of, Clara, not a poky old house near the mine, tucked away at the far end of England. I can offer you a position in society. I can offer you clothes and jewels.'

She knocked away the hand that was grasping her with a quick blow. She could feel the imprint of his fingers burning on her skin and knew that her face would be marked but she did not care.

'True,' she said coolly, staring at him, her green eyes luminous with fury. 'You can offer me all those things. But you do not know that I will accept them.'

He laughed then, as if he were truly amused. 'But of course you will, Clara. You will not be able to refuse me. Not when you know it will mean bankruptcy and disgrace for your father.' His teeth flashed, white and regular under his golden moustache. 'Because I am going to have you, Clara. That is one thing I am decided upon.' His eyes were on her, intent, watchful. 'I have wanted you since the first moment I saw you and I am used to getting what I want.'

Clara's hands, hidden in her full skirts, clenched until she could feel the nails gouging small half-moons in the skin of her palms. Her voice steady, she replied, 'I should have thought that a man would have more chance of acceptance if he talked about love, not want; if he wanted to help his fiancée's family, not ruin them.'

He shrugged impatiently. 'Love. Want. What's the difference? We both know you're going to accept me, so why are we wasting time like this?'

She showed her small teeth in a tight, angry smile. 'Perhaps,' she said gently, 'I am waiting for you to propose in the accepted style?'

167

'On one knee?' He grimaced. 'Well, my love, if that is what it takes.'

He dropped gracefully onto one knee, his well-manicured hands clasped over his heart. 'Clara, Miss Pentreath.' His voice throbbed with simulated passion. 'Will you do me the honour of agreeing to be my wife?'

Clara paused a second, her eyes on his, then a broad smile lit her elfin features. 'Mr Blacklock,' she said, cordially, 'Edward.' Her voice hardened, became louder. 'Please believe me when I say that I wouldn't marry you if you were the last man on this earth!'

It was so unexpected that she could see him struggling to take in her words, then he was on his feet in one quick, lithe movement. 'The last man on this earth, eh?' His voice grated with fury. 'We'll see about that. You don't think that I would really make your father bankrupt – is that it?'

She had to force herself not to flinch from him as she replied; 'I am quite sure that you are the sort of person who will do what he says he will.'

She gave a brief prayer of thanks that his threats had no power over her any more. She and her father were free from the grasp of this man for ever. The Captain would suffer a few bad moments when he heard from her mother that Clara had refused Blacklock, but that would soon be over. After one look at the sample of tin that Adam had left her, she knew that he would be so delighted that he would back her decision completely.

Blacklock was staring at her under lowered brows, trying to understand the reason for her behaviour.

'I am that sort of person,' he assured her. 'And I have said that I will marry you and that is what I am going to do.'

'Despite my views on the matter?' Clara forced herself to smile but she could feel her cheeks tight with tension. 'And how will you do that, may I ask?'

His mouth twisted. 'Oh, I'll find a way, never fear. And then you'll wish that you had accepted me the first time that I asked you.'

Clara could not suppress a shiver, his face was so malignant and determined. She had to remind herself again that they were free from him now. He had no power over her. She would defy him to the last.

'When that happens, I'm sure you will remind me of your threat,' she said proudly. 'But for now, Mr Blacklock, the answer is "no". I will not marry you now and I can foresee no circumstances in the future that would be bad enough to force me to accept your offer then.'

She could feel her knees shaking under her long skirts as she added, her voice full of bitterness, 'Nothing would ever make me marry the person who was responsible for parting me for ever from the man I love.'

It took him a few seconds to find his voice, and when he did, it was no more than a grating whisper. 'So, you love that filthy animal, do you? You prefer him to me?' He paused. 'It makes me even more glad that I took the actions I did. In fact,' he added, 'it makes me hope that the Preventative man, Nancarrow, dies of his injuries. I would like it even more if that rat, Trevelyan, is hanged from a gibbet as he deserves.'

Clara went white with shock and clutched at the table. The room whirled around her. She had known nothing of this, had heard no rumours.

He saw her reaction and laughed. 'Yes, that's right, Clara. The animal you love is not just a criminal, he's a murderer as well.'

He laughed again and moved towards the door, then turned, his hand on the door knob. 'But don't think that knowing you loved Trevelyan will stop me marrying you, Clara, because it won't. Quite the contrary!'

His grey eyes undressed her, moving over her body with insulting slowness and she saw his tongue flick quickly across his lips.

He said, 'It will merely add an extra piquancy to our union.'

Then he was gone, and the door swung noiselessly to behind him.

Edward rode thoughtfully away, his face dark. He was still determined to marry Clara. She was all he wanted, all he could ever imagine wanting. Attractive, spirited, the grand-daughter of an earl, she would make an admirable wife, enhancing his social position and arousing his desire in bed.

He licked his lips again, imagining her slender voluptuous body exposed to him, fantasising the battles they would have. He would win, of course, but she would fight him every inch of the way. Suddenly, his longing for her was paramount. He *had* to have her, and soon. He had intended to see Laity, to urge him to greater efforts in his hunt for Adam Trevelyan, but this was more important.

Clara had already defied him, and her mother. Would she have the strength to withstand the pressure that her father could bring to bear on her?

Reaching a decision, he swung his horse around and spurred it into a fast canter towards Wheal Susan.

Hugh's heart dropped as he saw Blacklock turn into the mine workings. He had seen little of the man recently, probably because he had been too busy laying the trap for Adam, Hugh thought angrily as he walked to meet his antagonist.

If Blacklock had wanted to ruin the mine, he couldn't have done it better, he decided. The new vein of tin ore had to be in that part of the mine. And now he had lost both Adam and Norman.

He had tried to persuade the other miners to take over the pitch but they had backed away with superstitious dread, refusing even to visit the abandoned face. Word had got around that it was bad luck. They cited Adam's accident, the fact that he had been caught smuggling, even the lack of good air.

'Tes the knackers, Cap'n,' they had said, shaking their heads. 'The little people. They've ill-wished that pitch. Bain't no use our working it, the trouble will only come to us then.'

One and all, they had given him the same advice. 'Let that pitch bide, Cap'n. If you do try and work'n you'll only bring bad luck on all the mine.'

Well, he hadn't worked it. He hadn't even had the heart to go down there himself since Adam's precipitous departure two nights before. Yet here was bad luck, appearing as regularly as ever. He forced his face into a welcoming smile. 'Any sign of your fugitives yet?'

'None,' said Edward shortly, swinging himself off his horse. 'But we'll get them. There's nowhere for them to go. They only know mining and I've got friends around Camborne who are keeping an eye open in case they turn up there.'

Hugh suppressed a sigh of relief. He had seen through Clara's apparently innocent enquiry about references for assisted emigration, and had deliberately concocted the reference so that it would suit Adam and Norman, leaving the paper lying on his desk. It had gone when he came back later. And Clara had not been down for breakfast this morning for the first time since she came home from school. He could only hope that she had managed to get it to the two men. They were good souls who didn't deserve imprisonment, just for indulging in a little free-trading. Why, he had done it himself when he was younger.

Edward glanced quickly around the mine workings. 'Let's go into the Count House. I wish to speak with you alone.'

Hugh's heart dropped but he led the way to the white-washed building, dismissing Grenfell with a curt nod of the head. He shut the door behind the purser and leaned against it, his hands in his pockets in a relaxed pose. 'Well?' he began. 'I haven't found that lode yet, if that's what you want to ask me.'

Edward's grey eyes stared at him expressionlessly. 'I'm not asking this time, I'm telling.' He tapped his fingers irritably on the inkstained table. 'I'm withdrawing my support. As of now, this mine is bankrupt.'

Hugh felt the world reel about him. There was a drumming in his ears, a red mist in front of his eyes. For a second he thought that his head would burst. Then he managed to find his voice.

'Why? For God's sake, why?'

Edward shrugged. 'The price of tin is down again. And I've lost patience with this elusive lode. The fact is, this mine is not viable and I'm cutting my losses.'

'Your losses!' Hugh could not control his anger now. It boiled in his veins, vibrated in his head. 'You've never made a loss on this mine. You've made a fortune out of us. You've taken us for every penny you can and now you're closing us down on a whim.'

'The reason does not matter,' Blacklock said bleakly. 'For the past couple of years you've been keeping going on my money. Now, I'm stopping that facility. I want my money back and I intend to get it.'

He clapped his tall hat on his head and moved towards the door. As he left, Blacklock turned back to the stricken man and gestured at the activity around them. The songs of the bal-maidens floated out over the hammering of the tin stamps, and buddle boys screamed and shouted at each other as they they paddled through the slimy mud, separating out the tin ore from the pulverised rocks.

'I should send them home at once if I were you. It's the kindest thing. There's no money to pay them.' He swivelled on his heel and was gone.

Hugh stared after him blindly, unable to take in the enormity of the disaster. Automatically, he made his way to his sanctuary in times of trouble, the great engine house which provided the motive power for draining the mine.

Ben Pasco was there as always, a rag in his hand as he buffed the already gleaming brass to a yet brighter finish. He swung round as Captain Pentreath pushed the door open and made his way, staggering slightly, to the seat by the pressure gauges. 'You all right, Cap'n?'

'I'm – all right.' Hugh's voice was a weak thread. He forced a smile at the man. 'Go and get some air, Ben. I'll look after her.'

He waited until the door had closed then slumped, his head in his hands. All he had worked for, all he had achieved – gone into nothing. How would Susan cope? What would happen to Clara?

He vomited suddenly, messing his trousers and the floor but he did not care. Compared to his other problems, what did that matter? And his head hurt so much, so agonisingly much. It got in the way of his thinking, of his planning. He groaned, huddling closer around the pain, his hands pressing into his head as if to contain it that way.

But his hands could not stop the sudden bursting inside his head. His eyes opened suddenly, wide with surprise, then he fell from the chair to lie unconscious in the pool of his own vomit.

And the first that anyone knew about it was when the great engine, untended for too long, exploded, blowing the pistons through the granite walls as if they were not there.

Chapter 21

Clara glanced uneasily at her mother as she sat by the empty fire-place. Her embroidery hung loosely in her hands and she rocked gently, unceasingly, backwards and forwards, giving no sign that she had heard the maid's announcement.

Clara cleared her throat. 'Show Mr Brightman in, please.' Gently, she reached out and shook her mother's shoulder. 'The attorney is here, Mama.'

Her mother's faded green eyes were empty of all expression as she nodded slowly and stood up. She had lost weight visibly in the few days since her husband's death, Clara thought. Or perhaps it was the effect of the deep mourning in which they were both dressed. The dull, black crêpe robbed all colour from her mother's face, as Clara knew it did from her own. Her fair hair half-hidden under her cap showed more silver than blonde.

Clara steadied her mother with a strong hand, helping her to a chair in front of the large table. It had seemed more suitable to her that the reading of the will should take place in a formal setting, and in this, as in everything else since the news of Captain Pentreath's death, her mother had made no objection. She was still in a state of shock.

'Mr Brightman.' Clara moved forward with extended hand and a welcoming smile. The attorney had always been a favourite of hers as a small child. He was short and round, reminding her, with his quick, alert movements, of a robin. Now he squeezed her hand warmly, his face serious, managing to convey a nice distinction between friendship and business.

Lady Susan roused herself at his entrance. 'So good of you to call, Mr Brightman. It has been an age since you last came to see us. You mustn't stay away so long in future.' Her face creased grotesquely into a parody of her old, social manner.

Clara saw the surprised look on the attorney's face and intervened quickly. 'I'm sure you must be very busy, Mr Brightman. Perhaps it would be a good idea if we were to get these formalities over as quickly as possible.'

He nodded, relieved, and moved behind the table. 'The will is quite straightforward, ladies.' He smoothed the thick parchment with nervous fingers. 'Apart from a few small legacies to the servants, the whole of Captain Pentreath's fortune is left to you, Miss Clara.'

Clara knew that the will was meaningless. The debts her father had left would eat up almost all the estate. Nevertheless, she could not help exclaiming, 'But my mother! Is there no provision for her?'

Before he could reply, Lady Susan broke in, 'I have my own money, Clara. My dear father made me a good settlement when I married your father.' Nodding complacently, she sank again into silence, her hands constantly twining and intertwining in her lap.

The attorney stiffened slightly. Seeing Clara's expression he said diplomatically, 'I am sure that your father knew he could rely on you to look after your mother, Miss Clara.'

Clara watched him carefully. Her suspicions were aroused. She said thoughtfully, 'That seems a very simple will for a man in my father's position.'

The attorney nodded, his whole body jerking forward from the waist in a quick, bird-like movement. 'The simplest wills are the best, Miss Clara.'

Before she could speak again, her mother broke in, 'I really do not know why my husband is so late, Mr Brightman. It is not like him to keep you waiting. I really must apologise on his behalf.'

Clara's eyes met those of the little lawyer and despite the horror that ran through her she almost smiled at his shocked expression.

She rose swiftly and went to her mother's side. 'You look tired, Mama. I think you should rest. Why don't you let your maid help you to bed while I talk to Mr Brightman.'

The attorney quickly echoed her. 'Do not put yourself out on my behalf, dear Lady Susan. I shall be quite comfortable here with your daughter.'

Lady Susan smiled graciously but made no move to go. It was as if she had forgotten already what they had said. She simply sat, never ceasing her constant rocking motion, her fingers moving as if they had a life of their own.

Clara took her mother's arm, pulling her gently to her feet. 'You will feel better after a sleep, Mama. You are overwrought.' Carefully, she shepherded her mother through the door and saw her into the capable hands of her maid, then she returned again to the attorney.

'Now that my mother has gone, perhaps we can speak openly, Mr Brightman,' she began, seating herself at the table opposite him.

He shot her a worried look. 'Openly, Miss Clara? In what way?'

She said baldly, 'My father's financial position was by no means as good as it would appear from that will. Am I correct?' She was proud that her voice did not betray the fear that she felt whenever she contemplated the future.

There was a long pause, as if he were considering the best way to break the news. 'I had a visit from Mr Blacklock yesterday.'

'And?'

He sighed. 'I am afraid, Miss Clara, that towards the end of his life your father behaved very unwisely, very unwisely indeed.' He bowed at her in brief apology. 'I am talking in financial terms only, you understand.'

He cleared his throat. 'The result is, I am afraid, that this house and the farm now belong to Mr Blacklock.'

Clara had suspected it before, but the bare statement brought the horror of it all home to her. With a sudden movement she rose from the table and walked restlessly around the room. 'So if he chooses, we are homeless?'

'That is the position.' The lawyer fiddled uneasily with the papers on the table. 'Of course, Mr Blacklock is a gentleman. He may not insist on his full – er – pound of flesh.'

'I wouldn't rely on that,' Clara said bitterly. She knew all too well that he would take every penny to which he was entitled. The only way to stop him would be to marry him. 'Are there any assets which he doesn't own?'

'There are your own personal possessions, of course, jewellery and such like.' Clara had a brief vision of her pearls, lying in Adam's hard brown hand. 'And there is the mine.'

Mr Brightman took a deep breath. 'I have to tell you, Miss Clara, that that mine is the cause of all these problems. It has been a good mine in the past, but your father was unable to come to terms with the falling off in output in recent years.' He blew his nose, loudly, into a brightly coloured handkerchief, as if repudiating any suggestion that he had played any part in Captain Pentreath's downfall. 'For instance, my dear, he recently bought up many of the shares in the mine, so that he, and now you,' he bowed at her with his quick, bird-like movement, 'at present own nearly seventy per cent of the mine.'

'And I suppose I can't sell those?' Clara knew the answer even before she asked the question.

'They are worthless. Even before the accident, you would probably have found it impossible to sell them but now, with the pumping engine in ruins and the mine flooding . . .' He sighed, spreading his hands in a hopeless gesture. 'Of course, in the future, if the price of tin were to rise . . .' Like every businessman in Penwith he was intimately acquainted with the tin market.

Clara moved to the window and stared out at the glorious day outside, her eyes damp with unshed tears. It was worse than she had thought. Edward Blacklock had known the true situation, she realised that now. That was why he had been so sure that he could force her to marry him.

Well, she would not do it. Not while there was any other option open to her. She was willing to face hardship on her own behalf if that was necessary. Anything would be preferable to marriage with a man who had driven away the man she loved and, she was certain, had caused her father's death. But she had no right to inflict such privations on her mother.

Her heart turned over again as she remembered Lady Susan's behaviour since her father's death. She had swung from apparently inconsolable grief to a kind of absent-minded lethargy, occasionally not even seeming aware of what had happened.

Clara remembered the look on the lawyer's face when her mother had mentioned her marriage settlement. Turning back, she asked more hopefully, 'Presumably Edward Blacklock cannot touch my mother's marriage settlement?' That, after all, was the purpose of such a device. To ensure that a loved daughter was not left in poverty after the death of her husband.

Mr Brightman shook his head. 'I am afraid, Miss Clara, that there is a problem about that.'

She raised her dark brows questioningly. 'Such as?'

He fiddled with his papers again, as if unwilling to see her face as he broke the bad news. 'There was no marriage settlement.'

It took a few seconds for the information to sink in. 'What! But my mother said –'

The attorney said swiftly, 'Your grandfather was extremely angry when Lady Susan decided to marry your father. If I may say so, unreasonably angry.' He coughed apologetically. 'He believed in breeding above all else. There was no way he would consider your father as a suitable son-in-law, so when your mother insisted on marrying him, he refused to give her a penny in settlement.'

Clara felt herself sway. 'But my mother said . . . She has always believed . . .'

'That was your father's doing,' Mr Brightman replied smoothly. 'He knew how hurt your mother would be by such a reaction from your grandfather so he lied to her. Told her that he had achieved such a settlement. In face, the monies that your mother received each year from her so-called settlement came straight from your father's pocket.'

Clara turned away, leaning her burning forehead against the cool glass. It was typical of her father to do such a thing. From what she had already discovered about their relationship, he would do almost anything to spare her mother pain. He had put her mother first in all things. And now, Clara thought angrily, he had left it to her to sort out the mess he had made as a result.

'Would –' She had to struggle to get her voice to work properly. 'Would my grandfather take my mother in, do you think? In the present circumstances?' It did not matter what happened to her, she could look after herself. Somehow or another she would work her way out of this mess. But her mother would never stand the disgrace of poverty.

Mr Brightman shook his head. 'I fear not, Miss Clara. The Earl is implacable. He prides himself on never changing his mind.'

'I see.' Clara felt depression flooding over her. 'So there's no way out?'

He shuffled his papers again. 'If you will forgive me, Miss Clara.' He scrutinised her carefully. 'You are an attractive young lady, well brought up, well-educated. You no longer have the advantage of wealth, of course, and that will severely limit your options. But even without it, you should be able to attract a young man who will be happy to provide for your mother also.'

Clara gritted her teeth. 'I see,' she said coldly. 'So your advice, Mr Brightman, is that I sell myself to the highest bidder?'

He looked affronted. 'I do not advocate a marriage without affection, Miss Clara. But in your position . . .'

'In my position, you consider that the only option.' She could hear the tears in her voice now and swallowed hard. Then, with an effort, she straightened her back and advanced on the little lawyer.

'Thank you for your time, Mr Brightman.' Her voice was calm and under control. 'Perhaps you can see you own way out. I ought to go and tend to my mother.'

'Of course, Miss Clara.' He bowed over her hand. 'And if there is anything I can do . . .'

'I think, Mr Brightman,' Clara said bitterly, 'that we are unlikely in future to be able to afford your services. But I would like to thank you now, on my mother's behalf, for the way you assisted my father.'

She maintained the bright, social smile until he was out of the room, then she slumped miserably in a chair.

177

Distraught, she ran her fingers through her hair. It was worse, even, than she had feared. She and her mother were to all intents destitute; they had no home, no money, no friends.

And whatever hope they had for the future rested with her. Clara could understand now why her father had left his estate to her. It was obvious to her now, as it must have been to him all along, that Lady Susan's grasp on reality was not strong. She would never have coped, even if the mine had been successful. And now . . . Dry-eyed, Clara sat with her chin in her hands, and stared blindly at the empty grate as she tried to find a way out of her troubles.

The room was drowned in dusk when the maid came again. 'Mr Blacklock, miss.'

Clara roused herself with an effort, stretching to get the stiffness out of her body. She should have realised he would come today. This man would be unable to wait any longer to bring her to heel, to win his battle with her.

She awaited him, standing up, her back straight, her head high. She was pleased that her eyes were not red with crying. The situation could not be helped by tears. Her only way out of this mess depended on herself.

'Clara.' He took her ice-cold hand in his and bowed over it with his customary grace. 'Accept my condolences on your father's death. Words alone cannot tell how sorry I am.'

'Can't they, Mr Blacklock?' Her voice was cool, controlled. 'Perhaps that's a good thing. I don't think that I would believe any protestations of regret that you would have made, in any case.'

He stared at her blankly as if he had not expected such an unwelcoming reception. 'But of course I regret his death, Clara.' He forced a smile. 'You know how much you mean to me, how much I have wanted you, and for how long. Do you really believe that I could do anything other than grieve with you?'

'Yes, I do, Mr Blacklock,' Clara said spiritedly. 'I personally think that you must be delighted at the way events have turned out.'

Her emerald eyes met his fearlessly. 'My father was in debt to you, but he did not like you. If matters had really come to a head, there was always a chance that he would have backed up my refusal to marry you, at whatever cost to himself. You no longer have that worry now, do you?' She waited a moment, then: 'Now you have only myself to deal with.'

'Clara!' If she did not know better, she might have been taken in by the shocked horror in his voice. 'Grief has made you irrational. You are not yourself.'

'On the contrary, Mr Blacklock,' she said defiantly, 'I am truly myself now, for the first time in my life.' She stared at him, her face set. 'You see, I have nothing left to lose. My father is dead, I have no money, my mother is – unwell,' she swallowed abruptly. 'All I have left is myself.'

'And that is why I am here, Clara.' He leaned towards her and she could feel his breath on her cheek, smell the expensive cologne that he used.

'You have lost so much. I did not want you to think that you had lost everything, that I would withdraw my offer for your hand because of your changed circumstances.'

He took her hand in his. It lay there, as cold and motionless as a dead bird. 'I know that this is not the time when a man should usually talk about marriage, Clara, but I wanted you to know that my offer is still open. I will marry you, as soon as you wish. Our union is more important than the empty conventions of society.'

His grasp tightened. 'Tell me "Yes", Clara. You know that you have no money. What other course is open to you? Say you will marry me and make me the happiest of men.'

She did not move, did not speak. He pulled her towards him, enfolded her in his arms. 'Say "yes", Clara. Please.'

She freed herself, pushing him away with unexpected strength. 'Before I give you an answer, Edward, I have two questions I want to ask you.'

He nodded. 'Anything, Clara.'

She turned away from him, pacing the room, steeling herself for what must come. 'Did you go to see my father on the day he died?'

She watched him closely, saw his momentary hesitation before he broke into speech. 'Are you trying to catch me out? There must have been men at the mine who saw me and I'm sure the word has got back to you. Yes, I did see your father. But, on my life, Clara, he was well when I left him.'

She nodded briefly, her green eyes never leaving his face. 'And now tell me, Mr Blacklock, in your opinion, do I have any alternative to marrying you?'

This time he did not hesitate. 'You have no alternative.' His voice was definite. 'You have no money, no prospects, no friends. Unless you marry me, you have no chance of sustaining the life of a gentlewoman.'

'I see.' She showed no signs of dismay, standing quietly before him, looking paler and more delicate than usual. The mourning emphasised her fragility, made her look more vulnerable than he had ever seen her look before.

His face lit up with hope. 'Then you will marry me?'

When she spoke, her voice was quiet and composed.

'No, Mr Blacklock, I will not marry you. I may not be able to live the life of a gentlewoman, but at least I can live an honest life, one without lies and pretence.'

Her eyes blazed with a sudden passion. 'Mr Blacklock, you are responsible for the death of my father, the possible death of Adam Trevelyan and the breakdown of my mother. You are responsible for fifty men being without jobs because of the closure of the mine. As far as I can tell, you have not one whit of regret or remorse for any of those tragedies.'

Her voice broke then, the tears running unchecked down her cheeks. 'I would have to be starving before I accepted your proposal of marriage.'

For long, silent seconds, he stared down at her, his grey eyes cold and strangely empty. Then he spoke, his voice calm and passionless.

'Then starve,' he said, and walked out of the room.

Chapter 22

'Oh, stand still, you stupid animal!'

Clara could hear the tears in her voice as the cow lashed out with her hind foot, knocking against the heavy wooden bucket and sending the pitifully small amount of milk sloshing against the sides.

Clara buried her head in the cow's side, grateful for the warmth as the easterly wind screamed across the open field and bit viciously through her clothes.

Who would have thought she would have come to this? And so quickly?

As the cow quietened, she watched her hands, once white, now red and chapped, squeeze the milk from the unresisting udder. A smaller amount each day. The cow was growing visibly with her next calf and soon even this small amount of milk would stop.

And the cow would need extra feeding soon, Clara thought worriedly, especially with the weather so cold. Frosts were rare in this part of Cornwall but already they had had days when the temperature had not risen above freezing and there had been flurries of snow.

The furze-bushes she and Ma Downing had gathered from the moors in the autumn burned all too quickly. The huge pile at the back of the house was already less than half its original size, and it was still only the beginning of December. If only Adam had been able to prepare for the winter before he had had to flee.

At the thought of Adam she felt her eyes prick again. Five months and no word. She had argued with herself, knowing that if he had taken a ship for Australia, it might be nearly a year before they got a message to say that he was safe, but his loss was a constant emptiness inside her.

With a sigh, Clara stripped the last of the milk from the cow and got to her feet. In the distance she could see the waters of the Atlantic, dark grey with white tips whipped up by the wind the locals called

181

the 'Black Easterly', the horizon punctuated by the rash of mine chimneys that lined the coast between Pendeen and St Just.

Automatically, her eyes sought out the chimney that marked the place where the Wheal Susan lay drowned to the adit. It was dead, now, the engine house ruined by the explosion that had killed her father, the dinner service used at the Account Day dinners sold to a local inn. Even the wooden buddling racks had disappeared, salvaged by the local people who coveted every scrap of wood in this treeless landscape. Clara suspected that some of the wood Ma Downing had brought back had come from the mine, but she had never asked. That mine had been a living being to her father, and she could not bear to think of it dismembered and vandalised.

It was too cold to linger here, where the rising wind seemed to come straight from the Russian steppes, but she hated the thought of returning to Adam's tiny cottage where there was no privacy and where her mother waited with her constant complaints and strange, irrational behaviour.

She had never realised before what a luxury privacy was, but then, she admitted to herself, walking slowly up the hill, the wooden bucket banging against her legs at every step, she had never before appreciated even more simple things, like a warm room, and enough and varied food.

The memory of the Great Alhambro floated into her mind and her lips twisted in a wry smile. He had been right about one thing, she decided. Now she really did know the meaning of the words 'to want'. And things could only get worse.

She heard the sound of the horse's hooves when she was partway up No-Go-By Hill and Clara tensed automatically. Surely it couldn't be Edward Blacklock again?

It sometimes seemed as if he haunted her. Although he had never offered her marriage again, he seemed to be a constant visitor. His excuses were impeccable. He came to 'inform' her of her financial position or 'request' her advice on the disposal of the estate. But these were just excuses. All the time, Clara could feel his grey eyes watching her with an intensity that scared her.

His elegant, black-clad figure only emphasised the poverty of the cottage, but she knew that he had not given up hope. His eyes told her that he still desired her; his actions, that he was determined she would one day be his.

But she would never marry him. He had killed her father, driven away her lover, ruined her life. She suspected that he had been the reason she had been unable to get work in Penzance. As a banker, his influence extended to all parts of the community, pulling the small businessmen into his power. If he had made it clear that he was against the idea of her working, there was scarcely anyone in the area who would dare to go against him.

She thought again of the dwindling store of money hidden behind a loose stone in the wall of the cottage. She had sold all her jewellery, even some of her clothes. There was very little left to sell now. Poverty stared her in the face. But what was poverty compared to the moral degradation she would feel if she were to accept his offer, merely for the sake of an easier life?

Clara placed the wooden bucket carefully on the ground and turned to face the on-coming rider. Attack, she had discovered, was always the best form of defence where Blacklock was concerned. Her chin held high, she waited, her heart beating nervously, for the rider to appear between the high Cornish hedges.

'Miss Pentreath.' She had to stop herself from sagging with relief when she saw that it was Lieutenant Laity. She saw him glance at her closely and she knew, miserably, that he was comparing the attractive, pampered young lady of before with the wind-blown and unkempt female he now saw before him. Her black dress, new after her father's death, showed the marks of hard wear and she had long ago given up her fine, hand-made boots for the heavy but hard-wearing ones of the common woman. Her fine, pale hair had blown loose in the blustery east wind, but even that seemed duller and thinner than it had in the old days.

'Lieutenant.' She dropped a brief curtsey, half-expecting him to ride on by but to her surprise he dismounted.

'That bucket is too heavy for you, Miss Pentreath. Allow me to carry it home for you.'

His kindness almost brought tears to her eyes. Is this how low I've sunk? she wondered. Brought down by a few kind words from a man I would once have considered had a duty to exert himself to please me? But it was a relief not to have to carry the unwieldy bucket back up the hill, banging against her already bruised shins.

'You have a cow?' the Lieutenant asked, glancing into the bucket as he hefted it easily in one hand, the other leading his docile horse. 'That is very enterprising of you.'

'Half a cow,' she admitted.

He laughed. 'I hope you have the useful half, then, not just the half that eats.'

She forced herself to smile at him. 'Happily, it is divided by time rather than space. We milk the cow in the morning and the Eddys have the evening milk.'

'A sensible arrangement,' he said approvingly. 'One cow would be too much for a small family.'

'If it's milking well,' she agreed, thinking unhappily of the shrinking volume of milk the cow was giving. What would they do when she dried up completely? It was possible to buy milk from a farm but it would deplete her rapidly diminishing store of money. She sighed involuntarily.

At once, the Lieutenant slowed. 'I'm afraid I was walking too fast for you, Miss Pentreath.'

She shook her head. 'It is my fault. I don't seem to be as active as I once was.' As soon as the words were out she bit her lip, wishing she could recall them. She didn't want him to think that she was complaining.

His eyes on her face, he said gently, 'Forgive me if I am impolite, but you seem much paler than I remember. I hope you haven't been ill?'

Clara could not help the brief grimace that crossed her face. Pale? No wonder! It was probably the result of too much worry and not enough food, but she couldn't tell him that.

'I was unwell after – after my father died,' she admitted, remembering the sickness that had wracked her every morning for weeks. 'It was a result of the shock, I think, but I'm quite well again now.'

'And living in Mr Trevelyan's cottage,' the Lieutenant said cheerfully. 'I've always thought it looks a very cosy little house, nestling against the side of the hill.'

Clara did not know where to look. The very lack of condemnation or comment in the Lieutenant's tone made her feel all the more embarrassed.

As if he had seen her discomfort, he went on, 'I saw young Phil in Mousehole the other day. He's really fallen on his feet, hasn't he? Running his own yawler already, and good at it too, from what I hear. That young man was wasted down the mine.'

Clara could not let this pass. 'I would have got him a job in a mine if it were possible. Adam – Mr Trevelyan – was very against Phil working on the boats. But with the mines closing down, not just Wheal Susan but the others round here as well, it was impossible.'

She fought down a memory of the death of the mine, so unnecessary, so untimely. If only she had told her father in time, if only she had not driven Edward to punish her father for her disobedience. But regrets were useless. She dragged her mind back to the present.

'Dick Thomas in Mousehole is some kind of uncle of Phil's. And it was Phil's idea that we should live in the cottage.' She could not bear to think that Lieutenant Laity might condemn her for moving into what was virtually Phil's house then throwing him out of it.

It had taken all the money that Adam had left to pay the Thomases to look after Phil and teach him their trade. They had no son of their own and if he proved himself, he would make a good living there, possibly even taking over the family boat in time. But she knew that Adam would have condemned her for her actions. She remembered again his anger when she had suggested the sea as a way of life for Phil.

As if he could read her mind, Lieutenant Laity said, 'It is a much better life for a boy, being in the open air, with other boys his own age.'

'But Mr Trevelyan thought it was too dangerous.'

He laughed. 'Each to his own. I'd never let a son of mine even go down a mine. I would consider that far too dangerous. But the sea – I'd be happy if he chose that. It's always the way. You understand the risks in your own job, and exaggerate those of another's.'

'I suppose so.' Clara felt comforted by his words. If Adam's dislike of the sea had been simply prejudice, then perhaps she hadn't done so badly, apprenticing Phil to a fisherman.

She said tentatively, 'You seem to hold no grudge against Mr Trevelyan?'

He smiled. 'Ladies never understand a man's attitude to his work, and why should they? The truth is, Miss Pentreath, I admired Mr Trevelyan greatly as a man but I have my duty to do. If I catch a man smuggling I must arrest him, whatever my feelings are to him. But, in fact, I never did catch him, could not even identify him as one of the smugglers that night. There is only the evidence of Mr Blacklock and Grenfell against him at the moment.'

Clara was silent. It was wonderful to hear Adam spoken of so admiringly, to meet someone who appreciated his good qualities, but it just made her life seem emptier than ever. No Adam. No father. Just her ever-present responsibilities and worries dragging her down, as even her body seemed to these days.

It was almost a relief when the cottage came into sight around the corner, low, squat, mean – a bitter contrast to the ancient elegance of Penalverne House. In the rising wind, the rocks swung and banged against the rough stone walls. They weighed down the ropes that held the thatch secure against the gales, but their banging was a constant irritation to her nerves, keeping her awake at night and hammering into her head like driven nails during the long, dark days.

She turned again to the Lieutenant. 'I can carry the bucket from here,' she said, reaching out a red, chapped hand. She hoped that he would take the hint but he simply smiled and shook his head.

'I must pay my respects to Lady Susan now that I am here.' He hitched the horse's reins over the gatepost and smiled at her reassuringly. 'I am not one to forget my friends, Miss Pentreath.'

She lifted her head proudly, refusing to let him see how ashamed she was of the humble cottage, of the poverty implicit in every item of rough-hewn furniture.

She forced a welcoming smile. 'My mother will be delighted to see you,' she lied.

With an effort, she pushed open the door, hiding, as she always did, the despair she felt as she entered her only home. Outside, she could forget the claustrophobia of the tiny cottage, her mother's increasingly irrational behaviour, the constant drag of poverty. Indoors, there was no escape.

Lady Susan was slumped in front of the fire as always, her embroidery held slackly in one thin hand. As Clara entered she turned her head, her hair now almost white under the cap she wore, the still fashionable ribbons hiding her sagging jaws.

'Clara. You're here at last.' Her voice was as autocratic and self-assured as ever, strangely vibrant in her shrunken body. 'We must leave at once. Your father will be wondering what has kept us.' She got to her feet, the embroidery dropping unnoticed onto the earthen floor.

Ignoring the Lieutenant's gasp of surprise, Clara hurried forward. 'Look, Mama, a visitor. Lieutenant Laity has come to visit us.'

The Lieutenant came forward, bowing low over the hand that Lady Susan extended. 'I am pleased to see you in such health, madam.' Clara could see no difference in manner from the way he had always acted when he had visited them at Penalverne.

Lady Susan smiled graciously. 'You have only just caught us, Lieutenant. My daughter and I were just on the point of going home.' She threw a meaningful glance at the broad back of Ma Downing, bent over the table where she was kneading bread. 'Poor, but very deserving, you know,' she added in a loud whisper. 'The Earl, my father, always insisted that we should be charitable to the deserving poor.'

The Lieutenant clasped her hand more tightly. 'You are to be honoured for your charity, ma'am. But please sit down. There is no occasion to stand on my account.' He pressed her gently back into the chair and drew up a three-legged stool. 'Very inclement weather for the time of year.'

Clara breathed a sigh of relief, and handed the bucket of milk to Ma Downing. 'I'm sorry.'

The old woman cocked a bright eye at her. 'And for what, my handsome?' She nodded her head at Lady Susan, condescending graciously to the Lieutenant. 'If things were like they are in her head, she'd have a right to talk about me like that. And I'd be grateful for

186

the charity, too.' She grinned toothlessly, slapping and thumping the pallid dough with gusto.

'But things are not like that,' Clara said. She pulled off her bonnet, the once-fashionable brim now limp and shapeless after exposure to the vagaries of the weather. Wearily, she smoothed back her fine hair. 'I am afraid that one day you will take offence and go.' Her voice was a quiet murmur, almost drowned by her mother's stronger tones.

'And what for should I do that?' Ma Downing asked. 'She can't help it, poor lady. It's all gone too fast for her and she's like Tregony band, three scats behind. She don't mean no harm, and I don't take no offence. It's no good growing old if you don't grow wise. And I tell you, Miss Clara,' she nodded fiercely, 'you don't get rid of me that easily. I'm happy as a cock on his own dungheap, here. It'll take more than a poor old lady wandering in her wits to get rid of me, I can tell you.'

Clara reached out and embraced the older woman and was pulled closer in a bearlike hug. Suddenly, Ma Downing stiffened and pushed her away.

'You're putting on a brem bit of weight, young Clara.' Her voice was suddenly sharp, inquisitive.

Clara nodded sheepishly. 'Not like my poor mother. She seems to be getting thinner every day.' She heard a change in the conversation behind her and turned back to the Lieutenant.

'I must be going, Miss Pentreath.' He bowed over Lady Susan's hand. 'It was a pleasure to meet you again, ma'am.'

'Come again, Lieutenant.' Her mother sighed. 'We see so few people since my husband died.'

Clara accompanied the Lieutenant to the door. Pulling it closed behind her she said, 'You need not return again, Lieutenant. As you can see, we don't live in the style any more where we can make visitors welcome. And to be honest with you,' her green eyes glanced meaningfully at the low cottage behind her, 'I doubt if my mother will remember that you have been here for more than a few minutes.'

He took her roughened hand in his strong brown ones. 'Miss Pentreath.' His voice was soft, throbbing. 'I must tell you that I have the greatest admiration for what you are doing. There can be few young ladies who would carry on so bravely under such a reverse. And without even a mother to help you!'

Clara bit her lip to stop it trembling. His kindness was suddenly more than she could bear. 'Thank you, Lieutenant, but you are too kind. I am only doing what I have to; there is no merit in that.'

'But you have so many responsibilities,' he insisted. 'Your mother, that old woman, even young Phil.' He squeezed her hand. 'Your father would have been proud of you.'

She turned away, her eyes filling with tears at the mention of his name. She missed him more than she would ever have guessed, his wisdom, his laugh, his confidence. If he had still been alive, even life in this cottage would have been bearable – an adventure instead of a burden that dragged at her weary shoulders day and night.

She could feel the Lieutenant's eyes upon her but she could not meet them. The loss his words had evoked was too strong, too raw.

He said hesitantly, 'I hardly like to mention the matter to a lady, but thinking of your father has just reminded me that I have been negligent.'

She forced herself to turn back and face him with tolerable self-control. 'Really, Lieutenant? I can't believe that.'

He thrust a hand into his pocket. 'The fact is, Miss Pentreath, just before your father died, we had a small bet. He won it, but I am afraid that I completely forgot about it in the tragedy of his death.'

A dreadful suspicion rose in Clara's mind but she tried to speak naturally. 'Fancy. And may I ask what you were betting on?'

For a moment he looked embarrassed, then he laughed. 'Actually, Miss Pentreath, it was a horse race.'

'And how much did he win?' Her voice was cool and controlled, giving no sign of the emotions that boiled within her.

'Twen – er, fifty guineas.'

She stared up at him, noticing the way he had to force himself to meet her eyes. He said awkwardly, 'I have only just remembered it. I don't have the money on me at the moment, but if you will allow me, I will bring it to you tomorrow.'

Her green eyes were enormous, unblinking, and when she spoke her voice was soft. 'No, Lieutenant.'

He stared down at her, startled. 'I – I beg your pardon?'

'I said "No", Lieutenant.' A small, humourless smile played for a second around her lips. 'I meant,' she explained, 'that I will not allow you to bring it to me tomorrow.'

His face reddened. 'I can let you have some now.' He took his hand from his pocket and extended it. Golden guineas winked and glittered in the thin winter sunshine. How much was there? Five guineas? Seven? More than she had in the house. By itself, enough to see her and her mother safely through the winter.

For a second her resolution failed her at the sight of the desperately needed coins. Then she rallied.

'I am afraid that you have misunderstood me,' she said quietly.

He shifted guiltily under her steady gaze. 'M – misunderstood you?'

Her anger was a spear of white lightning. 'Yes, misunderstood me, Lieutenant.' Her voice was a whiplash, her green eyes blazing. 'I may be living in reduced circumstances, but I am not a charity case. I do not need, nor do I expect, to be given money by those I once considered my equals.' Her voice throbbed with passion.

His colour mounted, but he argued staunchly, 'This isn't charity. It belonged to your father and now it belongs to you.'

She shook her head. 'No, Lieutenant, it belongs to *you*.' Her lips twisted into a parody of a smile. 'You see, Lieutenant, my father believed that horse sense was what stopped horses betting on men. He would bet on many things, but only where he could use his judgement and thought he had a good chance of winning. Pugilism, for example.' She paused, then said with finality: 'He *never* bet on horses.'

Their eyes locked for several seconds, then the Lieutenant bowed. 'Forgive me, Miss Pentreath.'

'There is nothing to forgive, Lieutenant,' she said softly. 'But I think it would be better if you did not visit us again. We – we are no longer part of your world and it will be easier for us if we are not constantly reminded of the fact.'

He bowed his acquiescence. 'But I may speak to you when I meet you by the way?'

Clara nodded silently, and watched as he mounted and rode out of sight, then she slumped back against the wall of the house, her hands pressed over her eyes.

Oh, how she had wanted that money! Her need had been a physical hunger. The sight of the coins had almost made her mouth water. But she had refused them.

Was this how Adam had felt, she wondered, when he threw back the hundred guineas he had won? Had he experienced this burning need for money? It wasn't for herself that she hungered after it, dreamed of it at night. It was for her mother.

Lady Susan's grasp on reality was weaker every day. How long would it be before she lost it for ever? Clara drew breath in a deep, sobbing sigh. And how long would her mother's body hold out, once her mind had gone? She was looking older, thinner, frailer every day. At this rate she would not survive the winter.

Suddenly, the thought of returning to the dark, claustrophobic cottage was unbearable. Anything was better than that. She just wanted to be out of it all, away from the constant demands of her mother, the never-ending presence of Ma Downing.

Swiftly, Clara peered through the door. 'I am taking the laundry down to wash it,' she called out to Ma Downing. 'Look after my mother, please, while I'm gone.' She reached in and grabbed the heavy flasket, hefting it awkwardly in her arms. Washing might be cold and hard work, but it would give her a couple of hours of peace, hours which she could use to try to discover a way out of her troubles.

Chapter 23

In the cold morning air, steam writhed and billowed above the pool where the waste hot water from the Wheal Carcy pumping engine collected. It was a favourite place for miners' wives to do their washing but the cold wind that whistled up the zawn had, today, discouraged all except one lone woman, her black head bent over strong red hands as she pummelled the heavy, wet linen.

Clara grimaced. She had wanted so much to be alone, to be away from the pressures of other people's personalities, their constant chatter and the need to respond to them with politeness. Laity's offer of money had shocked her to the core, brought home to her the depths to which she had sunk.

She felt as if she had stepped onto a slippery slope. Everything had happened so quickly. Battered mentally and physically by the shock of her father's death, she had had no chance to stand back and examine the way her life was going. It had been all she could do to cope with each day as it came, accepting Phil's offer of the cottage with gratitude, throwing herself into the never ending tasks that living without servants seemed to necessitate.

Now, suddenly, she had seen herself through the eyes of another. Distressed gentlefolk! Her lips curled in derision. Another year of this life, she realised suddenly, and no one would even be able to recognise that she had once been a lady.

And what of her mother? Clara had provided her with food and shelter, but was that really enough? Should she, for her mother's sake, accept Edward's offer? Every instinct in her body cried out against it, but she realised suddenly that she had to decide. Time was running out. Her mother's life and sanity were at risk.

'Oh, Adam,' she breathed as she dropped the heavy wicker flasket onto the damp earth that surrounded the pool. If only she could hear from him, if only he were still alive! She dragged her thoughts away

191

from a vision of him, coming back, rescuing her, taking all her troubles onto his broad shoulders. She was the only one who could solve these problems. She pulled a heavy petticoat out of the flasket and dumped it into the water, enjoying a brief moment of physical pleasure as the hot water warmed her chilled hands.

'You needn't go and stir all the dirt up.' The sharp voice brought her head up, swiftly. The other woman was staring angrily at her across the small pool. 'Just because you think you're better'n we, you've no call to ruin our clothes. I've as much right to be here as you have.'

The black hair and rosy cheeks were familiar. Clara racked her brains to place the face. A bal-maiden – that was it – a bal-maiden at Wheal Susan, and, it came to her suddenly, the sister of the man Adam had escaped with.

'It's Miss Willcock, isn't it?' A sudden hope flooded through her. 'Have – have you heard from your brother?' Just one word about Adam, she prayed, just one word to say he is well, is still alive.

'What's it to you?' Molly demanded. 'Going to run blabbing to the Navy man of yours, are you? I saw you up-long, just now, talking to him, thick as thieves.'

'No, of course not.' Clara fought down the anger she could feel rising inside her at the unfair accusation. But she could not tell this woman the part she had played in helping the men escape, and there was just a chance that she knew something about their whereabouts.

She lowered her head so that Molly would not see the tension in her face, rubbing at the cotton with the coarse yellow soap that gritted uncomfortably under her fingers. 'I thought that you might have heard something from them, either of them,' she added, realising suddenly that the brother might be illiterate.

Molly gave a coarse laugh. 'It's not my brother you care about, is it? It's Adam.' Her voice rose in pitch. 'Your fancy man. Smiling at him, leading him on with your la-di-dah ways, visiting him at all hours.'

Her bold blue eyes swept Clara from head to foot, lingered on the bonnet, softened and misshapen by months of wind and rain, the mud-bedraggled hem of her skirt, the once-white hands now red with the cold and the action of washing.

She snorted. 'He wouldn't be so taken if he could see you now, would he? Just like one of us you are now. But what good is that to me? He were my man, he was, and you took him from me.' Her voice broke on a sob. 'I could have made him happy. We could have been wed on the money he were making at the mine, but no, you had to

192

come along, all sheep's eyes and soft talking, turning his head, giving him ideas.'

Tears stood in her eyes as she suddenly wailed, 'We could have bin brem happy but for you.'

Clara felt herself grow cold and a bitter bile rose in her throat. Adam had courted this common, loud female? She noticed for the first time, beneath the well-worn skirts and thin shawl, that the girl had a well-developed figure, that her face, if common, was attractive, the bold eyes a brilliant startling blue under her black hair. Even in her present state, she exuded an animal magnetism.

It had never occurred to Clara that Adam had had other women friends. He was the first man in her life, and he had seemed so superior to the common run of miners that she had assumed that he held himself aloof from them. Instead, he had gone out with this girl, even, if she was telling the truth, thought about marrying her!

She remembered again the times she and Adam had spent together, so few, so short. They had seemed so open and honest with each other, heart speaking to heart. And all the time, there had been vast parts of his life he had kept hidden from her; he had never even let her see that they existed.

Their last night together flashed irresistibly before her eyes. It had been so meaningful for her, so wonderful. But what had it meant to him? Had he been just a common man taking advantage of a young woman, knowing that he was going away, that there would be no come-back? And how many other women had Adam taken on the high cliffs, under the canopy of stars? This one? Others?

Only pride kept the sudden tears at bay. Only a lifetime of training enabled her to rise to her feet and face her persecutor, back straight, head high.

'Don't be ridiculous.' Her voice was crisp, incisive. 'Adam Trevelyan was a free man. If he did not marry you it was because he did not wish to marry you.' And she let her disdain show on her face as she eyed the girl standing before her.

Molly's hands clenched. 'You think yourself so high and mighty. Well, so you might have been once. But not now. Now you're just like the rest of us. If he could see us now, Adam wouldn't look twice at you! You know nothing about making a home for a working man or comforting him after a long core underground.'

Clara gritted her teeth. 'Then you have nothing to worry about,' she snapped. 'If Adam ever comes back, he'll marry *you*. And personally, I shall dance at your wedding.' Head high, her face white, she stared proudly at Molly, praying that her tears would not flow, that the girl would not see her distress.

'Wedding!' Molly's voice rose to an unladylike shriek. 'There'll be no wedding! Don't you understand? Ain't you got no eyes?'

She pressed her skirts back against her body, outlining the smooth curve of her stomach from waist to thighs. 'Can't you see?' Tears were streaming down her cheeks. 'Well, you're the only one that can't! I'm pregnant, you stupid fool, pregnant! And I haven't got no man!'

The earth seemed suddenly insubstantial, as if at any moment it would float from under her feet. Clara fought for breath, trying to hide the shock and dismay she felt, trying to act as if her world hadn't suddenly fallen upside-down.

'Are you sure?' The words were out before she could stop them and she cursed herself for her stupidity, but Molly seemed to take them at face value.

'Course I'm sure,' she said truculently. 'You must think I'm brem stupid! I've had it all, sickness in the morning, my courses stopped, this.' She patted her stomach. 'I'm going to have a child right enough. And me without a man, I'm at my wit's end!'

Clara sat down suddenly on the hard earth, her head reeling. The litany of symptoms rang through her head. Sickness, monthly courses stopped, the growing stomach. She dropped her head into her hands, cursing herself for a stupid fool. Why hadn't she seen? How could she have been so blind?

But it had all seemed so reasonable. The changes in her life, the pressures she was under, surely it had been no wonder that her courses had dried up? And the sickness? She grimaced again as she remembered the first weeks at the cottage, the constant stench of the pig, until Ma Downing killed it for the feast day, as was traditional. The sight of raw meat – anyone would have been sick, surely? Any delicately reared lady?

And what if she had let her corsets out? She wasn't used to carrying heavy weights. Her muscles had grown. And as she no longer had a maid to lace her tight, as had happened in the old days, it was only to be expected that her waist would grow larger.

But she knew! Whatever her mind said, she could feel her body acknowledging the truth she was trying to deny, accepting the inevitability of a suddenly altered future. Inside her, unknown, unsuspected, Adam's baby was growing.

The bile rose suddenly in her throat and she retched, her body shaken by the spasms. To her surprise, she felt an arm around her shoulders, a hand supporting her forehead. 'Here,' Molly's voice was less sharp, concerned. 'Don't you take on so! It's me that's having the baby.'

She retched again, spewing up the remains of the Sky Blue and Sinker that she had once disdained and now ate hungrily every morning. The very thought of her pregnancy distressed her. With an effort she pushed herself upright, wiping her mouth with a lacy handkerchief, whose silken softness mocked her present state.

Molly sat back on her heels. 'What's the matter? Didn't you know about having a child?'

Clara wiped the mingled sweat and tears with the back of her hand. 'I – I suppose so. We'd discussed it at school when the teachers weren't around.' She stopped, the memory of that innocent time suddenly heartbreakingly poignant.

'But you must have seen other women,' Molly insisted. 'You had enough servants at your house.'

Clara shook her head. Any maid who found herself pregnant would have been dismissed instantly, as soon as her mother's sharp eyes had noticed it. She found herself breathing an unexpected thank you for her mother's present state. If she found out about Clara's condition it would kill her.

But Ma Downing had known, she realised suddenly, remembering the old woman's remark about 'putting on weight' and her sharp glance. At least she had one woman she could turn to.

But she wasn't the only one with problems. With an effort she turned back to Molly. 'What are you going to do?'

Molly shrugged. 'What can I do? I tried to get rid of it, but nothing worked. I could go away and have it, but what then? What is there for someone like me to do? All I do know is spalling tin, and round here, all the mines are closing down. They won't take on a woman with a bastard if they've got other women to choose from. I'd just end up on the streets, selling myself for the price of a night's lodgings and a glass of gin.'

'So you're going to stay on here?' Clara could scarcely get the words out. The thought of seeing this woman around, of seeing, in time, Adam's child by another woman, made her want to vomit again.

Molly shrugged. 'The old besoms round here are pointing at me and chattering, but they're my kind. They won't let me starve.' Her pretty face grew hard for a moment. 'Just make me pay for my mistake every minute of every day for the rest of my life.' She kicked angrily at a stone, sending it into the pool and they both ducked as the hot water splashed high into their faces. 'If only I could get him to marry me!'

Clara bit back her hurt. 'There's no chance of that,' she said curtly. 'Even if he's still in the country, he couldn't come back. Not with the Preventatives after him. And besides, no one even knows where he is.'

Molly stared at her. 'Don't know where he is? 'Course I do!'

Despite herself, Clara felt joy flooding through her. 'You know where Adam is?'

The blue eyes stared down at her. 'Daft as a brush, you are. 'Course I don't know! But it isn't Adam who's the father, it's Sam Grenfell. And the bastard refuses to marry me.'

Relief made Clara suddenly weak. She had to bow her head to hide the tide of colour that washed over her face. 'Grenfell!' Her voice was suddenly vibrant, her lips trembled. She let out her breath with a gasp.

'Grenfell,' Molly confirmed, her face dark with fury. 'He takes me out, gets me drunk as a lord on what he calls "The Doctor".' She snorted. 'Doctor! I'll doctor him if I ever gets the chance. He's been brem bad to me.'

'But do you want to marry him?' Clara queried, struck by the girl's anger. 'If you feel like that about him – well,' she stammered, realising the awkwardness of her comment, 'I mean, after A – Adam, he's, er, not much of a man.'

How could anyone who had gone out with Adam ever walk out with Grenfell? She could not imagine. She compared his thin frame and receding hair with Adam's muscular body, and had to bite her lip to keep back the moan of anguish that suddenly rose in her throat.

To her relief, Molly did not take her comments amiss. 'Well, he's one of Pharaoh's lean kind,' she admitted and gave a short laugh. 'Looks like two hellen clapped together, if truth be known,' and, seeing Clara's mystified expression, she translated. 'Slates, if you like. He's no thicker than two slates put together. Especially when you get his shirt off. And no great shakes as a lover either. But any man's better'n none when you're in my shoes.'

Clara felt herself blush at the woman's outspokenness. 'Surely he must know that he's the father?'

''Course he do know! Clunking like a toad, he was, when I told him about it, his Adam's apple bobbin up and down like a pump beam. But he's gentry, near enough, and I'm common. There's no way he'll wed me.' Her eyes filled with tears. 'He has all the fun, and I do all the paying! My life and soul, 'tis a brem unfair life!'

Clara said impulsively, 'I'll help you if I can.'

Molly stared down at her, disbelief in her eyes. 'You? What can you do? You're like me now. No money, no friends, no good!' The old antagonism was back in her face, the brief moment of sisterhood forgotten. With jerky movements, she leaned over and piled her wet washing into her elderly flasket. 'You look after your own problems, miss. Seems to me, you've got enough of 'em.' And with a flounce of her head she heaved the heavy basket off the ground and stalked off.

You're like me now! Thank God Molly didn't know just how true that was, Clara thought, bending again to her washing. But she would know soon enough – so would everyone. And they would all despise her.

A fallen woman! She had heard the phrase, used it herself, but had never thought that she would be one. Molly's bleak résumé of the options open to her rang in Clara's ears. But Molly had chosen the one course that was not open to her. She had no friends in the village. She was an outsider, a pariah. Neither villagers nor gentry would help her once her condition became known.

And there was her mother. Even in her present confused state, she had times of rationality. It wouldn't be long before she realised what had happened. With her haughty ideas of the behaviour to be expected from the grand-daughter of an earl and their present lowly status, the knowledge could kill her.

Clara dragged the wet clothes from the pool, wringing them between her hands, grimacing at the now familiar spurt of pain in her elbows that the action set up. She had never realised before how wearing on the body was the unrelenting toil of a common person. Then she lifted the flasket and set off on the long trudge uphill to the cottage.

Lost in her worries, she scarcely noticed the damp from the clothes dripping onto her skirts, the chafing of her legs against the wet material. She had to do something. But what? Even marriage to Edward was no longer an option. He would hardly take her, knowing that she was carrying Adam's child, and in common decency she would have to tell him.

As she approached the cottage, the door opened and Ma Downing poked her head out. 'Your ma is wanting you. Fretting something awful, she is.'

Clara nodded. 'In a minute. But I have something to say to you first. In private,' she added, casting a glance at the small cottage.

Ma sighed and came out. 'Be quick, then. The Lord knows it's cold as Pharaoh's heart out here.'

Clara took her courage in both hands. 'I'm going to have a baby.' She kept her eyes fastened on the woman's face, alert for the smallest expression.

Ma Downing nodded. 'I've thought that for a long time, and I knew it today when I felt your belly. Near five months gone, I reckon.'

Clara nodded. 'About that.' Her throat was tight with unshed tears.

'And it's that there Adam's, I'll put money on it.' Ma Downing read the answer in her face. 'Well, I can't say I'm happy for you. 'Tis a sore trouble to a woman at the best of times, and having no man don't make it no easier. But there 'tis and couldn't be 'tisser. Naught you can do about it now but grin and bear it.'

Clara swallowed the lump in her throat. She knew that she should be grateful for the old woman's matter-of-fact attitude. Any sympathy and she would lose all her self-control, throw herself wailing into Ma Downing's arms, pour out all her fear and her distress. But what good would that do? It was her problem, her life. She had no right to burden other people with her problems.

'Ma,' she hesitated for a moment, afraid of the answer. 'You will stay with us? This won't make you leave?'

The old woman gave a laugh that shook her chins, sending her pendulous breasts quivering. 'Leave? Why should I do that?' She looked around at the small cottage, the lime-washed walls glimmering white in the dull December light, the low, thatched roof. ''Tis better than being on the Parish, my handsome. Ess! And better than being on the road! If you want me to go, you'll have to prise me out with a shoe-horn, I reckon.'

Clara gripped her hands together. 'And after – you know, after the baby is here . . .' She took a deep breath. 'Will you stay and look after the baby – if I leave and get work? I'll send you money,' she added quickly.

The old woman looked at her shrewdly. 'What do you want to go away for? This here is your home.'

'But I can't get work here,' Clara said desperately. 'And if I take the baby with me, I won't get a job anyway. Not as a teacher or a governess, and they're probably the only jobs I'm qualified for.' A sudden mocking gleam lit up her face, a smile which she had not given for many months. 'I may not look it now, but I am well-educated.'

'I never doubted it for one minute,' Ma Downing said stoutly. 'It fair mazes me the way you can read all them old books of Adam's. All them black marks creeping across the page, just like the tracks of a padji-paws on cream.'

Clara closed her eyes. For a second her old life appeared before her. The table laid for dinner, the multitude of dishes. And always, on the jelly, the marks of the newts that had crawled across the jellies when they had been put in the coolness of the well to set.

With an effort, she brought herself back to the present. 'But please, will you look after the baby?' A quavering voice called fretfully from the cottage and Clara glanced quickly at the door. 'I know you

198

wouldn't be able to handle both a baby and my mother, but I have a plan for her.'

Ma Downing nodded cheerfully. 'I'll do it, my lamb. Never you bother.'

The voice called again from the cottage, more irritably this time. 'Clara? Clara! Where are you? I want you this minute.'

'It's your ma,' said the old woman. 'You'd better go in. She's as restless as a toad on a hot shovel.'

Clara nodded, moving towards the door. Ma stopped her, laying a not-unkind hand on her shoulder. 'I'm brem glad you told me, maid. A trouble shared is a trouble halved, and I'll do what I can for you. But one thing I *do* know,' she added forthrightly. 'It went in a lot easier than it'll come out.'

Clara blushed, then gave her a quick peck on the cheek as she hurried past her to Lady Susan.

Her mother glanced up as she entered the cottage. 'There you are, Clara. At last! I've been calling you this half-hour or more. We must hurry home. I am expecting the Earl, my father, at any moment, you know. It would be a poor welcome if we were not there when he arrives.'

As her mother's thin body thrust itself from the chair, Clara hurried over and took her arm. 'Soon, Mama, we will leave soon. But I have something to say to Ma Downing first. Why don't you sit down while you are waiting?' She picked up the embroidery and placed it in her mother's hand. 'You can do your needlework. I won't be long.'

Her mother took it listlessly, turning the material over and over in her thin hands. She never set a stitch these days, and in any case, the light in the room was too poor for such close work, but the familiar feel of the needlework calmed her.

Clara knelt by the chair and stroked her mother gently on the cheek. 'I'll look after you, Mama,' she promised.

A faint spark of awareness awoke for a second in her mother's clouded eyes. She reached out a trembling hand for her daughter, pulling her closer. 'I don't like it here, Clara.' Her voice was tremulous and Clara had to lean closer to make out the words. 'I want to go away from here. I want to go home.'

Clara felt her eyes prickle with unshed tears. Something had to be done. 'You will, Mama,' she promised fervently. 'You will.'

Chapter 24

'Sweet lovers love . . . the spring!'

Isabelle Kingsley played the last few notes of the song, her long fingers lingering on the piano keys, then smiled up at Edward Blacklock. He looked so handsome, leaning over the piano to sing while he accompanied her in the song; his evening clothes perfectly fitted his elegant figure, and his golden hair was very attractive in the candlelight.

She knew that she was looking her best. This room itself might have been designed to show her off like a piece of jewellery in a case, for the rich red drapes at the windows and covering the top of the grand piano were a dramatic foil to her white skin and dark hair. Surely Edward Blacklock must appreciate her, seeing her in these surroundings.

'Bravo, Miss Kingsley!' Lieutenant Laity clapped his hands enthusiastically. 'That was wonderful. Your daughter is very musical, Mrs Kingsley.' He bowed to the lady sitting quietly by the fire, her proud eyes never leaving her daughter's face. 'And the voices blend so well together.'

Isabelle let her lids drop modestly down, hiding the pleasure that she felt. Dear Laity! He always said exactly the right thing. She bowed gracefully to Edward across the piano. 'It is all due to Mr Blacklock. His voice is particularly pleasant.' Then she ran one white hand across the keyboard in a soft *glissando* so that he could admire her slender fingers.

Isabelle was aware that she was looking particularly charming tonight. The blue of her dress, unusually dark for a young girl, emphasised the colour of her eyes until they glowed almost sapphire in the soft candlelight.

Not that she was so young any more. She could feel panic rising within her at the thought and her brow contracted automatically in a frown, which she hastily smoothed out. She was twenty-four now. No longer a young debutante. It was time, and past time, that she should have found a husband.

If only Edward had proposed before Clara Pentreath had arrived back from school. Isabelle had been so certain of his affections and, after all, who else could he marry in this area? Without being conceited, she had always known that she was the most attractive girl around, and one of the richest.

And Edward had seemed so attentive. Not over-eager, but then, he was a gentleman, and one expected even courtship to be conducted with propriety. It had seemed pre-ordained.

Until Clara Pentreath came along . . . Isabelle played another *glissando*, louder and faster this time. Clara seemed to have bewitched him, though it was hard to understand why. She was a dab of a girl, hardly came up to Edward's shoulder, and with that strange hair, so fine and pale as to be almost colourless. What could he have seen in her? She didn't even act like a lady sometimes, laughing with the men and joining in their conversation as if she were a young man herself. Yet they seemed to like it, had never turned from her to Isabelle, sitting elegantly beside them, behaving with perfect decorum.

She glanced up at Edward where he leaned on the piano top, giving him the full benefit of her huge, dark eyes. 'I hope that you are not finding the business of being an executor too arduous? It must take up a great deal of your time, especially considering the poor state in which Captain Pentreath left his affairs.'

'Not too arduous.' His voice was abrupt, his grey eyes expressionless. Surely he didn't still harbour a *tendre* for the daughter of a bankrupt? And he a banker and smelter!

Lieutenant Laity wandered over from his seat by the fire. 'I happened to meet Miss Pentreath this morning,' he remarked. His eyes were on Edward Blacklock as he spoke. 'I thought she looked very ill, and her mother does not seem to have recovered at all from the shock of her husband's death.'

Edward grunted unsympathetically. 'Lady Susan has never recovered from the shock of marrying a commoner. She is one of those people who always seem to think that the past was better than the present.'

'And you don't think that in this case she might be correct?' Laity raised interrogative eyebrows. 'Any gently-born woman would find it a strain, living in a miner's cottage like the one I saw. And for the daughter of an earl, it must surely be even more difficult.'

Edward stared aggressively at the other man. 'What are you

201

suggesting, Lieutenant? That I am not carrying out my duties as a trustee correctly? Let me assure you, what I am administering is not so much Captain Pentreath's assets as his debts. If the truth were known, I have lost more than I care to reckon on his death.'

'And Miss Pentreath has no assets at all?' the Lieutenant persisted.

'The controlling interest in a worthless mine. I would sell that if I could, but there are no buyers.'

The Lieutenant's glance did not waver. 'I have heard rumours,' he said tentatively, 'that just before the Captain died, a new, rich lode of tin was found.'

Edward laughed, throwing back his head. 'And you will find that rumour going round about every mine that has ever closed down, especially once it is flooded and the truth cannot be checked.' His grey eyes flicked contemptuously across the Lieutenant's face. 'You will never make a businessman, Lieutenant, if you cannot learn the difference between hard fact and wishful thinking.'

Isabelle broke in swiftly. 'But it is sad that Lady Susan and her daughter are reduced to such poverty.' She smiled as the two men turned to her, pleased to have captured their attention. 'Surely something can be done? Cannot the Earl be informed? He would assuredly not allow his daughter and grand-daughter to live in such reduced circumstances.'

Edward said calmly, 'It is like you to be so concerned for another, my dear Miss Kingsley, but you are judging by your own sweetness of temper.' Despite the compliment, his grey eyes passed over her as if he could not see her. 'Mr Brightman, the solicitor, has already contacted the Earl. The reply, from his man of affairs, was that the Earl had thrown off his daughter on her marriage and that she was no longer any concern of his.'

Isabelle gasped. 'But that is appalling, unnatural.' She turned to the two men. 'Surely something can be done to help the poor lady?' Her blue eyes were opened to their widest.

'Perhaps if *you* were to contact the Earl, Mr Blacklock, he would not be able to refuse you?' She did not have to pretend to the earnestness she projected. If the Earl were to remove his daughter then Clara would go too. And with her out of the way, Isabelle had no doubt of her ability to bring the desirable Edward Blacklock to hand.

Lieutenant Laity said warmly, 'Miss Kingsley is, as always, as charitable as she is lovely. Surely a personal application could not fail to move the Earl's heart?'

'If Lady Susan were to appear in person,' Edward replied calmly, 'it would not move him. He is as proud as the Devil and boasts that once he has made up his mind nothing will move him.'

202

He shifted slightly, his grey eyes expressionless, one finger reaching automatically to stroke his golden moustache. 'And I would remind you, Lieutenant,' he added coldly, 'that I am the trustee of Miss Pentreath's estate. I can assure you that I have carried out my duties to the letter and any court of law in the land would support me on that. There is no occasion for anyone else to interest themselves in her affairs. Do I make myself clear?'

Lieutenant Laity bowed slightly, his face unreadable.

Edward Blacklock went on: 'Miss Pentreath and I understand each other perfectly. She already knows that there is a remedy for her present situation. Whenever she cares to accept it.'

Isabelle's eyes widened involuntarily with shock. What remedy was that? she wondered, her heart sinking. Edward couldn't, he just couldn't, mean to marry Clara . . . Or could he?

And if he did, what would become of her? Was she destined to sink into spinsterhood, at the beck and call of her parents? All her looks and hard-earned accomplishments were wasted on the half-gentlemen that populated this distant part of England. She couldn't bear it! She felt the panic rise again in her throat, her corset suddenly hampering her breathing. That must not happen. She could not allow that to happen!

Her fingers clenched involuntarily on the keyboard and the discordant note echoed loudly through the room breaking the tension that she could feel between the two men and waking her mother with a start.

'Perhaps,' she suggested, her voice sounding strained in the sudden quietness, 'we could sing another song.' She turned to Laity and gave him her most winning smile. 'Can you sing, Lieutenant?'

'I'll have to drop you 'ere, miss. I don't go no nearer.'

Clara peered through the driving snow that weighed down her long, dark lashes. They were in country that was strange to her. Here, tall trees surrounded the narrow Cornish road and gateposts, topped with stone pineapples signifying hospitality, loomed in the gathering darkness.

The driver pointed his whip at the dimly-seen path that led through the gateway to disappear under the shadow of the trees. 'It's down there, miss. One of the side gates to Trevival.' He looked at her curiously. 'You *are* expected, aren't you? Only the old Earl can't abide beggars.' He caught the flash of her emerald eyes and hastily backed down. 'Begging your pardon, Miss.'

'He will see me.' She tossed the few coins she had promised him into his lap, too angry to argue.

She had burned her boats, she knew that, had burned them in Camborne when she had sold her mother's betrothal ring, their last valuable possession, for money to complete the journey. She had got them both here. If the old Earl refused to help, she knew that she had barely enough money to travel home again, not even using the slow, cheap waggons that crawled between one town and the next, their canvas roof and sides doing nothing to protect their passengers in the freezing weather.

Gently, she shook her mother awake. The older woman was slumped between the driver and herself. The long journey from Penzance had been hard on her. At first she had been angry, obstreperous, amusing the other passengers by demanding in her loud, well-bred voice why they weren't using their own carriage? Why Hugh Pentreath wasn't there to help them? But, as the long hours passed, she had sunk into an apathetic stupor, scarcely rousing when they stopped at the small towns along the way.

Only in Bodmin had Lady Susan seemed aware of her surroundings, recalled by the scenes of her youth. She had exclaimed at the changes, the gas-lights in the shop windows, the new fashions, the paving stones where she remembered seas of mud. For a brief hour, she reminded Clara of the woman she had once known, her faded eyes brighter, her shrunken body once again upright and vigorous.

But this final journey, on an open cart in the driving snow, had broken her slim grasp on reality. Now, she mumbled and complained, almost too stiff with cold and lack of movement to keep her feet as Clara helped her down from the cart.

Clara waited until the farmer had driven out of sight in the swiftly deepening gloom, before she crouched by her mother in the snow, pulling her bonnet straight and wrapping her cloak more tightly around her as if she were a child.

'We're at Trevival, Mama. Do you understand? Trevival. Where you used to live.'

'Trevival. Home.' Animation shone briefly in her mother's lack-lustre eye.

'Yes, home, Mama. I'm taking you to see your father.' And pray God he's home and that he will see us, she added fervently to herself.

She could not believe that once he saw his daughter, the Earl of Bodmin would refuse to take her in. If the driver of the cart thought that they were beggars, if as slight a friend as Lieutenant Laity were moved to offer them money, then surely that old man's heart would be softened by the sight of his daughter's plight.

It was for that reason that she had gambled with the last of her money to get her mother and herself to this lonely spot, six miles outside Bodmin town. Her grandfather had not been softened by her father's pleas or the visit of his solicitor. Clara had doubted whether he would respond to a letter from herself, however she pleaded with him in it. But the sight of his youngest daughter, destitute, her mind wandering – surely he would not be able to refuse to succour her in that situation?

And it was her mother's situation that concerned her. Clara knew that it would not be long before everyone could see the evidence of her pregnancy, and once that happened she would be shunned by polite society. But her mother must not suffer for her action.

She shook her mother slightly again, trying to bring her back to reality. The driver had told her that she was still a mile from the house. It was impossible for her to drag her mother that far; she had to find a way to energise the woman, interest her enough to make the effort to walk the distance herself.

'Look around you, Mama.' Clara instilled all the enthusiasm, all the energy she could into her voice. 'Do you recognise where we are?'

Her mother's head turned slowly, blindly, as if she were almost beyond the reach of Clara's urgings, then her eyes focused on the pillars. A smile, the smile of a young woman, trembled for a second on her lips. 'We're home!' There was a note of joy in her voice that Clara had never heard before. 'We're home, Clara!'

'Yes. Home.' Clara shook her lightly again to make her attend. 'But we are a long way from the house, Mama. We have to walk.'

Her mother raised her head haughtily, a travesty of the imperious young girl she had once been. 'Send a servant for the carriage, Clara. It's too far.'

'The carriage can't get here because of the snow, Mama.' Clara spoke distinctly, authoritatively, pitching her voice above the whine of the icy wind. 'You have to walk. But once we're there you'll be safe, won't you? Safe and warm.'

Let it be true, God, she begged as she took her mother's arm and led her into the teeth of the wind. If her grandfather were not there, if he refused to take them in, Clara doubted if her mother's sanity or her health would stand the shock.

Clara gritted her teeth. Why did this have to be the worst winter in memory? Why, just for once, couldn't things work out for her? She was doing her best. As it was, she stood alone against the world, the responsibilities for three other lives resting heavily on her shoulders. Surely she deserved some help from on high?

The drive was lined with trees that cut out the pale light of the winter's dusk, making the pathway glimmer with a ghostly luminescence. The snow hid the unevenness of the ground, so that Clara's

205

feet, throbbing with cold, stumbled and slipped at every step. Her heavy skirt was soon weighed down with the mud and snow that clung to the hem, making every step an effort, chafing painfully against her icy legs.

It was no wonder her mother had sunk into a dull lethargy, Clara thought, supporting her as best she could as the wind gusted erratically from all points of the compass. It caught at their skirts like sails, so that they staggered drunkenly together under its buffeting. It snatched the breath from their mouths and blinded their eyes, while above, the trees groaned and roared, unseen against the pitch-black sky.

A mile. Only a mile. A twenty-minute walk on a good day. But not today, not in these conditions. Her mother sagged against Clara more heavily as all light faded from the world.

The snow settled on her face like a veil, filling her mouth as she shouted encouragement at her mother, urging her to make one more effort, just one more. That they would soon be there, with warmth and shelter waiting for them, just a bit further on, just a little bit further. But each time, her mother's response was more feeble, her weight on Clara's shoulder leaden now.

If only she could sit down, Clara thought, gasping with the effort, the cold air burning in her lungs. Just for a minute. Just to ease her arms and her back. But she dared not. If she stopped, if her mother sank further into her apathetic stupor, there would be no hope for either of them. They had to keep moving.

When she caught her first glimpse of the house, it seemed a mirage. Dim lights gleamed in the darkness, mysteriously high. It was several seconds before she realised that she was seeing the lights in the upper windows of a tall building, itself invisible against the blackness of the night.

'See, Mama? We're here!' But the older woman did not raise her head, simply staggered blindly forward, one step after another as Clara guided her round the sweep of the drive until she could see the front steps, half-hidden by the snow, rising at her feet.

She hauled urgently on the iron bell-pull, one arm still supporting her mother. They must really look like beggars now, she thought. Wet, filthy, exhausted. The appalled expression on the butler's face when he opened the door confirmed this.

Clara straightened herself automatically, her voice, thank heavens, springing clear and bell-like through her frozen lips. 'Please inform the Earl that Lady Susan Pentreath and Miss Pentreath are here to see him.'

He hesitated, worried by the contrast between their appearance and the younger woman's well-bred voice and autocratic manner. Clara raised her brows, her emerald eyes flashing. 'At once, if you please.'

She saw him recognise the quality of a lady. He backed away, bowing, and she stepped for the first time over the threshold of her grandfather's house, almost lifting her mother with her.

'If you will wait here, Miss Pentreath.' The butler was obviously not sure enough of their status to show them into a comfortable private room, but what did it matter? After the conditions outside, even the entrance hall, its black and white squared floor and panelled walls offering no extra comfort, seemed like heaven.

Carefully, she lowered her mother onto one of the carved wooden chairs that stood against the walls. 'Mama. Mama!'

Lady Susan's head fell forward. Exhaustion – or mental withdrawal? Clara did not know, but her mother would be quite unable to help her in the forthcoming interview. Clara chafed the cold, unresponsive hands, trying to stifle the nervousness that rose inside her.

She had to persuade her grandfather to give shelter to Lady Susan. Whatever it cost her in dented pride, she *had* to humble herself for her mother's sake. With Lady Susan in safe hands and Phil settled in Mousehole, Clara knew that she could cope alone. After the baby was born she could find work – as a governess, even as a school teacher, somewhere outside Cornwall. Her earnings would be risible, but enough to support herself, with a little over to send to Ma Downing and the baby. It would keep them all going until Adam could send for them.

Adam. As always at the thought of him, her heart beat faster. His loss was an aching void that deprived her life of meaning. His silence, a constant source of fear. How long before she heard from him? How long?

If he returned to her, then her present problems would be a minor irritation, to be laughed at in later years, when time had softened the cutting edge of remembered poverty. If he didn't . . .

In the dark nights, tossing uneasily beside her mother on the uncomfortable bed, a thin mattress stuffed with straw supported by ropes tied to the rough, wooden frame, the future seemed so uncertain.

If Adam had gone to Australia, it might be nine or ten months before she heard from him. *If* he had reached it. Not all boats that set out for that distant destination landed safely. And, when they did, not all passengers survived.

But if he were alive, if it was humanly possible, she knew that he would contact her, would call her to him. She knew him in her heart

207

as she had never thought to know another person. She could trust him . . . to the ends of the earth, to the end of time. As he could trust her. She sighed.

'Well?'

The harsh word rang through the hall like the croak of a crow. Clara rose slowly to her feet, settling her mother against the wall lest she fall off the chair. Her heart was thudding nervously and she hid her trembling hands in the fullness of her damp skirt, determined to betray none of the fear that rushed through her at the uncompromising monosyllable.

Her head erect, her back straight, she turned to confront her grandfather for the first time.

Chapter 25

'Well?' The croak came again. 'Who are yer? What do yer want?'

Faded emerald eyes surveyed her suspiciously from either side of a beak-like nose. She had imagined that an earl would be tall, burly, but he was no taller than she, shrunken and dried-up inside his parchment skin. His black tailcoat and tight black trousers with an instep strap emphasised his slender frailty.

But there was no weakness in the glance which swept over her, nor any sign of friendliness. His eyes were as cold as the snow outside.

He tapped impatiently on the chequered floor with his ebony stick, his hands gnarled and twisted with rheumatism. 'Well, girl? Lost yer voice?'

Taking her cue from him, Clara dropped him a brief, formal curtsey. 'My lord.' She rose, her eyes assessing him carefully. The servant must have told him who she was or he would not have been here now, but he chose to pretend that she was a stranger.

Well, she *wasn't* a stranger. She was, as her mother constantly used to remind her, the grand-daughter of an earl. Drawing herself up and forcing herself to meet his gaze, she said calmly, 'My name is Clara Pentreath, as you have already been informed.'

His eyes narrowed. She could see that he wasn't used to being treated as an equal. He snapped, 'And what has a Miss Clara Pentreath to do with me?'

'I have brought you your daughter, Lady Susan,' Clara announced succinctly.

His expression did not change; he did not even glance at the woman slumped almost unconscious against the wall. He said coldly, 'I have no such daughter.'

'You may wish that you did not,' Clara's voice was quiet, 'but that does not alter the situation. My mother, your daughter, is in terrible distress. I,' she dropped her eyes, humiliated by the admission she

209

must make, 'I have no money, no means of keeping her.' She had to force out the next words: 'We have no proper home.'

Despite the cold she could feel herself grow hot with shame at the thought of begging. 'I am unable to look after her as she deserves, as her health demands.'

Then sheer desperation helped her to meet again his cold stare. 'My lord, Grandfather,' her voice faltered, recovered, 'I can do no more. I have brought her to you.'

His expression grew harder, more remote. He barked, 'She stopped being my daughter the day she married your father.'

'She can never stop being your daughter.' Clara gripped the wet material of her skirts in passionate entreaty. 'She is of your blood. You cannot deny her now, when she needs help so desperately.' She choked suddenly. 'You have a duty to look after her.'

The faded eyes flashed briefly before he hid his anger under lids as wrinkled as a tortoise's.

'Duty? You talk to me about *duty*?' He pointed his stick at Lady Susan. 'And what about her duty? Where was that when she disobeyed me? Where was that when she ran away to marry yer father? A common man! A miner! A peasant!' He spat out the last word.

'My father was not a peasant!' She could not let the insult pass. She insisted furiously, 'He was a good man, a loving father, a caring husband.'

The Earl gave a bitter laugh. 'So caring that he left you penniless. So loving that he did not even provide you with a home. Every vagabond in England can claim to be a good father if that is how yer judge things!'

'And in what way does he differ from you?' Clara asked, her voice vibrant with emotion. 'If he left us with nothing it was because he died with nothing, spending every penny he had to keep my mama comfortable during his life.'

Her face was pinched with disappointment and despair as she stared at her grandfather. It was obvious already what his decision would be. She had wasted the last of their pitifully small amount of money and risked her mother's life, in order to come here to listen to her father being insulted by a man who wasn't fit to black his shoes.

She concluded bitterly: 'Papa did his best for us and failed because he lacked the money. You, my lord, intend to leave us penniless despite the fact that you have wealth enough and to spare.'

For a brief second his face reddened, as if she had struck home, but then he retaliated, 'If your mother had been a dutiful daughter, I would have been a loving father. It was not I who threw her out, it was she who ran away.'

210

'To marry the man she loved,' Clara insisted. 'Was that so wrong?'

The Earl hammered his stick on the ground, his gnarled fingers, dry as parchment, trembling with the force. 'Love! Love!' he sputtered. 'Plebeian humbug! What has love to do with marriage? Marriage is to do with property, blood-lines, power!'

His faded green eyes glittered furiously at her under lowered brows. 'And yer mother knew that. Good God! That was what she was reared for. That was what she was bred for! Love!' His voice quivered with indignation.

'And you denied her love.' Back straight, head high, Clara reined in her temper, spoke quietly. 'If you had found her a husband, she would have been dutiful, she might even have been happy. But that wasn't what you had planned for her, was it?' Her voice dripped sarcasm.

'She was the youngest daughter, so she wasn't going to be married off for power or prestige, like your other daughters. Susan's role in life was to stay at home and look after you. Be your servant, my lord.' Her scorn was palpable.

He almost flinched under her attack. 'It was my decision, my right.' She could hear the self-justification in his voice. 'She was my daughter!'

'She was a person,' Clara flashed back. 'A person in her own right. But you wouldn't see that. You denied her any rights of a life of her own, normal happiness. Her needs were to be subordinated to your wishes.'

She faced him angrily across the black and white tiles, flinging her cloak back as she placed her hands on her hips, defying him with every bone in her body.

'Her job was to look after you, to carry out the personal, the sensitive tasks that a servant cannot do, but that a daughter can.' Her voice shook. 'No wonder she left. No wonder she married my father.'

Her bright emerald eyes challenged his faded stare. 'She was right,' she said. 'She had the courage to know what was best for her and to do it.'

She took a deep breath and her eyes swept over him consideringly, as if he were a horse she was thinking of buying. When she spoke again, her voice was more reasonable. 'I wonder if you have the courage to do what is right now, and to admit that you made a mistake in the way you treated her, all those years ago.'

His face was purple; for a moment she feared lest he were going to have an apoplexy. 'I have never been spoken to like this in my whole life!'

211

Clara turned to look at her mother. The older woman had slid down in the seat, her fingers picking aimlessly at her cloak. Her eyes were open now, and staring at the Earl, but they were blank, uncomprehending.

Clara pointed a shaking finger at the slumped figure. 'Look at her, look at your daughter. If that doesn't move you, then you must be made of stone.'

She turned back to the Earl, holding her hands out towards him, desperate to make him understand. 'My mother is ill. She is wasting away. She no longer knows what is real and what she remembers from the past.'

Her voice shook. 'I'm asking you to save her reason, her life! Forget the past. Think of now, of the future. She is your youngest daughter and she is dying!'

She swallowed the hot, bitter tears that rose in her throat. 'Please.' Her voice was a whisper. 'I'm not asking you to take her to live here with you. I'm not asking you even to treat her as a daughter once more. But surely, from common humanity, you can find it in you to help her as you would any other distressed gentlewoman. Just provide her with food and shelter – a home where she can dare once again to live in the present.'

'A home,' he echoed harshly, his voice grating in the icy air of the hall. 'Provide a home for a faithless daughter? And for her ill-begotten offspring and her forthcoming bastard.' He laughed bitterly. 'Not much to ask for, is it?'

Clara froze. It took two attempts before she could make her voice sound the word. 'B-bastard? What do you mean?'

He laughed again, pointing his stick at her body. 'Don't lie to me! Don't deny it! By God, my wife had children enough, aye, and I've seen enough maidservants in the same condition. Do yer think I'm blind, girl? Do yer think I'm a fool?'

His green eyes gleamed with malicious pleasure. 'You're breeding, girl! Five months gone, by the look of it. And if you were going to do it you'd have been married by now. But you ain't! You're going to have a bastard and you're trying to fool me into providing a home for it.'

Clara tried to speak but the words would not come. The accusation had stunned her. The world seemed strange, distant, hushed.

As if from far away, she could hear the Earl's voice; 'Well, I ain't going to do it. You're just like your mother, bitches in heat, both of you, running after any man that will have yer.'

He hammered his stick on the ground again. 'I won't have it, do you hear? I won't be tricked and manipulated like this. You've both

212

made your beds and you can lie on them, do yer hear me! And as far as I am concerned, you can lie on them until you rot!'

Fury surged through Clara's body. 'Rot?' she exploded. *'Rot?'*

The sound echoed through the hall, setting the chandeliers aquiver, then it spread, remorselessly, throughout the old building. As the shout died away silence fell once more, watchful, waiting.

'No, *Grandfather*. I shall see to it that we won't rot. You have refused to accept your responsibility, but I shall not do that.' There was pride in Clara's glance, in the way she stood. 'I will accept that responsibility, for my mother, for myself – and yes, for my child.'

Her green eyes met and clashed with his. 'You need not fear that we will ever trouble you again,' she said. 'I wouldn't demean myself as to ever mention your name. And you need never fear that you will be embarrassed by an illegitimate grandchild.'

Her mouth tightened as she stared at him. 'I can only be glad that my child will never know from what inhuman and cruel roots he comes, that he or she will grow up knowing only love and affection and honourable behaviour.'

She leaned towards him, her voice no more than a chilling whisper. 'You will never see your great-grandchild, if I have any say in the matter. As you never knew or saw me. Never! Never! Never!'

It was the Earl's glance which dropped first. He limped over to the front door and threw it open. Snow spiralled in, settling momentarily on his black clothes like dandruff, then melting into droplets that shone like diamonds in the light of the chandelier.

'Are yer going? Or do I get the servants to throw yer out?'

Suddenly she was exhausted, worn out by the travelling and the emotions of the last quarter of an hour. Her mind was numb, her body seemed to move by itself. As if from a distance, Clara saw herself walk across to her mother and gently rouse her. Slowly, speechlessly, they moved to the door.

As she felt the blast of the wind, her mother pulled back, making a faint mewing sound. Still lost in the strange weariness, Clara heard herself whisper reassuring words, saw herself help her mother down the steps, into the biting wind and the swirling, billowing snow, heard the bang as the door slammed shut behind them, cutting them off from light, from help, from hope.

Her arm about her mother's waist, Clara stood still for several seconds, the snow beating unheeded against her face. Her gamble had failed. There was no hope now for her mother, none at all. All that she had achieved was to waste the last of their money, subject herself to shame and ridicule, and strand them both miles from home in the worst winter she could remember.

A more violent gust than usual caught at her skirts, sending her teetering wildly for a moment, then she and her mother fell headlong into a drift of deep, soft snow.

The shock of the cold brought Clara to her senses. She struggled to her feet, dragging her mother up with her. They could not stay here. They had to find shelter or they would die.

She shook her mother roughly, forcing her into the painful present. 'Which way to the stables, Mama? Which way?'

Together they staggered around the side of the great house. Clara kept them well away from the windows – not that anyone was likely to be looking out of them on a night like this. The wind whistled around them as they crossed the stableyard, covering their footprints with driven snow almost as soon as they made them.

She could see lights on above them; the stable boys must be billeted above the horses, benefiting from the heat of the animals. But the coach-house was dark and silent.

Clara helped her mother into its quiet gloom, feeling her way to the biggest and most luxurious of the coaches there. The Earl's travelling coach, that would do. She settled her mother and made another foray to fetch horse blankets from the tack room. Probably there was a dog around somewhere, but on a night like this, it, too, must be lying low and keeping warm.

'Sleep, Mama. We're safe now. Sleep.' Clara stroked the greying hair from her mother's brow as she sank swiftly into peaceful forgetfulness. Safe for a few hours. But they would have to leave before the stable boys awoke and discovered them. Her pride would not let them be thrown off her grandfather's land as if they were common vagrants.

Eyes open, shivering with cold, she stared into a bleak future.

'Edward Blacklock will see me.' Christopher Kingsley brushed the snow off his shoulders with energetic hands, trying to hide the nervousness he always felt when he had to see Blacklock on business. The man had such a damned cutting way of talking, as if he knew that he owned you body and soul. And the present poor state of Kingsley's finances did not improve matters.

The clerk who moved forward to usher him to the big office seemed vaguely familiar, but it was several seconds before Kingsley recognised him.

'You're that fellow who used to be purser out at Wheal Susan, aren't you? Grumble, or something. What are you doing here?'

'Grenfell, sir.' The eyes were lowered obsequiously. 'Mr Blacklock was good enough to offer me a situation after the mine was closed, sir.'

'Bad business, that.' Kingsley stopped for a moment, frowning at the floor. He had seen Clara around but he had always tried to avoid her. What could he say to her? She was his class (secretly, he admitted to himself that she was above him, whatever her father may have been), but she was poor. What could you say to a young girl in those circumstances?

If she had been a bal-maiden he could have chucked her under the chin, thrown her a few shillings to satisfy his conscience. But you couldn't do that to a girl you had dandled on your knee, for heaven's sake. Nor, unfortunately, could you invite her to dinner, not when she was living in that poky cottage.

He was aware of a polite cough. 'Mr Blacklock is waiting, sir.'

He roused himself with a start, walking into the office with an exaggerated swagger to hide his sudden nervousness. 'Well, Blacklock, old man. How are you?'

The thin smile did nothing to make him feel more at ease. Cold-hearted bastard, he told himself, sitting uncomfortably on the hard wooden chair that contrasted starkly with the magnificent mahogany desk behind which Blacklock was installed.

'Another of our meetings, eh?' he joked, under the scrutiny of the light-grey eyes that surveyed him as if they were valuing every item of clothing. 'Getting a bit too regular for my peace of mind.' He tried to give a jolly laugh but it sounded hollow even to him.

'Rather too regular for me, also.' Blacklock's eyes returned to a ledger which lay in front of him. 'Your business has gone downhill again since our last meeting.'

'Oh, come now,' Kingsley wriggled uneasily. 'Things aren't that bad.'

'No?' There was nothing but polite enquiry in the voice of the man opposite him, so why did it make him feel as if he were being slowly flayed alive? 'Things look pretty bad to me.'

'It's because the mines are closing down,' Kingsley said. 'Damn, you know we do most of our business with the mines. And when the price of tin goes down, the mines close, or they lay off men. Either way, they buy fewer candles, less gunpowder, less soap . . . less of everything. But it's only temporary – everybody knows that. In a while, the price of tin will rise again and the mines will re-open. We'll be making a fortune.'

He could feel the sweat on his forehead and despised himself for it. 'Your father always understood,' he ended up, unable to keep the aggrieved note out of his voice.

'My father is dead. The business belongs to me now.' Edward Blacklock's long fingers strummed lightly on the desktop as his eyes thoughtfully considered the man in front of him. Kingsley could feel the sweat under his arms now, despite the coldness of the day. If Blacklock refused to give him any more credit . . .

'Very well.' Blacklock's light voice sounded as calm as if he were discussing the weather. 'You can continue with the arrangement for another three months. On the same terms.'

Kingsley had to stop himself mopping his brow. Saved again. For another quarter. Now that the tension was over he felt suddenly weak with relief. He slumped down in the uncomfortable chair, digging his hands deep in his pockets, his legs sprawling apart.

'Everyone's having a difficult time at the moment. The world seems full of bad news.' He knew he was babbling but he did not care. 'I heard today that Ben Pasco was killed in an accident at Wheal Poverty.' There was no response from the man opposite him but that did not matter. He was talking to calm himself down.

'Poor old bugger fell off a ladder.' He blew his nose in a large, spotted handkerchief. 'Used to work at Wheal Susan, you know. Captain Pentreath had him running the engine house. He was too old, really, to go climbing ladders, but then you have to get what work you can these days.'

The long elegant fingers still strummed lightly on the desktop. There was no alteration in the gaze of the light-grey eyes.

Christopher Kingsley surveyed the results of his nose-blowing, then folded his handkerchief and tucked it into his pocket. 'He was one of the lives in a cottage on my land. Now there's only one life left. Not that it will do me any good.' For a second he frowned, trying to look like a hard-hearted businessman. 'With Adam Trevelyan fled the country, how will I ever know when the cottage reverts to me?'

The strumming fingers were suddenly still. Kingsley looked up to see Blacklock staring at him but when the younger man spoke his voice merely sounded bored.

'Which cottage would that be, then?'

'Adam Trevelyan's, of course. The one Clara Pentreath is living in. Not that I grudge it to her, poor girl,' Kingsley added quickly. 'She can stay there as long as she wants as far as I'm concerned, and welcome.'

Edward Blacklock stroked his moustache with a long finger. 'And this house is held for three lives?' he asked.

Kingsley nodded. 'That's right, Adam's father built it on a useless bit of my land years ago, with the usual agreement that it would revert to me when the three designated lives had died.'

He listed them on his fingers. 'One was Adam's sister, but she died

216

of the cholera when she was just a child. One was Adam, and the other was Ben Pasco.' He shrugged. 'Using children as a life is always dangerous. The young 'uns pop off so quick if there's any fevers around. So I suppose they chose Ben, who was a hearty young man in those days, so that the cottage would still be there if any other children came along.'

He sighed. 'All that family. Good hard-working people, all of them, and all dead. All except Adam, and he's had to flee the country.'

Edward said slowly, 'But he might be dead.'

Kingsley shrugged. 'No way of telling. No one's heard of either of them since that day, not even when that Preventative man recovered. They could be living somewhere up-country, or abroad. Who's going to know now?'

'Or they could be dead,' Edward repeated.

Kingsley stared at him curiously. 'What does it matter? You don't think I would turn that poor girl and her mother out, even if I knew that he was dead, do you? Good God, man, I'm not such a brute as that!'

Edward leaned back in his chair, his finger still stroking the golden hairs on his upper lip. 'You call it being a brute?' His voice was quiet, gentle. 'Myself, I would call it being a businessman.' He sat up suddenly, a faint smile playing around his handsome mouth. 'The sort of businessman to whom I would be willing to allow credit.'

The words were so softly spoken that it was several seconds before Kingsley realised what Blacklock was saying, then he leapt to his feet. 'Are you telling me that if I don't turn that poor girl out of her house . . . ?' He stuttered to a halt.

Blacklock smiled. 'What I am telling you is that I only lend money to businessmen. If you haven't got the business sense to make the most of your assets, then I would have to reconsider our agreement to extend your loan.'

Kingsley stared down at him. 'What's behind this, Blacklock?' His voice was harsh, all pretence of civility gone. 'Why are you persecuting that poor girl?'

'Persecuting?' His voice sounded hurt, innocent. 'I'm not persecuting anyone, Kingsley. Though I do think it is time that Clara Pentreath came to her senses.' There was a faraway look in his eye, and a bead of sweat appeared on his forehead as he murmured, 'I have waited as long as I can.'

'And you expect me to throw her out of her cottage?' Kingsley demanded furiously. 'A young girl and a woman who has been

217

recently widowed?' He leaned over the desk, pushing his face furiously into Blacklock's. 'I won't do it, I tell you! I will simply not do it!'

Edward shrugged his elegant shoulders. 'I can't make you, of course.' His voice was quiet, reasonable. 'We always have a choice in life.'

'I'm glad you realise it,' Kingsley said angrily, straightening up.

Edward smiled at him gently. 'And your choice is this,' he went on. 'Is it going to be Clara Pentreath who is made homeless . . . or Isabelle Kingsley?'

Chapter 26

'My life and soul!' Ma Downing looked up from the pastry she was rolling out and peered through the small, distorting panes in the window. 'Here's that there Mr Kingsley from Pendeen. They do say he's a brem hard magistrate, but a good one for a laugh.'

Clara froze for a moment, her hand on her mother's feverish brow, then she leapt to her feet.

'He mustn't see me like this!' She grabbed for her cloak, hanging ready on a nearby peg on the wall. Her waistline had extended visibly in the few weeks since she had returned from Trevival, but she had still not come to terms with the fact that she was having an illegitimate child.

Hastily, she swung the cloak over her shoulders. It fell in voluminous folds over her full skirts, hiding her thickening body.

Ma Downing threw a cynical glance at her. 'And how do you think you're going to hide the young one when it comes? Look brem plum, you will, going round with a seven-year-old boy under your clothes all the time. Tell the truth and shame the devil, that's what I always say.'

'Later, Ma. Not now.' Although her heart thrilled to the thought that she was carrying Adam's child, she could not yet bring herself to face the shame and censure that would fall on her when news of her pregnancy became known.

Especially not from Mr Kingsley, one of her kind, one of her father's oldest friends. Once the gentry knew of her fall from virtue she would be cut off from their society even more than she already was by her poverty. Lack of money would not prevent true Christians like Lieutenant Laity from seeking her society on occasions; lack of chastity would put her irrevocably beyond the pale.

Clara pulled on her bonnet and ran for the door. 'Why, Mr Kingsley!' She hoped the breathlessness in her voice would be attributed to surprise. 'How pleasant to see you again. What brings you here?'

His round red face was strangely grave as he took off his top hat, twisting it awkwardly between his hands. 'Miss – er – Miss Clara.' His voice was husky and in another man she would have suspected that he was embarrassed. For a second, she wondered if he had heard a rumour of her pregnancy and had come to berate her about it, but she dismissed the thought. It would be his dowdy, acidulated wife who came on that errand . . .

'You wanted to see me?'

'Er, well, your mother, er . . .' His voice died away.

Clara said, 'She is ill at present, Mr Kingsley. She has a low fever and has been suffering from it for some time.' Ever since that ill-fated journey to see the Earl. Clara put the thought out of her mind.

'I hope it is not contagious,' she went on, knowing very well that it was not, 'but I would not wish to put your wife or daughter to any risk. It might be best if you were to say what you have to say to me out here.' She forced a confident smile and moved down the path to the gate where Mr Kingsley's horse was tethered, forcing him to follow her. Ma Downing had long ears and Clara had a premonition that it might be best if this conversation were kept private. 'Shall we walk along the road while we talk? The movement will keep us warm.'

When he did speak, his choice of words surprised her. 'I don't know if you've heard that Ben Pasco was killed in a mining accident last week?'

She nodded. 'I knew him when I was a child. He was one of those who grew up with my father and he had a great respect for him.' Her face darkened. 'He was too old to work down the mine. My father allowed him to mind the pumping engine and he did it very well.' The thought of the engine that had blown up, killing her father brought a lump to her throat and she had to swallow before she went on, 'I attended his funeral, Mr Kingsley. I thought it would be expected of me, even in our present circumstances.'

'I am sure you did quite right.' But there was no warmth in the man's voice and his face was set in frown. He said abruptly, 'I don't know if you are aware, but Ben Pasco was one of the lives against which your cottage is held.'

She nodded. 'I think I had heard that. But there is no difficulty, is there? He wasn't the last life.'

Kingsley would not look at her. Instead, his eyes followed the straight lines of the leats, clearly visible now that the bracken had died back. They transversed the craggy hillsides, carrying the water, precious and strangely scarce in this area of high rainfall, from small

220

inland streams to feed the insatiable thirsts of the mine engines that ringed the Atlantic cliffs.

'It seems that he *was* the last life.' The words were dragged from him, reluctantly.

Clara said stupidly, 'But Adam was one of the lives!' Then realisation struck her. She felt a cold sweat break out on her forehead and the baby jumped in her womb, responding to the sudden shock that ran through her. The world span around her and she put out a trembling hand to the hedge to support herself. 'You've heard that he's dead!'

Automatically, Kingsley responded to her distress even though he did not understand it. 'No, no,' he said heartily. 'I haven't heard anything definite,' then, realising he was weakening his case, he added swiftly, 'but neither do I know for sure that he is still alive.'

This was enough for Clara at the moment. One hand pressed against her swollen belly under the all-enveloping disguise of her cloak and her eyes closed in a brief prayer of thankfulness. There was still hope. He might yet come, take her away from this. She could still imagine a life where they were together, loving, supporting each other. She concentrated on taking deep breaths, calming herself for the sake of the baby, his baby, lying under her heart.

'Miss Clara?' She jerked her eyes open. Mr Kingsley had stopped and was staring down at her, his face concerned. She could hear the echo of his voice in her ears but she had completely missed what he had said.

'I – I'm sorry. Could you say that again, please?' Her thin face lit up with her brief, elfin smile.

He seemed reluctant for a moment, then it all burst out. 'I do not know that Trevelyan is dead, but equally, there is no evidence that he is still alive. Under the circumstances . . .'

Clara felt the blood drain from her face. 'You are evicting us?' Her voice was little more than a whisper. Disaster stared her in the face. Without the shelter of the cottage, they were lost. Where could they go?

They barely had money enough to survive the winter and she had no hope of earning any until after the baby was born, sometime in April. Her mother, she, Ma Downing, the baby – all cast onto the dubious mercy of the Parish, scraping a bare existence on the few bitter scraps of charity which were all that the righteous councillors provided. Living in the workhouse – a fate that even the poor, who were inured to suffering and degradation, avoided at all costs. How would her mother endure it? How would Clara herself?

Panic spread through her. Without a second thought, she cast her pride to the winds, throwing herself onto Kingsley's mercy. It could not happen! It must not!

'Mr Kingsley, please.' She reached out, laid a trembling hand on his arm. 'You can't do this to us, surely? Not to my mother – it would kill her.'

She gripped his arm with all her strength. 'It may be the law, but you don't need the cottage, you don't need the money. And you don't even know for sure that Adam is dead.'

Tears stood in her eyes, rolled unheeded down her pale cheeks. 'Please, Mr Kingsley, for the sake of my mother, for the friendship you had with my father, please change your mind. Please let us stay.'

He jerked his arm away, turning his back so that he could not see her beseeching face. 'You have until the end of the month to get out.' His voice was rough and loud, then he had moved and was striding quickly back down the road. She heard him swear at his horse as he mounted it, then he was gone, the hoofbeats dying away on the cold winter wind.

Clara collapsed in a heap, crouching over her precious, secret burden. Her arms wrapped round herself and she rocked to and fro, hardly aware of the frantic keening sound that issued from her lips. It was over. It was all over. Her brief, desperate dream of keeping them together was gone.

The workhouse. Degradation. Humiliation. Living surrounded by the lowest of the low, the drunkards, the half-witted, the mad. Getting up each morning to carry out menial tasks. Separated from her child, if he were male. Her arms tightened around herself. Oh God, oh God! Let there be a way out of this. A way that would not entail the ultimate misery of the workhouse where poverty was treated as a crime and humanity was denied.

The baby moved again, responding to her distress and she pressed her hands against her quivering belly. Edward Blacklock was behind this, she knew. Mr Kingsley wasn't a cruel man, he was even kind in a careless way. If he had done this, it was because Edward had found some means of pressurising him.

But even that way out was denied her. He would never marry her, knowing that she was big with Adam's bastard. There was no solution for her, for them all. None. None. None.

The cold fingers of the wind searched through her clothes, bringing her finally to her senses. Slowly she raised her aching head, her eyes swollen with tears, her body stiff and cramped, contorted as it was around her unborn child. The words from Ma Downing came back to her, mocking her. 'There 'tis and can't be no 'tisser.' Well, she thought bleakly, nothing could be 'tisser' than the workhouse. Reality had to be faced.

She climbed stiffly to her feet. Whatever happened to her family, at least she had kept her word to Adam; she had done her best for Phil. Adam might not like the fact that he was working on the fishing boats, but at least she had saved him from the workhouse and given him a hope, however slim, of a better future. For herself, that hope had almost disappeared. Only if Adam came back soon could she find a way out of the shame and poverty that awaited her. She tried to keep her thoughts on that faint gleam of light in the surrounding darkness.

Slowly, she stumbled back up the road, forcing her numb feet to carry her. Her mother and Ma Downing must be told but her mother, at least, would be unable to appreciate the horrors that awaited her.

Ever since they had returned from the abortive visit to the Earl, Lady Susan had run a slight fever. Her breathing was difficult and she coughed frequently. None of the herbs with which Ma Downing had physicked her had done any good, and there was not enough money for a doctor. And she was still unaware most of the time of her real situation, constantly talking about Captain Pentreath as if he were still alive, harking back to the days when the only time she would have entered a humble cottage was when she was paying a charitable visit.

The little window glowed dimly through the grey January afternoon. Ma Downing had lit the crude lamp that burned cheap pilchard oil. Unconsciously, it cheered Clara with its promise of shelter and warmth, however temporary. She pushed open the door with an eagerness she did not often feel.

Ma Downing glanced up at her entrance. 'You got your mother then?'

Clara felt herself grow cold. 'No. Where is she? What happened?'

'Went out she did, saying she was going to find your da.' The old woman saw the look of horror on Clara's face and added quickly. 'I couldn't stop her. Real determined she was. And I knew you couldn't have bin far off, so I let her go.'

'She didn't pass me.' Clara thought hard. Penalverne or the mine; they were the only places her mother was likely to have gone. But which one?

'What did she say before she left? What was she talking about?' Clara's voice was abrupt, anxious.

'Said that she never saw your da these days, that he was working too hard. She said she were going to see him and give him what for.'

The mine! She was going to the mine! 'And when did she leave?'

The woman shrugged. Time meant little to her. 'It were just after you'd gone out. A brem while, any road.'

Clara turned and ran down the path, leaving the door to slam behind her. It was nearly two miles to Wheal Susan, a long way on a cold winter's afternoon for a woman already frail and ill. The setting sun was low in the overcast sky, giving a fading grey light that made it difficult to pick out the rocks and stones that littered the muddy road. Clara hurried as quickly as she could.

Surely someone would see Lady Susan, would realise what was wrong and stop her. But with Wheal Susan closed down there was less traffic in the area, and on a day like this with a bitter wind, all who could would be safely indoors. Besides, which of the village women could stand up to her mother? Obedience to women of Lady Susan's class was bred into them. They would not interfere.

She was breathless now. Her back ached from the weight of the baby which seemed to be dragging her down, but she forced herself on. Her mother was her responsibility. She had to find her.

The early January dusk was already falling as she turned into the entrance to the mine. It was the first time she had been there since her father had died and she felt her heart contract at the desolation that lay around her.

The Count House walls, once a spotless white, were blotched and stained. The buddling frames had disappeared, vandalised by villagers desperate for wood. She hurried between the derelict buildings, slipping on the greasy ground. The mine had been closed for nearly six months but no weeds softened the abandonment. The ground was poisoned by the waste from the mines. It would be years before anything would gain a foothold.

'Mama! Mama!' Clara's voice echoed hollowly off the ruined walls. The only answer was a thin rain that began to fall, almost invisibly out of the sky, beading her cloak with tiny drops that glistened like miniature diamonds. 'Mama!'

Perhaps she was wrong, Clara thought. Perhaps her mother had gone to Penalverne after all. But she had to check the mine properly first. In the fading light it was a death-trap, the ground gaping suddenly where unexpected channels cut across the bare earth. The winding machinery had disappeared but the shafts gaped hungrily to the empty sky.

'Mama!' Clara walked unwillingly towards the ruins of the pumping house. The walls were breached where the explosion had ripped the boiler apart. The huge bob lay abandoned close by, having shattered the roof as it fell. Once it would have been sold to another mine. Now, when mines were closing almost every week, it was not worth the cost of transportation.

Surely her mother would not have gone in there? Clara had to force herself to enter the sagging doorway of the building where her father had died. The wreck of twisted metal was still there. Some of the machinery had been removed but the rest remained, the once brilliant brass green with verdigris, contorted by the forces that had passed over it. A piece of loose iron, high above her, clanged dolefully as it swung gently in the fitful wind.

'Oh, Father.' Clara leaned her head against the ruined wall, the desolation bringing back to her the strength of her loss. Hugh Pentreath had loved the mine. It had been his pride, the symbol of his success. By his own efforts he had dragged himself up from nothing to become the virtual owner of this, and then, just when he had been about to save it from bankruptcy, it had killed him.

Tears pricked at her eyelids but she forced them back. Mourning was a luxury she could not afford. She had to find her mother. She pushed herself away from the wall and hurried back through the mine workings again. 'Mama! Mama!' Surely she was here somewhere?

A faint cry, no louder than the mew of a drowning kitten, caught her ears. She turned towards it, shouting louder. 'Mama! Mama!'

'Here.' Weak, indistinct.

She moved forward more slowly now, her eyes searching the ruins around her in the swiftly gathering dusk. 'Mama! Where are you?'

'Clara.' It was almost at her feet. She paused, looking down. The main shaft gaped before her, the iron ladder leading down into thick darkness. Surely her mother hadn't gone down there?

'Clara.'

The voice was closer now. No doubt about it. Carefully, Clara knelt at the edge and peered down. The shaft was black but, just at the edges of her vision, was a glimmer of white. 'Mama?'

'I'm afraid, Clara.' The voice was quivering, almost unrecognisable. 'I can't get up.' A pause. 'Tell your father, Clara. He'll come. He'll rescue me.'

Clara bit her lips to stop their trembling. Once, she too had had that childlike trust in her father to put everything right. That was yet another of the losses she had suffered in the past months.

'He's not here, Mama. No one is here. Can't you climb up by yourself?'

'Of course not.' There was a touch of the old autocratic Lady Susan in the cross response. 'Fetch your father immediately.'

But that was impossible. If her mother wouldn't climb up, then

Clara would have to climb down. The shaft was dark, uninviting. The iron ladder was red with rust and slippery with rain. Clara hesitated. 'You can do it Mama,' she urged. 'Come on – climb the ladder.'

But there was no response.

With a sigh, Clara took off her cloak. Skirts alone would be hampering enough. She turned and felt for the first rung with a nervous foot. It seemed to be a long way down. Dear God, how had Adam coped all those years? How had Phil? She found the first rung and stretched for the next. Her skirts bunched up before her, pressing on her pregnant stomach, hampering her movements.

'I'm coming, Mama.' Step by slow step she lowered herself into the dank blackness. Below her, she knew, gaped a thousand feet of darkness, now drowned with cold, black water. Was it better to die in a fall or drown? She turned her thoughts away from the involuntary speculation with a shudder. 'I'm coming.'

Four rungs down and the dim twilight was almost entirely cut off. All she could see was the faint glimmer of her hands on the ladder.

'Mama. Mama.' She could hear the panic in her voice. Just to hear another human being! Just to know that she wasn't alone in this dreadful void.

'Clara.' The voice was still a long way away. Dear God, would this ladder never end? Her feet sought and slipped, her hands ached with the need to grip. Down, down, down.

'Clara.' The voice was close to her now. Clara's searching foot hunted for the next rung and couldn't find it. It flailed wildly in a sudden panic and touched something solid, off to one side. Of course, the resting platforms, a 'sollar', she remembered her father calling it. Where the men got off one ladder and prepared to descend the next. Thank heavens her mother had not gone any further!

She stepped onto the platform, her knees shaking with the strain. 'It's all right, Mama. I'm here.' She reached out in the darkness and touched her mother's body, pulling it into her arms. The woman's skin was clammy, cold as a dead fish, and her breathing rasped in her chest. Shudders ran through the thin form. How long had she been down here?

Her mother said fretfully, 'I came to find your father, but he's not here.'

'He's up above, Mama. We must climb back up to see him.' Clara stretched and straightened her cramped fingers. 'You have to climb back up, Mama. Do you think you can do it?'

There was a sudden resonance of the old Lady Susan. 'That is hardly proper behaviour for the daughter of an earl.'

'Nevertheless, Mama,' Clara spoke calmly, cheerfully, hiding the trepidation she felt inside, 'you must do it.' She took a deep breath. 'I'll help you. If I climb behind you, you need not worry about falling.'

It took all her courage to lean out in the blackness, above that unseen, unfathomable drop, and search for the invisible ladder. For a frantic second she thought that she would not find it, that they would be trapped there until daylight, and she knew, with a dreadful certainty, that if that happened her mother would not survive the night. Then her questing hand brushed the metal sides of the ladder and she caught and held it with a sigh of relief.

'Feel along my arm, Mama.' Her voice was calm and confident. 'Feel the ladder.' Her mother's body brushed by her in the darkness, and she felt her hand touch the metal by her own. 'Now step across.' Action by action, inch by inch, she guided her mother onto the ladder, got herself on it too, her body close behind her mother's.

'There. That's the most difficult part. Now all you have to do is climb. You can't fall. I'm right behind you. It's very easy.'

Easy! Easy for a man, perhaps, with unencumbered limbs. Not so easy for a woman. The rungs of the ladder seemed even further apart going up. At each step, Clara found, she had to lift her foot almost to knee-height to find the next rung, clinging with one hand to the wet and slippery iron as with the other she dragged her skirts and petticoats up to free her other foot. And all the time, she had her mother's skirts swaying in her face, filling her mouth, suffocating her.

She tried to drop further back, but without her comforting presence behind her, her mother would not move. Slow foot by slow foot they made their ponderous way up through the darkness. Only the gradually increasing dampness told Clara that they were making any headway at all. Up there, in the real world, it must be pouring with rain. Here, in a Hell of everlasting blackness, all she could feel was the water running over her cramped and shaking fingers, making the rungs even more slippery under her questing feet.

Up. Up. The climb had lasted for ever. Surely they must be nearly at the top?

Clara turned her head aside to free her mouth from her mother's voluminous skirts and panted out the encouragement that she herself no longer believed. 'Nearly there, Mama. You're doing really well. Just a few more steps.' She gasped as her foot slipped on the wet rung, saving herself by a quick grab with the hand that was struggling to control her skirts. 'Nearly there.'

The end, when it came, took her by surprise, blinded as she was by her mother's clothing.

Lady Susan, coming suddenly into the open air, flung herself onto the safety of solid earth. Her sudden movement, the swift thrust of her legs and sway of her skirts, hit Clara in the face and knocked her off-balance.

For a second she was flung off the ladder, one tired, cramped hand all that prevented her from falling a hundred feet into the blackness below. She screamed, flailing desperately with her free hand, her feet hampered by engulfing material. Then her second hand found purchase on the wet rungs. She managed to force a knee, covered with petticoats though it was, between two of the rungs, reliving some of the strain on her fingers.

Sweating, shaking, she leaned her head against the ladder, planning her next moves. It would be awkward to untangle her feet, get them back on the rungs again, but it could be done. She just had to stay calm, move slowly.

She had put more weight on her knee, releasing one hand to struggle yet again with her skirts when there was an ominous 'crack' just above her head.

She clung to the rung, frozen in disbelief, as one side of the ladder, very slowly and easily, pulled away from the wall.

Chapter 27

'Mama.' Terror closed Clara's throat and her voice was no more than a squeak. 'Mama!'

She clung to the loosened ladder, her knuckles white, afraid to move lest she should send the ladder, with herself attached to it, hurtling down to the inky waters far below.

'Mama!' She managed to get more volume to her voice now. In the silence of the night she was aware of small sounds, the dripping of water down the open shaft, the soft patter of rain falling onto bare earth, the harsh gasping of her mother's breath as she came closer.

'Clara? Are you there?'

Clara closed her eyes in relief. For a dreadful moment she had thought her mother too far gone to respond.

'Mama, please help me.' A scuffling noise and then the faint gleam of her mother's face staring down at her.

'Clara, what on earth are you doing down there? Get out at once!'

The voice was outraged, peremptory. 'Is this how I brought you up – to behave like a hoyden?'

Clara bit back the hysterical giggle that rose to her throat. 'Mama, I'm stuck. The ladder is coming away from the wall. I need your help.'

'Come up out of there at once.' She could hear the breath wheezing in her mother's chest as she spoke. The wait in the cold wet shaft had worsened the inflammation of her lungs.

Clara gritted her teeth. No time to worry about that now. One thing at a time. 'Mama,' she made her voice as confident and commanding as she could, 'give me your hand. If you don't help me I shall fall.' The ladder creaked alarmingly.

A long silence, then a cough, and her mother's voice: 'Are you really stuck, Clara?'

229

'Really.' She fought to keep her voice steady. 'You must help me, Mama. I can't get out without your help.'

'I'll get your father, Clara.' The voice was suddenly stronger, more determined. 'He'll know what to do. Stay there. We won't be long.'

Fear gripped her. 'Mama! Mama!' But over the noise of the falling rain she could hear the soft sound of her mother's feet moving away through the dark night.

The sob rose in her throat, taking her by surprise; hot tears rolled down her cheeks. There was no one to help, no one at all. Desperation flooded through her in the dank darkness.

She bit her lower lip with her teeth, thinking hard. If there was no one there, she would have to save herself. The ladder creaked again. How long before it gave way? She blinked. What did it matter! If she stayed where she was she would fall, either because the ladder had finally broken free or because she could no longer hold on. If she were to escape, she would simply have to do it by herself.

Cautiously, she released the fingers of one hand from their death-like grip on the ladder, and fumbled blindly with her hampering skirts. At every movement the ladder creaked but she closed her ears to the sounds. There was no other way.

One foot was freed, found a purchase on the wet, slippery rungs. She gratefully took her weight on it and froze as the ladder moved perceptibly under her. For long seconds, she held her breath, but nothing further happened. The ladder was still again, the only sound the soft splash of the rain.

Slowly she freed her knee, ignoring the pain as the muscles protested; slowly she worked her skirts free again. Found a foothold on the next rung. Creak. Freeze. Straighten knees. Move hands up the ladder. Creak. Free other foot. Put it on next rung. Take weight.

The ladder moved again, but her head was suddenly above the ground. She took a deep breath of the fresh air, savouring the salt on the wind, the rain blowing in her face. Nearly there.

After the blackness of the shaft, the surface seemed well lit, even under the rain-filled sky. She searched for something to take her weight but the nearest thing, a rusty metal stake, was still beyond her reach.

Creak.

Taking a deep breath, Clara concentrated on climbing the next rung, slowly, oh so carefully. Almost there . . . but then, suddenly, the final shift of her weight was too much for the rusted ladder. It bucked beneath her and there was a rending screech that tore at her ears.

Frantically, she threw herself upwards, her hands grasping for the metal stake. Her fingers gripped it, crushing the flaking rust, just as the ladder finally gave way and fell abruptly from under her feet.

The lip of the shaft caught her across the stomach as she hung, legs flailing, listening in terror to the crash and rumble of the ladder as it bounced off the walls of the shaft on its journey to the depths of the pit.

She could find no toehold. Her tired fingers were all that kept her from a dreadful death. But the rain at last was helping. The sodden earth was slippery under her body, allowing her to pull herself, inch by inch, out of the pit.

She got one knee up and, in a sudden convulsion of terror, heaved herself out of the grip of the mine, to lie, shaking and crying, face down in the mud while the rain beat down on her unprotected body like a benediction.

Clara did not know how long she lay there. Time was meaningless. It was a luxury just to be alive, to be above ground. Now, at last, she understood the look in the miners' eyes as they talked of returning 'to Grass'. Only someone who had risked death in a filthy pit could recognise the wonder of fresh air, of rain, of the open sky.

It was the cold that roused her at last. She climbed to her feet, groaning as strained muscles protested bitterly. She was wet to the skin, the whole front of her body caked in the thick, red clay that covered the surface of mine workings. Her back ached with a sickening intensity and she rubbed it, wishing that she could just go home, lie down, be warm and cosseted.

But her mother was here somewhere. She had to find her. Wearily, Clara plodded off through the derelict buildings, calling, searching.

Her mother was huddled in a corner of the deserted Count House. Clara bent over her, wincing at the pain that shot through her. 'Mama, wake up,' she urged softly. 'We must go home.'

The older woman was hot, almost delirious. Only by shouting could Clara get through to her, and only by taking most of her weight could she get her to move along at all.

No-Go-By Hill seemed interminable in the rain-soaked darkness. Her mother's breath rasped painfully at every step, while her own muscles shrieked as she forced them to almost carry the other woman foot by painful foot up the rough road. Her back ached as if it were broken in two but she could not stop, could not rest, until she had got her mother into the warmth and shelter of the small, isolated cottage.

Ma Downing's eyes widened at the sight of them. 'My soul and body! Whatever have you been up to?'

'She's ill.' It was almost a sob. 'We were stuck down the mine.' Tears of weakness prickled behind tired eyes.

'You sit yourself by the fire, I'll look after your ma for you.'

231

Gratefully Clara relinquished Lady Susan into the old woman's brawny arms, resting her head against the wooden chairback as she heard the two struggle up the uneven stairs to the small bedroom.

It was so good to sit in peace. So wonderful not to have to struggle. Her wet clothes clung to her shivering body but she was too tired to care. If only her back would stop aching, if only the strange feeling of heaviness would leave her.

The pain came suddenly, doubling her up with a gasp. She felt sick, but it passed and she leaned back again, lulled by the lethargy of exhaustion. Twice more it happened before Ma Downing bustled down, her arms full of wet clothes.

'And what do you think you're doing?' The old woman's voice was sharp with concern. 'No more sense than a day-old chick, you haven't, sitting around in they wet things, cagged with mud. You get them off now, and sharp about it.'

Another pain racked Clara's body. She was scarcely aware of the woman's arms around her, steadying her, of her hands, warm and soothing, drying the sweat that beaded her forehead.

The spasm passed as the others had, and she clutched at Ma Downing's arm. These strange pains were frightening her.

Anxiously she asked, 'What is it, Ma? What's happening to me? Why . . .' her voice cracked suddenly. 'Why am I getting these pains?'

There was compassion in the old woman's eyes but no evasion as she answered baldly, 'You're having your baby. And I reckon it's a good three months too early.'

Phil checked over his shoulder that he had got the jolly boat into the correct position, then pulled in the single oar with which he had been sculling over the stern.

The mackerel fleet from Mousehole was coming round Carn Dhu Point, the forty boats under full sail, the waves creaming under their bows in the early January sun.

Thank God the season had lasted longer than normal this year, he thought, his eyes fixed on the *Sally-Ann* as she bore down on him at top speed. He enjoyed being a yawler, as the boys who rowed the jolly boats were called; he wasn't looking forward to the barren period each year which was almost upon them, when the boats stayed in the harbour and the only work was the retarring of hulls and the making and mending of nets.

All around him other boys jostled for position, lining their punts up with the oncoming luggers to which they belonged. But the *Sally-Ann* was ahead, almost on him now, her black hull with the distinctive red stripe looking enormous as she loomed ever closer.

Phil stood up, the rope coiled in his hand. This was the testing moment, when reputations were made or lost. His heart beating fast, he judged his moment then threw.

The coil of rope flew through the air, unwinding smoothly under its own weight and he sighed with relief as he saw Dick Thomas' hand catch it, safe and sure, before winding it swiftly round a cleat.

Phil could feel the relieved grin split his face as he crouched hurriedly in the boat, clinging to the sides with both hands.

Without a check, the *Sally-Ann* roared past him then the rope tightened with a jerk and the nose of the small punt rose high out of the water as it was pulled willy-nilly behind the bigger boat as she sailed at top speed for the moorings off Newlyn.

The speed, the wind in his face, excited him as nothing else did. It was even better than the games the boys played during the long days when the luggers were at sea, daring each other to get the small boats over rocks and into gullies which seemed impossible.

He had even once, during a rough sea, at high tide, got his boat across the centre of St Clement's Island off Mousehole Harbour. He had been lashed by Dick Thomas for doing it; that had been too dangerous even for him to countenance, and punts cost money, but it had been worth it. He was definitely top yawler at Mousehole now, even if he did come from St Just and had spent most of his life down a mine.

He glanced behind him over the water boiling and fretting in his wake. John-Henry had missed his throw again, forcing the *Aunt Mary* to turn round to pick him up. That would mean a belting, but the physical pain was far less than the sense of shame a yawler suffered at the disgrace.

Ahead, the long sandy beach at Newlyn was coming into view. The small pier was too small to take the number of boats and they were forced to anchor offshore, using the jolly boats to ferry the fish ashore.

As always, the beach was crowded, with children, women, and the aged 'jousters' who carried the fish in wicker baskets on their backs, all hurrying to help land the catch.

And behind them, slender as an oar, her strange fair hair looking almost white in the fitful sunshine, Clara Pentreath. Amongst the village women she stood out, elegant and ladylike, standing slightly apart from the others who crowded forward near the shore.

Adam! thought Phil. She had come to tell him she had heard from Adam! And he felt a despair run through him at the thought. His uncle had been good to him, looked after him when he was all alone, taught him and fed and housed him. But Adam was a miner to the marrow of his bones. He would fight to get Phil back down a mine, back to the life Adam knew and loved. And away from the life his nephew now knew and loved.

A shout from above made him look up. Dick Thomas was grinning down at him. The lugger had come to a halt, the jolly boat hauled to her side, while Phil was lost in thought.

'There's Miss Clara waiting for you.' There was no worry in the older man's voice. 'We've brem few fish this trip, reckon the season's over at last, so we don't need your help. I'll take you in to talk to her – we can land this catch without you, lad.'

He dropped easily into the punt, taking the long sweep oars that the men used to row the small boat. As he pulled for the shore, Dick Thomas asked, 'Reckon she's heard from Adam?' He nodded towards the slender, black-clad figure.

'P'raps.' Phil could not hide the dismay he felt. He would not go back down the mine!

Halfway to the shore, Dick rested on his oars, his eyes on the boy. 'About the future.' His voice was slow and thoughtful. 'God never gave me and the missus no children.' He spat briefly into the sea. 'Reckon we could do worse than let you have the boat when my rheumatics get too bad for fishing.' He bent again to the stroke.

Phil felt his face break into a foolish grin. Exultation flooded through him, depriving him of words. Adam could not make him go below ground, now. He had a future, a profession. He would be a boat-owner.

Dick Thomas saw the grin, read his mind. 'That do you, mate?'

Phil nodded, his eyes shining. 'That'll do me proper!' He struggled to keep a manly sternness in his voice, but knew that his face betrayed him.

The grin was still there as he ran up the beach to Clara. She was looking thinner than he remembered, and paler, and her emerald eyes were huge. He gave her a quick peck on the cheek and reddened with embarrassment as she caught him to her, holding him close with an intensity he could not understand.

With a wiggle, he pulled himself free. He was almost as tall as she, he realised with a shock. 'You've heard from Adam?'

Clara shook her head, her eyes sad. 'Not a word. Nor has anyone else that I can find out.' She examined him, holding him at arms' length. 'You've grown.'

He laughed. 'The fishermen say I'm like a weed. Show me a bit of sun and I shoot up.'

'And there was no sun down the mine.' She shivered suddenly, pulling her cloak closer around her. 'Are you happy, fishing?'

234

He nodded. 'Dick Thomas say he'll leave me his boat when he gets too old.' Enthusiasm and pride bubbled in his voice despite his effort to appear calm.

'And you want that?' She was strangely insistent.

'More'n anything in the whole world.'

'Then I don't have to worry about you.' There was a weariness in her voice. She said softly, 'Things are not so well with us. Ben Pasco has died and Mr Kingsley is claiming the cottage back.'

'He can't do that!' Phil said hotly. 'Adam's still alive.'

'But we can't prove it,' she sighed. 'And my mother is ill,' she paused, 'very ill. An inflammation of the lungs. She may die and I can't afford a doctor.'

He understood. 'Dick Thomas will help,' he said eagerly. 'I've been a brem good yawler, and he's always saying he's grateful to you for letting him have me.'

'It isn't that.' He watched as small, white teeth gnawed at her lower lip. She had always been so strong, so sure of herself, he could not understand her strange lack of certainty.

Slowly, her eyes on him, she said tentatively, 'Mr Blacklock has asked me to marry him.'

'Cor!' Phil could not hide his amazement. 'He's brem rich! He's even richer than your da was! You'll be all right with him.'

She turned away from him, her shoulders slumping. 'Yes, he's rich.' There was a choke in her voice and he stared at her, bewildered. 'But what about Adam?' He could hardly hear the words.

'But he's not here!' Phil knew that she wanted something from him, but he could not understand what it was. The conversation was meaningless, one of those strange exchanges that grown-ups seemed to have amongst themselves where he could tell they were discussing things that somehow weren't actually mentioned.

Making a valiant effort, he said confidently, 'We'll hear from him one day, don't you fret.'

'But that will be too late!' She turned back to him and he was horrified to see that tears sparkled on her long, dark lashes.

'Too late for what?' he asked, mystified but she only gave a small, shaky laugh, dashing her hand across her eyes.

'I'm sorry, Phil. It's my fault. You're just too young. I should have realised . . .'

He said stoutly, 'I'm ten now, and good for my age. Dick Thomas says so.'

'I know.' She reached out for him, pulling him to her again, and this time he recognised her need and stood quietly in her embrace. 'It's just that . . .' she swallowed convulsively. 'If Adam ever asks . . . If you ever see him again . . .' Her voice was choked now with tears. 'Tell him – tell him I had no choice, will you, Phil? Tell him I didn't want to do it.'

'You can tell him yourself,' he said.

'Perhaps.' She put him away from her. 'I'm glad to hear your news, anyway. I'm glad to know that you are happy and provided for.'

'Happy as a cock on his own dunghill,' he joked, and she smiled at him through her tears and turned slowly away.

The desolation in her attitude struck him suddenly and he ran after her. 'What's the matter, Clara? Where are you going?'

'I'm going to accept Mr Blacklock's proposal,' she whispered.

And she walked swiftly up the beach while he stared silently after her.

Chapter 28

The footman entered on silent feet. 'A Miss Pentreath to see you, sir.'

Edward felt a jolt of surprise. She had come! At last, she had come. 'Show her to the library.' His voice sounded cool but his hands were shaking with excitement. As he heard the door close behind the servant, he lowered the forkful of ham back on the plate and buried his face in his hands. She had come!

He had almost given up hope. She had held out so long! There had been days when he was sure that she would never submit, whatever pressure he could bring to bear, that she would never come to him; days when he had feared she might take her own life, marry a miner or fisherman, anything to deprive him of her.

On those days, he had ridden to St Just, had called to see her on any pretence he could find, just to feast his eyes on her face, on her body. Even her hatred fired his need, and the village women he had been accustomed to turn to were no longer enough.

He could no longer pretend that their heavy bodies were hers, slender yet voluptuous, that their rough hands were her small, delicate fingers. He had lain awake at night, groaning with his insatiable need for her. He had sacked a maid because her blonde hair had been a constant reminder of her. Every time he had come unexpectedly upon the woman his heart had leapt painfully for one fleeting second, until recognition came.

And now Clara was here. To accept his offer, surely to accept his offer? He pushed away his breakfast plate, his appetite suddenly lost. He must get control of himself, hide the desperation of his need for her. She was the petitioner and she must be made to realise that.

He unclasped the watch from its chain and laid it on the table in front of him. Ten minutes, he decided, he would make her wait for ten minutes. And his eyes remained fixed on the hands as, imperceptibly, they moved to the time when he could see the woman he loved.

She was standing by the window when he entered. His heart sang at the sight of her, even more slender and delicate than she had been in the old days when he had courted her openly.

She turned slowly at the sound of his footsteps, her hands clasped together in front of her, her expression quiet and determined. In the cold winter light he could see the ravages that her recent life had inflicted on her fine-boned face, and he would have regretted it, had there been any other way to bring her to him.

She bowed her head slightly. 'Mr Blacklock.'

'Edward,' he corrected her gently, and felt a glow as she repeated the name. Submission. He had got there at last. 'You wanted to see me?' His voice was cool, urbane.

For a second she hesitated. 'I – will you – that is,' she faltered, began again. 'You once asked me to marry you.'

Exultation flooded through him but he would not make it easy for her. 'As I remember, you refused me, Clara. Quite hurtfully.'

A quick blush stained her pale cheeks and as swiftly fled. Her hands twisted together. 'May I ask if you are still of the same mind?' Her voice was almost inaudible with embarrassment.

He could not contain himself any longer. He moved towards her, his hand outstretched. 'Does this mean that you will marry me?'

She raised her chin. 'There are certain conditions,' she said, and he stopped short. Damn the woman. She was the petitioner, didn't she realise that? What right had she to make conditions?

Her hands were locked together, the knuckles white. 'My mother is ill, very ill.' Her voice trembled slightly. 'An inflammation of the lungs. She may be dying. We – I – can't treat it. She needs a doctor. Quickly.'

He could hear the desperation in her voice and a surge of anger went through him. It had not been his carefully-laid plans that had brought her to him then, just a random event that might have occurred at any time. Even in her submission, she was still denying him his triumph.

'And your other demands?' he asked coldly.

'That my mother live with us after our marriage. And that the old servant who looks after us should also be housed here.'

'In the best bedroom?' he asked silkily, and she blushed.

'In the servants' quarters. She is a good worker.'

The very smallness of her demands showed how desperate she was, he thought, stroking his moustache as he watched her. 'And that is all?'

'One more.' He braced himself. This would be the big one.

Her head high, emerald eyes staring into his, Clara said, 'I want Sam Grenfell to marry the woman he has got with child.'

238

He almost laughed out loud. What had Sam and some village wench to do with her? It was a preposterous request. But why not meet it? It would be amusing to see Sam leg-shackled to some coarse woman.

His eyes on Clara, he moved to the wall and tugged sharply on the bell-pull. He could see the sudden tension in her body, the way her face seemed to get suddenly thinner and paler. She *is* desperate, he thought. She is afraid I am going to throw her out, refuse her. I am her last chance. Folding his arms, he stood silently until the footman opened the door, then he gave his orders without turning.

'I want a message sent to Dr Crawford. He is to go *at once* to treat Lady Susan Pentreath for a serious inflammation of the lungs.' He gave the directions succinctly, watching as the tension left Clara's body.

'I have demands of my own,' he stated as the man left the room. He saw her brace herself again but when she spoke her voice was under control.

'And they are . . .?'

Her calmness angered him. 'That you and your mother move out of that cottage at once. I refuse to marry a woman who lives in a hovel.' He thought quickly. 'You can move in with the Kingsleys until the wedding.'

'Perhaps Mr Kingsley will not wish to have us,' she replied.

'He'll do as I tell him,' Edward snapped.

She still stared at him. 'What do you have over Mr Kingsley?' Her voice was cool, interested.

'Power,' he said harshly. 'The power to make him do what I want. The same power that I shall have over you after we are married.'

At this, her green eyes widened. 'You will only have the power that I give you,' she said, positively.

Her naivety made him laugh. 'Clara, as your husband I shall have all the power I need.'

'And that is why you are marrying me. To exercise your power.' It was a statement, not a question; she knew the answer, there was no point in denying it.

She went on quickly, 'Are there any other demands you wish to make?'

Her nearness, her defiance of him even when she should have been crawling, begging for him to marry her, excited him as it always did. He wanted to take her now, crush her to him. He could hear the quiver in his voice as he said, 'One other.'

He took a deep breath. 'We will be married within the next month.'

Her face went white. 'So soon? But I . . .' Her head drooped. 'I have been ill.' Her voice was a muffled whisper and a pulse beat wildly at her temples.

So that was it. He could see it now in the translucent skin stretched over her slender bones, in the shadows under her eyes.

'As soon as possible, then.' Her weakness moved him as he had never been moved before; it even subdued his need for her body. To hide his emotion, he said with a leer, 'I don't want a sick bride in my bed on our wedding night.'

Her hands twisted convulsively, then were still.

'And, of course,' he went on, 'I need not state that I shall expect you to love, honour and obey me, as you will promise in the wedding service.' He gave a short laugh. 'I well remember your stalwart views on the subject, Clara. I am sure that you will make an admirable wife.'

She bowed her head. There was a desolation about her that tore at his heart-strings. He wanted to take her in his arms, to whisper words of comfort into her ear, but he did not know how. A despotic father, boyhood at a public school, swift, lustful couplings with village women . . . what did they teach him about how to love a woman like this, at once vulnerable and aloof?

Well, at least he would know how to treat her in bed. At the thought he could feel his body betraying him, so he moved hastily to the bell-pull to order a carriage to take her home. It would not be long now before she was his.

But the memory of the look he had caught when she mentioned her mother dying troubled him. He would have to get them moved to the Kingsleys' immediately, he decided. If Lady Susan was as ill as Clara said, she would need warmth and care.

Because, if she died, he would have lost his last hold over Clara Pentreath.

Clara dismissed her maid, holding herself upright until the woman had left the room, then she sank to the seat in front of the dressing table and stared at her reflection in the flickering light from the candles.

In her white nightdress, heavily decorated with lace and ribbons, she was more covered up than in the low-cut evening gowns she had been accustomed to wear at parties. Yet she felt so vulnerable, with her hair flowing over her shoulders and clinging to her skin, still electric from the brushing the maid had given it.

Behind her, the great bed gleamed richly, the covers already thrown invitingly back. How could she go through with it?

But she had to, she reminded herself. Already, that day, she had vowed herself, body and soul to the man who would shortly be coming to claim her, the man she already hated and feared as she had hated and feared no one else in the whole of her life.

She dropped her head in her hands, running her fingers through her hair. 'Oh, Adam!' She whispered. 'Why didn't you write? Oh, why didn't you send word?'

If there had been any hope, would she have given in like this? She doubted it. Even her mother's illness would not have moved her, if she had known that Adam was still alive, that he still loved her.

She rose, and moved restlessly to the windows, pulling back the heavy curtains. Outside, the spring night was balmy and clear. The stars shone brilliantly in the black velvet of the sky.

If he had loved her, she would have heard from him by now. If he had wanted her, he would have got word to her somehow. But there had been nothing. No letter. No word sent even to Phil. Either he was dead or he cared nothing for them; and his loss was an emptiness that ran through her life like a flaming spear. Unconsciously, she pressed her hands against her abdomen, now flat again, and empty. Empty like her life. Empty like her heart.

The door flew suddenly open and she whirled round. He stood there, her husband, her owner, his golden hair shining against the darkness of the corridor behind him. His grey eyes seemed to devour her, and she had to stop herself from crossing her arms protectively across her body.

'Well, Clara?' His voice was a pleasant tenor, showing no trace of the copious amounts of wine she had seen him drink this evening. He moved towards her, graceful, athletic, handsome. 'So you are my wife. At last.' His hand came out, strong and swift, catching her chin and lifting it until she was staring him straight in the eyes.

'Edward.' Clara forced herself to acknowledge him. She would not look away, would not give him the pleasure of seeing how frightened she felt, even though her heart was hammering so hard she could feel her whole body throbbing in time with its beats.

His lips curved in a wolfish smile. 'And you are prepared to love, honour and obey me?'

'I made that promise.' She had to fight to keep her voice level, twisting her hands together in the fullness of her night-robe lest their trembling betray her.

'And yet, it seems to me that you haven't been very enthusiastic about our union. You made me wait the full three months I gave you. I might almost have thought that you were an unwilling bride, the way you kept putting off the happy day.'

'My mother was so ill, and I was – pulled down by the life I had

241

been living.' Despite her best intentions, she could not meet his eyes as she told the lie. 'You said you did not want a sickly bride.' She tried to inject some lightness into her voice but it rang hollow and false, and she knew without looking at him that he had noticed it.

'And that is the only reason?'

She knew he was playing with her, enjoying the sight of her writhing under his questions and her temper snapped.

'You know what I think about you.' She had no problem in meeting his eyes now. 'I hold you, and you alone, responsible for the death of my father, the illness of my mother, the ruin of our mine.'

With a quick movement she slapped down the hand that was grasping her chin. 'I agreed to marry you because I had no option if I were to save my mother's life.' Her beautiful eyes glared up at him, lit with the fires of her disdain. 'Don't expect me to say now that I married you for love. We both know better than that.'

'Your mother's life was safe weeks ago.' He stroked his moustache with a careful finger, his eyes lingering on her pale face. 'But you did not seem to be eager to marry me. I have spent a long time wondering what the reason was.'

'And what was it?' She could feel herself shaking with fear even as she looked him full in the face.

'That you were waiting to hear from another man. One whom you might have preferred to me, despite his lack of obvious qualifications for the position of husband to Miss Pentreath.'

She swallowed nervously, the sound audible in the silent room. 'I don't know what you mean,' she said, and cursed the tremble in her voice.

'Oh, I think you do,' he answered, his voice suddenly cold and bitter. 'I think you know exactly what I mean.'

She stared up at him, her eyes enormous in her pale face. 'Why are you doing this?' she demanded, her voice no more than a harsh whisper. 'Why are you torturing us both like this?'

'Perhaps it's because I love you,' he said, his eyes suddenly blank and unreadable. 'Perhaps it's because I wanted you to love me, even just like me or feel grateful to me because I had rescued you from an intolerable position.' He swung away, pacing the bedroom floor with his long legs.

'But I'm not even going to get that from you, am I? Not even gratitude! Certainly not love.'

'Gratitude!' she repeated, her temper rising. 'Why should I feel grateful to you? You didn't rescue me from an intolerable position, you put me into it!'

Tears stood in her eyes but she blinked them back. 'Men had found

242

tin in Wheal Susan. We could have kept the mine open, we could have paid you back what we owed, but before my father could be informed of that, you closed the mine down and killed him.'

She stifled a sob. 'I could have worked in Penzance, earned enough to keep my mother and myself decently but you stopped that. People were afraid to help us because *you* had scared them off.'

She stared at him scornfully. 'And then you dare to say that you did it because you love me. You don't know what love is!'

'And you do.' His voice was quiet but the anger underscored every word. 'You know exactly what love is, don't you? Because you already love someone else.'

Clara gripped the dressing table for support. 'I don't know what you mean.' Even she could hear the dismay in her voice.

'Don't deny it. I know, you see,' he told her. 'I know that you love another, a *peasant*.' She flinched at the scorn in his voice. 'I know that the woman I love, whom I *married*, dammit, is unworthy of me, and yet,' his voice broke, dropped, so that she had to strain to hear the next words, 'I still love you.' It was almost a groan.

Coldness dropped around her like a cloak. This wasn't suspicion, she realised suddenly. He knew!

Unable to help herself she moved towards him. 'How do you know?' She could scarcely force the words past her trembling lips. 'What evidence do you have?'

He reached into his pocket and pulled out several sheets of notepaper. The pages were grubby and creased, as if they had been pored over again and again. He waved them angrily in her face. 'This is the evidence. A letter to you from another man, a criminal. A love letter.'

She could not read what the pieces of paper said, he was moving them too quickly, but she had no doubts as to the identity of the writer. Her heart leapt painfully in her chest. Adam! They had to be from Adam!

'How did you get those?' she demanded. 'What right had you to read a letter addressed to me?'

'Right?' His face twisted in a grimace that suddenly showed her his inner pain. 'Why, the right of an executor to open post addressed to a dead man. The right of a friend to save a bereaved family hurt. The right of a fiancé to open a letter addressed to his love.' His grey eyes burned down at her. 'Are those rights enough?'

'What does he say?' Her desire to know overcame her caution, her commonsense. She moved forward, reaching for the letters. 'Is he well? Where is he?'

He lifted the letter above his head, out of her reach. 'He wanted to

243

know if he could marry you. If your father would consent to an engagement.'

'A-a-a-gh!' It was a long drawn-out moan, a lament for what might have been, for the death of hope. Clara stood stiff with shock for an everlasting moment as the enormity of what she had done washed over her.

Adam *had* loved her. He had not forgotten her. And she had betrayed him, doubted him, given herself in marriage to the man who had ruined him. She covered her face with her hands, battling the desolation that emptied life of all meaning.

As if from a great distance, she heard Edward speak again, his voice dripping scorn. 'My woman, the woman I wanted to marry, to be linked to a common criminal, to be touched by an animal like that!'

'Not an animal. No. A man. A real man.' She lifted her head in anguished denial and the pages he still held aloft caught her eye.

'Give me those.' She sprang at them, but he was too quick for her, jerking them swiftly out of her reach.

'What?' he demanded. 'Let my wife, my new bride, start our married life by carrying out a correspondence with another man?' His voice was heavy with irony. 'What of your vows, my dear? What of the promises you made only a few hours ago? To love, honour and obey. To foresake all others. Don't you remember?'

His mouth twisted in a cruel smile. 'Because *I* remember, very well. And I know that you are now legally a part of me. You have no possessions but what I allow you, no money but what I give you, and,' his teeth flashed white in the candlelight, 'no correspondents except with my agreement.'

He held the papers to the candles on the dressing table, fending her off easily with one hand as she struggled to stop him. She moaned again as they caught fire, blackening and shrivelling before her longing eyes, the flames devouring the words she lusted after.

For a second the writing stood out, silver grey against blackening paper, then it was consumed for ever and he dropped the fragments to the floor, grinding them out on the wooden floorboards with a cruel heel.

She stood stiff then, her eyes fixed on his face. 'I hate you.' Her voice trembled with the force of her emotion. 'You have ruined my life, ruined *his* life. What you have done is unforgivable.'

He advanced on her, his face a mask of fury but she did not flinch; she defied him with every bone in her body. 'I will never love you.' It was a promise, a vow. 'I will never be your wife.'

'You already are my wife.' His voice was harsh. 'Forget him. He is

244

beyond your reach now. You don't even know which continent he is on. As far as you are concerned, he is dead.'

He pulled her to him and his voice was suddenly husky with anticipation. 'But you are my wife. Now. For ever. And I will teach you what that means.'

Before she could move he had gripped the material at her throat, ripping it from neck to waist with a sudden, convulsive movement. She fought then, with nails and teeth, twisting like a wild animal in a trap but he was too strong for her.

Even when she realised that her struggles only served to excite him, she still fought on. Her pride, her anger, would not allow him anything. And when it was all over, she huddled in a tight ball on the far side of the bed, curled round her anguish as round a precious relic, and cried herself to sleep.

And never knew that on the other pillow, a bare foot from her, hot, bitter tears were silently cried by a man who wanted to love but who had learned only to hate.

Chapter 29

'A letter! A letter!'

Adam straightened up abruptly, shading his eyes as he watched Norman race down the dusty track between the shacks, waving the letter over his head as he ran.

At last! For over a year he had waited, sweated, hoped, prayed. And now a letter, at last!

He forced himself to stand still, schooling his face so that none of the passing men would see the churning anxiety inside him. He was an under-captain now, with a position to uphold. He could not afford to let his men see him acting like a schoolboy. The copper mines at Burra Burra were no different, when you got down to it, from the tin mines of St Just, and the men were exactly the same. They would respect you – but you had to earn it.

He dragged his eyes from the running man, concentrating on cleaning his nails with a sharpened match, but his hands were shaking so much he jabbed it painfully into the quick. Fool, to care so much.

He greeted Norman with unaccustomed roughness. 'Anyone would think you were daft as a besom, to look at you now.'

Norman grinned cheerfully, ignoring the insult. 'The mail has just come – our first letter ever.' He held it out, delighted, but it took only one glance for Adam to see that it wasn't from Clara. The writing was sprawling, unformed.

'From our Molly,' Norman said, inserting a grimy thumb. He glanced up. 'You don't seem very excited.'

'I am.' But his heart was heavy. Surely she could have written? Surely her father should have replied, even if it were only to tell him that Clara was not for him? Hopeless to remind himself that ships were becalmed, held up, sometimes for months. Possibly even sunk. Perhaps he should write again? The first letter could have gone astray.

246

'My God! It's all been happening since we left!' Norman's exclamation cut through his thoughts.

'What has?' he demanded. Even though the letter wasn't from Clara it might mention her.

'Wheal Susan's closed down, and –'

Adam leapt to his feet. 'What? But there was tin there – I found it!' Surely Clara had recognised the specimen he gave her for what it was? She couldn't have been so ignorant that she wouldn't have known good tin ore when she saw it? And even if she had, the Captain would have seen it the next time he checked underground. No one could have missed it, a seam of ore, black and soft as butter in the white hardness of the quartz.

'Perhaps it wasn't good quality.' Norman was immersed in his letter, hardly listening to the noises around him as the miners prepared their evening meal. The smell of roast goat rose fragrant on the soft air but for once his attention was not on the coming meal.

'My dear soul, listen to this! Our Molly's wed – and to Grenfell, that stick of a purser! However did she catch him, I wonder?' Norman raised amazed eyes. 'And he's working in Blacklock's bank in Penzance!' He shook his head, disbelievingly. 'She were a fine gert maid, but I'd never have thought she'd manage that.'

He turned back to his letter and Adam was aware of a sudden silence. Norman was crouched over the sheet of paper, unmoving, a still centre in the noisy flow of human life that made up the mining settlement.

'What is it?' he demanded suddenly. 'What have you read?' Norman made a movement as if to hide the letter but Adam was too quick for him. He snatched the coarse paper out of his hand, his eyes running swiftly over Molly's ill-spelt writing.

Clara's name jumped up at him. '*And that stuck-up Miss Pentreeth has gon and wed Mr Blakloke.*' Adam stood still, feeling as if he had been punched in the stomach.

Blacklock? It was impossible. It *had* to be wrong! She would never have married Blacklock!

He became aware of Norman pulling at his arm, shouting at him: 'Adam, Adam. Don't take on so, lad.' The sounds, the hands, seemed a million miles away.

But he could only stand there, frozen in time, staring at the paper in his hand, the fateful sentence leaping out at him as if it were printed in red. '*And that stuck-up Miss Pentreeth has gon and wed Mr Blakloke.*'

'Adam.' Hands gripped his shoulder now, were shaking him so that he could no longer focus his eyes on the paper. But it did not matter.

247

The words were burned for ever on his brain. '*That stuck-up Miss Pentreeth . . .*'

'Adam, talk to me.' With an effort Adam tore his eyes away from the letter. Norman was staring up at him, his face dark with worry.

'I'm sorry. I've taken your letter.' He pushed it gently into Norman's suddenly nerveless hand, then turned away. With great concentration, almost as if he were drunk, Adam walked slowly to the scrubland behind the mine workings.

Clara married. If it had been anyone else, he knew that he could have coped. What was she ever but an impossible dream? He wasn't good enough for her, he knew it. And she couldn't wait for ever. There would be pressure brought on her to marry, by her father, and her mother Lady Susan. He knew that. He could have understood.

But Edward Blacklock! The man who had ruined him, exiled him. How could she have married him? That was betrayal. That was unforgivable.

He stood alone in the gathering darkness. Around him, the world was filled with alien noises. A parakeet screeched eerily, like a flying ghost. Creatures of this new, strange continent rustled and scuttled just out of sight. Slowly, silently, the stars appeared.

But not his stars! Not the stars that had smiled down when he lay with Clara on the Cornish cliffs, made her his own, pledged himself to her with his body. These stars were foreign. There was nothing here that linked him with the old days, nothing at all – except his memories of her, his love for her.

And that was gone. Gone for ever. With one action she had betrayed him, betrayed his love, betrayed his life.

Since that night on the cliffs, everything he had ever done had been for her, every penny he had earned saved against the day he could call her to him.

And it was all gone! Wasted! Thrown away by a woman who put position before love, wealth before honour.

Pearls before swine. The phrase came unbidden to his mind. He fumbled briefly at his neck and pulled out the soft leather pouch that he wore, tucked down inside his shirt. With a swift movement he untied the cord, and poured the contents into the palm of his hand.

Under the Southern Cross, the pearls gleamed with a life of their own. They were Clara's pearls, the ones she had given him, that he had kept safe. He had taken them out when times were bad, burying his face in them as if they still held the faint scent of her body. He would have starved rather than sold them, They were hers, and he held them in trust for her. For a faithless harlot!

Adam gripped the smooth globes between his fingers, snapping the

248

silken thread that held them, then, with one, heartbroken gesture, he flung them far into the starlit night.

Dawn was paling the eastern sky when he pushed open the door to the shack. Norman was sprawled, still dressed, in a chair and his eyes creaked open as Adam loomed over him.

'I were brem worried.' He rubbed his eyes roughly, trying to drag himself awake. 'I looked everywhere for you, tried all the bars.'

'I walked.' Adam stood still, his eyes unreadable in the dim light as he stared down at his friend. 'That letter –' his voice was hard, all emotion hidden '– did it say anything about Phil?'

Norman sat straighter. 'Molly said he's well, and very happy.' There was an earnestness in his voice that awoke Adam's suspicion.

'And where's he working now Wheal Susan has been knacked?'

Norman said unwillingly, 'He's got a job fishing. But Molly did say he were brem happy,' he added quickly.

Fishing. Adam turned away. Clara knew what he felt about the sea, knew what his ambitions were for the boy. He could feel again her light touch on his sleeve, hear her voice, soft, clear, different from the loud coarseness of the bal-maidens. 'I'll look after Phil for you.'

But she hadn't! She had deliberately taken him away from work that would have provided him with a good future. She had risked the boy's life because she couldn't be bothered to use her father's influence to find him work down a mine.

She was false, false through and through!

'Do something for me.' His voice was abrupt. 'When you write to Molly next, just tell her one thing.' He had to struggle to get the next words out. 'Tell her, tell her I'm dead.'

Norman gaped at him. 'But what about Phil . . .?'

'Forget Phil.' Adam's voice was harsh with pain. 'He's made his own life now. He doesn't need me any more.' He turned away, rubbing a hand roughly across his face. 'My life isn't of value to anyone in Cornwall. It will be better if they all think I've died.' He strode quickly across the room and bent to drag the blankets from his bed.

Norman watched him, surprise and alarm jerking him fully awake. 'What're you doing? Are you mad?'

'Mad? No, I'm sane. At last, I'm sane.' Adam stood up, his arms full of bedclothes. 'I'm through here. I've had enough of respectability. I'm fed up with flogging my guts out for someone else, working my way up from tributer to under-captain and then on.'

'You're giving up mining?' Norman was incredulous.

'I'm mining for myself from now on. I'm taking my own risks, making my own way.' Adam's face was white and set. 'Money is the

249

only thing that matters in this life. All the rest of it – respectability, honour – they're just snares, invented to keep men down. They're meaningless. Money is what counts, and if you don't have it, you're rubbish.'

He took a deep breath, his chest swelling under his coarse shirt and Norman could see the pulse that beat crazily at his neck.

'Well, I've seen through them at last. If money is that important, then that is what I shall get – or die in the process.'

'You mean . . .'

'I'm going to Ballarat,' Adam said tersely. 'They've struck gold there. There are fortunes to be made and I'm going to make one.' He glanced over at Norman. 'It's up to you whether you come or stay.'

'Come – to look for gold?' Norman let out a whoop that echoed down the small street. 'You bet I'm coming!'

Adam dragged his spare pair of boots from under the bed. 'There's one thing you must understand.' His voice was muffled by his position. 'I intend to make my fortune, but if I don't – well, I won't be coming back. Do you understand?'

He straightened, staring at Norman with an expression of absolute determination and the other man sobered abruptly. Adam meant exactly what he said: he was going to make money or die in the process.

And from the look in his eyes, he didn't care which.

'Stop the carriage!' Clara's voice rang out sharply. As the coachman pulled the smart landau to a halt she swung round in her seat, peering past the edge of the raised leather hood. Surely that was Molly Willcock? She corrected herself, Molly Grenfell. She waited until the footman had handed her down from the carriage then she hurried back towards the small figure. Blacklock's servants mustn't over hear this conversation.

Clara saw the small figure recognise her, then hesitate briefly before she walked on, hefting the small baby she held higher in her arms. At the sight of the child, Clara felt her heart contract. Her child would have been that age, now, hers and Adam's. If it had lived. She closed her eyes briefly, fighting back the pain that lanced through her at the thought.

'Mrs Grenfell.' She forced a welcoming smile. 'I must congratulate you. I haven't seen you since your marriage.'

She had expected smiles, thanks. After all, it had been her intervention that had saved the woman from a life of shame. But she was treated to a small curtsey, the briefest that politeness allowed from the wife of an employee.

Clara tried again. 'You have a fine child. May I see her?'

'It's a boy,' Molly said gruffly, but she turned the baby slightly so that Clara could see his face.

'A handsome child.' Clara touched the soft pink cheek. Hers had been a boy. Oh God, would the pain never end? Her hands shook with the anguish of her grief.

She swallowed convulsively, recalling the reason why she had stopped. 'Have you heard yet from your brother?' There was no time for the social niceties; she *had* to know about Adam. If only she could tell him what had happened, share her pain . . .

Molly stared at her, her blue eyes contemptuous. ''Tidn't my brother you're interested in, is it? It's Adam Trevelyan you want to know about.'

'Well, what if it is?' Clara felt oddly defensive. 'He was a – friend – of mine. Surely there is no harm in asking about him.'

''Tis all right for the gentry to have friends, I reckon,' Molly said angrily. 'When a poor girl like me has one, everyone looks down their noses at her.'

Her hostility was so obvious that Clara retaliated. 'It seems little enough to ask, especially when I . . .' Her voice tailed away.

'When you what?' Molly demanded. 'When you made Sam Grenfell marry me like I was a heifer on the farm, to be mated to the bull the farmer thought best?'

'But you wanted to marry him!' Clara was caught off-balance by the venom in her voice.

'I wanted him to marry me,' Molly corrected her. 'I wanted him to *want* to marry me. That was what I really wanted.' Her blue eyes swam with unshed tears. 'You gentry, you think that people like us don't have feelings. You think that you've got to be rich to have any pride. Well, you're wrong, I tell you! I had me pride, and you shoved my nose in the dirt.'

She swung the baby onto her other shoulder as if moving him away from Clara's contaminating presence. 'How would you like to be married to a man who didn't want you? Who threw the fact in your face every time he saw you? Who went on and on about how you've ruined his life? How he could have done better for himself without you?'

Clara stared at her. 'I'm sorry.' The words were inadequate, but what more could she say? 'I did it for the best. I did it to help you.'

'You don't know what help is.' The tears were streaming down Molly's face now. 'You come, playing the Lady Bountiful to a hurt miner and he gets his eyes dazzled by your pretty ways and your fine talk. And what happens? He has to go to Australia. And it was all your fault. I do know all about it. Sam Grenfell told me how your husband laid a trap for Adam. And all because of you.'

She sobbed suddenly and the child set up a thin wail, infected by his mother's seething emotions.

Unconsciously, she soothed him, her eyes still fixed on Clara's face. 'And now you want to ruin his life again. You want to keep him dangling after you even though you've already got a husband of your own.'

'I just want to send him a message.' Clara felt helpless in the face of the other woman's antagonism. 'Just one message.'

'He's already had the only message about you that I'm going to send him,' Molly said furiously. 'And that was, that you'd married Mr Blacklock.'

'You've told him that!' Clara closed her eyes in anguish. This woman, so bitter against her, would have delighted in breaking the news as suddenly as possible. 'But I wanted to tell him about it. I wanted to explain . . .'

'You wanted to keep him dangling after you,' Molly repeated crudely. 'Well, it's too late! You can't do it. He's where you can't get at him any more.'

Clara's face paled. 'What do you mean? Where is he? What's happened?' She reached out unthinkingly, her hands on the other woman's shoulders, shaking her as if she could shake the truth out of her, while the baby screamed in distress.

Molly pulled herself free with an angry jerk. 'He's dead, that's what I mean! Norman wrote and told me. My lovely Adam's dead! And it's you that killed him, you and that no-good husband of yours!'

Chapter 30

'You are home, madam.'

The butler's voice filtered slowly through Clara's misery as she lay, pressed back against the squabs of the comfortable carriage. With an effort she forced her eyes to open, open on a world empty and meaningless. Carefully, one finger at a time, she uncurled her clenched fists. Her universe might lie in ruins about her, but one still had to keep up appearances.

'Thank you, Bennet.' The words came out accompanied by a quivering, polite smile, but she stumbled on the carriage step and only the butler's quick reactions saved her from a fall.

'Are you well, madam?'

Her voice was husky again, her eyes burning with tears she dare not shed. 'Quite well.'

He handed her carefully up the steps, obviously not believing her. 'The master is home and luncheon will be served whenever you are ready.'

At the thought of food, Clara felt her stomach churn. All she wanted was to be alone, to wrap herself round her hurt, but she would not get that privacy here, not with the servants and Edward always around. And Edward must not know, not yet. She could not bear his triumph, his delight, when he learned that his rival was dead. He would know it sometime, but not today, not while the shock still coursed like ice through her veins and the world was empty of love and hope.

'You may serve luncheon in ten minutes' time,' she instructed, and went upstairs to get ready.

But not all her willpower could help Clara to force one mouthful of food past her lips. She pushed it around on her plate, talking with a brittle gaiety to Edward about the work of the bank while her body shuddered convulsively. For once she matched Edward's intake of wine, glass for glass, hoping the alcohol would dull the pain inside.

253

At the end of the meal he pushed back his chair. 'I think you should have a rest after luncheon, Clara.'

His invariable words when he took her upstairs . . . as if their bitter couplings when they retired at night-time weren't enough. For eight months she had fought him, every time, struggling with a ferocity that was all the greater for being silent. She had even marked him, with teeth and nails, until he taught her better by whipping her for her rebellion. But it hadn't been the pain of the whip that had stopped her, it had been his excited gasps as he swung again and again at her and she had realised, disbelieving, that he got as much pleasure from this as from their embattled love-making.

For a second her heart quailed then pride took over. She bowed her head in acquiescence; reluctant to let herself down in front of the servants. Slowly, she made her unwilling body move towards her husband, feeling his hand burning her arm through her sleeve as he escorted her to their room.

But when the door closed behind them, the horror of Adam's death loomed starkly. What did anything matter? She could no longer feel that by giving in to Edward she was betraying the love that Adam felt for her. He was dead. Dead and gone. She would never again see the smile in his blue eyes, never feel the touch of his mouth on hers, the glory of his arms around her. He was dead, and in dying, he had killed all emotion in her.

Wearily, she turned to Edward. Let him do as he wished. Today she would not fight him, had no energy to struggle. She made no movement or sound as he forced her back across the bed, throwing her voluminous skirts up over her head.

Hidden by the enveloping folds, she covered her face thankfully with her hands. *Oh, Adam. Adam.* The tears squeezed silently past her closed lids. If only she could have held him, just once more, touched him, heard him speak her name.

Edward's hands, hot and hard, spreading her thighs meant nothing to her. Even when he pulled aside her divided drawers, ramming his fingers into her innermost parts she stayed quiescent, detached. Her body seemed to belong to someone else; only her mind and her memories belonged to her. *Adam. Adam.*

But the love-making did not proceed as it had always done. Even in the midst of her despair, Clara became vaguely aware that it was taking longer than usual. Once he had overcome her opposition, Edward would mount her swiftly, battering her unmercifully for the minute or so it would take him to reach satisfaction. But this time, the probing fingers lingered uncertainly. There was a long pause.

'Help me.' It was no more than a whisper. He reached under the skirts for her hand, pulled it down, laid it on his groin. 'Help me, Clara.'

Something was wrong. Always before, his body had been rampant, powerful. Now his manhood lay under her fingers, soft, flaccid, motionless. Too miserable to care, her fingers moved on it for a few seconds, then dropped away as another wave of misery overcame her. *Oh, Adam.*

Then the bed shook as her husband pulled himself away. There was a soft rustle of clothing being adjusted then the door banged shut.

Unbelieving, she heard his feet hammering down the stairs, a shout for his horse, the slam of the front door and she was alone. Alone, at last, with her misery. She curled into a small ball, pulling the pillow over her head to stifle her sobs, and gave herself up to the pain that racked her. *Oh, Adam.*

The afternoon passed in a rage of mourning and despair. By the time her maid came to dress her for dinner, Clara could barely rouse herself enough to mutter that she was unwell before sinking again into lethargy. In her prison of emptiness she was scarcely aware of her maid undressing her and helping her into her nightdress. Even when Edward came to bed, smelling of drink, and fumbled impotently with her before stumbling back downstairs to the brandy bottle she lay inert, lost in the dark dream of her loss.

The maid brought up her morning tea, asked anxiously if the doctor should be called, begged to be allowed to send word to Mr Blacklock. Clara lay unmoving, the blankets pulled tight around her body, a shield against the world. If Adam were dead she wanted to die. What was the point of life if she could never see him again, never hear his voice, know that he was looking at the same sun that she saw, breathed the same air? She kept her ears closed to the maid's worried enquiries, waiting for her to leave so that she could be alone again, lying in the dim room, wishing for death.

'Well!'

The door was slammed open with a bang that jerked Clara's eyes wide in shock, then the curtains were thrown violently back with a rattle of curtain rings and the winter sunlight streamed in. Ma Downing stood over her, arms akimbo, her red face wrinkled with disgust. Clara had never seen such a look on her pleasant features before.

'Well!' she repeated furiously. 'And suppose you tell me what you think you're up to, lying here like a pig in its own muck, setting all the household by its ears.'

Clara groaned, covering her eyes with her hands. 'Go away, Ma,' she begged. 'I'm not well. I can't stand the light. I'm tired to death.'

'Tired, is it?' the old woman demanded. 'And why's that, then? Arranged too many posies, have you? Pricked your finger with your tapestry needle?' Her voice dripped sarcasm. She moved forward and stood over the bed, so close that Clara could smell the scent of old woman's flesh and stale sweat that brought back instantly her time in Adam's cottage.

At the memory her eyes pricked with tears, but she fought them back. Once she gave way to crying she was afraid she would never stop. Better by far to sink into a decline, to lie here until death claimed her than to make an hysterical show of her emotions, be the butt of jokes and scandal.

'Please, Ma,' she begged again. 'Leave me alone. Just go away and leave me alone.'

She heard the woman cross heavily to the door, the snick of the catch, and she breathed a sigh of relief. Then the footsteps returned.

'So what is it, my handsome?' Mother Downing asked, sitting on the edge of the bed. 'What's happened to make you act like a dying duck in a thunderstorm?' She gently smoothed back Clara's tumbled hair with a rough hand.

The caress was too much for her. A sob broke and the tears came streaming down her cheeks. 'Adam's dead, Ma. Adam's dead and I can't go on living without him.' She reached out despairing hands to the woman. 'You do understand, don't you? I loved him. I loved him and now I want to die.'

The old woman snorted. 'Oh, I understand.' There was an abrasive note in her voice that Clara had never heard before. 'I understand very well.' She stood upright and pointed a red, bulbous finger in Clara's face. 'A man you once fancied passes on and you think you can upset all the rest of the world just because you feel brem unhappy.'

'But I didn't just fancy him.' Clara almost wailed the words. 'I loved him, Ma – I really loved him. You know that.'

She sniffed. 'I know only one thing,' she said, 'and that is, you married another man, and you've been cheating on him all this time. Loving Adam! What about your marriage vows, eh? What about them?'

'But Edward knows,' Clara sobbed. 'He's always known that I loved Adam.'

'That was when you were unwed,' Ma Downing said staunchly. 'That were then, and this is now. You haven't got no right to love another man, not now you're wed. Mr Blacklock's kept his side of the bargain. Your ma may not know where she is but she's well and happy. And you've got silks for your back and beef for your belly. He's kept his side of the bargain, now it's up to you to keep yours.'

Clara could feel the tears trickling off her chin. 'But I can't, Ma, I can't! I'm so unhappy!' Her fists beat impotently on the counterpane.

'And what's that got to do with anything?' the old woman demanded. 'God never put us on this earth to be happy. He put us here to do right. And if being unhappy is the price you have to pay, then you pays it, and you keeps your chin up and a smile on your face while you're paying it.'

She leaned forward, thrusting her fat red face up close against Clara's. 'Grieving won't bring him back,' she said fiercely. 'If grieving would have brought anyone back, do you think I'd be a widow now? You have your memories of him. Thank God for that, and show your thanks by living like a good Christian, not wailing and howling like a poor heathen what don't know no better. Now, you get out of that there bed and get dressed, and start acting like a lady instead of a baby what's lost its teat.'

With businesslike hands she stripped the bedclothes back and without knowing how she got there, Clara found herself standing by the bed, her head swimming. She made one final attempt. 'But Ma, I can't face the servants. I'll cry, I know I will.'

'Then get out and stay out until you can act proper,' Ma said unsympathetically. 'Now, do you want me to help you dress, or do I tell that po-faced maid of yourn to do it?' Her thick red fingers fumbled at the ties on Clara's nightdress. 'What you want is some fresh air. Give anybody the vapours, it would, frowsting in here without a bit of real exercise. No wonder you feel like dying. When you feel like that, you got to go right out and start living. Work's best, but if you can't do that then go for a brem long walk and thank God you've still got the health to do it.'

'Not walk,' Clara whispered. She couldn't bear the faces of the people she would meet, their greetings or conversations. 'I'll order my horse and ride out until I feel better.'

'That's it.' Ma Downing patted her shoulder. 'That's the little maid I remember. I always knew you had guts.'

'Not guts, Ma.' Clara's voice was constricted but she managed a shaky laugh. 'Not guts! No lady has those.'

Ma snorted. 'Then you're no lady, because I can remember well enough you puking them up when you was carrying last year.' She saw Clara's horror-struck face and lowered her voice. 'All right, 'course I won't tell nobody. But if you got yourself in the family way again, you wouldn't have no trouble with all these vapours. Too much

257

time on your hands, that's your problem. You want to milk a few cows every day, and look after a handful of children. That would stop your fancies.'

A handful of children! But she had only wanted one. Adam's child. And he had died.

Ma was right – it *was* a relief to be out in the open air, spurring her horse to a frenzied gallop as if she could leave her unhappiness behind her. The speed, the physical movement took control of her senses, dulling the pain that tore through her. Clara rode, simply for the physical relief it gave her and it was with a shock that she came to herself and found she was staring at the rotting remains of Wheal Susan. Strange, she thought, that now, when her present life was empty and meaningless, she should go back to a place that once had meant so much to her. Once it had been her father's life, the foundation of his fortune, the passport to her parents' marriage.

Now it just represented death. She threw the reins over a piece of rusting machinery and walked slowly through the ruined buildings, her heart breaking again at the desolation she saw all around her.

The winter sun highlighted the stains that besmirched the once-pristine walls of the Count House, thrust pale fingers of light through the gaping holes where once smartly painted doors and windows had defied the weather.

Who had stolen them? she wondered. Men who had once worked at the mine, whose livelihoods had died with the explosion that had killed Captain Pentreath?

She leaned her head against the granite walls of the engine house. So many deaths! Her father. Adam. Her child, the child she had killed unknowingly while she had struggled to save her own mother's life. And her mother, now lost for ever in the world of her childhood. That, too, was a kind of death.

And Ma Downing had blamed her for not keeping her marriage vows. Clara covered her face with her hands. Here, in this place, she could accept that at last. But had it been so wrong? Surely she had done everything she could, everything that could be expected of her. She had sacrificed her body, her youth, her future for the sake of her mother's health.

Surely it was not too much to ask that she should be allowed to keep her dream? That sometime, somehow, Edward would die, that she and Adam would be together again. She had even imagined them working together here, at this mine, opening it, working it, mining the vein that Adam had discovered.

But she had never wished for Edward's death. It had been a fantasy, the only way she could face up to a loveless marriage with a man she hated and feared.

And now even that dream was taken from her. She had no hope for the future; no happiness, nothing. Just the grey dullness of duty and propriety. Just carrying on, loathing each day as it came, knowing that tomorrow would be no better.

The memory of her first meeting with Edward came back to her. She, in her too-small, too-tight riding habit, defying her mother. Her proud words, 'When I marry I shall give my first allegiance to my husband' rang in her head.

And now she was married, and to the very man who had heard that promise. And she was being expected to keep it. Without love. Without hope. Without end.

She groaned. 'Oh God. Help me.' It was too much, too much to bear. She had lost everything and now she had lost even hope. At nineteen, the years stretched ahead of her terrifyingly vacant.

How could she live like this? She was a fighter, not an endurer. As long as there was a battle to be fought she could rouse her courage and her energy. But she could not just endure from day to day, existing in a stultifying slough of despair and misery.

The cold breeze plucked at her skirts, and far above, a gentle clanging made her look up.

High above, silhouetted against the pale winter sky, the winding gear still stood, like a crown on the head of a fallen king. One rusty piece of metal, loosened by neglect, swung slowly in the wind, tolling away the destruction of the mine.

Wheal Susan, too, was dying. Under her feet, the tin ore lay drowned in blackness, the ore for which her father and Adam had sought so desperately. Its loss seemed an abomination, another death.

Then, even as she gazed upwards, a ray of sunlight shot momentarily through a gap in the clouds. For a second the winding gear blazed golden, almost blinding her with its brightness. Then the clouds closed, the brilliance faded.

But not from Clara's mind. It seemed an omen, a portent.

Why should the mine die? There was tin down there. It could pay its way. And the price of ore was rising again. She straightened, the colour sweeping back into her pale cheeks as the thought came to her.

Marriage with Edward she could do nothing about. She would have to endure it, using every ounce of strength and discipline, to act, at least, like a perfect wife. But here was something to fight for, something to give her life a meaning beyond the mere tedium of existence.

She would re-open the mine. As a memorial. To her father. To the child she had lost. And to Adam.

She filled her lungs with the fresh Atlantic air, smiling as new life flooded back through her body. Her life wasn't over. She would carry on again. She had found a reason to live.

Chapter 31

'You've done well tonight.' Lieutenant Laity paused, a cigar in hand, smiling down at Edward Blacklock as he lay back in the leather armchair.

'I do well every night.' Edward could not keep the note of pride out of his voice. He ran his fingers lazily through the pile of sovereigns that lay on the table beside him. The gold coins glimmered in the yellow gaslight, ringing against each other with a soft chime that seemed to cut through the conversations of the men around them.

Lifting his coat-tails, Laity seated himself in the chair beside him, signalling to a passing waiter for a drink. 'And you play here often? It seems to me that you are always here when I come in.'

'Where else is there?' Edward threw back his brandy in one gulp. 'Dead-and-alive hole! But it's the only decent hotel in Penzance. Only one this side of Truro, for that matter.'

He cast a disparaging look around the room. On the small balcony from which the death of Nelson had been announced to a stunned crowd, three musicians played softly, their instruments almost drowned out by the chatter of men relaxing without their womenfolk on one of the hotel's special evenings.

The card tables were emptying now as the players enjoyed a drink with their friends before making their way home along the muddy roads that surrounded Penzance in all directions.

He ran his fingers through the pile of coins again, admiring their heavy resonance. 'Why didn't you play on my table?'

Laity laughed. 'You play too deep for me. I play cards for the fun of it, not for the excitement. I get that in my work.'

'You'll never win much that way.' Edward's voice slurred slightly. He peered up at Laity under lowered lids, his fair hair falling in a damp lock across his brows. Beads of sweat glittered on his moustache.

'Or lose much either.' Laity dug in his pocket for change to give the waiter who had brought his brandy. 'We don't all run banks.'

'As if that is a help.' Edward's face darkened. He was fed up with all the complaints and worries from his chief clerk. That was all he met with these days. The happy social round that he had been a part of while he was single had drifted away on his marriage. At first he had been too enthralled by Clara to want to share her. And now . . . drinking and gambling were his only escape.

Clara might be his wife but she was not his lover, was not, in some strange way, even *there* any more, when he tried to force himself on her in their bed at night. It was as if she was not aware of him during those hot, panting moments.

Edward closed his eyes, feeling wretched. It had been so different during the first months of their marriage, when she had fought him every time, rousing him to a passion he had never experienced before, to a lust that drove him home during the day-time to slake his needs on her.

What did it matter that she did not bother to disguise the fact that she did not love him? That their conversation was limited to mere politenesses? Just to look at her across the dinner table, knowing that, in a few hours, she would be his for the taking, had been reward enough.

But in the last few weeks, that had all changed. She no longer seemed to resent him. In fact, she was pleasant, friendly even – the way he had always dreamed she might be.

But in bed, even his worst blows could not rouse her to defy him. And without her struggles, he was helpless.

For the first time in his life he was unable to perform like a man.

The memory of that charlatan of a fortuneteller came suddenly back to him – the small, smelly tent hung in black, the flickering light. And his words, harsh, gleeful words, full of ill-omen. 'You'll get what you want. But by that time you won't want it any more.'

And he had got what he wanted. He had got Clara. But the Great Alhambro had been wrong about one thing; Edward still wanted her. Oh God, how he wanted her! Wanted her with an intensity that burned in his mind night and day, blinding him to everything else. But when he went to her now, his treacherous body let him down.

He waved his hand violently in the air. 'Waiter! More brandy – and quickly!' he shouted, ignoring Laity's shocked surprise. Pious prig, sitting there, implying that he was spending too much on gambling. As if there was anything else to do in this godforsaken dump.

'Still after Isabelle Kingsley?' Edward demanded with malicious pleasure. 'You won't get much cash with her, you know. Her father's heading for the rocks, just like the rest of 'em.'

Laity drew deeply on his cigar. 'Really? Not that I would let such a matter affect me where I loved, but I understood from Mr Kingsley that business was picking up, now that the price of tin had risen again and more mines were re-opening.'

Edward felt a frisson of panic. Now that he thought about it, he hadn't seen Kingsley at the bank for several months. He must have seen the figures, he assumed; the clerks were always shoving ledgers full of figures in front of him whenever he showed his face at the bank. But they had lost their interest for him since his marriage with Clara. He could no longer concentrate as he used to. Her face, her body haunted his thoughts, and recently it had got worse. The less he could make love to her the more she obsessed him. It was only when a pile of sovereigns depended on the turn of a card that he could put her from his mind.

He took the glass from the waiter's hand and swirled the golden spirits around in it. 'The price of tin is always going up and down. I can't be bothered to keep a track of it day to day.' But that might lie behind Clara's sudden demands that he should re-open Wheal Susan, he realised. As if he would ever throw good money after bad, resurrecting a drowned mine that hadn't paid its way for years before its final decay.

Laity's laugh broke in on his thoughts. 'And here was I thinking that I was getting to be a real Cornishman because I have got in the habit of always knowing what the price is.' He sipped his drink. 'And how is Mrs Blacklock? I haven't seen her for several months.'

'She's well.' Edward could not keep the satisfaction from his voice. Whatever the state of their marriage, he knew that from the outside it looked like a match made in heaven. Clara had too much pride ever to let an outsider know the truth of their relationship.

'And will we have the pleasure of seeing her over Christmas? You seem to have kept her very close since your wedding.'

Edward could feel the brandy roaring hotly through his veins. Why not? he thought suddenly. It would be good, after his humiliation in bed, to see the envy and admiration in other people's eyes when they looked at his wife and saw his elegant house. And at least he had no doubts about Clara's faithfulness. She had never been interested in any other man – except one! And Grenfell had brought the news of his death a few weeks ago.

'I don't see why not.' Edward sat up straighter in his chair. 'We'll have a party at Christmas,' he decided. 'Liven up the place with some fun and jollity.'

And that might be just what Clara needed, he thought, lurching unsteadily towards the hotel stables. She was still a young woman. Perhaps, in his jealous pride at marrying her, he had confined her too much at home. It would do her good to act as hostess for a big party, and it might bring her out of herself. Whistling to himself and jingling the sovereigns in his pocket, Edward Blacklock's lips curled in an anticipatory smile.

'A party?' Clara's eyes gleamed like emeralds in the morning sun. 'Here?'

'Of course here,' Edward said gruffly, lifting his tea cup with a shaking hand. His head was pounding unmercifully but he had not forgotten his decision of the night before. 'It will give all the old biddies a chance to see how we live. They've been dying for a quiz round ever since we were married. We can put all their noses out of joint, the load of shabby-genteel merchants.'

Despite herself, Clara found her interest caught. She glanced around the elegant morning room, seeing as if for the first time the rich curtains, the shining furniture, the heavy oil paintings in their handsome frames that hung on the walls. She had begun to take her luxuries for granted, summoning servants without a thought as she had in the old days at Penalverne, simply accepting that, at her least word, a worn carpet would be replaced, the silk chair-coverings renewed.

It would be fun to throw a party, she decided. She had been alone at home for too long. And it would be something she could do for Edward, to help keep the promise she had made to herself that she would be the best wife she could to him.

She had even steeled herself to endure his love-making, but that resolution at least was never put to the test these days. Although he fumbled occasionally for her body he no longer forced himself on her. Perhaps that was what happened in all marriages.

The thought of a party lifted her spirits. It would be fun to show off to all those people who had despised her because she was the daughter of a mine captain, and who had ignored her when she was in desperate need . . . For the first time ever she found herself in agreement with Edward. They would give a party, she decided, that would really make the locals sit up and take notice.

Edward moved towards her and placed a hand on her shoulder. 'You must be pleased. For the first time since our wedding you look really happy.' His voice sounded unlike him, almost humble. He said tentatively, 'It won't be too much for you?'

She threw back her head and laughed with genuine amusement.

264

Too much for her? She who had carried wooden pails of milk up No-Go-By Hill every day? Who had heaved heavy flaskets of wet clothes around even when she was pregnant? Too much – to organise a party in a house full of servants? 'I think I can manage it,' she assured him, laughter bubbling in her voice.

Suddenly, moved by an impulse she scarcely understood, she placed her hand over the one that Edward still kept on her shoulder.

His fingers, warm and slender, moved under hers. 'I want the best for you.' His voice was awkward, as if he found the words hard to say.

Guilt flushed through her. They had been married nearly ten months and, until Adam's death, she had given him no support, scarcely talked to him more than the bare necessity of living together demanded. But he had done all she asked, saved her mother's life, treated Clara with consideration except when they were in bed together. And she had punished him, punished him for wanting her, for using all his powers to make her his, for not being Adam.

She remembered with an inward shudder last Christmas, the constant hunger and cold, her fear for her mother, for her growing child. Edward, at least, had saved her from a repetition of all that.

Impulsively, she pressed his fingers into her slender shoulder. 'We'll have the best Christmas party ever,' she promised him. After all, Adam was dead, Adam's child was lost for ever. But possibly, just possibly, there was a new life on the way, and she was still young. Now was the time to forget the past and look forward to the future. If the party went well, she might even manage to make Edward change his mind about Wheal Susan.

She tilted her head back until she could look up into her husband's light-grey eyes. 'A good Christmas,' she repeated, and submitted as his lips came softly down to kiss her forehead.

'Lieutenant!' Clara came forward in greeting. 'We had almost given up all hope of you.'

Around her, she heard the noisy talk of a successful party slacken off then rise again as the guests took in the latecomer's arrival. She smiled up at Laity whom she had always liked, suddenly conscious, under his bright eyes, of the becoming cap of lace and ribbons that signified a married woman, perched on the back of her piled-up hair; she was wearing a chignon for the first time ever tonight.

'Mrs Blacklock.' Laity bowed over her hand. 'How can I apologise? Believe me, only urgent family business could have kept me away from your party.'

'Nothing serious, I hope?' Clara led him further into the drawing room, feeling again a thrill of pleasure at the sight.

The massed candles added an extra dimension to the elegant room, reflecting a millionfold in the cut glass and in the deeply faceted mirrors that lined the walls. Even the mahogany reflected endless candle-flames in its polished surfaces and the rich draperies glowed with a lustrous sheen in the soft light.

She knew that it was foolish to feel pride in such unimportant things, but she could not help herself. After the poverty she had endured it was pleasant to hear the gasps of her guests, to see the envy in Isabelle's eyes as she took note of each discreet luxury that breathed 'wealth' to a discerning viewer. It was good to know that, at last, she was safe from the spectre of poverty, that neither she nor her unborn child would ever want again.

Instinctively, her hands strayed to her stomach, still flat and youthful. Only the fact that she had been pregnant before had enabled her to recognise the signs so quickly this time. When should she tell Edward? she wondered, throwing a glance to where he stood across the room, his fair head gleaming in the candlelight. Perhaps on Christmas Day? It would make a good present for him. He had never mentioned that he was disappointed that she had not become pregnant before, but every man, surely, wanted an heir? Especially when he had as much to leave as Edward did . . . She smiled secretly, amused to find herself caring what Edward thought, thinking about how to please him.

She realised guiltily that she had missed Laity's reply to her question. He saw her momentary discomfiture and repeated himself. 'My sister-in law's funeral. And now my elder brother is ill.'

She turned to him then with real concern. 'I hope it is not serious.'

'I'm afraid it is. He is suffering from the consumption that killed his wife. We hope for the best, but . . .' He shrugged, then forced a polite smile. 'As he is my father's heir that obviously leads to further problems.'

'Indeed,' Clara murmured discreetly. 'It must be a considerable worry for your parents.'

He grimaced. 'Not, it seems, as great a worry as my present occupation, which they have always thought dangerous. I suppose I am being selfish, but I have no desire to give up the Navy and move away from here.'

Clara saw his eyes wander across the assembled guests and realised that he was searching for Isabelle Kingsley, then he turned back to her again. 'I have won a temporary reprieve, but if,' he corrected himself, '*when* my brother sadly dies I fear I shall have to give up the sea and learn to manage the estates. And I can tell you, Mrs Blacklock,' he smiled his engaging smile at her, 'it took considerable address to win even that concession from Sir Henry under the circumstances.'

A brief wave of perfume alerted them to the arrival of Isabelle. 'Sir Henry!' She looked flabbergasted, her dark hair adorned only with pink flowers, pretty in the soft light. 'I never knew that your father was a knight, Lieutenant.' She caught his arm, leading him away from his hostess, chattering swiftly.

Clara watched them go with a twisted smile on her lips. It only needed the prospect of a title to make the Lieutenant completely irresistible to Isabelle, she decided, amused. But he seemed happy to allow himself to be captured. And who was she to carp? She had married Edward purely from financial need, and Isabelle was only doing the same. And marriage to a rich man was what they had both been educated for.

Mr Kingsley came towards her, his wife by his side. 'I loved the sight of the Christmas bushes in your windows as we rode up,' he enthused. 'When I was a boy, every house would have one, but now they seem to have disappeared completely, taken over by this German fashion for Christmas trees. A lot of nonsense.'

'They are more decorative, I think,' Clara smiled. It had been hard to forgive Kingsley for the way he had threatened to evict her. So much harm had followed from it – her mother's illness, the loss of her baby – not even the knowledge that he had been forced to it by Edward had enabled Clara to treat him other than coldly when she had stayed at his house before her wedding.

But that was all behind her. Tonight, she was determined that no bitterness from the past should ruin the evening. She moved to the window and twitched open the curtain so that they could see the bush. Despite its name, it consisted of two hoops, tied together at right angles and covered with greenery decorated with oranges and nuts. Inside, a candle burned.

'We put one in every window,' Clara explained. 'I think they help to bring a little Christmas cheer to those who pass by who may be too poor to afford such fripperies themselves.'

'A lovely idea,' Kingsley said gruffly.

'And one thought up by my wife.' Clara had not heard Edward approach, did not know that he had listened to the conversation. 'It was her idea to make this a traditional Cornish Christmas.'

'And very nice, I'm sure,' Kingsley said heavily. Clara bit back a smile. She knew that he did not share his wife's and daughter's appreciation of music. The imminent arrival of a choir from Paul Church to sing carols was something he was rather too obviously dreading.

'But I also think that we should move with the times,' she said swiftly. 'Carols for those who enjoy them, and for those who don't,' she smiled at Kingsley, 'there are card tables laid out in the library.'

She met the sudden brilliant gleam in Edward's eyes. 'My wife,' he said proudly, 'is an excellent woman, Kingsley, and thinks of everything.'

She lowered her eyes demurely, pleased with the approbation in his voice. This had been the first party she had ever organised by herself and she was glad it had gone so well.

But her head came up quickly as Edward went on, 'We might as well go to the library now, don't you agree? I'm sure we can make up a table. Old Boyns is always ready for a game, and Trewellard hasn't got a note of music in his body.'

He bustled around, suddenly full of vigour, rounding up the men he knew would be willing to leave the conversation of mixed company for the sake of a little card playing.

Clara watched him, baffled. The party had been going so well, and he had seemed so pleased with her. So why this sudden flight to the library? The choir wasn't due for an hour yet as he knew very well, and she had not intended to let it be known that there was alternative entertainment for those men who found all singing little better than caterwauling, until their actual arrival.

She had planned a wassail bowl, too. It was ready in the kitchen – a big wooden bowl already decorated with ribbons and such flowers as she had been able to find, for in this climate, even in mid-winter, there were always a few in bloom.

But the ceremony of passing round the bowl would lose much of its flavour if the head of the house wasn't there to do the honours and encourage the assembled guests to drink.

Her eyes followed her husband's fair head as he led the men towards the library. There was a small crease between her brows and somewhere, deep down, she felt the first small stirrings of unease.

Chapter 32

When Edward entered the room, Clara laid down the baby dress that she was sewing. 'Well?' She spoke crisply.

'Well, what?' He flung himself sullenly into the big armchair that stood beside the fireplace and closed his eyes thankfully. In the spring sunlight that flooded the room, Clara could see the incipient bags under his eyes, the soft flesh around his chin. He had gone markedly downhill over the last few months.

'Well, where were you the last three days?' She tried to keep her voice level, to hide the irritation she felt. It was getting too easy to fall into stupid rows about nothing. Sometimes, she almost wished she were back in the relationship they had had last autumn. They might not have spoken much then, but at least they had been polite to each other.

'Truro. I told you.'

'You told me you would be away for one night.' She managed to keep her voice unaccusing.

'One night, three, what does it matter?' He kept his eyes shut as if the bright sunlight hurt them. 'You don't miss me from your bed and the business runs without me.'

She flinched away from his mention of beds; that was too dangerous a subject to bring up. Instead, busying her hands again with her sewing, she said calmly, 'That's where you're wrong. You *are* needed.' She raised her emerald eyes to watch his reaction. 'Mr Trevaskis has resigned.'

His eyes shot open, bloodshot and bleary. 'Trevaskis? From the smelting works? But why, for God's sake, why?' He dragged himself out of the chair and began pacing the room, wincing as he passed through the light from the window. 'I pay him a good salary, even gave him time off when his wife was ill. What more could I do?'

'Given him what he had asked for, perhaps?' Clara suggested. 'He

269

said that he had been requesting new furnaces for months and you kept putting him off. Now output is falling.'

'He's the manager – it's his job to keep the output up.' Edward shrugged. 'I'll go and see him. Ten guineas a year more and he'll stay.'

Clara shook her head. Under her small lace cap her hair shone like spun silver in the sunlight. 'He won't stay. He's got another job already – manager at Chyandour. Their old manager is ill.'

Edward swore. 'I thought we smelters were supposed to stick together, not pinch each other's best men.' He paced the room angrily for a few turns before coming to a decision. 'I'll put Grenfell in. He'll soon stop all this nonsense.'

Clara watched him carefully. 'And the new furnaces?'

He turned on her furiously. 'I'm not made of bloody money! Those furnaces are good for another few months at least.' He walked to the bell-pull and tugged it angrily. 'I need a brandy,' he muttered. 'I come home after working in Truro for three days, and what do I get? Complaints and bad news! What sort of a welcome is that?'

He swung round as the sitting-room door opened. 'A bottle of brandy,' he ordered shortly. 'And quickly.'

Clara waited until the servant had passed out of earshot before saying bitterly, 'It wasn't work that kept you in Truro, and you know it. You were gambling again. And you lost.'

It wasn't even a guess. After all these months she knew the signs only too well. When she had first mentioned her concerns about gambling to him Edward had laughed, pouring his winnings into her lap in a great golden heap. 'What does it matter if I gamble?' he had asked her. 'Why work when I can make money this way?'

But recently the money, once handed out so easily, had stopped. As her pregnancy progressed she had seen her husband become first quiet and then irascible. His days at the bank and the smelting works had become less and less frequent, and his absences longer.

Now he swung round, pouring out all his frustration onto her as if it were all her fault. 'What is it to do with you? I give you enough housekeeping, don't I? And you live in the finest house in the neighbourhood!'

'For the moment.' She knew it was unwise but she could not help herself. The worries she had tried so long to deny suddenly surfaced. 'But how long will that last if you carry on the way you are doing? If you ignore your business and spend your days drinking and your nights gambling, what sort of future are you building for your child?'

'Oh, very wise words!' He turned on her, mockingly. 'And you know all about it, of course. The daughter of a bankrupt! A woman I saved from the gutter! You know all about running a successful business.'

'I know that businesses don't run themselves,' she said stubbornly, refusing to rise to his taunts. 'I know that Trevaskis wouldn't stay because he could no longer carry out his work properly. I know that if you put Grenfell in he will simply run the business down by cutting costs instead of building it up by good management and investment.' She stared at him defiantly. 'I know all those things.'

'Then it's a pity you don't know your place,' he retorted, his cheeks reddening with fury. 'You should support me, not find fault with everything I do. Your job is to run the household and bear my children. Who I choose to run the smelting works is nothing to do with you.'

Furiously, she jumped to her feet and confronted him, her back straight, her hands folded protectively over her swelling belly.

'It is to do with me if I see you wasting our child's inheritance,' she snapped back at him. 'It is if your manager comes to tell you he is resigning and you are not available because you are in Truro gambling your money away and it is I who have to deal with him.'

'Oh, of course,' he broke in resentfully. 'Everything is to do with you. You are the centre of the bloody world.'

He strode to the door. 'Well, you can run your little world without me! I'm going out to where I am appreciated, to where I can get a drink.'

He jerked the door open and stormed through it, almost knocking down the servant who stood just behind it, the tray with the brandy on tilting dangerously as he brushed past with a curse.

Clara heard his footsteps echo through the hall then the slam of the front door. There was a long silence, then she bent to pick up the baby dress that had fallen from her hands during the altercation.

'You had better take that back,' she advised the staring servant. 'And please tell Cook that Mr Blacklock will not be in for dinner.' She waited until the door had closed before she sank into her seat and pressed her hands to her belly.

Under her fingers, new life stirred. It brought back memories of the first child, so wanted, so mourned, and the grinding poverty she had endured at that time. Her lips tightened and she felt a great determination rise within her. This child would never know that sort of poverty, she vowed to herself. Not if she had to kill to prevent it.

Her mother's suite was quiet as Clara pushed open the door. The change to better surroundings had helped Lady Susan physically but her mind still wandered. She was happy in her pleasant sitting room, thinking herself back once more at Trevival and Clara encouraged the belief. What did it matter?

Ma Downing looked up from the saffron bun she was eating. The smell of warm yeast and the rich crocus savour made Clara's mouth water, reminding her that she had been too upset to eat after Edward had stormed out.

The old woman greeted her affectionately. 'Your ma's asleep, but you're welcome as a breath of spring.' Her rheumy eyes slid quickly over Clara. 'You're looking vexed as fire,' she said anxiously. 'You shouldn't be gettin' yourself worked up about things in your condition. Here, sit yourself down.'

Clara sank gratefully into the chair and gave Ma a twisted smile. 'You didn't fuss over me like this the last time.'

'Well, there were no point,' Ma said stoutly. 'What can't be cured must be endured, they say, and I reckon you did your bit of endurin'.'

'And it's not over yet.' The words were out before she could stop them. Cross with herself, Clara bit her lip. She had come here to take her mind off her worries, not to take Ma Downing into her confidence.

Better feelings had never hindered Ma. 'Problems with your man?' she guessed. 'They do say downstairs you hadn't seen hide nor hair of him for three nights, and you expecting him back days ago.'

Irritation drove her wearily to her feet. 'I hate the way there's no privacy in this house,' she said furiously. 'What is it to do with the servants if Edward decides to stay in Truro for a couple of extra nights? It's none of their business.'

'It's their livelihood,' Ma corrected. 'You can't blame them for keeping a weather eye on the two of you.' She watched Clara's restless pacing and her face softened. 'What is it, my handsome? Has he got another woman?'

Clara paused, a feeling of incredulity flooding through her. She had never thought of that as a reason for Edward's absences. 'Perhaps,' she said slowly.

Ma nodded. 'He don't fancy you now you're growing big, that's what it is. Some men are like that. Now my Jack couldn't get enough of it. "It's like havin' three in a bed," he used to say.' She laughed fatly, her stomach heaving with her hoarse chuckles. 'Mind you, he weren't exactly against it when I wasn't expectin'. But that's men for you.'

'If it were just another woman, I could stand it.' Clara bit back the thought that she would actually welcome such a situation. 'But it's more than that.' She turned to the older woman and lowered her voice. 'I think he's gambling.'

'That's what men do.' Ma Downing was unsympathetic. 'That, or drink. And being gentry, I reckon he'll do both.' She shrugged. 'Well, he can afford it.'

Clara's lips tightened. Was she worrying for nothing? But she remembered the way he had poured the gold sovereigns into her lap when she had first raised the subject. Several times he had come home with winnings of fifty pounds, and once with nearly seventy.

He had urged them on her, telling her to buy herself some new dresses or trinkets, but the memory of her time in Adam's cottage had been too vivid. She would have given her soul then for fifty pounds.

She thought suddenly of her first child, born too soon. No vicar would have allowed it in the graveyard, illegitimate as it was, but there might have been a way. Sextons had been known to bury such children secretly, in a secluded corner – if well bribed. But the money had not been there, and Ma Downing had taken the tiny body from her and thrown it down a disused mine shaft like unwanted rubbish, the normal fate for such mites.

Clara swallowed the lump in her throat. With that memory to haunt her, she could not now throw that money away as if it were worthless. The coins were still there, locked in the drawer in her bureau, and even now, the memory of them gave her a feeling of security.

But if Edward had been winning those amounts, it stood to reason that he was also in danger of losing them. And certainly, he had not recently shown any signs of winning. But she could not complain to Ma Downing about her husband's behaviour.

With an effort, she gave a seemingly casual shrug of her shoulders. 'I suppose the reason I'm blue-devilled is that the manager of the smelting works has left and Edward is talking of putting Sam Grenfell in his place. He doesn't know the first thing about the business.' She forced a laugh. 'It's just prejudice, I suppose, but I can't stand the man.'

'Like a wet week, he is,' Ma agreed. 'But he worked all right for your da. I don't see why you need to worry. You leave all that to the men.'

'As if they'll do any good,' Clara said bitterly. Dear God, she had far more business sense than Edward. If only she were running things . . . She grimaced. She was a woman, and pregnant to boot. There was no way she could intervene even when she was sure that she could run the smelting works and the bank better than Edward.

She walked over to the window and stared out across the fields at the trees that crowned the nearby hill. After the barrenness of St Just

273

she had been accustomed to find the gentler, tree-clad slopes of Newlyn Coombe soothing, but for once the sight of the trees did not exert their usual influence. She stared at them with unseeing eyes, lost in her thoughts, drumming her fingers unconsciously on the sill.

The memory of Grenfell's pale face rose before her. Ma Downing was probably right about him. Her father had found no fault with him, and he seemed to have been loyal to Edward.

But she knew that she would never trust him.

As soon as she saw him, Molly knew by the glint in Grenfell's eye that something had happened. She quickly swallowed the words of complaint with which she had planned to greet him and leaned forward eagerly, her eyes searching his face. 'You're looking like the cat that's found the mouse.'

To her surprise, he put his arms round her and pecked her briefly on the cheek. 'Mouse?' he chuckled. 'Not a mouse, my handsome. I've caught myself a bloody great big rat.'

He sat himself in the hard wooden chair by the table and threw back his head, laughing.

Molly seated herself opposite him, her strong elbows planted on the table. 'You've been given a rise at work,' she guessed.

'Better'n that. Guess again.'

'What could be better than that?' Despite the difficulties of the marriage, Molly loved the fact that her husband worked in the bank, that he was, as near as made no difference, a gentleman. 'They've been and made you chief clerk?'

He shook his head.

She could think of nothing else that was likely to account for his good humour, so she experimented with wilder fantasies. 'Bloody Blacklock's died and you're his heir.'

'Nearly as good as.' He paused for effect before announcing: 'Trevaskis has left the smelting works and I've got the job!'

Molly felt as if she had been slapped. Banking was a gentleman's job. Sam was able to work in an office in Penzance, warm and dry, and come home at the same time every evening with regular pay. But smelting was scarcely better than mining, even if you were a manager. Still, if it meant more money . . .

He saw the look on her face. 'You don't understand.' He leaned forward, lowering his voice. 'Blacklock's drinking even more heavily than before. We hardly ever see him at the bank and he never goes near the smelting works, even though it's practically on his own doorstep.'

'So?' She frowned, unable to see where he was leading her.

'So I've got a free hand.' His face split in a wolfish grin. 'The ore from half the mines in St Just go through the smelting works at Newlyn Coombe, for all that it's run by only twenty men and a couple of boys. And it's from the smelting works that Blacklock gets all his money to keep the bank going.'

Molly's blue eyes blazed in the dimness of the poky little room. 'And all that tin is worth a lot of money.' She could see what he was leading up to now, and her heart leapt at the thought. Here, at last, was a way to get back at Blacklock and Clara for foisting this marriage on them as if she and Sam were belongings rather than people. And if they could make money out of it too . . .

'And Blacklock doesn't know or care what happens out there.' He was building on her thoughts, rubbing his hands together with satisfaction, his knuckles cracking.

Her face was alight with mischief. 'That'll teach him,' she said with satisfaction. 'That'll show him he can't carry on as if he was God, making you marry me and all.'

'And we'll be rich.' He could see it already before his eyes, bags and bags of cash, all sneaked from under Blacklock's nose.

'Just give me a few months to work my way in,' he cautioned, 'and then . . .'

They clasped each other in greedy arms, rocking to and fro, ignoring the thin crying of the child upstairs.

Chapter 33

Clara moved her swollen body awkwardly, trying to find a comfortable position. Despite the drawn blinds, the parlour was hot and stuffy. Flies spiralled ceaselessly around the ceiling even though the glass fly-trap on the table was black with their drowned bodies. Their constant buzzing rasped at her nerves.

Would this baby never be born? The instinctive fear she had had of the birth had gone now, driven away by the desperate wish to get it all over with, to be free of the dragging weight that made her days and nights a misery.

She fanned herself lethargically. The house was only a mile from the sea, but in the shelter of Newlyn Coombe, no breath of wind stirred the sultry July air. Clara thought longingly of the moors around St Just. Even in the hottest weather there was always a breeze there. In her present uncomfortable state she would have given anything to be able to feel the fresh wind on her face.

But St Just was as inaccessible to her as the moon. No lady would ever dream of showing herself in public in this advanced stage of pregnancy.

She spread her legs, supporting her stomach more comfortably on her thighs. Edward was hardly ever home now, and on his rare appearances he tried to avoid her. His disgust at her ballooning shape was all too obvious.

She did not blame him, she thought wearily. Her appearance even sickened herself. Her slender body seemed taken over by the mass of her belly, the blue veins snaking lividly across her white skin.

It would soon be over, she reminded herself for the tenth time that morning. Within a week, at most, according to Ma Downing, the child would be born. Surely the existence of a new life would justify all this discomfort?

The door-bell pealed through the house but she scarcely noticed it.

It would not be for her; she was at home to no one until after the birth. Clara rested her head against the chairback and closed her eyes.

The sound of loud voices broke through her lethargy. She could hear Bennet, the butler, remonstrating, then another, unfamiliar voice, arguing forcefully – frantically even. There was a note of desperation in it that reached her, even through the torpor of late pregnancy. For a minute she listened, straining her ears to make out the words but they were muffled by the heavy, close-fitting door of the room. Only the urgency in the voice came through.

She could not ignore its appeal. With an effort she heaved herself out of her chair and opened the door, taking care to keep her swollen body out of sight.

'What is it, Bennet?' she demanded.

He turned to her in obvious relief. 'A – person – from the bank, madam. There seems to be some sort of trouble.'

The visitor pushed roughly past the butler, twisting his tall shiny hat nervously in his hands. 'We need Mr Blacklock urgently, mum.' His voice was high with tension. 'He's the only one who can help now. If he doesn't come . . .'

'He's not here.' She could see the worry deepen in the man's face and made her mind up. This was a crisis; she couldn't ignore it. Unwillingly, she pulled wider the door to the parlour. 'You'd better come in here.' She moved hurriedly, placing a high-backed chair between them in an attempt to hide her advanced pregnancy. 'Now, what is the matter?'

He was a lowly clerk from the bank. She could see it in the ink-stains on his fingers, the way his cheap collar had wilted in the heat. He swallowed nervously, his Adam's apple bobbing above his disordered neckcloth.

'There's a run on the bank, mum. There's hundreds of them, standing outside, shouting. They all want to take their money out. And we can't pay it, mum.'

She frowned. 'You mean the bank doesn't have the money? But surely –'

He broke in swiftly. 'Not in cash, mum. You see, people give us their money to hold and then we lend it to other people. That's how banks work. But it all depends on trust, see. People have to trust us to look after their money for them. If they all try to take it out at once, the bank will collapse because it just can't be done.' He twisted his hat convulsively between thin, bony fingers. 'It's not the bank's fault. There's not a bank in England that could stand that, mum.'

Clara thought hard. She knew nothing about banking. For her, it had just been a mysterious way in which Edward had made his money. But she could identify the significant fact in the clerk's nervous explanation. 'So why has everyone suddenly lost confidence in our bank?' she enquired.

There was a long pause. She could hear again the droning of the flies, the noisy click of the clerk's Adam's apple as he tried to swallow. He ran a damp finger around the inside of his tight collar, completing its ruin. 'I couldn't say, mum.' His eyes shifted uneasily.

'I want to know the truth,' she demanded. 'How can I help if I don't know what's going on?'

'It's said – they say . . .' He took a deep breath and forced the response out in a rush. 'They say Mr Blacklock has gambled away all the money, mum.'

'I see.' She could feel the blood hammering at her temples and the baby moved urgently in her womb, responding to her distress.

'I'm sure it's not true, mum.' The clerk moved towards her, anxious to disassociate himself from such slanders. 'But it's what they are saying in Penzance.'

She pressed her hands to her stomach. Surely this couldn't be happening? After all the sacrifices she had made, surely she couldn't be facing a lifetime of abject poverty again? And what of the child?

'Is there no way of stopping it?' She despised herself for the note of panic she heard in her voice.

'If Mr Blacklock was there,' the clerk said, 'he could stop it, maybe. If he just showed himself, showed that he was still interested in the bank, that would help. And lots of people are frightened of him, begging your pardon, mum.' He sketched an apologetic bow in her direction. 'If he was there, he'd scare them into keeping their money in.'

'But he isn't here.' Clara had gained control of herself again, the momentary panic conquered. 'What else can be done to stop this?'

He paused. This was beyond his experience but her determination reached him. 'I suppose if one of our big customers was seen to be putting money in,' he said slowly, 'that would help. But they won't. They're all there, outside the bank, shouting and hollering for their money. You won't get no one in Penzance to put money in at a time like this.'

Careless of her condition, Clara moved away from the chair and began to pace the room. The enormity of this crisis was more important than polite conventions. 'What about the smelting works?' she asked suddenly. 'Isn't that the basis of the bank's wealth? Surely while that is doing well, there can be no concern about finance?'

The clerk looked as if he wanted to sink through the carpet. 'The

278

chief clerk tried to tell them that, mum, when they first came. But there's some that say that the smelting works isn't doing well, so that didn't help at all. Made things worse, if you ask me,' he added with a rare flash of individualism.

Clara continued her pacing, ignoring the evident discomfort of the clerk at her condition. 'And how much money would be needed to save the bank?'

He gaped at her. 'I dunno,' then, seeing the flash of irritation in her eyes, he added hastily, 'it would depend on who was putting it in, I suppose. If it were someone they would trust, five hundred pounds might save it. Otherwise . . .' He shrugged, helplessly.

Five hundred. The bags of sovereigns that Edward had given her came suddenly to mind. Clara paused. Her experience of poverty had sunk deep in her consciousness. Every instinct told her to keep that money. If the bank and the smelting works were to close, it might be her only protection against starvation; not just her own, but that of her mother and child.

Her lips twisted as she remembered Edward as she had last seen him two days ago, his face mottled with the signs of over-indulgence. In his present condition, he would be yet another liability, and she knew that he had used his financial powers too cruelly in the past for there to be any help from his previous victims.

But there was her child. She could feel its presence, as much, now, in her mind as in her body. Was she willing to let that child be born into poverty and disgrace?

For a few seconds she wavered, then moving swiftly to the bell-pull she gave a vigorous pull.

'Tell the coachman to bring round the landau,' she ordered crisply.

'But madam!' The butler was scandalised.

'My carriage,' she repeated. 'At once.' Ignoring her swollen belly she ran for the stairs, already fumbling at her waist for the key to the bureau. Would the money be enough? Or was she throwing away her last asset in a hopeless attempt to put right Edward's mistakes? It was too late to worry now, she told herself grimly. The die was cast. She could only pray that she reached the bank in time.

She could hear the noise of the crowd as the carriage drove past the Market House. The voices were angry, interspersed with catcalls and whistles. She tightened her grip on the bags that she held on her knee. 'To the bank,' she ordered as the coachman hesitated at the sounds.

The terrace outside the bank was packed with shouting male bodies, struggling for a place in front of the locked doors. Shutters were pulled close over the downstairs windows but from the first-floor window, the pale face of the chief clerk peered nervously out. He was attempting to reason with the crowd but his voice was lost in their furious cries.

'Give us our money.' Clara could hear the constant refrain from many different voices. 'Thieves. Liars. Give us the money that belongs to us.'

For a moment her courage deserted her. Surely nothing would satisfy these men but the full restitution of their savings and the fall of the bank. Then her head went up and she straightened her back. If the bank failed, it would not be because Clara Blacklock had lacked the courage to try to save it.

The elegant landau had drawn up at the bottom of one of the flights of steps that led from the road up to the terrace that ran down one side of Market Jew Street. Lowering her parasol so that she could be recognised, and pulling her short cape around her in an attempt to disguise her condition, Clara rose unsteadily to her feet in the well-sprung open carriage. Standing, she was almost on a level with the men on the terrace.

Nervously, she cleared her throat. 'Gentlemen.'

Her words were lost in the bedlam of angry male voices. She tried again, louder this time, but with the same result.

This was impossible! Throwing convention to the winds, she flung back her head and screamed at the top of her voice.

The high-pitched shriek cut effortlessly through the deeper shouts. Instantly, there was silence as the men turned as one to see the source of the sound.

The clerk had exaggerated when he had said that there were hundreds of men besieging the bank, Clara realised. In actual fact, there were probably only fifty staring down at her with shocked expressions. But that was enough to make her wish that she was anywhere else.

With an effort she lifted her chin and stared defiantly at them. 'May I ask, gentlemen, what is the meaning of this unruly behaviour?'

For a few seconds there was an abashed silence then a voice shouted from the rear of the crowd, 'We wants our money, that's what the reason is.' Other voices took up the cry. 'Our money. Give us our money.'

Imperiously, she raised a gloved hand and the voices died away again. 'And why do you want to take your money out?' she enquired, her voice low and reasonable. 'Is there some problem with the bank that you should suddenly lose faith in it?'

Under her emerald eyes, the front rank of men shuffled awkwardly but from the back the voice rang out again. 'The problem is your husband.'

Another voice took up the refrain. 'That's right. Drinking our money away, he is.'

'And gambling,' a third shouted. 'That's sinful, that is. We're working men, we worked for our money. And we're not going to let some drunken blackguard put our families out on the streets. We want our money.'

'Give us our money! Give us our money!' The horses moved nervously at the chorus and Clara had to clutch at the side of the carriage for support.

'Well!' She forced a tone of light amusement into her voice, praying that the men would not see the fear that was welling inside her, rousing the baby to painful kicks. 'Really! What a to-do about nothing.' She let her eyes wander over the crowd of men. Christopher Kingsley was there, she noticed, and other men who only months before had been overawed by the richness displayed at her Christmas party.

She made sure that they were aware of her glance, then she said lightly, 'It's a good thing this has happened now, isn't it?'

There was a mystified silence. 'I mean,' she went on sweetly, 'it is less than a year ago that some of you,' she stared particularly at Kingsley, 'owed a great deal of money to the bank. You didn't think then that it was unstable.'

Her lips broke into a smile that lit her pale face. 'How strange it is that now that the price of tin has risen, and most of you have paid back the money you borrowed, you should suddenly think that the bank can't cope.'

Her emerald eyes bored through the men staring silently down at her. 'It seems to be a strange reward for the way the bank supported you during your times of hardship.'

For a second she thought that she had won them over, then the voice from the back shouted again, 'It's not the same. If we go bust, the bank always get its money. But what do we get if the bank goes bust? Bloody nothing!' There were murmurs of agreement.

'And why should it go bust?' she asked pleasantly.

'Because your bloody husband doesn't give a damn about his business,' one man called out.

'Because he's a drunk and a gambler,' another added, and she heard a muttered addendum from the back of the crowd, 'And a lecher.'

She set her teeth and refused to let her embarrassment show. 'A comprehensive range of accusations that could be thrown at more than my husband if the rumours I hear are correct.' Her stare moved deliberately over the men in front of her, resting meaningfully on her erstwhile guests and she saw them fidget, abashed under her scrutiny.

The men followed her gaze and there was a ripple of laughter. Methodism had reduced the amount of drinking in the working classes, but most prosperous businessmen went to church and considered that they had a right to drink as much as they liked.

She sensed the lessening of antagonism and went on quickly: 'But that is no reason to lose confidence in a man's ability as a businessman. This bank is as sound as it has ever been, backed up as it is by the profits from the smelting works.'

'What profits?' demanded the heckler from the back, though she noticed with relief that the tone was quieter now, as if the owner were less sure of himself.

She gave them a brilliant smile. '*These* profits, gentlemen.'

She reached down into the carriage and picked up a small cotton bag.

Holding it high above her head she tilted it slowly. A cascade of gold tumbled out, glistening blindingly in the bright sunlight. There was a sudden silence as the money poured in a gilded stream onto the seat beside her, and the ringing sound as a few stray coins slid further onto the floor of the carriage could be easily heard.

'Not bad for a smelting works which is supposed to be losing money.' Clara turned again to the watching men. She bent and picked up a second bag. 'And then there's this!' She shook it. The gold clinked reassuringly inside its cotton covering. She tossed it casually down onto the seat and picked up a third.

'Tell me, gentlemen, do you really think that a bank backed by a smelting works which makes profits like that is not suited to look after your money?' She raised her emerald eyes enquiringly.

'It is your decision,' she went on calmly. 'You may take your money out of the bank if you wish. It is nothing to do with me. But my father used to say that bankers always stuck together.' She shrugged lightly. 'You may find another bank less willing to take your account if you are known as the sort of man who panics at a wild rumour.'

She raised her eyes to the chief clerk who was goggling at her from the upstairs window.

'Open the doors, will you please,' she requested crisply. 'Some of these gentlemen wish to withdraw their money. And send some clerks down to collect this gold. Men you can trust,' she added sharply. 'There is a great deal of cash here and I don't want any of it to go missing.'

Already the crowd outside the bank had lessened, she was pleased

282

to see. And most of the remainder seemed to be there just out of curiosity. As the three bank clerks carried six bags of gold into the bank there was a murmur of amazement.

'Home, please,' she told the coachman, sinking wearily onto the seat. She leaned her head back against the squabs and waited for her heart to stop racing.

Thank God she had emptied the bag containing the gold and not one of the ones filled with farthings and small stones from the garden, she thought with a wry smile. As long as the chief clerk didn't open the bags in public the crisis should be over for the moment.

A sudden pain made her gasp and writhe. The baby! Now, of all times, it had chosen to come. With an effort she caught her breath. 'Drive home quickly,' she amended, doubling over as the contraction gripped her.

But even the pain could not drive out the thought that filled her mind.

That crisis was over. But how long would it be until the next one?

Chapter 34

'The Joes are coming! The Joes are coming!' The words ran like a shiver of fear through the clustered miners.

Adam straightened his aching back and checked hastily that his licence was safely in his pocket. The gold-field police only believed the evidence of their eyes; to be caught without your licence meant being chained to a log for hours until someone fetched your licence from the tent. All around him, the sudden disappearance of men showed that not all the miners were as careful – or as honest.

It had happened to him once and he did not plan to let it happen again. The thirty-shilling licence issued by the new State of Victoria only bought the right to a month's mining. A shilling a day, he thought bitterly; more really, because no one ever worked on a Sunday. At that rate, even an hour away from the mine was expensive. And it wasn't as if he and Norman were finding anything, for all their hard work.

The nearest Joe moved towards him, his once smart red and green trousers mired to the knees. Adam resignedly held out his licence for inspection, mopping the mixture of sweat and rain from his forehead. The man gave it only a cursory glance before hurrying off to where a scuffle had broken out nearby. Another unlicenced miner caught. With these constant checks, it wasn't worth trying to buck the system, Adam thought, however expensive it was.

He wiped his hands on his trousers then hefted the handles of the wheelbarrow and trundled it through the yellow clinging mud to the edge of the creek, winding it between the closely packed men, all panning their pay dirt for gold.

'Got anything?' He tipped the barrowload of earth onto a heap next to where Norman was rocking what looked like a child's cradle.

Norman grimaced. 'Not enough to fill a croggan.' He straightened wearily. The cradle acted as the buddles did in a tin mine. The soil

284

was mixed with water and agitated and the heavy gold sank to the bottom while the lighter earth was washed away. He kicked it with an angry foot. 'I suppose these contraptions do work?'

'They do for everyone else,' Adam said shortly. 'Some people have found a fortune while we've been here.'

'And others have lost all they had,' Norman retorted. 'The men in the next tent are leaving today. They came to say goodbye – asked me if I wanted to buy their cradle.'

A brief smile lit Adam's brown face. 'If we buy another one, we'll buy one that's good at finding gold,' he said. 'Not that their cradle was at fault. I saw them working once when I went to get my licence.'

'And?'

He shrugged. 'Too slow to carry a cold dinner, I thought.'

'Well,' a weary grin crossed Norman's face, 'like you're always telling me, laziness isn't worth nothing unless it's well followed up.' He bent to rock the cradle again. 'But we're working hard enough, and what have we got to show for it?'

What indeed? Adam thought. They couldn't work harder. It was scarcely daylight each morning when they crossed the frosted ground to the square of mud they were licensed to dig, and they never stopped until the dusk gun shot from the Gold Commissioner's tent warned the miners that night was closing in. And they had done it every day now for almost two months, and still, to use Norman's words, they didn't have enough gold dust to fill a limpet shell.

He swore. At this rate, the money they had so painfully accumulated at Burra Burra would soon be gone. It wasn't just the licence, everything here cost more. Flour, salt, potatoes, everything had to be carted seventy miles over bad, mud caked roads from Melbourne, and the prices reflected the fact. It sometimes seemed to him that only the merchants were making money out of these gold fields.

For a brief second the image of Clara's pearls flashed before his eyes but he forced it away. He could not have used those pearls anyway. They were tainted with her dishonesty and treachery. No good would ever have come from them or anything that they bought. He was glad he had thrown them away, he reminded himself angrily, glad to be free from a woman like that.

Norman emptied another shovelful of soil into the cradle. 'How much longer will our money last?' His voice was carefully non-committal.

'We've enough to pay for next month's licences,' Adam said curtly.

'But not enough to eat while we're using them.' It was a statement, not a question.

285

Adam's temper rose. 'You don't have to stay. You can go back with the others if that's what you really want.'

Norman stopped working the cradle. 'And you?'

Adam's head jerked back. 'I'm not leaving,' he said harshly. 'I told you that before we arrived. I came here to make my fortune and that's what I'm going to do, or die in the attempt.'

'Dying in the attempt is one thing,' Norman said heatedly. 'Slaving and starving over a hole in the ground that hasn't produced as much gold in two months as some men find in one shovelful is another.'

'You reckon we can do better anywhere else?' Adam asked crossly.

Norman moved closer and lowered his voice. 'Frenchy John says they've found gold a bit further up north. Mount Alexander, he said.' Norman's eyes gleamed. 'It's not far. We could be in at the start, choose our claim, make a fortune.'

'Or lose the little money we've got left on a wild-goose chase,' Adam broke in curtly. 'Forget it! I find my fortune here or nowhere.'

'And if you don't find it?'

'You know the answer to that.' Adam turned away. 'But you needn't stay. Go where you choose, on to this new place, back to Burra Burra. It's all the same to me. But I'm staying here.'

He stared down at Norman, his blue eyes cold and determined. 'I've learnt my lesson. Money is all that's important in this world and if you haven't got it, you're nothing! So I've made my mind up. If I can't live life as a rich man I'll die as a poor one, and I'll make it here or nowhere!'

'Well, you'll die bloody soon the way things are going,' Norman said coarsely. Suddenly, his eyes softened. He reached out a muddy hand and gripped Adam's shoulder. 'Why don't you think again, Adam? Is it worth it? Clara was only a woman. There's plenty more in the world.'

The name coming so unexpectedly tore at Adam. It was the first time either of them had mentioned her since that day at Burra Burra when the letter had come.

'I'm not thinking about women,' he said, hiding his hurt in a display of anger, 'I'm thinking about me. All my life I've been kicked in the teeth because I don't have money. This is my chance, my last chance. I'll find gold here or else . . . '

He turned away, leaving Norman to continue with the cradling. Looking for gold was essentially the same as looking for tin, Adam reflected as he waded through the clinging yellow mud, back to the waterlogged pit in which he worked. Only here, there were no big organisations that kept the profits and paid the workers a pittance. Here it was each man for himself. What you found you kept.

286

Only he wasn't finding enough. He gritted his teeth. Others were. Every day, you heard of new finds, of men who had found nuggets of gold, of men who could get one hundred pounds' worth of gold dust in just one pan of dirt.

But he worked as hard as any of them and had got nothing. With a curse he began to shovel earth furiously into a basket as if his life depended on it.

'The Joes got Frenchy John today.' Norman pushed his empty plate away from him. 'Bloody interfering lot!'

Adam grunted. 'So he won't be going to Mount Alexander, then.' He stretched his feet out to the sullen fire. The damp wood spat and hissed but the rain had stopped at last. He glanced up at the clear sky and shivered. There would be another sharp frost tonight, he thought. Even though it was almost November, there was still no sign of spring.

He glanced across at Norman, his blue eyes catching the firelight. 'And you?'

'Reckon I'd better stay here and help you,' Norman said gruffly. 'It's probably just a wild rumour anyway.' He sighed. 'But if it's just started up, they won't have got the Joes there yet. I could kill for a beer.'

'And me.' The no-alcohol rule bit deep. But it was a long way to the nearest town just for a drink, even supposing they could have afforded it. There were illicit stills in the camp but the stuff they produced was expensive – and dangerous. He couldn't risk going blind. His mind went again to the problem of money. It was always the same! Money was the basis of everything. Here he was, in the middle of a gold field, and it looked as if the thing that would stop him making his fortune was lack of money!

He said carefully, 'Our money should see us through to the end of next month. With care.'

'With tight belts, you mean,' Norman corrected. He sighed. 'I was getting fed up with mutton, anyway.' He poked the sputtering logs with his foot. 'Do you really mean to stay on after the money runs out?'

'I told you,' Adam said shortly. 'The only way I'll leave this place is with a fortune in my pocket. And if I don't find one, they can throw my body in the workings and cover it over with waste for all I care. I'm not leaving here poor.'

He looked round at the tents which surrounded them, a small township, each tent full of dreams of riches. They glimmered in the darkness, the lamps glowing luminously through the thin walls. 'If you

287

leave, I could sell the tent. A newcomer would buy it, and the weather will be getting warmer soon.'

'You can sell it even if I don't go,' Norman said. 'It can't be colder outside than it is in.' He moved closer to the fire. 'If only this was Cornwall! At least there we knew how to make a bit of money on the side when we had to.'

There was a thoughtful pause, then Adam sat suddenly upright and pounded him on the back. 'You've got it! You've got the answer!'

Norman gaped at him. 'What do you mean? How can we smuggle here?'

'Ssh!' Adam hushed him swiftly. 'Don't say the word.' He glanced around him. Tents were close, with other miners relaxing around their fires, enjoying a rare break in the rain in this unusually wet spring, but if they kept their voices lowered no one would overhear.

Adam leaned closer. 'You're not the only one round here who would kill for a beer, I reckon.'

'Beer!' Norman's eyes glistened. 'We could do it with *beer*?'

'Why not?' Adam asked. 'That's what men want.' Then his face clouded. 'No, that's not on.' He saw the disappointment in Norman's face. 'Too bulky,' he said succinctly. 'We'd be caught for certain if we tried to bring anything like that into the camp. The Joes aren't fools.'

He stared into the fire, lost in his thoughts. There had to be a way of earning money that would enable him to keep working here. There must.

He said slowly, working it out as he spoke, 'Beer's out, like I said, but maybe – whisky?'

Norman grimaced. 'It's not the same.'

'Not to you, maybe,' Adam looked up, his dark face split by a humorous grin. 'But to men who are desperate for a drink? Just think how most of the men act as soon as they strike lucky. First thing they do is go to Melbourne and blow the lot on women and drink.'

'And you always despise them for it,' Norman reminded him.

'Money's too important to waste like that,' Adam agreed. 'But, equally, it's too important not to have any. Besides, it's like the brandy. We never drank that ourselves, remember?'

'We had beer up the kiddleywink in those days,' Norman said gloomily.

At the mention of the kiddleywink, Adam felt his heart contract. His homeland. He'd lost it for ever. And all because of Edward Black-lock – and Clara, he reminded himself. Even if there was some way to

288

escape the charges of smuggling, he could never go back to Cornwall while Clara was there.

For a second her image hovered before him, her fine, pale hair and slender, voluptuous body. He forced it away. She wasn't his, he reminded himself bitterly. Not his, as he had once dreamed, but Blacklock's now.

At the thought of Clara and Blacklock together, his hurt erupted in sudden fury,

'Well, go back to Cornwall if you feel like that,' he snapped. 'Go back and live on salt cod and spend your days in blackness until you die coughing your guts up before you're forty. Go back and see whether you're going to get transported straight back here for smuggling or whether you just get hard labour in prison. What do I care!'

He jumped to his feet and strode off, his emotions goading him ever onwards. He stormed up to the top of the low hill, nicknamed 'Golden Point' by the miners because of the riches they had found there. In some places, the hill was honeycombed with their holes, only a narrow wall of earth left to separate one pitch from the next.

He slowed down. It would be easy to break a leg here and that would ruin his only chance of ever striking it rich. He came to a halt and stood, leaning against a wattle tree, fighting to control the anger that seethed within him.

It was strangely quiet up here. In the day-time, the whole air vibrated to the sound of hundreds of cradles constantly rocking, rocking their way to wealth or despair. Now they were silent. The night was dark but the town of tents below him glowed luminous in the cold air, lit from within by a thousand lamps.

A sudden shout broke the silence. Even from a distance, he could tell it was a shout of joy and triumph. Another miner who had struck it rich, he thought despairingly. When would it be his turn?

He lashed out with his foot at a nearby pebble and it bounced and rattled along the ground before striking against a gumtree. If I were lucky, he thought, that pebble would be a solid nugget of gold. But he was not lucky. Ever. Even when he had made that find at the Wheal Susan, he had made no money out of it. And here he was, on what men said was one of the richest goldfields ever found, and he couldn't earn enough to feed himself.

He knew what had brought on this uncharacteristic mood of self-pity. It had been the thought of Clara, of Cornwall. The two were inextricably linked for him. He would never again be able to think of the cliffs around St Just without seeing her body, pale in the glorious starlight; never think of the Wheal Susan without seeing her, on her horse, her face white and strained as she stared down at him.

And she had betrayed him, betrayed the love and trust that he had thought they shared, thrown his love and devotion in his face and left him for his worst enemy. And all for money. The one substance that Blacklock had and he could not get.

Adam gave a long, shuddering sigh. He must not, dared not, think about the past. It did not exist any more. For him there was only the present and the future. And the real concern with both, he reminded himself, was how to make money.

It was an hour before he could trust himself to make his way back to the small tent. On the way, almost automatically, he picked up the pebble he had kicked so viciously. You dare not throw away any opportunity.

Norman glanced warily at him as he crawled through the opening but his only comment was, 'You've persuaded me. I'll stay on here.'

Adam grunted. 'What changed your mind? The thought of the mines or the thought of prison?'

'Salt fish,' Norman said briefly. 'Mutton may get boring over here but we never had a chance to eat it back home.'

'This is our home now,' Adam reminded him curtly, then, in apology, 'if you're willing, I thought you could make the trip to Melbourne for the goods.' His voice shook with laughter. 'At least it will give you a chance to drink some beer.'

'You've worked out how we can do it, then?' Norman's voice was eager. He had always enjoyed the thrill of smuggling, just for its own sake, Adam remembered.

'I've worked it out,' Adam confirmed. 'But first I've got to find a way to talk to Frenchy John.' He rolled himself carefully in his blanket. By morning the ground would be covered with frost, and anyone who wanted a good night's sleep made sure that he was as well covered as possible.

'Why him?'

'Because I reckon he escaped from the penal colony on Tasmania,' Adam told him. 'I want to find out how we can get off the place before I risk getting us sent there.'

And that was the most likely result of any attempt at smuggling, he thought wearily. This place wasn't like Cornwall. There was so much still that he didn't know about it and in smuggling, knowledge was your best defence against being caught. But it had to be risked. He would not go back on his word. He would not leave here until he had made his fortune.

290

The next morning he took the pebble out of his pocket and examined it carefully. But it was just a pebble. That's the way it is, he thought philosophically. Fate seemed determined that he would never be a rich man. And he was equally determined that he would. His teeth flashed in a humourless smile. Let's see which of us is right, he thought, reaching for his shovel.

Chapter 35

'I'm surprised you want to change your claim.'

Adam shrugged casually. 'You know how it is. Greener pastures.' He had high hopes of this new pitch. It was a 'shicer' – a shaft that had already been given up by one group of miners, but he was sure that there was gold there. He had examined the lie of the land with care and it seemed to him that the rock strata dipped just where his new pitch was. If that was the case, then maybe the last diggers had given up too soon.

The policeman looked at him quizzically, his tanned face whitened by the sunlight streaming through the thin canvas walls of the Commission's tent. 'But you seem to have found a good bit of gold in these last couple of months.'

Adam swore under his breath. He had taken payment for the whisky in gold, which he had handed in as if he had found it himself. The police would soon have got suspicious if he had seemed to be able to live without any income. Now it looked as if his ploy had backfired.

He made his blue eyes meet the policeman's intent gaze. 'I'm greedy. I want a real find, not these piddling little bits. An ounce here, an ounce there – what good is that to a man?'

The policeman drummed his fingers on the licence forms spread over the table, his eyes never leaving Adam's face. 'And you're prepared to risk losing the "ounces" for the chance of getting a fortune. You're a gambler, Trevelyan. How will you feel if the man who takes over your claim finds a fortune?' He held Adam's eyes for several seconds longer. 'Of course,' he added softly, 'he might not find anything there at all.'

The Joes were suspicious! Adam could feel the sweat break out on his brow. Thank God it was so hot in the tent! Even the policeman had rivulets of sweat running down the creases in his lean cheeks.

Adam forced a grin. 'I'd prefer the latter, myself,' he said. 'I'd be sick as a shag if he found more than I did.' He raised an eyebrow in mock enquiry. 'You wouldn't want the next man to find more than I did, would you?'

Under his blue gaze, the policeman dropped his eyes. 'Of course not.' He fiddled with the papers for a few seconds as if gathering himself for another attack. 'At least you don't go and blow all your findings on drink and women like some of them do.' He stared suspiciously at Adam again. 'As your partner does, for example. He's off to Melbourne again, I hear.'

There was no doubt now. There were on his trail right enough! And Norman was due back tonight with a load of whisky . . . Adam threw his head back and forced a laugh. Even to his ears it sounded hollow.

'Not women where Norman is concerned, I think. Not unless he's changed a lot since we left Cornwall. Beer is what he's after. That's all he ever talks about, this weather. Beer. Beer. Beer.' He wiped his forehead roughly with his hand. 'Not that I reckon he's far wrong. At this moment I'd give a sovereign for a pint, and I bet you would too.'

'Alcohol is forbidden in the gold fields,' the policeman said swiftly, though Adam noticed the way his tongue had licked his lips at the mention of drink. 'We clamp down hard on people who have it here. And on those who bring it in.' His eyes bored into Adam's.

Someone must have talked. This wasn't a casual conversation. Adam shrugged, feeling his blue serge shirt sticking to his shoulders. 'Well, don't look at me. As you said, I'm one of the sober ones.' He glanced at the paper that lay under the Joe's hands. 'Now, what about my licence? I'll never make my fortune if I spend all day chatting to you.'

He stowed the precious bit of paper in his pocket as he walked slowly between the tents that made up the administrative section of the township that had grown by the river.

Even with the licence in his pocket, Adam knew that he was taking a risk in leaving the mine. A claim that had not been worked for twenty-four hours could be claimed by someone else, and there were always claim-jumpers who would move in even if the mine had been left just a few hours.

Briefly, he hesitated, his eyes staring blankly at the Union Jack flag that hung limply from a nearby tree in the hot air. This was his best chance so far of finding gold. Dare he risk it?

He had to, he decided. There was no choice. He had to warn Norman, even if it meant that they lost the claim, even if it meant that they both got caught. He could not let Norman suffer alone for something that he had started.

He threw a quick glance over his shoulder to make sure that the Joe wasn't watching him then angled swiftly away from the river.

He knew that something was wrong well before he came on the scene. There was a tension in the woods, a quietness. Even the galah birds were silent and the only noise was the faint rustle of leaves in the hot wind.

Adam moved carefully forward. If Norman were anywhere, he would be here, waiting for darkness to fall before he covered the last short stage of his journey to their agreed meeting place. The rented bullock cart, its load disguised so that it looked like any one of the dozens of carts used by men making their way to the Ballarat gold fields, should cause no comment. There was no reason for anyone to doubt that it was anything other than what it seemed, until it reached the area where Norman might be recognised by a nosy Joe.

The sun sank, red-gold in the burnished sky. Its dying beams, sliding under the thick foliage of the gum and acacia trees, suddenly caught some metal in a brazen flash.

Adam stopped abruptly. Only the police wore clothes that would reflect the light like that; their shiny buttons were laughed at throughout the gold fields. He dropped to the ground and wriggled silently forward until he could peer around a tree.

The bullock cart was there standing in a small clearing. It looked as it always did, piled high with cradles and tents which they supplied openly to the merchants at Ballarat. Adam raised his head, puzzled. Perhaps the flash he had seen was the sunlight glinting off a piece of metal on the cart.

He was just getting to his feet when a sudden movement caught his eye and he dropped swiftly to the ground again. He had been right first time. The Joes had found the whisky. He could see it piled at the foot of a nearby boxtree, under guard by the policeman whose buttons had flashed the warning. It would be hidden from anyone near the bullock cart.

So. They had found the whisky and set a trap. And they were expecting someone to spring it. But where was Norman?

Suddenly he froze. Behind him he could hear stealthy footsteps. He rolled swiftly under a sheltering bush, praying that he had not chosen the haunt of a deadly redbacked spider or death adder.

The footsteps drew closer. Adam buried his head in his arms lest the pale flash of his skin should give him away. The footsteps paused momentarily by him. He held his breath.

'Seen anything?' The words were spoken right over his head, and so unexpected that he jumped involuntarily.

'Nothing. And we won't if you stand there shouting your mouth off like that.' The answer came in an angry hiss.

The Joe above him was unmoved. 'I don't think there'll be anyone to catch. What if he's telling the truth and this was his first trip? We'll be here all night for nothing.'

The policeman by the whisky said angrily, 'That's what you're paid for, to stand and wait. It's not our fault if nobody comes, but it flaming well will be if they come and we scare them off.'

'All right, no need to shout. You're the one who's doing the scaring, I reckon.' There was a pause then he added, 'Not but what it's all right for you. You've got your back to the tree. I have to walk around here.' He glanced quickly over his shoulder. 'God knows what's in these woods. There could be natives, ghosts, anything.'

'Ghosts.' The scorn was palpable. 'That's the trouble with you new boys; you haven't got the guts for the job. One gliding possum and you're running for home crying for your mother.'

'I don't . . .' the man began then, nervously, 'what was that?'

Adam grinned to himself as the cuckoo-like call of a boobook owl rang out over their heads.

'Oh, for God's sake!' He could hear the contempt in the policeman's voice. 'Come and guard the whisky then, if it makes you feel safer, poor little chap.'

The policeman by Adam took up the offer with alacrity. He must really feel nervous, Adam thought with a sudden surge of sympathy, remembering how alien he had found Australia at first, the strange birdcalls and the crackling sounds made by wombats. Even he had thought of ghosts the first time a gliding possum had flown over his head in the darkness, making a low whirring moan as it leapt from tree to tree. And then there were the gumtrees glimmering in the dark, so different from the treeless headlands of Cornwall to which he was accustomed.

He watched as the Joes changed places, then he wriggled back out of sight and climbed to his feet. Norman must be around here somewhere, and Adam was honour-bound to rescue him. He moved silently through the trees, straining his eyes and ears for any sign of human life.

For over an hour he continued his search, managing to avoid being found by any of the police who staked out the wood, even though one of them had tripped over his leg as he lay hidden and had cursed loudly, taking it for a fallen branch. He had almost given up hope when he finally found Norman. His hands and feet were tied together and there was a gag in his mouth to keep him quiet.

When he saw Adam crawling softly towards him through the darkness he signalled urgently with his eyes.

'I know,' Adam breathed in his ear. 'I can see him. And hear him.' There was only one man left to guard the prisoner and he was asleep, leaning against the bole of a stringy-bark tree. His mouth was open and the loud snores had been what had finally led Adam to the right place.

He leaned over Norman, cutting through the ropes with his knife. Thank heavens they hadn't chained him as they usually did, he thought, then realised that the police had used ropes so that the rattle of chains would not alert Norman's accomplices.

He removed the gag carefully, then, leaving Norman to rub some life back into his feet, he searched for a large stone and crawled towards the sleeping Joe. There was a muffled thud and the snores stopped to be replaced by quieter breathing.

Norman limped painfully towards him. 'What did you do that for?'

'To keep him quiet. Someone would have come soon to wake him up. You could hear those snores half a mile away.'

'Well, we'll be gone from here soon.' Norman stretched and Adam could see him wince in the dim starlight as the blood flowed painfully back. 'Just give me a couple of minutes and we can be well away.'

Adam nodded to their left, his hands busy tying the gag around the Joe's mouth. 'The cart's down that way, isn't it?'

'Yes. They've staked it out. I told them I was working alone but they didn't believe me.' Norman shrugged. 'If we go the other way we shouldn't have any problem.'

'To hell with that,' Adam said forcefully. 'They've got our whisky back there. I'm not leaving without that! We need the money.' He rolled the Joe over, tying his hands with the remains of the ropes that had been used on Norman.

'But there are four of them,' Norman hissed. 'All strangers. I think they've been brought up from Melbourne specially. They're all armed.'

'So, we take care.' Adam frowned. 'I had to abandon one load of goods for the Revenue men when I left Cornwall. I'll be damned if I leave another for the peelers in Australia.'

He fumbled through the Joe's uniform. The man woke up at his touch, and squirmed, grunting furiously. 'Don't they have any whistles or rattles out here?'

'What do you want a whistle for?' Norman demanded.

'Just an idea. But if he hasn't got one, we'll have to think of something else.' He stood, frowning briefly, then his face cleared.

'How are your legs?'

Norman wriggled his toes again. 'Fine now. I reckon I could keep up with you, no trouble.'

'You're not going to have to keep up with me,' Adam said. 'You're going to have to run like hell in the other direction. Think you can do it?'

Norman's head came up. 'What are you planning?' he asked suspiciously.

'Just to get our whisky back.' He searched through the pile of kit the Joes had stacked and emerged with more rope and an old pair of grey-white long underpants. 'I'll need a fair amount of time to get ready.' He stood for a moment lost in thought. 'Long enough to get down to our pitch in Wheal Susan and back to grass again. Think you can remember it?'

'I'll never forget it,' Norman grimaced. 'And then?'

'Then you shout for the Joes. Sounding as like the Joe there as you can. And if you can find a whistle or a rattle in the kit there, use that as well. Anything to get them to come here and leave the whisky.'

'They'll probably still leave one on guard,' Norman warned.

Adam's teeth flashed white in a brief smile. 'I've got plans for that.' He became more serious. 'Once you're sure they're coming, make yourself scarce. And quickly. Get right away from here. I'll meet you back at the tent.'

He dropped a hand on Norman's shoulder. 'You're the only friend I've got in the world,' he said gruffly. 'I can't afford to lose you.' He turned abruptly and walked off, the rope slung in a loose coil around his shoulder.

He made his way inside the three circling watchers, sliding carefully on his belly until he was close to his target.

The night was darker now, the pile of whisky barrels invisible against the dark bole of the tree though he could still see the pale face of the man on guard peering nervously into the darkness, his gun at the ready. Adam grinned, sliding under a dense bush while he made his final preparations, then he lay still, waiting.

Norman's performance was better than he could ever have hoped. The woods rang with his shouts and he added to the noise by hitting together what sounded like two billy cans. The effect was as if a tribe of Aborigines had attacked all at once.

The Joe on guard jumped visibly and let off his gun in a nervous reaction, adding to the commotion and sending roosting birds shrieking into the air. Adam lay still, straining to catch the sound of the three hidden watchers.

He heard one yell, 'Stay by that whisky. If you move I'll have your guts for garters,' and then there was the pounding of feet as the men ran to the rescue of their comrade.

Adam stayed where he was until he was sure that the other men were well on their way then he rose carefully to his feet.

The guard was peering nervously after his departing comrades, his rifle clutched to his chest. Adam tiptoed forward until he was within a few yards of the man then let out a soft moan.

The guard swung round so quickly that he caught his feet in a tree root and stumbled almost up to Adam. For a long petrified second he stared at the apparition before him and even in the darkness Adam could see the blood drain from his face.

He was closer than Adam had intended, too close. If he regained any particle of common sense . . .

Adam moaned again, waving his arms in the air. At the same time a light breeze blew through the trees, not much, just enough to move the leaves in a soft whisper. And enough to flutter the ends of the underpants that Adam had tied over his head, the legs partly stuffed with twigs and leaves so that they stood like two horns above his head.

In the darkness his naked body, protected from the sun, gleamed pallidly. The Joe was transfixed with horror for what seemed to Adam like minutes. Then the breeze blew again, fluttering the loose hanging legs of underwear until they reached out like hands.

The Joe let out a moan, even more harrowing than the one Adam had given, then dived for the security of the woods, dropping his rifle as he went. Adam hauled off the underpants and picked the rifle up, grinning. Dressing up as a ghost had been a favourite trick of the Cornish smugglers in the old days, though they had given it up now. The Revenue men were too sophisticated to fall again for that old ploy. It was good to know that the old ideas still worked, even in this new land.

He fetched the rope and swiftly climbed the tree under which the Joes had piled the whisky. If one old trick had worked, so might another. The last place they would look for the whisky would be right above the spot from which they had lost it. Within a few minutes he had hoisted the kegs up into the branches and made them fast. They would be safe there until the hue and cry died down.

He dressed swiftly, one ear cocked for sounds of the returning Joes, but he could only hear shouts and yells in the vicinity of their camp. He pushed back the thought that they might have caught Norman; he was too wily to let himself be trapped twice. And, like Adam, he had been raised on stories of the Cornish smugglers. He might well have prepared a surprise for the policemen on his own account.

Taking the Joe's rifle with him Adam hurried away from the scene, grinning broadly.

He stopped once, abruptly, at an unexpected noise in front of him, but it was only the bullock, placidly chewing cud. For a second he hesitated, but there was no sound of imminent pursuit and, after all, the cart was still fully laden. And money was money.

Adam could hear the noise of the cradles, like a constant beat of muffled drums, long before he drove out of the trees and could gaze down on Ballarat spread out before him. He had been told the name meant 'Pleasant Resting Place' in the Aborigine language, but no one who could see it now would so describe it.

The tents, interspersed with rough shacks and even with shelters made from tree boughs, covered all the ground between the trees and the creek. Amongst them were the workings, rough holes dug without thought to anyone's safety, some of them already abandoned, others with a rough windlass standing sentinel. And everywhere, the miners, their rough red and blue shirts bright under the sun, scurrying like ants as they pushed their barrows of pay dirt to the creek.

Even that had shrunk now. The area of swamp that surrounded it in winter had dried up, and the creek itself had become smaller, its edges thickly crowded with the rocking cradles, in places two or three deep, as men frantically searched for the magic mineral that could transform their lives. The gold that he could not find.

So he drove the cart openly down into Ballarat, submitting to a careful search by the police with rare good humour. After all, at least four such carts arrived every twenty-four hours, and as Adam pointed out, it wasn't illegal to bring in much-needed supplies, even if he had taken over from the regular driver who had gone back to Melbourne for personal reasons.

But he knew that that would be his last smuggling trip. The Joes could not prove anything, but they would not forget. From now on, he was a marked man. He could not subsidise his mining by smuggling any more. Now his back really was against the wall.

He could find gold. Or he would starve.

Chapter 36

'Dammit!' Adam threw his spade down in disgust. He leaned against the rough earth wall of his claim and wiped his forehead morosely with a dirty handkerchief.

The afternoon sun was low in the sky and the bottom of the pit was in darkness, lit only by a flickering tallow light. No breath of wind disturbed the fetid air here, sixty feet below the ground.

'Dammit,' Adam swore again, kicking furiously at the earthen side of the pit. They had laughed at him for taking over a shicer that other men had given up on, and teased him for digging deeper than any of the other miners.

'Trying to dig your way back home?' they'd joked. 'Think there's another river down there with gold?' But he had ignored them. And now look at what he'd found!

He hammered his heel furiously into the clay which he had uncovered. Clay! Like glue when it was wet and like rock when it dried. There'd be no gold dust mixed in with clay.

He slumped against the walls. Others had found gold. Sometimes it seemed as if everyone in Ballarat had found gold except for him. He had become used to hearing the shouts of triumph, to seeing men who a few days earlier had been dressed in rags suddenly become rich overnight. He had seen them riding off to Melbourne on their expensive new horses, their eyes bright with anticipation as they foresaw the pleasures ahead of them. For once, they could eat what they liked, where they wanted. They were *rich*!

Yes, he reminded himself, and he had seen the same men come back, days or weeks later. Some of them still had money, but many didn't. But their stories! Buying champagne for everyone in the pub! Lighting their cigars with five-pound notes! The women they had had! Even though he despised them for wasting the power that money gave them, he had listened with all ears, half-envying them, even though he knew that he would never be like that.

And he was poor, and getting poorer. He stared again at the clay he had uncovered. No time now to get another claim. No way he could even pay next month's licence fee. This was the end of the road for him. He had said that he would starve here if necessary, and now there was no getting away from it. He had to do what he had said he would do.

He had failed. He faced the fact squarely, his face bleak. With all his hard work, all his experience, all his efforts, he had failed. This was the end of the line for him. There was no more hope, no more future. Just failure and an unmarked grave. He would lie here amongst all the other victims that the gold had claimed, men who had died of dysentery or chicken pox; of thirst or drowning.

A shot reverberated through the air. The rifle shot from the Commission tent, marking the end of the day's work. Well, as far as he was concerned, it was the end of his life's work. There would be no alluvial gold dust in clay.

Wearily, Adam climbed the sixty feet up out of the airless pit, ducking under the heavy wooden windlass he had fitted up to help him raise the dirt. Winter was almost on them again, though you wouldn't know it during the day. But the nights were already getting colder and Norman was complaining about the light frost that silvered the ground on clear nights.

As if on cue, Norman appeared. 'Found anything?'

Adam shook his head. Why tell him the bad news? Let him eat his damper and mutton stew in peace. He waited until Norman was drawing on his pipe before he broached the subject he had been turning over in his mind ever since he first saw the streak of blue marl clay under his feet.

'It's time you were going back to Burra Burra.'

'What?' Norman's face was a mask of surprise. 'But why? Don't you want me here any more?'

Want him? Adam felt his throat tighten at the question. Norman was someone he had always taken for granted, someone who was always there, whose faults and failings Adam knew as well as he knew his own. Norman was all he had left in the world now. Phil had gone his own way, Clara was lost to him for ever. Norman was the only person in the whole world who cared whether he lived or died, and for that very reason he had to make him go away.

'You'll be better off at Burra Burra,' he said harshly, ignoring the pain that lanced through him at the thought of the loneliness he would feel when Norman went. 'They would make you an under-captain if you went back, I'm sure of it. And that's the real life for a Cornishman – real mining, dealing with copper.'

Norman's eyes were fixed on his face, his stare unblinking. 'And you?' he demanded. 'What are you going to do?'

'I'll carry on here.' Adam did not mention his vow to die here; the possibility was now too close, too real. 'If I find anything, I'll share it, you know I will. And you can come back when I've struck it rich. You can help me spend it.' He tried to force his face into a smile but his cheeks were stiff with emotion.

Suspicion lit Norman's face. He jumped to his feet. 'Something's happened, hasn't it?' His voice was sharp. 'What is it? What's happened?' Then, more slowly, 'What have you found?'

It took long seconds for the question to sink in, then Adam too leapt to his feet. 'Found?' he queried, his voice shaking with fury. *'Found?'* His voice cracked on the word.

He stared at Norman with disbelieving eyes. 'You think I've found gold, don't you? You think I'm trying to get you away so that I can keep it all to myself.' He punched one fist into the palm of his other hand, trying to control his anger, to hide his disappointment.

'Well, you have found something, haven't you?' Norman insisted. 'Don't try hiding it from me; I know you too well for that. You've found something and you don't want to let me know.'

Emotion had loosened Adam's tongue. 'Yes, I've found something all right,' he said, and despised himself for the way his voice shook. 'But not what you think! Nothing like you think!'

He stared down at his accuser, his erstwhile best friend, standing beside him. 'I've found clay,' he said, tasting the bitterness of defeat on his tongue.

'Clay?' Norman faltered. He hesitated. 'But . . .'

'Yes, clay!' Adam broke in. 'A great joke, isn't it? Adam Trevelyan, the great miner. Read all those books, did all that studying, worked like a dog for seven months on the richest gold field on earth and all I've managed to find is clay!'

He swung away but Norman caught at him. 'So that was why you wanted me to go away!' His voice was quieter, the light in his eyes dimmed. 'Not because you'd found gold but because you'd found clay.' He knew the devastation Adam must be feeling. The other miners had made their best finds in the quartz gravel seams that criss-crossed the area.

Adam dropped again to sit by the fire. He felt tired, beaten, bone-weary. He was twenty-five years old and he had worked since he was nine, studying alone in the evenings after a full day's work down the mine. He almost welcomed failure, he realised suddenly. At least it meant an end to labour, an end to responsibility. Norman was the only one dependent on him, now. Get Norman off his hands and he could rest at last.

'Clay,' he said quietly. 'So no gold. And no money for another licence. And no time to dig elsewhere. This is the end of my dreams, Norman.'

He raised his head and his blue eyes blazed in the firelight. 'But not the end for you, Norman. You don't deserve this. I dragged you into this, made Cornwall too hot for us, brought you out here, even took you away from Burra Burra. But this is the last thing I'm going to ask of you.'

His face was serene now, the anger of a few minutes ago wiped away as if it had never been. 'Go back to Burra Burra, Norman.' He was almost pleading. 'There's life for you there, a good life. You can make money, get yourself a wife, rear children. You can be happy in this country.'

'And you?' Norman's voice was hoarse, catching in his throat.

'There is no future for me,' Adam said quietly. 'Perhaps there never was. All I ever had was dreams. They were what kept me alive, kept me fighting.'

He stared into the fire, his eyes soft. 'I wanted a good life, a rich life. I was prepared to suffer now so that I could have that life in the future. But I realise now, it was all a delusion. There is no better life for me. And without that dream . . .' He shrugged, relapsing into silence.

Norman dropped to his knees beside him. 'You can still do it, Adam,' he insisted. 'You can still make it.'

Adam shook his head, a small smile curving his lips. 'No. But you can.' He reached out, clutching at the coarse serge shirt that Norman wore. 'You can have a better life, you can make your dreams come true.'

When Norman didn't reply, Adam grasped him, roughly. 'You must do this for me,' he insisted. 'It's the last thing I shall ever ask you. You can't let me down now.' There was no mistaking the sincerity in his voice. 'Let me at least have the satisfaction of knowing, at the end, that I haven't ruined your life as well as my own.'

Norman bowed his head. 'But it's such a waste! All your knowledge, all your reading . . .'

Adam shrugged. 'Perhaps all life is a waste, really. Perhaps it's just that it takes us a long time to realise it.'

After Norman had gone to bed he still sat up, staring at the fire. Knowledge! He gave a short laugh. What good had it done him? Other men had come here not knowing one end of a shovel from

303

another and gone away rich. And he – dear God! back in Cornwall he had pursued knowledge as if it was the key to the universe. Even when he had no thoughts beyond the Wheal Susan, he had devoured those books on mining that Clara had lent him, even those that dealt with subjects he had never for a second imagined he would have anything to do with. Like gold mining . . .

The smile died on his lips. Suddenly he was back again in the small, dark cottage, the wind howling in from the Atlantic. And he was sitting in front of the small window, making the most of the dim light that filtered through the thick, distorted panes. Before him was one of Captain Pentreath's books. He could see again the small, cramped print, read the words . . .

Suddenly, he was up on his feet and running, running through the quiet camp, leaping over the half-seen corners of the tents and mounds of baggage, black and formless in the deceptive moonlight. At the claim he slithered swiftly down the makeshift ladder he had constructed, jumping the last ten feet and landing with a thud that jarred his back teeth and brought him to his senses.

Careful, he reminded himself. Out here, a broken leg could be a death sentence. Even a sprained ankle would mean disaster. He breathed deeply, waiting until his heart had slowed down and his eyes adjusted to the faint glimmer from the tallow dip he had lit.

The vein of clay shone lighter against the dark earth. Adam had himself under control again now; even his immoderate hopes that for a moment had overcome him were now firmly battened down. Once again, he was a working machine, cold, logical, knowledgeable.

He swung the pick. The point sunk deep into the earth, tearing it back, exposing still more of the seam of clay. He swung again and again and now the pick bit deep into the clay itself.

The camp was asleep. Dimly, he could hear the noises of the night, the bark of dogs, the braying of mules, but they were muffled by the sides of the pit. Far louder was his own breathing, the grunts of effort as he swung the pick again and again.

He was putting off the moment. He knew it. First he couldn't wait to try out his idea: now he was terrified in case it had been wrong.

The floor was littered now with broken earth. He had no excuse to put off the moment any longer. He laid down his pick and in the dimness he knelt, riffling through the soil with shaking fingers.

Norman crawled slowly from the tent, his hair on end but his eyes alert and concerned. 'You didn't come to bed last night.'

'I couldn't sleep.' Adam turned to the fire, pouring hot water over

304

tea leaves that had already been used until they could scarcely colour the water. 'There was no point in keeping you awake as well.'

Norman stretched, enjoying the warmth of the sun, then paused suddenly. 'But you let me sleep on.' Around him, tents were already emptying as men made their way to their diggings and in the distance there was a line outside the butcher's tent as men bought the mutton for their dinner before the heat and flies could get at it.

Adam shrugged. 'There's no hurry now. I thought you deserved a lie-in. God knows, we've had few enough in our lives so far.'

Norman put down his mug, his face concerned. 'This isn't like you, Adam. I've never known you so down before. You're always the one who thinks we can win through despite everything. And now you don't seem to care any more.' He reached out a friendly hand and grasped Adam's faded sleeve. 'What is it? Has something happened?'

'You could say that.' Adam was surprised himself at the calmness he felt. All these years of fighting and struggling and now, when it was all over – suddenly all he felt was tired. As if he wanted to lie down and sleep for a month.

He reached under the rough log on which he was sitting and threw something to Norman. His friend's hand shot out instinctively, catching it before it could fall into the fire.

Norman turned the small pebble over in his fingers, his mind so concentrated on Adam's strange behaviour that it was long seconds before the implications of what he was seeing sunk in. Then the glint of yellow metal, flashing in the sun, made him blink.

He held the smooth nugget closer to his eyes, running his fingers over it, feeling its deceptive heaviness. 'W-where did you get it?' His voice caught roughly in his throat.

'In our claim.' Adam watched him with amused eyes. 'In that clay I told you about last night.'

Norman cleared his throat. 'But it's gold! A nugget! It's two or three ounces – that's ten quid. Ten whole quid!' His voice rose. 'You realise what this means? We can stay here, carry on looking.' He began to move impatiently around the fire. 'Why didn't you wake me earlier? There might be more there,' he said excitedly. 'This could be the day we really make a find!'

Adam reached behind him again and shied three more pebbles at his friend. Norman caught the first two in eager hands, wincing as the third caught him on the knuckles and bounced back to lie in the ashes of the fire. Careless of the heat, he raked it clear with his free hand. All three were gold.

'But this,' his eyes were shining, 'this is IT! This is what we've been searching for all these months. And not dust, my God, but nuggets. Real nuggets! We've done it! We've done it! We've done it!'

He began to dance around the fire, the nuggets clasped in his hands. 'Gold! Gold!'

Suddenly he stopped and stared down at Adam, who was still motionless, sitting watching him with a twisted grin on his face. 'Is this all?' he asked suspiciously, and reading the answer in Adam's very stillness, 'it isn't, is it?'

Adam shook his head and moved his body to one side. Behind the stump, half-covered by a rough piece of sacking, a small pile of nuggets glistened in the autumn sunlight.

'Dear Lord!' Norman was on his knees beside them, lifting first one and then another, turning them to examine the soft patina of richness. 'But how? When you said you had struck clay . . .'

Adam nodded. 'Then I remembered what I had read in one of Captain Pentreath's books, that some people thought that clay was formed where a river had dropped its load of silt, and I thought, if modern rivers drop gold, then why not ancient rivers?' He shrugged. 'It seemed worth a look.'

Norman was still turning the nuggets in his hands. 'And you found all this.' His voice was disbelieving. 'All this – and at seventy shillings an ounce . . .' He jumped to his feet again, gripping Adam by the shoulders. 'We've done it! We're rich! Rich!'

'Keep your voice down you fool.'

But Norman's simple pleasure moved Adam. This is what he should have felt, not simply the sudden surge of relief that the failure he had seen approaching so irrevocably was gone, but pleasure in his findings. Yet he knew he could never feel that. It wasn't the value of what he had found that was important to him, it was what he could do with it. Wealth signified power, an escape from a half-life of poverty and despair. The ability to lead his own life as he chose.

And although gold could achieve all that for him, the mere sight of it did nothing for him. The work wasn't over yet. The gold had to be wrung from the ground, assayed, turned to wealth. *Then* he would be happy.

But never happy in the way that Norman was, he knew that, and briefly regretted the loss of an innocence that could delight in the mere sight and touch of a few pretty pebbles. Once, he too had believed that wealth could bring him happiness, but the loss of Clara had taught him different. All it could do now was to compensate him for his loss.

He made an effort to hide his sombre feelings, forcing his face into a grin. 'There's plenty more where that came from. I was too tired to carry on digging.' And too disillusioned, now that his dream had come true. 'You see what you can get,' he suggested. 'And don't let on just how big a find we've made to anyone else. I want us to get what we can from the claim before every treasure-hunter in Ballarat is digging around us.'

'Well, I think we deserve a break.' Norman wiped the mixture of rain and sweat off his forehead, leaving a muddy streak, and glared furiously at Adam in the dim light of the taper. 'We've got enough. Let's go and spend some of it.'

'We have not got enough.' Adam paused in his work of sifting the soil that had been dug out from the tunnel. It was real mining, now, following where the clay led, deep under the soil. And, just as in Cornwall, there were the same problems of water and lifting the mullock or waste out of the mine.

'We could go away just for a bit,' Norman suggested. 'Just until we get some better weather. All this rain is making the ground dangerous.'

'If you're too frightened to work underground, just let me know,' Adam said furiously. 'I'm not afraid of a bit of darkness, even if you are. And as for having enough, this is our only chance, remember that. Luck like this isn't going to come twice in anyone's life. We stay here until it runs out.'

'But we've got enough,' Norman repeated. He wiped his filthy hands down the side of his soaking, clay-streaked trousers. 'With what we've got we can buy a farm, or a business. For God's sake,' he shouted, suddenly losing his temper, 'we can almost buy a bloody bank!'

Like Blacklock's. Adam felt his face grow stiff at the thought. 'That money is between the two of us,' he pointed out. 'That doesn't make us so rich.'

'It makes us rich enough to get away from all this.' Norman had had enough. 'Why stay here, huddled in a freezing tent, when we can employ men, a manager.'

'We could be cheated,' Adam broke in. 'How can we trust them?' He pointed at the pile of nuggets he had found already that morning. This claim was rich, rich beyond belief. It had yielded steadily now for four months and there was no sign of it stopping. 'How can we trust other people with that?'

There was a long silence. Above them, rain drummed on the makeshift roof they had built to protect them from the worst of the weather, sliding in rivulets down the rough-hewn walls to puddle around their feet.

307

Norman said quietly, 'It's got to you, hasn't it, this gold? It's all you want out of life now. Not pleasure, not happiness. Just gold.'

'No!' It was a despairing shout. How could he be so wrong? Adam said, 'It's not the gold that matters, can't you see that? It's what it does for you, what it gives you.'

He began to pace around the bottom of the shaft, his booted feet squelching and slipping in the mud. 'This.' He bent to pick up a nugget, brandishing it under Norman's nose. 'This isn't gold, don't you see? It isn't even money. It's power. And that's what I want it for, for the power it will give me.'

He dropped the nugget and it half-buried itself in the mud at his feet. He kicked at it disdainfully. 'In itself, it's nothing. But it's what it can buy me that's important.' In the dim light, his eyes held a fanatical glow. 'It can buy me respect. It can buy me a place in society. It can stop me being kicked in the teeth by some bugger who isn't fit to tie my shoelaces but who happened to be born into a family with money.'

Norman threw back his head. 'It can't buy you Clara,' he said cruelly. 'And that's all you really want, isn't it?'

Adam turned on him. 'I wouldn't speak to her if she came to me on bended knee,' he said bitterly. 'I wouldn't give her a penny if she were starving. I would rather throw a loaf of bread to the gulls than give it to her, even if her life depended upon it.'

'And you dream of her at night,' Norman taunted him. 'You cry out her name in your sleep.'

Fury rose in Adam until he could taste it. He knew Norman was only saying these things to anger him, to get back at him for keeping him away from the bars and women of Melbourne, but the words were too hurtful, too vicious.

'Are you going to bloody well work, or do I stuff you up that tunnel with my boot up your arse?' he demanded.

Norman knew he had gone too far. In a mood like this, Adam was capable of anything. Swiftly, he ducked down into the low tunnel that led through the clay to the face where they were working.

Adam stood still, his fists clenched, his face red with fury. Bloody whinger! He was always the same. Always trying to get off work. He had done it in Cornwall and he was doing it here. No matter that he was getting more for an hour's work than he could have earned in a month back in Cornwall; all Norman bloody Willcock ever wanted to do was cut loose and enjoy himself.

He felt it before he heard the noise. A gentle movement under his feet as if an animal, under the mud, had rolled over. Then the sound, soft, insidious, terrifying.

He was at the mouth of the tunnel even before the back-blow of air belched from it, fetid, muddy, deadly.

'Norman!' It was a cry of despair. Careless of his own safety, Adam dived into the narrow tunnel, tearing with his bare hands at the piled soil that blocked the way. 'Norman! NORMAN!'

When they found him, his hand, bloodied and broken, was gripping Norman's ankle. He had dug his way so far but could go no further.

With care, they tunnelled deeper but it was hours before they could free Norman's body from the fall, his eyes, that had shone in the fresh air of Cornwall now filmed and dulled by the deadly clay of Ballarat.

Chapter 37

Clara gazed down at the sleeping baby in her arms, feeling her heart contract with tenderness and fear for him.

He was so small and helpless, his tiny forehead furrowed as if, even at four months, he already realised that life was a struggle. Or was he picking up her concerns? Clara wondered guiltily, her arms automatically rocking the tiny creature. Did he somehow feel the worries that kept her awake, night after night, as she lay waiting for Edward to return from his current gambling or drinking hole?

Lady Susan's querulous voice cut across her thoughts. 'Let me hold him, Clara. Give him to me.'

She turned unwillingly. It caused her a wrench even to hand the child to his highly trained nurse. Letting Lady Susan hold him made her break out in a sweat of fear. But it seemed to calm her mother.

Ma Downing broke in soothingly, 'She'll mind the babe, never you fret. Brem taken with him, she is.' She took the child with practised ease. 'Here you are, my lady. As bonny a boy as you could see in a month of Sundays.' She laid him in the other woman's arms and Lady Susan immediately bent over him, her worn face breaking into a happy smile.

Clara hovered, unable to ignore the unease she felt whenever anyone other than herself held the child. But Lady Susan rocked the child competently enough. Watching her, Clara wondered suddenly if her mother had ever held her like that when she was a baby. It seemed impossible. In her childhood Clara could only ever remember being hugged by her father. Her mother had always pushed her away, pleading ladylike behaviour and a need for self-control. Was it, she wondered suddenly, because she had only been a girl, or had Lady Susan repressed the feelings she so patently felt for Jamie because it did not accord with her view of motherhood?

310

Almost in answer to her thoughts, Lady Susan began crooning a song Clara was certain she had never heard as a child.

'See saw, Marjorie Daw,
Sold her bed, lay on the straw.
Gipsies come and carr'ed her away,
Threw her over Newlyn Quay.'

'Mama,' Clara broke in, unable to contain her curiosity. She came nearer, knelt at her mother's feet, looking up into her face. 'Mama, did you ever sing that to me?'

But Lady Susan was lost in a world of her own. Gazing at the small pink face she tenderly brushed back a wisp of whitest-blond hair, as soft and light as thistledown. 'Who's a lovely boy then?' Her voice was an adoring whisper. 'He's the very image of the Earl, so he is. A true heir to Trevival, aren't you my beauty?'

Clara jumped abruptly to her feet. 'An heir to Trevival', indeed. Her mother was rambling again. Jamie would never be allowed to even visit the place. And if Edward did not stop his drinking and gambling, Jamie would have no inheritance at all.

Her worries flooded back again. How could she stop Edward? What could she do? Any comment she made on the situation just made things worse, driving him out ever earlier in the day, complaining that she was nagging him.

He had even blamed her for her actions at the bank, forbidding her ever to go there again, ever to even mention business matters to him. 'You did no good,' he had told her furiously. 'They would never have really taken their money out. You just made a laughing stock of yourself, turning up like that. And in your condition! Do you think I want my wife to expose herself like that to the hoi-polloi?'

She paced restlessly across the room, driven by her agitation. He had made no mention that she might have harmed the child by her actions, she realised suddenly. His only concern was for his reputation. But he was unable to see how he himself was endangering it by his actions, she thought, feeling the panic rise in her throat. He would not recognise that if she had not acted as she had done, they would already be bankrupt.

If only he would open up Wheal Susan. That, at least, might hold off the doubters. Other mines were being re-opened as the price of tin rose. But Edward refused categorically to do so.

She moved to the window, pushing aside the luxurious red brocade curtains. Outside, the short December afternoon was wearing away, drowned by the streaming rain that almost hid her view of the valley.

It brought back all too clearly her memories of that other December, two years ago, in Adam's small cottage. She felt her mind shy away from the very name. Don't think of him. Don't remember him. Sanity comes only from living in the present and the future. Not the past.

But the future was nearly as bleak, she decided. Two years ago she had agreed to marry Edward for her mother's sake. Now, it seemed inevitable that they would again be penniless, but with a child to care for as well. Her breath misted the glass and as she rubbed it clear she saw a horseman trotting slowly down the drive. Edward.

Moved by a sudden resolution, she turned to Ma Downing. 'Watch out for Jamie, please. I shall be back as soon as I can.'

Whatever Edward felt about it, she had to have one last try to make him see sense, she decided, lifting her skirts as she ran down the broad, gleaming staircase. She was a mother now. She had responsibilities that took precedent over her vows to be a good wife.

The front door flew open with a bang before she reached the foot of the staircase and Edward barged through. Clara paused, aware instantly that something was terribly wrong.

Edward threw his wet coat at the footman. 'Brandy in the library. At once.' Without acknowledging her presence, he strode swiftly across the hall and the door slammed behind him.

Clara followed more slowly, aware that her heart was thudding painfully in her chest. Dear God, what had happened now? Not another run on the bank. Not that!

He was sitting behind his desk, his head in his hands when she softly pushed the door open. At her entrance he glanced eagerly up but his face fell as he recognised her. 'I thought you were the butler. Where the hell is my brandy?' He jumped to his feet and marched to the fireplace, jerking on the bell-pull with such force that Clara almost expected it to come away in his hand.

'Edward! What's the matter? What's wrong?' Alarmed, she moved forward, put her hand on his arm.

He shrugged her off. 'Wrong? What should be wrong?' His voice was heavy with sarcasm. He swung away from her as the door opened. 'The brandy. At last!'

He was pouring it before the door had closed behind Bennet, his hand shaking so much that the decanter clinked against the glass. Then, with one swallow, he downed it, coughing as it burned his throat.

Instantly, he poured another glass, but now he was calmer. He turned to Clara, the glass in his hand, and she was shocked at his grey pallor. He took another swallow, smaller this time. 'You want to know what has happened?' He laughed harshly. 'I'll tell you what has happened. Grenfell has left my employ.'

312

Clara's first feeling was one of relief. She had never trusted him. Then she looked again at Edward. Grenfell had been his man, even while he had worked for her father, but it was ridiculous for Edward to get so upset just because he had left. Edward had never shown any loyalty to anyone but himself for as long as she had known him.

She said slowly, 'That's not all though, is it? Other men have left but I haven't seen you react like this before.'

He took another mouthful of brandy before he replied. 'All? Of course it's not all! He's left me, and he's taken the last month's profits with him. And God only knows how much more besides.' He finished the brandy and turned to refill his glass.

Clara felt her knees turn weak. 'The profits?' she asked stupidly. 'The profits from the smelting works?'

'The whole bloody lot! He sold the tin to some bugger I've never heard of and had the money transferred God only knows where.' Edward sank into his seat, his head in his hands. 'And I only found out because the chief clerk wanted to know why the payment hadn't reached the bank.'

He groaned. 'All that money! And we owe the mines for the ore. We haven't paid for the coal, the wages, nothing! And if he'll do this, he's probably been milking the smelting works for months. The clerks said that the income seemed much lower than it should have been, but no one told me.'

No one had told him because he had cut himself off from the day-to-day work of the bank, blasting with anger anyone who tried to bring any business to his attention. Clara knew that. She sank slowly into a chair opposite him, trying to think of a way to save the situation. 'But you can have him arrested . . .'

He gave a harsh bark of laughter. 'Arrested! If I knew where he was! He's been off "sick" for almost a week. And his family have been away "visiting relatives" only no one knows where.'

Clara shut her eyes, trying to control the panic that rose inside her. All Molly's relatives lived locally, she knew that. The whole situation showed evidence of being a well-thought-out plan. She took a deep breath, trying to fight down the sick feeling that rose inside her, the feeling of terror at the thought of Jamie, homeless, penniless. She had to think clearly. Edward was panicking. She had to be the one who worked out what they could do.

She said slowly, 'It's only one month's money, when all is said and done. We can arrange to pay our bills. You own the bank. You can get a loan if there isn't enough money in our account. And the smelting works is still there . . .'

He interrupted. 'It's not still there. Grenfell hasn't spent a penny on it for months. All the furnaces are leaking, the output is rock bottom. They'll all have to be replaced.'

'So, we replace them,' Clara said. 'What's the problem?'

He jumped to his feet, thrust his face, red now and blotchy, close into hers. 'Money!' he yelled. 'That's what's the problem! Money! Money! Money!'

She flinched at his sour, alcoholic breath. 'But the bank . . .'

He sat slowly down. Despair dragged at his features. 'The bank,' he stated definitively, 'is finished as well.'

They stared at each other across the polished mahogany of the desk. Clara couldn't breathe. Her chest was gripped in a tightening vice. With an immense effort she managed to force words past her stiff, cold lips. 'F-finished?'

Shock suddenly took her and she could feel the shudders running down her spine. Frantically, she dug her nails into her palms, fighting for the ability to cope with these revelations.

'Finished.' There was a touch of relish in the way he said it, as if he enjoyed seeing her for once at a loss. 'There's no way you can do your conjuring trick this time, Madam Know-It-All. This is the end. Of the smelting works, of the bank, of the house . . .'

'The house?' Something snapped inside her. Leaping to her feet, she screamed at him, 'This is your fault, all yours! You lost that bank, you gambled away your son's inheritance, you ran down the smelting works.' Tears trickled down her cheeks, then dropped off her chin. Unconsciously, she wiped them away, her eyes still fixed on her husband. 'Why?' Her voice broke on a sob. 'Why did you do it?'

'Why?' He rose to his feet, his face pale with anger, the red veins of alcoholic abuse showing up more clearly now. 'Why do you think? Because I had a wife who didn't love me, that's why! A wife who always knew better than me, who hated me, who despised me.' He turned away, his shoulders drooping.

'How could I concentrate on the business when all the time I was longing for you, wanting you, wanting one word of love, of submission?'

He swung round, his face twisted with fury and hate. 'But you wouldn't submit to me, would you? You would never give in to me the way a wife should. Always, always, you fought me, defied me . . .'

Clara stared at him, made breathless by the unexpected attack. 'But I . . .' Her voice died away as she remembered the months she had fought him in bed. But she had been submissive since. Her eyes lowered as she said sombrely, 'I have not fought with you now for over a year.'

'But don't you see, that's not what I meant! I wanted you to . . .' His voice died away and he turned from her again. 'Oh, what's the use!' There was bitter defeat in his tone. 'You wouldn't understand. You never have understood.'

For a second she wavered. He looked old, suddenly, old and afraid. Her heart went out to him. Then she rallied. Feeling sorry for Edward was a luxury she could not afford. Her existence was at stake, hers and her son's. Forcing herself to stand straight and defiant, she said, 'I understand one thing only too well. Whether you blame Grenfell or myself, the facts remain. You have ruined two good businesses and left your family homeless and penniless. As your wife,' her voice dripped sarcasm, 'might I be allowed to ask whether you have any plans for the future?'

He shrugged. 'How can I have? Plans need money.' He lowered his head into his hands.

Clara stared at him in fury. He couldn't give in like this, he couldn't! They had to fight, to scheme, find some way to salvage at least a competence out of this wreck of their fortune. Their son's happiness, perhaps even his life depended upon it.

She hadn't gone through two years of purgatory, being married to him, just to end up back in the gutter again. She would not allow all her self-sacrifice to be thrown away like this.

'You can't just give up,' she snapped. 'You're a man! Act like one, for God's sake.' She moved towards him, caught him by the arm, shook him roughly. 'Fight, Edward. Fight.'

He shrugged her off, not even bothering to answer.

So, it was all down to her again. Clara felt the weight of responsibility settle heavily on her shoulders. Oh God, why did it always have to be her?

Perhaps Edward was right. Perhaps she was stronger than he was, even though he was a man. She took a deep breath. If that was her fate, she would have to bear it, carry him as well as all her other responsibilities. It was no more than her father had done all through his life.

It was as if the thought of her father released a valve in her mind. Suddenly, the answer came to her.

'The mine!' Her voice vibrated with happiness and relief. 'Edward, there is still Wheal Susan. We can work that. You can borrow money for that easily enough, now that the price of tin is rising. And there is tin down there. A-Adam found it before he – went away.' She had to force herself to say his name, the name that had never been mentioned between them since their wedding night.

She could see that her words had got through to her husband.

Slowly, his head came up, his back straightened. 'The mine!' She could hear hope in his voice.

Cautiously, she warned, 'We'll never be as rich as we were when you had the bank.' She looked around the library with its leather-bound books, the rich red draperies, the pleasant glow of well-polished mahogany. 'We could never afford to live in a house like this. But we won't be penniless!' She could smile now, her eyes blazing with confidence. 'We'll have an income.'

Edward was staring out of the window. 'The mine,' he repeated. 'Of course, the mine.'

Clara felt as if her heart would burst. Jamie would not be reared in poverty. There was a future for him. She said happily, 'It will be wonderful to have it working again. It will mean so much, not just to me but to the people of St Just.'

Edward nodded absently. 'I'm just wondering about the price.'

'What does that matter?' Clara asked scornfully. 'You can borrow the money to open it easily.'

He turned and looked at her. 'Open it?' He raised his eyebrows. 'My dear Clara, we've got to think about the future. I'm not going to open it.'

'Then what are you going to do?' she asked, puzzled.

He laughed, the first careless laugh she had heard from him for months. 'Do? I'm going to sell it, of course.' His grey eyes were alight with excitement and he stroked his moustache with a gentle finger.

'With what I get for the mine I can go to London,' he said feverishly. 'That's where the real action is. That's where they play for the big stakes.'

As she stared at him disbelievingly, he added, 'I'm a lucky gambler, Clara. With money like that, I will even have a chance to win enough to save the bank.'

'But . . .' The blood drained from her face. 'You can't sell it, you can't!' Her voice was high with shock. 'It's mine. Wheal Susan is mine, left to me by my father. You can't sell it!'

'Oh, come.' His voice was impatient. 'You can't be that ignorant, Clara.' He moved towards her, staring down at her with a superior smile on his face.

'When you married me, my dear, all your possessions became mine – to do with as I liked. Wheal Susan belongs to me now. And I intend to sell it.'

Chapter 38

'Mrs Blacklock! What a pleasant surprise. And to think I was about to ride out to see you.' Mr Brightman bowed swiftly over Clara's hand. 'At least you have saved me a cold, wet drive. But come in, do come in and get warm.'

Didn't attorneys' offices ever change? Clara wondered as she looked around the gloomy little room. He had one of the most successful practices in Penzance but the walls were murky with the soot and dirt of years and the hard outlines of the piled deed boxes were softened and blurred by a thick covering of dust. It was just as she remembered it from her occasional visits with her father more than ten years ago.

The only spot of colour in the room was the fire which burned cheerfully in the small iron grate. Thankfully, she held out her hands to it, rubbing them together to encourage the blood back into her numbed fingers. It had been foolish to decide to ride in such wintry weather, but her mental anguish demanded some sort of physical relief.

The attorney smiled at her, his eyes brighter than the dim gaslights which combatted the gloom on this dark winter afternoon. 'I haven't seen you properly since your father's death, Mrs Blacklock, but that's always the way it is with attorneys, I fear. People only see us when there's something wrong.'

Had he heard a rumour of what had happened, or was he just being tactful? She took advantage of the opening he had given her. 'And I'm afraid that's why I'm here, Mr Brightman. I have a problem and I've come for your advice.'

He bowed, swift and neat as a sparrow. 'I am honoured, Mrs Black-lock.' He bobbed to her again.

'You may not be so pleased when you hear what I have to say,' she commented dryly. She threw her wet cloak over the back of the chair and settled herself across the scratched desk from him.

317

'My husband has lost both the bank and the smelting works through gambling.'

She could see that he knew it already. Of course, news like that would race through the district. Probably he had known it even before Edward had plucked up the courage to tell her. He nodded, his bright eyes intent on her face.

Clara took a deep breath and went on, 'He has told me he intends to sell Wheal Susan in order to raise money again.'

She looked at him, expecting an intervention, a comment, but he merely sat watching her, his small, inkstained hands folded across his swelling waistcoat.

Desperation rose in her. She leaned forward, her hands gripping the edge of the desk. 'Mr Brightman, he can't do that!' Her voice trembled despite herself. 'That mine was my father's life and he bequeathed it to me. It's the only asset that we have left to provide for my son. Edward can't sell it. He can't!'

He cleared his throat. 'Unfortunately, it isn't that simple, my dear Mrs Blacklock. The mine was left to you when you were single. Now you are a married woman.'

'But what does that have to do with it?' she almost shouted. 'Other married women own property, they have their own incomes even.'

He rose to his feet, scarcely taller standing than sitting, and began to pace the office, his hands behind his back, his feet automatically fitting themselves to the bare patches he had worn in the carpet over the years.

'That is not actually correct,' he explained, his face concentrated and blank. 'The Queen, God bless her, is, legally, the only married woman in England who owns property in her right. But . . .' He held up a small hand imperiously, stopping her before she could say more.

'The ladies you referred to do *not* own their own property. In law, on marriage the husband becomes the owner of all his wife's property.' He turned to her. 'Exceptions are made for items of personal clothing et cetera, you understand.'

Clara gritted her teeth. 'I am not discussing items of clothing,' she said sharply. 'I am talking about a mine.'

'Quite so.' Unperturbed, he continued his pacing. 'Where a woman owns or is likely to inherit property, it is possible to tie this up in a marriage settlement so that she retains the benefits of that property, even though she is not the actual owner.'

He turned to stare at her. 'Mrs Blacklock, if no settlement was made out at the time of your marriage, then your husband is now the

318

true owner of all your shares in the mine. As such he can dispose of Wheal Susan as he thinks fit.'

Clara sat back in her chair letting the legal explanation wash over her. She had taken in the important point. By not having a marriage settlement agreed before the wedding she had handed over everything to Edward.

It was so obvious, now that it was pointed out. The memory of those days rose again before her eyes. She had been weak from hunger, ill and distraught from the loss of her baby, desperately worried by her mother's illness and the imminent loss of a roof over her head.

She had heard of marriage settlements, of course, but they were something that parents concerned themselves with. She had never realized their true significance.

Despair washed over her. Edward had won. Despite everything she had done, her child would be destitute, reared in poverty. It did not matter how much money he got for the mine, she knew that he would gamble it away within a few months.

'So I can't stop him.' Her voice was quiet, resigned. All hope was gone. All she could do now was accept the inevitable and make what plans she could for the future. There was no point in hiding from the facts. She was still young, she still had strength and courage. Somehow she would win through, would give her son the life she wanted for him.

'It's not that simple.'

The attorney's words took her by surprise. 'What do you mean?' she asked. 'If the mine belongs to him . . .'

'Oh, it does. No question of that.' The attorney turned to her. 'But there is a new factor to be considered.' He watched her gravely. 'Am I right in believing that you are unaware that the Earl of Bodmin died recently?'

'My grandfather?' she asked in surprise. 'I knew nothing about it.' And no wonder. She had been so wrapped up with her new baby and, in the last few days, with the problems of their imminent poverty that she had had no contact with the outside world.

Brightman nodded. 'That was the reason I was planning to visit you. I received a letter today from the Earl's London attorneys.' He coughed. 'As your father's legal representative, they assumed that I would be able to contact you regarding your grandfather's death.'

Clara glanced up, surprised, and he held up a warning hand. 'Do not, I beg of you, be thinking that you have been left a fortune in his will.'

Despite her desperate situation a smile curved Clara's lips as she

319

remembered her only meeting with the Earl. After the way he had shown her the door she had expected nothing. Her green eyes sparkled with suppressed humour as she assured him gravely, 'You need have no fears about that, Mr Brightman. I expect nothing from my grandfather's will.'

He nodded. 'A very sensible attitude in view of the bad relations that existed between your father and the Earl.' He cleared his throat. 'However, as it happens, you *are* a beneficiary.' He paused to watch her reaction.

'Don't tell me.' Her memory of the old man was too unhappy even for this to raise her hopes. 'He has left me the proverbial penny?'

'No, indeed. Not a fortune but not that.' He bowed towards her again, more sparrow-like than ever. 'He has left you the mineral rights to Wheal Susan.'

She had almost forgotten that her grandfather owned them, even though that was how her parents had met. Someone always owned the mineral rights to the land which was being mined. Often it was either the Crown or one of the large absentee landowners like her grandfather. Mining was allowed, provided that they received a certain percentage of the value of the ore mined. Some landowners had become millionaires because of the mines worked on their land. And some land was owned by the most unlikely people.

She remembered her father telling her once of an old woman in St Ives who had left a field to a favourite donkey in her will. When copper had been found under it, the donkey had become very rich! How unfair it was that a donkey could own land, but a wife couldn't.

She glanced up to see the attorney peering down at her with bright, interested eyes.

'It makes no difference,' she said crossly. 'I suppose I should be grateful to my grandfather, but I suspect he did it to put me down, to show me that as far as he was concerned I was just a mine captain's daughter.'

She shrugged. 'But what does it matter? He's dead now, whatever his reasons for acting as he did. And this is just something else for Edward to sell or gamble away as the mood takes him.'

Mr Brightman bobbed forward triumphantly. 'But it isn't!' he said, his face splitting in a cheerful smile. 'That was what I meant when I said that there was a new factor to be considered. He has left you the mineral rights in the land, yes! But your grandfather, Mrs Blacklock, was a rich man, and rich men only stay that way by controlling their assets very carefully.'

She frowned. 'What are you trying to say?'

'That the land and the rights in it have been tied up in such a way that your husband cannot touch them.'

As she glanced up, amazed, he added quickly, 'Don't believe that this was any particular act of favour on his part. I understand that a similar trust was set up for all the Earl's female relatives.'

'I would take nothing my grandfather did for me as a mark of particular favour,' she said dryly. 'But I cannot see how this alters anything. I may get an income from the mine if it is worked again, but my husband can still sell Wheal Susan.'

The little man seemed about to burst with excitement. 'But he can't!' he broke in. 'You haven't considered, Mrs Blacklock!'

He rubbed his hands together. 'He can only sell the mine on the assumption that the Lord of the Manor allows a search for minerals on his land. Or hers, of course.' He bowed to her again. 'If you were to rescind those rights, the shares in the mine would be worthless.'

'Then I *can* stop him!' She was on her feet, emerald eyes flashing with excitement. 'I can keep the mine!' She caught the attorney's hands in her own. 'Thank you, Mr Brightman. Thank you.'

He smiled. 'But do not be too hasty, Mrs Blacklock. Reflect. If the mine is worked by someone else, they bear all the costs, all the dangers. And if they find tin, you are assured of an income.'

She knew what he was saying made sense, but she was not going to let anyone else work the mine her father had discovered. She would rather be poor!

'And if we work it ourselves, we make even more money,' she said gaily. 'Our share of the profits plus the landlord's share.' Ten per cent of the gross profit. The mine would certainly be viable now.

The attorney said warningly, 'Only if you find tin,' but she laughed at him. The tin was there. She knew it.

He saw her to the door. 'Your grandfather's death was not the only one recently. Did you hear that Lieutenant Laity's brother died?'

Something else she had missed. 'Poor man. And it will mean that he will have to give up the Navy.' A sudden thought struck her. 'How will that affect Isabelle Kingsley, I wonder?'

He twinkled at her. 'Not badly, I think. I believe the young man will reach an understanding there before he leaves the area. And of course, there's another wedding in the area today. Ben Pasco's daughter is marrying.' He shook his head. 'Not a good day for it. Such weather!'

Trust an attorney to know all the gossip, Clara thought, as she gratefully accepted the help of the stable lad to mount her horse. The wind had risen and the animal circled and jibbed as the sleet buffeted his face with each squall. She wrapped her cloak more firmly around

321

herself as she forced his head into the wind, her heels driving him on. Even if she were not eager to tell Edward what she had learned, it was too cold today to ride slowly.

It was a relief to hand the horse to a servant and step into the sudden quiet of her entrance hall. It was unheated, but after the fury of the weather outside it seemed a haven of warmth and peace.

Thankfully, she stripped off her gloves and let the butler take her cape. 'Send Mr Blacklock to me in the drawing room, please.'

The butler folded her wet cloak in his usual imperturbable manner. 'The master is not at home, madam.'

Oh God! Not gambling again! Hiding her irritation, Clara asked, 'Did he tell you where he had gone?'

'Yes, madam. He has gone to St Just to show a possible purchaser around the mine.'

Chapter 39

Adam clung to the rail of the merchantman, his legs braced against the pitching of the deck. Sleet hurtled down around them until it was impossible to see for more than a hundred yards in any direction. And that wasn't enough, he knew, not with the ship bucketing along as she was with the storm roaring and baying at her stern.

A figure lurched out of the flying sleet to his side and Adam recognized the tall figure of the first mate. He sketched a rough salute and shouted over the din, 'Captain's compliments sir, and he asked me to tell you that we are making for Falmouth.'

'What?' Adam blinked spray and sleet out of his eyes. 'But I only took this ship because he promised we were not landing in Cornwall.' He had to pitch his voice at its loudest to carry over the scream of the wind.

'The cap'n knows that, sir. That's why he asked me to tell you.' He saw Adam's expression and added hastily, 'We're almost round the Lizard now and we daren't ride out a storm like this in the Channel. We'll be safe enough at Falmouth until it blows itself out.'

He saluted again, then made his way aft, fighting against the force of the wind.

Cornwall! Adam swore under his breath. The one place he had vowed not to visit, ever again. He would not, *could* not bear to be in the same county as that faithless Clara. The county which Norman Willcock had loved so much and would never see again.

As always at the memory of his friend his guilt overwhelmed him, more bitter than the wind that scoured his face with ice particles. If only he had not sent him back up that tunnel . . . If only he had talked to him for just a few minutes more . . .

He cursed again, rejecting these sorrowful thoughts. He had always lived by the philosophy that you should never look back. What was done was done; you should keep your eyes on the future. But how could he do that when his Cornish past was so close to him? When the very land of his birth that he had left behind him was forcing itself into his future?

If he had a future, he thought, watching the mountainous seas lifting the ship as though she were a leaf and hurtling her forward. It was quite possible that he could die here, on this ship, along with the gold that he had struggled so hard to get, accompanying them all to the bottom.

Because he would not leave this ship without the gold; he was determined on that. His find had cost him all he had, more than he would ever have dreamed possible. Clara, Phil, Norman – each in their way was the price he had paid for the cold metal now locked in strongboxes in the hold. That gold was the only thing left that made life even barely tolerable. If he couldn't have it, he would rather die.

The ship staggered under another onslaught of wind as it gusted suddenly from another direction. For a brief moment, the sleet whirled upwards and the white curtain was lifted, and he saw it: land – horribly, unbelievably near.

But it wasn't the sight alone that sent him sliding and gasping towards the stern as quickly as he could along the tilting, bucking deck. It was the profile of the land, glimpsed only for a half-second but as familiar to him as his own fingers.

Because the promontory he had seen wasn't the flat-topped land of the Lizard. It was the unmistakable conical hump of Cape Cornwall.

The captain was standing near the man at the wheel and Adam grasped him urgently by the shoulder. 'You've got to pull out. You've got to pull out,' he shouted over the noise of the storm and the creaking of the ship. He gestured broadly to port. 'You're nearly on the rocks.'

The Captain shook him off impatiently. 'It's all right, Mr Trevelyan. I know what I'm doing.' From long experience his voice carried easily over the noises of the storm. 'In a few minutes we'll be round the Lizard and in quieter waters. There's nothing to worry about.'

A wave sluiced over the stern, sending Adam staggering but he forced himself back to the other man, shouting into the wind: 'It's not the Lizard, you fool. It's Cape Cornwall. You've got to pull out!'

The Captain turned to him. 'Mr Trevelyan, I know you don't want to land in Cornwall but it is I who am responsible for this ship.' He gasped as another wave pounded over them then caught his breath and went on. 'I am going to shelter off Falmouth and that is an end to it.'

'But you're not off the Lizard,' Adam yelled. 'You're off Cape Cornwall and if you turn in now you'll be on the Brisons.'

The man turned to him, his face contorted with anger. 'I'm the Captain, Mr Trevelyan. I know where I am.'

'You're off the Brisons,' Adam howled – then was hurtled agonisingly forward as, with a grinding shriek, the bows of the ship impaled themselves on the hungry rocks.

Shivering with cold, Clara rode her horse between the deserted buildings of Wheal Susan. Where was Edward? She knew that he could not have ridden home or she would have passed him on the road.

She guided her horse to the Count House, white on white through the driving sleet. Through the open doorway she could see from the wet marks on the floor and the table that men had been here recently – almost certainly, Edward and his potential purchaser. In weather like this they would need somewhere sheltered to discuss business. But they had left, yet had not gone back to Newlyn.

She gnawed at her lower lip. Where could they have gone? To an inn to celebrate the sale? No! The thought came to her clearly. If the man was interested, Edward would take him to his attorney to tie up the details straight away. He needed the money too badly to be willing to waste even a day. And she knew where his attorney lived, on the outskirts of St Just.

Clara swung the horse's head around and urged it out of the slight shelter in the lee of the Count House and into the full force of the wind. They were both tired but she had to go on. She dared not let the sale go through and risk losing the only source of income which could provide for her son.

By the time she reached the attorney's house she was chilled to the bone. Only the urgency of her mission gave her the strength to slide stiffly from her horse and throw the reins to the unwilling servant who came, huddled under a sack, to take charge of the animal.

'Mr Blacklock,' she demanded of the man who opened the front door to her.

He hesitated, taken aback by her windswept appearance and the peremptory demand, but she had already heard her husband's voice from the front room. Impatiently, she swept past the servant and pushed open the door.

The conversation came to an abrupt halt at her sudden arrival and the faces of the three men turned to her in disbelief. Be calm, Clara reminded herself. Jamie's future depends on you.

She raised her chin, her emerald eyes sparkling with determination. 'Gentlemen,' she said, and gave them a brief scrutiny. Edward was glowering at her suspiciously, the attorney Mr Trenow was just as she had remembered him, untrustworthy-looking, and the third man was a stranger.

She threw back her hood, feeling the wet tendrils of hair fall round her face as she did so, then struggled with her cape. It was heavy with rain, rubbing painfully against the sensitive skin of her throat and she was grateful when the stranger moved forward to help her emerge from its wet, clinging folds. Clara smiled a brief thanks at him as he placed it dripping over the back of a chair, then she moved forward to confront her husband.

'Edward, I'm sorry but you cannot sell Wheal Susan.'

Irritation crossed his face. 'For God's sake, Clara. We've had all this out before. Wheal Susan no longer belongs to you. It's mine and I have every right to sell it.'

Mr Trenow broke in hastily, 'That is correct, Mrs Blacklock. The law is quite clear on this matter.'

'And,' asked Clara quietly, 'is the law clear on who is the Lord of the Manor?'

The attorney looked surprised. 'Certainly. It is the Earl of Bodmin.' He smiled mockingly at her. 'Your esteemed grandfather, I believe.'

'My *late* esteemed grandfather,' Clara corrected him.

'Quite.' The Earl's death was obviously no news to him. 'But I assume that the new Earl will inherit the rights to that land, along with the rest of the estate.'

'Then you assume wrong,' Clara said crisply. 'My grandfather has left the mineral rights in trust for me.'

She saw the swift glance that passed between the attorney and her husband. There was no doubting the consternation that they both felt. She pressed home her advantage. 'I think I should make it clear that I have no intention of allowing any mining on that land, unless it is under the control of my own family.'

She turned to the stranger. 'I am sorry, sir, if you have been called out on a fool's errand in such bad weather. Believe me, I have only just discovered this news myself and I came as quickly as I could in case delay could lead to an injustice being done.'

He bowed, any dismay or irritation he felt disguised by his training as a gentleman. 'You have done more than enough, madam. To come yourself, in such weather, is beyond the bounds of what one could expect.'

'Quite,' Edward broke in. 'You could have sent a servant.'

She stepped towards him, her anger raised. 'A servant, Edward? When I didn't even know that you were going to negotiate the sale today? Or where you would be meeting?' She held his eyes. 'And if I had sent a message,' she asked quietly, 'do you expect me to believe that you would have passed this message on?'

The stranger interrupted swiftly. 'Whatever the truth of the matter, it is obvious that we can go no further with this business until the question of ownership has been cleared up.' He bowed his goodbyes and left.

There was a long silence in the room. The only noises were the rattling of the window as the gale howled and battered at the side of the house. Finally, Edward spoke.

'We'll detain you no longer, Trenow. I am sure I need not tell you to check on the truth of this ridiculous story.'

The attorney bowed. 'But surely you are not leaving now? Mrs Blacklock must be tired out and the storm is at its height. In another hour or so it will have blown itself out. Stay to dinner and we can discuss the matter. I am sure that when your wife realizes that it is in her interest to allow the mine to be worked by someone else, this whole problem can be settled amicably.'

'We're leaving now,' Edward said curtly, throwing a look of hate at Clara.

Even with the help of the stable boy, Clara found it difficult to mount the horse, weighed down as she was by her wet cloak and her dread of the ride home with Edward.

She could see that he was in one of his worst moods, when he would lash out bitterly at everything and everyone. Well, words could not hurt her, she told herself, turning her horse onto the road that led from the attorney's isolated house at Boswedden towards St Just. And for once she had the upper hand. At least she would be able to save something from the wreckage that Edward had made of both their lives, save something for Jamie and his future. Set against that, Edward's anger and dislike counted for nothing.

He began as soon as they were out of earshot of the house, a diatribe that comprehensively covered her breeding, manners, behaviour and morals. Clara folded her lips, resolutely keeping silent. It was pointless to answer the individual charges; he was only venting his anger and despair on her. Only when he had come to a temporary halt, did she allow herself to speak.

'Understand one thing.' Her voice was as cold as the wind that whistled past them. 'That mine was my father's life. More, it was the cause of his death. I would be betraying his memory if I allowed anyone else to buy it. And I would be betraying my son. There is tin there, a fortune in tin. And I will do my utmost to make sure that it benefits my son and no one else.'

327

She turned to him, eyes slitted against the sleet. 'Remember that, Edward. That mine is for the benefit of my son. And while I live, no one will take it from him.'

They were travelling straight into the teeth of the storm now. Her horse turned its head away, walking sideways to escape the worst of the wind. It gave Clara an excuse to turn her back on Edward, pulling her hood closer around her as she stared blindly out to sea.

He would not forgive her for this, she knew. He would see her always now as the reason he had been unable to retrieve his fallen fortunes. But she had to do it, she had to. She could not let Jamie be brought up in poverty, just because she lacked the resolution to stand up to her husband.

For a brief second the wind let up and the sleet eddied, swirling abruptly upwards. Before Clara's startled eyes a ship appeared, ghostly, half-seen in the murk. She pointed. 'Look!' But the wind had picked up again, the sleet driving hard into her face, hiding all except their immediate surroundings.

She swung to Edward. 'A ship! Did you see it, a ship!'

'So what?' He was too angry with her to take in the implications. 'It's the sea. There are always ships on the sea. Or are you too stupid even to know that?'

She ignored his comment. 'It's too far in, Edward. It's heading for the rocks.' She pulled her horse around, using her whip to get the last ounce of speed out of its tired body. 'Those poor men. We must help.'

Like everybody raised on the coast, she knew the dangers of a wrecked ship. And she knew how necessary help was. Many a sailor had made it to the shore and, too tired to pull himself unaided out of the reach of the waves, had been battered to death on the rocks only a few feet from safety.

The wind at her back now, she rode furiously. The ship was invisible again, but she knew it was there, knew that it could not escape. It would ground, either on Cape Cornwall or the Brisons, just beyond. And God help the poor souls on board.

Edward stared after her. Stupid bitch. Minding everybody's business but her own. He heard again her words, spoken so proudly to her mother thirty months earlier. 'When I marry I shall give my first allegiance to my husband.' And had she? She had let him down in every way, lying like a rag doll in bed, regardless of what he did to her, so that his body, which was roused only by the writhings of his partner, failed him when he most needed to assert himself.

And she had fought him, first over the smelting works, and now over the mine, his one chance to get some money. He *knew* that if he had the stake he could win back what he had lost, but she wouldn't let him! Oh no, she would stop him retrieving even that amount of his self-respect!

Her words echoed hollowly in his ears. 'That mine is for the benefit of my son. And while I live, no one will take it from him.'

It was like a sign from heaven. While she lived! But if she died . . . then it would be his. The thought was irresistible. He could do what he liked with the mine – sell it, win back the smelting works, get another wife, a wife with money, a wife with whom he would not be impotent. And off Clara had gone, riding into the storm, into danger, in the vain hope of rescuing some shipwrecked sailors. The smile made his frozen cheeks hurt but he did not care. He turned his horse and rode after her into the gathering darkness.

Adam could hear the screams of the trapped men even over the noise of the wind and the sea. The masts had broken off short when the ship had run aground, pinning the sailors on the foredecks.

He pushed himself upright, shoving off the body of the Captain who had lain over him. Adam could see from the way the man's head was doubled under him that his neck was broken.

A huge wave broke over them, more forcefully than when they were still moving with the flow of the sea. It crashed against the stern of the boat, forcing her further onto the rocks, then washed over the deck sweeping men and broken spars over the side in a torrent of white water.

Adam caught desperately at the rail as his body was washed forward with the rush of water and held himself securely, ignoring the pain in his side where he had been crushed as the ship collided with the rocks.

Another wave hit as he managed to pull himself upright. He could hear the shriek of broken timbers as the ship settled herself more firmly onto the Brisons and then the shouts of the first mate, sounding half-hysterical. 'To the boats! Man the boats!'

Judging his run between the waves, Adam made his way back. He grabbed the mate's arm. He seemed too young to have this responsibility suddenly forced upon him, too immature.

'Not the boats,' Adam shouted in his ear, waving a hand at the maelstrom that surged around them. 'The currents here are too dangerous in weather like this. You'd be safer staying with the ship.'

The man shook him off. 'The boats! The boats!' There was a rush as those sailors still on their feet hurried to the side. Adam groaned. He had seen several ships wrecked here himself and heard stories of dozens more. Men had got ashore alive but it was a matter of luck. It

329

was safer to stay with the ship. He made his way forward, avoiding the tangle of ropes that cluttered the decks. 'It's safer to stay here,' he bellowed.

But they took no notice, frantic to leave the lifeless hulk, wallowing and screeching as the waves rammed it further onto the rocks.

At the last minute the first mate turned to him, indicating a place in the lifeboat. Adam shook his head. He would rather risk himself on board.

Besides, his gold was here, the gold that had cost Norman his life. He would not leave that. If the ship sank, so be it, they would go down together. Death was preferable to losing the only thing that made life worth living.

And if the ship survived, he thought, catching frantically at the rail as a bigger wave than usual scoured the decks, then he would be here to protect the gold from the ravening band of local men who would swarm on board as soon as it was safe to do so. Unless the Preventative men came to protect the cargo, of course. But no sensible man would voluntarily take to the seas on a night like this.

He watched the sailors lower the boats, willing them to survive even though his local knowledge told him that the odds were against it. The first boat swung clumsily down, but a huge wave swamped it before it was half-lowered, sweeping the men into the sea as if they were dolls. Adam closed his eyes, turning his head away. There was nothing he could do to help them.

Nothing he could do, now, to help himself.

'My darling.' As the door closed behind her father, Isabelle turned to smile sweetly at Lieutenant Laity. At last. She had done it at last . . . Even more than her love for him was the thankfulness that she would not now die an old maid.

Her sapphire eyes smiled up at him, and she came into his arms as naturally and eagerly as if she were one of the bal-maidens and not Miss Kingsley of Pendeen House. At last!

He held her to him, grateful that her father had had the tact to leave them alone together. One hand stroked her hair, the smooth dark hair that never seemed to be out of place, whatever the weather. 'You do understand, my darling, that we can't be married for a year?'

She gazed up at him, her blue eyes enormous with sympathy. 'Of course I understand. It wouldn't be right, not with your brother so recently dead.'

'And I shall have to give up the Navy.' He put her back from him so that he could gaze into her huge blue eyes. 'I will have to spend most of my time at our estate, now that I am the heir, but I'll come to

330

visit you as often as I can. And perhaps, now that we are engaged, your father will allow me to write to you.'

'I'm sure he will,' Isabelle made a mental note to sort this problem out as soon as the Lieutenant left the house. Nothing, but nothing must interfere with her engagement to him. The heir to his father's estates! She had to stop the shiver of pleasure that rose up her spine. One day, when his father was dead, they would be Sir Frederick and Lady Laity. In a sudden paroxysm of delight she hugged him to her.

'My little love!' He was half-amused, half-bewildered by her actions, so different from the ladylike, repressed Isabelle he had courted.

She pulled back, suddenly aware that in her happiness she was acting like a hoyden. 'I'm sorry.' She cast around for an excuse. 'The wind – it sounds so vicious howling round the house like that. Sometimes it quite scares me.' She smiled up at him. 'I am sure it will be different when we go to your home in Somerset.'

'If it means that you won't hug me then I shall hope that it is just the same,' he said gallantly, but she could see it was an automatic response. Dimly, above the rattle of the windowpanes and the howl of the gale, she could hear the noise that had attracted his attention, the sound of someone hammering on their front door.

They stood silent, their arms around each other, until the approaching footsteps warned them to separate. Christopher Kingsley put his head round the door. 'Lieutenant, er, Frederick,' he sounded awkward. 'There's a fellow to see you.'

'Lieutenant.' The figure was streaming with rain as he stood in the hallway, twisting his hat nervously in his hands. 'I'm sorry to bother you, sir, but there's a ship aground on the Brisons.' He cast apologetic glances at Kingsley and Isabelle who stood silently watching him. 'I'm sorry if I interrupted, sir. I thought you'd better know.'

Laity nodded. 'You were quite right. I'll be with you in a moment.' He drew Isabelle back into the drawing room and closed the door behind them.

She stood staring up at him, shocked and afraid. 'But you're not going out in this?'

'I must, my darling.' He took her hands in his, smiling down at her. 'It's my duty.'

'But you're going to give up the Navy, you said so!' She could hear her voice shaking but she did not care. She could not lose him now, not when they were so close to getting married! The wind gusted again so that the house seemed to shake under its impact and she shuddered.

He said firmly, 'For the moment I am still a naval officer, in charge

331

of the Preventative station at Pendeen. And part of my duties is to help ships in trouble.'

'But you can't help them, not in this weather.' Her voice rose, high and shaking. 'They'll all be drowned. And you'll be drowned too if you go out in this.' She threw herself into his arms, burrowing her head into his chest. 'Don't go. Just this once. For me. On the day of our engagement. Don't go. Let the men take the boat out without you, but you stay here. Please.'

He put her gently from him. 'I can't do that, Isabelle.' His voice was kind but strong. 'I have to do my duty.'

Duty? His duty would kill him! She saw the image of Sir Frederick and Lady Laity, so clear and close a few brief minutes ago, fading rapidly. She could not let him go!

'I thought you loved me!' Tears quivered for a moment on the ends of her dark lashes, then spilled slowly onto her cheeks.

'I do love you, Isabelle, but I have to do this.'

'You'll ruin my life for the sake of a few drowned sailors.' She clung to him again. 'Can't you see, if you're drowned I shall die. I can't live without you! Please.' Her voice was a heartbroken sob. 'You can't do this to me.'

She felt him hesitate, felt the doubt in his mind and hurried to press home her advantage.

'If you go,' she said tragically, 'I shall know that all your words of love were false. I shall know that you don't really love me or you couldn't hurt me like this.'

She pushed herself away and faced him, her head up, the slow, silver tears sliding down her pale cheeks. 'If you go,' she said, slowly and distinctly, 'our engagement is off,' and she turned from him, burying her face in her hands as sobs shook her slender body, waiting for the touch on her shoulder that would tell her that she had won.

Chapter 40

The taproom of the Commercial Hotel was a warm, smoky haven from the storm that raged outside. Phil lifted his glass of 'mahogany' – a mixture of gin and black molasses – and waved it genially at Dick Thomas. 'A brem good wedding!' His voice was slightly slurred. This was his first grown-up wedding and he was making the most of it.

Dick eyed the glass uncomfortably. 'Here, lad, you be careful. I know 'tis a warming drink but you don't want to take too much. We've got to get home yet and it's a brem long walk on a night like this.'

Phil took a quick swallow before the glass was removed from him. 'All the more reason to get good and warm, then.' The loud voices of the drinkers drowned the noise of the wind but he could see by the way that the lamp-flames fluttered and curtseyed that it would be a wild walk home.

'Well, young Phil, and are you ready to come back down the mines with us?' It was William-John Pasco, reeling drunkenly as he celebrated his success in giving his sister away.

Phil snorted. 'My soul and body! Working down there in the darkness, living like a mole.' He shook his head. ''Tis a man's life at sea. Fresh air and all.'

William-John waved a hand at the windows where the reflections of the lamplight danced as the panes rattled under the force of the wind. 'Plenty of fresh air tonight.'

'And we're not out in it,' Phil pointed out. 'But bad weather don't stop you going down the mine.' He gazed out of the window as if he were a hardened sailor. 'Any road, 'tis not that bad out at sea. A small boat should ride this as long as you keep away from the shore and don't get caught in no currents.' He grinned. 'I bin out in worse than this myself.' He felt pride rise in him. He knew that he was a good sailor; even the Mousehole men, born and bred, gave him that.

333

William-John dropped heavily onto a nearby stool. 'Well, you look good on it, I'll say. No one would take you for the little runt that used to work the wind-machine for Adam.' He grinned reminiscently. 'By God, you were no more than a skinned rabbit in them days.'

Phil wriggled awkwardly. He hated to be reminded of that time, spending eight hours on end in the stinking dark, his arms aching as he turned the great fan, trying to move the fetid air into the gallery where Adam was working, the interminable boredom.

Even the end of the core had brought no relief, for then he had to climb up endless ladders, clinging to the underside of some of them, his arms aching, the rungs too far apart for his short legs, water cascading over him. And all the time knowing that if his tired hands slipped, he would plunge screaming to his death in the dark, far below.

As if catching his unease, William-John said hesitantly: 'We were brem sorry to hear about Adam, lad. He were a fine miner and a good man.' He shook his head. 'Some terrible it were, him dying abroad like that.'

Phil turned his head away to hide the unmanly tears he could feel pricking at his lids. Despite his new life, he missed Adam every day, missed his rough kindness, his wise sayings, even, now that they were over, his lessons, which Adam had insisted Phil should do every evening.

He swallowed the lump that always came in his throat at the memory of Adam. 'He were – he were doing what he wanted.'

'And you left mining and gone to work on the boats!' William-John shook his head. 'No job for a proper man, that I reckon.'

Phil reached for the glass of mahogany where Dick Thomas had placed it on the rough-hewn table between them and took another swig, comforted by the way it warmed his throat and burned in his stomach. It gave him the courage to fight back his grief and turn to William-John with something of his old cheekiness. 'If you don't reckon it a proper job, whyfor did you let your sister marry a fisherman?'

William-John shrugged. 'And what mere man can ever stop a woman doing what she's set her mind on? You'll find that out soon enough, young Phil.' He swayed slightly on his seat as he raised a glass in welcome to John Henry who had staggered across to talk to his new brother-in-law. 'And how do you feel about your brother marrying away from the village?'

The young fisherman looked owlishly at him. 'I reckon she'll make him a brem good wife.' He waved his glass at the miner, not caring that the drink slopped over the side with the violence of his gesture.

334

'She must have a lot of patience. After all, she looked after you a good age.'

There was a roar of laughter and Dick Thomas slapped him on the back, spilling more of the drink. 'You're right there, lad. A fisherman's an easier husband than a miner. At least she'll get a bit of rest, like, while he's at sea.'

William-John broke in, his hackles rising, 'I tell you, a miner . . .' but the rest of his words were drowned out as the door burst open and a man almost fell into the taproom, the sack over his head white with snow.

Behind him, the wind roared and gusted, sending the lamps flickering wildly, and silence spread through the room as the men turned to the door.

The stranger was gasping for breath, coughing as the warm, smoke-filled air caught in his icy lungs.

'Quick, men.' In the silence his gasping words seemed to echo through the low-pitched room. 'There's a boat aground on the Brisons.' He doubled over in a paroxysm of coughing which told Phil that the stranger was a miner, already touched by the hand of death, the 'black consumption' as the miners called it.

Dick Thomas pulled the glass of mahogany from Phil and pushed it into the man's hand. 'How long ago?'

He took a deep pull, coughing again, before gasping out, 'Just happened. I saw un hit as I were coming along the cliff path.'

Already, the men in the taproom were on their feet, pulling on coats, doing up the bootlaces they had untied to rest their feet in their Sunday boots.

Phil saw Dick Thomas glance at him and knew that he had to act quickly or he would be left behind, considered too young to wait on the shore, struggling to pull the bodies from the ravening waves.

'I do know a quick way.' He raced out of the taproom door, glancing over his shoulder. Dick Thomas hesitated a moment, then followed him, and behind him came the rest of the Mousehole fishermen, heads lowered into the wind as they struggled up behind him.

Phil grinned to himself as they set off towards the cliffs. He wasn't going to miss this for anything.

Already, the weather was clearing, as if, having grounded the ship, it was satisfied. Although the wind still dragged at them as the group of men from the Commercial Hotel stumbled towards the shore, the sleet had stopped and the clouds lifted slightly.

At the top of the slope down to Priest's Cove, Phil stopped to catch

335

his breath. Below him, the sea crashed against the rocks, flinging spray high into the air. White foam streaked the surface of the sea and surrounded the distant Brisons with a turbulent collar of fretted water. And on the Brisons, canted high and awkwardly, loomed the great bulk of a seagoing ship, her masts mere stubs where they had broken off as she hit the rocks.

Peering through eyes slitted against the wind, Phil pointed. 'Look. They're trying to launch the boats.'

The men around him surveyed the scene with professional eyes, too accustomed to the sight of ships in distress to share his own seething excitement.

'Those sailors are brem fools,' Dick Thomas muttered. 'They can't be local. They'd be better off staying where they are. Tide's at full, now, and I reckon the wind's dropping. A couple of hours and they'll be high and dry.'

'They're not local, sure 'nuff,' William-John broke in. Although he was a miner, as the owner of his own boat he knew the currents around here as well as the fishermen. He gestured. 'They're trying to lower the boats on the land side. With the currents that set around they rocks, they'd be better off launching on the seaward side. They'd have a hope then.'

Even as they watched, they saw the small boat capsize, spilling bodies that disappeared instantly into the churning sea.

'Shall we get a boat out and rescue them?' Phil's voice was shrill with eagerness. 'There's plenty of boats in Priest's Cove.'

Dick Thomas paused, eyeing the sea carefully, then he shrugged. 'With the wind and the currents around here, we'll be better off on shore. That's where they'll fetch up, right enough. And if they're alive, they'll need help to get ashore, poor souls. Besides, in this sea, we'd never see to pick them up if we're in a boat ourselves.'

'There are ropes in the shed.' William-John was already running down the steep path, careless of the danger of a twisted ankle as he slipped and tripped on the mud and loose stones.

Phil raced after him, his heart thudding with adrenalin. He had been out at sea in weather like this, he had known drownings and deaths even in the few short years he had been a fisherman, but this was different. These were men he had never met, a ship he didn't know. There was no personal tragedy to affect him here.

He raced past the miner's small boats, drawn up for the winter well out of the reach of the waves and ignored the shout of William-John. Let him rummage around in the shed. Phil knew he would be sorting out ropes to tie round the waists of volunteers who would risk their lives, wading into the waves to drag out the bodies of the sailors as

336

they were washed to the shore. But the sea was more exciting now and he ran out onto the slipway.

Although the tide was ebbing, waves still crashed onto the small rocky beach, sending foam-edged fingers almost up to the foot of the low cliffs before they retreated again, dragging loose pebbles seaward in the backwash. Dick Thomas was right, Phil thought – the sea would cast up any bodies here.

He made his way carefully along the foot of the cliffs, his eyes searching the sea, being careful to keep out of the reach of the waves. In this weather, even a strong man could lose his footing and be swept out in the backwash before being hurled back onshore by the next breaker.

Ahead of him he could see two figures, a man and a woman standing close together. The wind caught at their cloaks, blowing them together and he wondered for a second if they were lovers having a private tryst despite the inclemency of the weather. Then the man saw him and the figures parted, the man walking swiftly off down the beach.

Phil hesitated; he did not want to interrupt anything. But the woman was standing alone now, staring out to sea, staggering slightly as the wind caught at her full skirts. Even as he watched, her bonnet came loose, one ribbon pulled away by the force of the wind, and it flapped and fluttered up over the cliffs, like a wounded bird. Then he recognized her fair, fine hair. 'Clara!'

She turned abruptly to him, one hand at her throat, then she recognized him and opened her arms as she had done in the old days when she had first moved into Adam's cottage on No-Go-By Hill. 'Phil!' She hugged him to her hungrily as if she longed for the touch of another person. 'What are you doing here?'

'Marrying off a friend.' He pulled away, affronted that she should think he was still a child to be hugged. 'Did you see the wreck, Clara?'

'Poor souls.' She stared at the outline of the ship, obscenely canted against the jutting crags of the Brisons, her hand touching her throat again as if it were sore. 'To be wrecked so close to shore.'

'It's the most dangerous place to be.' Phil stopped, jerking around as he caught sight of the male figure walking back towards them. 'Who's that?'

'Ed – Mr Blacklock.' He could hear the constraint in her voice even above the crash of the waves and the rattle of pebbles.

He glanced at her curiously, then at her husband. 'I wouldn't have thought he'd come to a shipwreck.'

'Strange, isn't it?' She gripped his arm with cold, unsteady hands.

337

'I'm glad you're here, Phil.' There was something about her that he could not understand. 'Stay with me. Please.'

'Well, as much as I can.' He didn't want to miss out on the rescues and besides, it wasn't as if she was alone. There was her husband here, as well as all the men from the taproom, fishermen and miners alike, pouring along the wave-washed beach, now, ropes in their hands and their eyes scrutinising the white-tipped waves.

Then he looked at her again and her pale, pinched face woke something in him. He reached for her hand and gave it a quick squeeze, hoping that the other men wouldn't see. 'I'll stay, Clara.'

Another wave crashed almost at their feet, the white foam bubbling over her short leather boots. Clara almost smiled as Phil pulled at her arm. 'Come back, Clara. If the sea catches your skirt you'll be washed in.'

She wiped the spray from her face with a shaking hand. Thank God the boy had arrived when he had. She had known that Edward would be angry with her for stopping the sale, but she had never dreamed that he would show it like that. She raised her hands to her throat again, feeling the bruises where his fingers had dug into her flesh. But surely it had just been a momentary loss of temper? He couldn't really have meant to throttle her. Nevertheless, she moved closer to Phil, grateful for his presence.

A shout roused her. There were fingers pointing out to sea and amid the surging waves she caught a brief glimpse of something pale. A man's arm flapped limply into the air as the waves turned the body over.

One of the fishermen was already breasting his way into the sea, a rope tied around his waist while three more men, feet firmly braced, held the other end. She moved closer, seeing the rescuer stagger and almost fall as the sea surged irresistibly against him. Then he managed another step, lunging forward and she heard his shout above the roar of the waves as he reached the figure in the sea.

'Take the strain, men!'

She recognised Dick Thomas and made her way to him. 'If there's anything I can do . . .'

'Aye, lass.' He was too intent on the rescue to treat her with his usual deference. 'The other women should be here soon, but if you can look after these bodies once they're out of the water . . .'

'Of course.' She swallowed the fear that rose in her at the thought of touching those drowned sailors. But the men were needed here, so she would do what she had to. She gripped her lower lip with her

338

teeth, watching heart in mouth as the rescuer, a strange seaman in his arms, was pulled closer.

Other men were wading into the shallows to help him, though they, too, had ropes in case they fell. He was almost within touching distance when a larger wave than usual lifted him off his feet.

For a second he wavered, but the weight in his arms unbalanced him and she let out a cry as he disappeared under the foaming water, still clutching the body.

'Pull, men, pull.' Dick Thomas' shout rang out and the three men leaned against the rope. For what seemed an impossible age there was no sign of the man then, another shout from the shallows, and he was dragged up by the scruff of his neck and pulled ashore by willing hands, seawater streaming from him, coughing and retching against the water he had swallowed but with the seaman's body still clutched to him.

She had time to see that other teams were at work now, other men breasting their way into the surges on the end of ropes, then, with a rush, the seaman's body was dropped at her feet.

Horrified, she stared at it as it lay, white and motionless on the rough pebbles. For a dreadful second she thought that she could not bring herself to touch it. Then Phil knelt beside it.

'Turn him over. Perhaps if we get out some of the water he might start breathing.'

Reluctantly, she knelt beside him, forcing herself to touch the cold flesh. Even with the two of them, it was difficult to turn him onto his face. Then Phil leaned forward, pressing on the man's back with all his weight.

Water trickled from his mouth. 'Does that mean he's alive?' Her voice wouldn't work properly.

'No.' He pressed again. 'Is he breathing?'

'No.' She gulped abruptly. 'There's nothing.'

'Reckon he's a goner.' Phil climbed to his feet, rubbing his knees where the pebbles had bitten into them.

Clara stayed looking at the body. Through the wet hair the pale skin of his scalp gleamed pathetically. She blinked back tears. 'He was somebody's son. Maybe a father.' She reached for the fastening of her cloak.

Phil stopped her. 'What are you doing?'

'It's for him,' she quavered. 'It's only seemly.'

He snorted. 'He don't need it. He don't need nothing now. We'll have his clothes off him, once we've finished here.' He put his hand on her arm. 'You keep it. You're still alive. You need the warmth, not him.'

Then two more bodies were being rushed up the beach towards her and the horror of her first death was submerged in new concerns.

She was struggling to turn over another of the bodies when she caught sight of her husband. 'Edward, come and help.' There was no time now to worry about that brief, frightening scene before Phil arrived. 'We need you.'

'Waste of time.' But he came, helping to turn the body over and using his greater weight to try to force the water from its sodden lungs.

The line of bodies grew. Were they all drowned, Clara wondered, pressing with all her weight on the shoulders of a boy who must have been younger than Phil. It was such a waste. And such a cruel fate. She raised her head and looked around her. Already the sea was further from her, the wind dying. If only the bad weather had cleared half an hour earlier, this tragedy would never have happened. The ship would never have sailed onto the Brisons if the lookout hadn't been blinded by the sleet.

'Here!' The shout made her look round. This body was bigger than the rest and Edward went to help the men who carried him up the beach from the ebbing waves.

'Reckon this one might have made it.' Dick Thomas dropped the man at her feet. 'Give a him brem few extra pushes. I thought I felt him move.'

'Let me, Clara. You're not strong enough.' Edward pushed her away and began to work on the man. She sat back on her heels, noticing for the first time how tired she was, her arms aching from the constant attempt to make dead men breathe again.

Suddenly, she gasped. 'He moved, Edward. I'm sure he moved.' Tiredness forgotten, she craned forward. He pressed once more on the man's back and this time there was no doubt. Clara's eyes widened as the man drew a rasping breath then coughed, retching up seawater.

'He's alive!' Her tiredness disappeared in delight. One, at least, had been saved from the waves. She leapt to her feet. 'I'll get someone to take him back to St Just. He needs warmth, protection.' And she ran swiftly back towards the slipway.

Edward sat back on his heels. He couldn't believe he was here, doing this. Only anger had sent him after Clara as she had raced her horse towards the shore. And hate . . . He shuddered as he remembered the feel of her throat under his hands. He must have been mad. That was no way out, not if there were a chance he might be discovered. He shivered as he remembered the shock he had got as he glanced up and saw Phil Trevelyan staring at him. If the boy had arrived a couple of minutes later . . .

The seaman beside him coughed again and moved, groaning slightly. Edward bent over him. 'You're safe now.' He was half-amused at the part he was playing. Fancy him acting the Good Samaritan! He helped the man to sit up slightly. 'We'll get you under shelter soon.'

The sailor coughed again and spat. 'Bloody weather!' he gasped. He eyed the sky balefully. Although the early dusk was falling, the stormclouds that had brought the sleet had passed on and a few stars were twinkling dully in the darkening sky.

Another body was dropped heavily onto the pebbles beside him and Phil moved across to try to resuscitate it. The rescued man turned his head painfully and swore as he saw the row of bodies. 'Christ! All of them dead!' He spat again. 'That bastard on board was right. We would have been safer where we were.' Another fit of coughing shook him as his body struggled to expel the seawater in his lungs. 'Some damn people have all the luck!'

Edward stretched his arms, feeling the ache in his shoulders where his muscles protested at the unaccustomed exercise. 'What luck?' he asked. Not that he cared, but anything was good that would give him a rest from the constant effort of trying to revive drowned men.

'That passenger. Said he came from round here. Perhaps I should have listened to him after all. But he was only some miner, what would he know about the sea? Made a bloody fortune digging up lumps of gold and now he's coming home to flaunt it.'

A cold chill seemed to grip Edward's heart and he felt his breathing constrict. It was impossible! Of course it was impossible! But he had to know for certain.

He struggled to keep his voice calm and casual. 'Do you know the passenger's name?'

'Yeah.' The sailor retched again and it was several seconds before he could continue. 'Typical Cornish swede-hopping name. Adam Trevelyan.'

Chapter 41

The shock was so great that for a second Edward was afraid he was going to vomit.

Adam Trevelyan. Not dead, after all. Not dead, but alive and rich, while he was facing bankruptcy, ruin, disgrace.

He leaned forward, digging his fingers into the pebbles on which he knelt in an agony of despair. To be bested by Adam Trevelyan! To be poor while he was rich, a failure while he was a success, to lose . . .

Dear God! It was too much! It was unbearable!

He groaned, softly. Beside him, the sailor raised himself further on one elbow, staring over his head out to sea. 'The ship's still there, then?'

He could not answer, lost in a world of misery. The seaman said, consideringly, 'I reckoned all that gold would pull her down, but with the weather improving, I reckon they'll be able to salvage it now, before she breaks up.'

The words slid insidiously into Edward's brain. Slowly, disbelieving, he raised his head. 'Gold?'

The man coughed again. 'From Ballarat. That's where he found it. That's one reason he wouldn't leave the ship, I bet. Afraid of the locals.'

Gold. Adam's gold. The gold he would use to rub Edward's face in the mud.

He was so lost in his thoughts that the dropping of another body close beside him made him jump. Dick Thomas grunted, 'Another dead one, I reckon. Yours is the only survivor so far.'

The only survivor. Which meant that he was the only one who knew about the gold. Edward swung round and examined the sea.

Even his landsman's eye could see that it was less rough than it had been, but it was still beyond his abilities to take a boat out to the Brisons.

He reached over, shaking Phil's shoulder. 'Could you take a boat out to the wreck?'

Phil gave up working on the latest body to be dropped beside them and stared out to sea. 'There's no point.'

'But if there's still a man on board?'

Phil shrugged. 'He'd be better off staying where he is, I reckon. By tomorrow we'll have him off as easy as winking.'

'But if that man is Adam?'

Even in the poor light he could see the colour leave Phil's face. 'Adam? But he's dead!'

The seaman roused himself. 'Not dead. He's come back, he's still on the ship.'

'Adam!' Phil turned to survey the sea again. 'I couldn't do it alone, but with someone else to help row, and another helping hand to get the boat into the sea . . .'

'Do it,' Edward commanded. 'Find another seaman to help you and I'll come with you.'

He watched as the boy raced down the beach, careless of the waves that washed around his ankles. Now if only Clara stayed away just a little bit longer . . .

He got up and moved to the body Phil had been working on, his hands sliding quickly across it.

'Dead?' The sailor was recovering by the minute. He'd be on his feet soon; there was no time to waste.

'Dead,' Edward confirmed, grunting with satisfaction as his hands found what he was looking for. He cast a swift glance up the beach but they were not being watched. The wind had moved round, casting up debris from the ship slightly further around the cove and the men had followed it, their eyes still searching the rapidly darkening sea for bodies.

He knelt by the sailor once again. 'You're feeling better?'

'Right as a trivet,' the man said, then his eyes widened with disbelief as Edward thrust the knife he had found between his ribs.

'This way.' Clara ran back along the beach towards the place where she had left the survivor, holding her wet skirts free of her ankles. The village men followed more slowly, hindered by the hurdle they were carrying to act as a makeshift stretcher.

The rescuers were further along the beach but she could see in the darkness the pathetic line of bodies.

Figures ran towards her out of the darkness, first a large figure that she recognised as John-Henry, one of the yawlers at Mousehole. He was a big lad for his age and very strong but she had always privately wondered if he were 'all there' as the locals called it. But there was no doubting the identity of the figure running behind him.

'Phil! Where are you going? What's the matter?' He shouted something at her but it was drowned by the wind and the waves. She wanted to run after him but she had other responsibilities. That poor man, the only survivor. He needed warmth, dry clothes. She turned back, her feet slipping and sliding over the rough pebbles as she made her way to the line of victims dragged from the sea.

As she ran, another figure passed her. It was Edward. What could have happened, she wondered, pressing on. Where were they all going?

As she reached the casualties strewn along the beach she slowed down and called out urgently: 'Hello? Where are you?' But there was no movement amongst the bodies; no one answered her call.

Briefly, she cursed Edward. He should have known better. Surely nothing was more important than to care for the poor sailor who had already suffered so much. The stretcher-bearers had still not caught her up. She moved slowly through the bodies, searching for the sole survivor. He must have fainted again, she thought, but he should be easy to identify. He was a big man, much taller than the other men who had been rescued.

That was him, surely. She dropped to her knees beside him, laying a gentle hand on his shoulder. 'There are men here, come to carry you to shelter.' But he did not move. She shook him lightly. 'Wake up. Please, wake up.'

His head lolled helplessly, just like that of the dead men she had seen. Frantically, she placed her fingers at his neck, feeling for his pulse but there was no flutter under her anxious fingers, and as she dropped her eyes searching for some sign of how he had died, she saw the handle of a sailor's knife, sticking out from between his ribs.

Adam leaned over the rail, peering into the gathering darkness. Now that the tide had ebbed, the ship was almost stable, only the stern moved slightly when a larger wave than usual ran up underneath it. He had been right to stay here, he thought, but with the improvement of the weather another problem loomed.

He knew his St Just men. They would risk their lives to rescue the sailors washed ashore, but if they learned that there was gold on this ship their greed would take them over. The instincts of a thousand years of wrecking would win out over their Christian principles. He might have survived all the other dangers only to die fighting for his gold with his one-time friends and neighbours.

He strained his eyes again. Surely that was a small boat? And it

344

had to be a local one, creeping carefully in from the seaward side. He loosened the knife in his belt, feeling his heart thud nervously, then a voice called out, ringing clearly above the suck and thud of the waves, a voice he had never expected to hear again in this life:

'Adam? Is that you, Adam? Are you there?'

'Phil!' He let his breath out with a delighted bellow. 'What in God's name are you doing here?'

'We've come to rescue you, Adam.' The small boat edged closer and he could see three figures huddled in it, two of them struggling with the oars to stop the waves sweeping them onto the rocks, although it was too dark now to make out which one was Phil.

The boy's voice came again. 'We can only get in under the stern, Adam. Can you drop a line?'

He grinned in the darkness. 'No problem.' It had been Norman's favourite phrase, one he had not used since his death, but now it sprang readily to his lips.

Avoiding the litter of broken spars he made his way to the back of the ship and flung one of the ropes he found over the stern, fastening it firmly. 'Can you see it?'

'We can see it, Adam.' There were low mutters in the boat and it edged warily closer to the stern of the ship. Then a figure rose suddenly, grabbing at the rope Adam had flung over and the boat pulled hastily away out of danger as the figure climbed awkwardly upwards, hand over hand.

It was too tall for Phil, Adam realised, fighting down disappointment, but it would have been silly to let a young boy take the risk.

The man was nearly at the top and Adam leaned forward to help pull him the last couple of feet onto the deck.

Stretched downwards, his body suddenly froze in shock as he recognised the man he was helping on board.

Edward Blacklock.

'But you've got to help me – you've *got* to.'

Dick Thomas turned to Clara and wiped the sweat from his face. 'I don't see what the problem is.' He stared out to sea where the black hulk of the wreck was almost lost in the gathering darkness. 'Phil's a fool to go out there, but if he's got John-Henry with him, they won't come to no harm. Phil's a good seaman and that there John-Henry has strength enough for two.'

'But there's something wrong!' Clara was almost frantic. 'I don't know why they've gone but he's in danger, I'm sure of it.' She shuddered in horror. 'I think – I'm afraid – my husband's gone, too.'

She could see by the look on his face that he suspected her of

345

having taken leave of her senses. 'Well, then that's one sensible head out there, at any road.' He patted her kindly on the shoulder. 'Don't you worry about it, Mrs Blacklock. They'll be right as rain, you'll see.'

'But . . .' She could feel panicky tears sliding down her face now. 'You don't understand. My husband, he's – I think he's just killed someone.'

Dick Thomas had been about to walk away from her, back to the other men who were still struggling in the darkness to see if they could rescue any other survivors, storm lanterns lighting their intent faces. At her words he whipped round, staring at her. 'And who would that be?'

She could see that he didn't believe her. 'That man off the ship who was recovering well. I left him with Edward while I went to get help and now . . .'

Her voice trailed off. How could she betray her husband like this? But Phil – she had promised Adam she would look after him; she dared not let him go off with Edward like this. Every instinct screamed at her that he had some mischief in mind.

Dick Thomas said, 'Maybe the man's heart gave out.' He sounded impatient. 'It can happen.'

'He had a knife in his ribs.'

The quiet words seemed to cut through the storm. The old fisherman looked at her for a moment then set off back up the beach at such a speed that she had to run to keep up. Silently, he shouldered his way through the crowd of helpers who were stripping the bodies before carrying them off for later burial. He knelt by the corpse of the big man, his hands running over his body and she saw the sudden stillness that came upon him as his hand touched the protruding handle of the knife.

'Christ!' He was on his feet in an instant. 'And Phil's gone off with that murdering bastard!' He began to run down the beach, his boots slipping and sliding on the pebbles. Clara ran after him, her wet skirt pulled up to her knees to free her feet, careless of the proprieties.

She caught up with him as he was wrestling to get one of the boats down the slipway and she dragged at it beside him, her breath rasping in her throat.

He paused for a moment. 'You're not coming! I ain't taking a woman out in weather like this, not even if he *is* your husband.'

She did not waste her breath arguing with him, simply bracing her feet and tugging at the heavy boat with all her strength.

After another doubtful glance at her, Dick Thomas began to pull again and slowly, the metal keel screeching as it slid across the rocks, the small boat moved down into the tossing waves.

'You get in,' Clara gasped. 'I think I can hold her long enough for that.' The water surged past her knees, catching at her full skirts, dragging her down, but she planted her feet apart, her hands clutching the stern of the small boat.

With a quick movement he was in, his hands already reaching for the oars he had put ready as she struggled desperately to keep the boat from being washed onto the shore.

He took a pull on the oars, the blades biting deep into the water and the boat jerked forward almost pulling her off her feet, so that she was thigh-deep in the eddying sea. 'Let her go,' he shouted over the noise of the waves on the pebbles. 'Get back before you're swept away.'

But her hands still clasped the tarred wood of the stern and, even as he took another pull on the oars, she flung herself forward and fell, headfirst, legs kicking wildly, into the boat.

A wave splashed into Phil's face, jerking him back into consciousness. Muzzily, he sat up, rubbing his chin. 'Wh – what happened?'

'Mr Blacklock hit you.' There was dull puzzlement in John-Henry's voice. 'I dunno what for, you weren't doing nothing.'

Phil struggled to remember. The wreck. He had been going out to the wreck. That sailor had said that Adam was on it. And he had called to him and then . . .

He sat up, ignoring the way the world span and lurched. 'Here!' He stared around him. 'What are you doing? We're nearly back at Priest's Cove again.'

'Mr Blacklock told me.' John-Henry rested on the oars, letting the waves toss the small boat hither and thither. 'He told me to put you ashore. And I was to come back at midnight.'

'Midnight! What for?' Phil demanded.

'Dunno. But he's gentry, isn't he? They do funny things. And you got to do what they say.'

'No, you haven't.' Phil pulled himself onto the thwart beside the other yawler. 'We've got to get back to the ship quick. I'll help you row.'

Obediently, John-Henry turned the punt once again into the wind. 'If you say so, but that there Mr Blacklock'll be all right, don't you worry. I lent him my knife in case he should get caught up in the rigging.'

'Oh, Christ!' Phil grabbed at the oar and pulled with all his strength, a feeling of dread bringing a cold sweat to his forehead.

*

347

Only the brief shimmer of light off the knife-blade gave Adam any warning at all.

He jerked himself backwards, away from the climbing figure, and the slash that was aimed at his eyes caught his outstretched arm instead. With a sudden twist he threw himself onto the poop deck, feeling the blade slice easily through the material of his overcoat and jacket and bite deep into his flesh.

Instantly, he rolled over and up onto his feet, but he was too late. Already Edward Blacklock was over the rail and moving towards him, the knife pointed threateningly.

The deck moved under Adam's feet as a larger wave lifted the stern and he heard the timbers shriek as the sharp rocks tore at them. He moved carefully backwards, his eyes slitted against the spray as he watched Edward's slow advance. 'Where's Phil?' His voice was sharp with anxiety. 'What have you done with Phil?'

Edward laughed. 'Don't worry about him. You'll never see that boy again.' He moved closer, weaving the knife in front of him, already adopting the half-crouch that Adam remembered so well from their fight at the Fair.

Adam felt his heart constrict. 'If you've hurt him . . .'

'Him? Why should I hurt the brat?' He lowered his voice, moving closer. 'It's you I hate. You! Throwing my money in my face at the Fair, mocking me, making a fool of me. And now this. Coming back with your ill-gotten gains, thinking you can be top dog now, steal my wife, lord it over me.'

The thought was so ridiculous that Adam almost laughed. 'I never want to see Cornwall again, you fool.' Then he had to jump swiftly backwards as Edward swung the knife viciously towards him. 'Don't you understand, I want nothing to do with any of you.'

'Rich!' Edward hissed the word between clenched teeth. 'Rich! You! A gutter rat!' He swung again and Adam dodged him, this time catching his foot on a piece of broken spar and only saving himself by a quick twist.

'I won't have it, do you hear? I won't let you do this to me.' Adam could hear the fury in his voice. 'I need that gold. I deserve it. And I'm going to have it.'

Edward moved forward, slashing wildly with the knife, while Adam searched around the littered deck desperately for something he could use to defend himself. He could see his death in Edward's staring eyes, see it in his set face, and it roused him as nothing had done since Norman's death.

To be hated like this by the man he had always envied, the man who had everything he had ever wanted, was the ultimate irony. Once

348

he had thought that only gold made life worth living, now it was life alone that he desired.

Another wave hit the stern of the ship and Edward staggered slightly as a wall of spray hit his back. Adam took advantage of his momentary distraction to hurdle across the glazed skylight of the companionway to the other side of the poop deck.

Frantically, he groped at his feet, searching for something, anything that would serve as a weapon or a shield. But the broken spars were still attached to their sheets. He jerked at the rail where it had been splintered as the ship ran aground. Out of the corner of his eye he could see Edward coming closer, knife outstretched.

With an effort Adam pulled a length of rail free and swung it wildly at Edward, but the shifting deck threw him momentarily off-balance and as Edward ducked, the wood splintered against the side of the captain's cabin.

Again Edward slashed at him and Adam backed away, ending up against the rail of the poop deck. He glanced swiftly behind him. He did not want to go down to the main deck, littered as it was with the fallen rigging, but he had no other option. Edward came nearer. The knife was a flash of steel, now, inches from his face.

With a desperate kick, Adam lashed out at Edward's face and, as he instinctively ducked, Adam put his left hand on the rail of the poop deck and leapt over it. But the pressure on his injured left arm was too great. As he jumped, it buckled under his weight and, with a cry of agony, he fell heavily onto the tangle of ropes and spars that covered the main deck.

Chapter 42

Clara clung to the sides of the small punt as it pitched and wallowed in the towering seas. Time and again she thought that they would be sunk by the oncoming waves, but each time the small boat rose miraculously to the crest before sliding precipitously down the other side.

'Look.' She pointed into the dimness where another punt rode the tossing waves. As Dick Thomas rowed closer, Clara strained her eyes. 'There's only one person in it!'

'Where is he? Where's Phil?' Dick Thomas' bellow cut easily through the noise of the wind and the waves.

'On the wreck.' The other man sounded scared though he was handling the pitching boat with ease. 'They both went on the wreck.'

'For God's sake!' Dick Thomas snapped furiously. 'Why the hell should they do such a stupid thing?'

'They said – Phil said,' John-Henry's voice quavered, 'they said Adam was on board.'

Adam! It was impossible. He was dead, dead and buried in some unknown grave on the other side of the world. But even as her head told her that, Clara's heart knew different. Adam was alive, was here, was in danger.

'I must get there.' Frantically, she threw herself at Dick Thomas, clutching at his shoulder. 'We must get to that ship.'

He shook his head. 'I couldn't land. The punt would be smashed up before we knew it.'

'But Edward's there, Phil's there.' Her need to be on the ship was a burning flame.

'They must have jumped for it.'

'Then I will!' Seeing him hesitate, she screamed, 'Take me there or I'll jump in the sea and swim for it.' She half-stood in the pitching boat, clutching her skirts around her. 'Take me there!'

350

Unwillingly, he turned the boat. 'You're a lady. You can't do things like that.'

Clara did not listen. Her whole being was fastened on the wreck. Adam! Adam alive, but in danger. She knew it with as much certainty as she knew her own name. Edward had always hated Adam. She leaned forward in the boat, urging it on.

The storm was clearing, even the thin clouds were scudding away before the dying wind, and in the dim starlight the wreck towered over them, only the biggest waves now reaching her stern.

'Like I said,' Dick Thomas remarked complacently, 'she'll be fine until the next storm.'

'But how do I get on board?' She stared up at the sides, seemingly unclimbable.

He pointed. 'The shrouds.' The foremast had broken off as the ship grounded, and its shrouds with their linking ratlines which the sailors used as a ladder when climbing the mast, hung down in great loops to the rocks. 'Can you climb them?'

Clara had a brief memory of the ladder in the mine, the day she had saved her mother and lost her baby. 'Yes.' If Adam were at the end of it, she would walk a tightrope. She gathered herself as the boat edged nearer to the wet, precipitous rocks, clutching her skirts in one hand. 'Tell me when to jump.'

'Now.'

It seemed impossible but she jumped anyway, throwing herself bodily at the rocks. And, miraculously, the timing was right. Her feet hit the rock and she dropped her skirts, clutching wildly for a handhold as her boots slipped and skidded in the wet. Then she was on her feet again, scuttling up out of the reach of the hungry waves, her knuckles bleeding as she pulled herself across the rough rocks to the side of the wreck.

The shrouds, close too, were a tangled mess, but they were a way up. *Adam. Adam.* His name sang in her head. She scrambled desperately up the cat's-cradle of ropes, not caring how they swung giddily under her weight.

The ship's rail had broken when the mast hit it and she squeezed through, her eyes searching the deck for any sign of the man she loved. And then she saw him.

Too far away to reach, Adam lay caught in a tangled mass of broken rigging, fighting for his life. And above him, Edward, despite Adam's efforts, was forcing a knife closer and closer to his unprotected throat.

'Adam!' The scream was wrung from her, shrieking across the deck, drowning out the noise of the wind. And Edward paused a

351

second, glancing up, his concentration broken, and as he did so, a small figure hurtled off the higher poop deck at the rear of the ship onto his back.

Phil! But he could not fight a man like Edward. Her breath rasping in her throat, Clara forced herself between the broken rails, falling forward onto the deck. Ropes caught at her ankles, a dead body rolled horribly under her feet, but her attention was on the three figures caught in a life-and-death battle just beyond her reach. 'Adam!' Her voice was a breathless cry. 'Oh Adam!'

Then Edward broke away. Powerless to help she could only watch in terror as he threw off Phil's clinging body and rose to his feet, the knife still in his hand. Then, with a surge, Adam was also on his feet. Phil hurled himself a second time onto Edward's back as Adam kicked out and the knife went soaring, glittering, out of Edward's hand to slide in a streak of silver into the turbulent sea.

Edward backed away, his eyes still on Adam but now it was man to man and Adam followed him. His right hand shot out, once, twice, catching Edward on the jaw, forcing him backwards, then a third time. In a sudden lull of the wind, Clara heard the blow connect with a bone-jolting thud, saw Edward teeter momentarily against the rail, then another wave caught the stern, the ship shifted with a screech of tortured timbers and Edward toppled slowly backwards into the foaming sea.

Stunned, she stood motionless, hardly able to breathe, and then Adam turned his head and saw her.

Long seconds passed. She could not speak, could not move. *Adam, alive. Adam, safe.* The words drummed through her brain but her body had been turned to ice. As if in a dream she saw the colour leave his face; he stared at her as though she were a ghost, as if she were the one who had been dead.

Adam. She tried to say the word but her mouth was dry, her lips still would not move. Nor could she walk towards him – her legs seemed rooted to the deck. Only yards apart, they stared at each other, motionless in the centre of the ceaseless motion of the sea and wind.

Then Adam turned from her; he turned his back, slowly, deliberately, finally – and she felt her heart break.

Tears coursed down her face, mingling with sweat and spray. Tears, hopeless, accepting. He did not love her. He had not forgiven her for marrying his enemy. She knew it, knew it as clearly as if he had spoken. Immovable, blinded by grief, she stood silent in her despair. Across the deck, only yards away, she could hear Phil's happy, excited voice, hear Adam's deeper answers but they meant nothing. She was alone. She would always be alone now. A sob rose in her chest, shaking her body, bursting out through her throat. Alone. For ever.

Then, slowly, she was aware of something shaking her hand. Impossibly, life was going on, someone wanted her attention. Dully, she blinked away the tears, staring at Phil's jubilant face.

'Clara, Mr Blacklock knocked me out! And then he tried to kill Adam. What did he do that for?'

She shook her head, unable to speak. The pressure in her chest was so great she felt as if it would burst. Tears coursed hopelessly down her cheeks.

'What's the matter, Clara? Are you sorry he's dead?' The shrill voice was anxious. 'Don't be sad, Clara. Adam's back now.'

She couldn't breathe. She was suffocating. Desperately, she dragged at her coat, pulling it loose from her neck, trying to get some air.

'Clara, what are those marks? Did Mr Blacklock do that on the beach? I thought he was kissing you. Did he hurt you?' he demanded angrily.

She nodded and the movement seemed to free something inside her. She could breathe at last, a great intaking of air that swelled her chest until she thought her stays would burst. Then she was sobbing, clutching Phil to her, weeping out all her hurt and her despair.

She was scarcely aware of gentle hands lifting her head, of fingers touching her neck.

'He did that to you?' Adam's voice was bleak.

She gulped. 'He wanted to kill me, I think. Because I stopped him selling the mine.' She raised her head then, staring at the frozen expression on his face. 'My father's mine, Adam. Yours. Ours. I couldn't let him sell it. I couldn't.'

'The mine.' His voice was sad.

Another sob rose inside her. 'It's never been worked, Adam. That tin – it's still there. Drowned. After my father died . . .' Sobs choked her. Another loss. She released Phil, burying her face in her hands, trying to hide from the coldness of his eyes, the condemnation in his face.

Phil said, 'Clara was wonderful, Adam. Even after she lost all her money she still looked after us. She even moved in with Ma Downing and me.'

Clara had to confess it, had to tell him the worst. 'I lost your baby, Adam. And I wanted him so much!'

'Dear God!' Suddenly his arms were around her, his hands, warm and strong, soothing her. His touch was a benediction. The tears flowed more freely, the terrible pressure in her throat eased. 'Clara.' She could hear the anguish in his voice but she could not answer it yet. 'Clara. My dear! My darling! If I had known . . .'

'I had to do it, Adam. I had to marry Edward. My mother . . .'

He caressed her, his arms holding her safe. 'It doesn't matter. Nothing matters. As long as you forgive me.'

'Forgive you?' She raised her head, astonished. 'But why? It's me –'

His mouth met hers, silencing her. She could taste the spray on his lips, but underneath, she could taste *him* – his own distinctive taste, one that she had never forgotten in all these years.

Phil's voice pierced through the happiness she felt blossoming inside her. 'There's boats coming, Adam. Lots of 'em.'

He was gone from her in a second, leaping to the side, and she heard the soft expletive he muttered under his breath.

She staggered after him. 'What is it, Adam? What's the matter?'

He laughed. 'I'm about to be robbed, if I know my own country-men. And probably murdered as well.' He turned to her. 'Get off this ship, Clara. If you stay on the rocks you'll be safe. They won't worry about a woman.'

'But I don't understand.' She clutched at him, bewildered. 'What is it? Why are they coming?'

He gave a harsh laugh. 'I would guess that they've picked up an-other survivor. And this one has told them about the gold.'

'Gold?' She could only stare at him.

He laughed again, but his face was sad. 'Gold, my love. I nearly died to get it, and it killed Norman. And it was only because I wanted you. It was – I thought . . .' He shrugged. 'What does it matter now? If I could have you I would be happy to be a pauper all my days. But it won't happen.' He kissed her gently. 'Take Phil and go, Clara. And remember me.'

She clung to him. 'I won't go, Adam, I won't. They can't do this. It's illegal.'

'Clara, my lovely. In some ways you're as innocent now as the day I met you.' He glanced again at the small flotilla, already nearing the Brisons. 'Go, Clara.'

But she pressed herself closer to him. 'I've found you at last. I shan't leave you this time.'

His lips sought hers, and he caught her to him, enfolding her in his strong arms. She closed her eyes in ecstasy at his touch. This was all she wanted, all she had ever wanted.

Her dream of happiness was broken abruptly. Phil's shrill voice rang out: 'They're going. Look – they're all turning around.'

Adam pulled away from her and strode to the rail. 'What the . . .?'

'Look.' He followed her pointing finger. Around the bulk of Cape Cornwall came a ship with all lights lit.

Phil jumped up and down. 'The Revenue cutter! The Revenue cutter! It's that Lieutenant Laity. He's come out in all this weather!'

'Well, I'll be damned.' Adam breathed a startled oath. 'It's the first ime I've ever been happy to see them.' He turned to Clara and pulled her into his arms again, holding her close. 'My darling, you're crying. What is it? What's the matter?'

She cuddled into him, dashing the tears from her eyes. 'Nothing, Adam, nothing at all.' She raised her head and smiled at him. 'For he first time, everything is all right.'

You have been reading a novel published by Piatkus Books. We hope you have enjoyed it and that you would like to read more of our titles. Please ask for them in your local library or bookshop.

If you would like to be put on our mailing list to receive details of new publications, please send a large stamped addressed envelope (UK only) to:

Piatkus Books: 5 Windmill Street
London W1P 1HF

PIATKUS

The sign of a good book